BELLA DONNA

FIFTH EDITION

BELLA DONNA

A NOVEL

BY

ROBERT HICHENS
AUTHOR OF
"THE GARDEN OF ALLAH," "THE CALL OF THE BLOOD," ETC.

PHILADELPHIA
J. B. LIPPINCOTT COMPANY
1909

COPYRIGHT, 1909
BY J. B. LIPPINCOTT COMPANY

Published October, 1909

Printed by J. B. Lippincott Company
The Washington Square Press, Philadelphia, U.S.A.

BELLA DONNA

I

DOCTOR MEYER ISAACSON had got on as only a modern Jew whose home is London can get on, with a rapidity that was alarming. He seemed to have arrived as a bullet arrives in a body. He was not in the heart of success, and lo! he was in the heart of success. And no one had marked his journey. Suddenly every one was speaking of him—was talking of the cures he had made, was advising every one else to go to him. For some mysterious reason his name— a name not easily to be forgotten once it had been heard— began to pervade the conversations that were held in the smart drawing-rooms of London. Women who were well, but had not seen him, abruptly became sufficiently unwell to need a consultation. "Where does he live? In Harley Street, I suppose?" was a constant question.

But he did not live in Harley Street. He was not the man to lose himself in an avenue of brass plates of fellow practitioners. "Cleveland Square, St. James's," was the startling reply; and his house was detached, if you please, and marvellously furnished.

The winged legend flew that he was rich, and that he had gone into practice as a doctor merely because he was intellectually interested in disease. His gift for diagnosis was so remarkable that he was morally forced to exercise it. And he had a greedy passion for studying humanity. And who has such opportunities for the study of humanity as the doctor and the priest? Patients who had been to him spoke enthusiastically of his observant eyes. His personality always made a great impression. "There's no one just like him," was a frequent comment upon Doctor

Meyer Isaacson. And that phrase is a high compliment upon the lips of London, the city of parrots and of monkeys.

His age was debated, and so was his origin. Most people thought he was "about forty"; a very safe age, young enough to allow of almost unlimited expectation, old enough to make results achieved not quite unnatural, though possibly startling. Yes, he must be "about forty." And his origin? "Meyer" suggested Germany. As to "Isaacson," it allowed the ardent imagination free play over denationalized Israel. Someone said that he "looked as if he came from the East," to which a cynic made answer, "The East End." There was, perhaps, a hint of both in the Doctor of Cleveland Square. Certain it is that in the course of a walk down Brick Lane, or the adjacent thoroughfares, one will encounter men of his type; men of middle height, of slight build, with thick, close-growing hair strongly curling, boldly curving lips, large nostrils, prominent cheek-bones, dark eyes almost fiercely shining; men who are startlingly un-English. Doctor Meyer Isaacson was like these men. Yet he possessed something which set him apart from them. He looked intensely vital—almost unnaturally vital—when he was surrounded by English people, but he did not look fierce and hungry. One could conceive of him doing something bizarre, but one could not conceive of him doing anything low. There was sometimes a light in his eyes which suggested a moral distinction rarely to be found in those who dwell in and about Brick Lane. His slight, nervous hands, dark in colour, recalled the hands of high-bred Egyptians. Like so many of his nation, he was by nature artistic. An instinctive love of what was best in the creations of man ran in his veins with his blood. He cared for beautiful things, and he knew what things were beautiful and what were not. The second-rate never made any appeal to him. The first-rate found in him a welcoming enthusiast. He never wearied of looking at fine pictures, at noble statues, at bronzes, at old jewelled glass, at delicate carvings, at perfect jewels. He was genuinely moved by great architecture. And to music he was almost fanatically devoted, as are many Jews.

It has been said of the Jew that he is nearly always possessed of a streak of femininity, not effeminacy. In Doctor Meyer Isaacson this streak certainly existed. His intuitions were feminine in their quickness, his sympathies and his antipathies almost feminine in their ardour. He understood women instinctively, as generally only other women understand them. Often he knew, without knowing why he knew. Such knowledge of women is, perhaps fortunately, rare in men. Where most men stumble in the dark, Doctor Meyer Isaacson walked in the light. He was unmarried.

Bachelorhood is considered by many to detract from a doctor's value and to stand in the way of his career. Doctor Meyer Isaacson did not find this so. Although he was not a nerve specialist, his waiting-room was always full of patients. If he had been married, it could not have been fuller. Indeed, he often thought it would have been less full.

Suddenly he became the fashion, and he went on being the fashion.

He had no special peculiarity of manner. He did not attract the world of women by elaborate brutalities, or charm it by silly suavities. He seemed always very natural, intelligent, alive, and thoroughly interested in the person with whom he was. That he was a man of the world was certain. He was seen often at concerts, at the opera, at dinners, at receptions, occasionally even at a great ball.

Early in the morning he rode in the Park. Once a week he gave a dinner in Cleveland Square. And people liked to go to his house. They knew they would not be bored and not be poisoned there. Men appreciated him as well as women, despite the reminiscence of Brick Lane discoverable in him. His directness, his cleverness, and his apparent good-will soon overcame any dawning instinct summoned up in John Bull by his exotic appearance.

Only the unyielding Jew-hater hated him. And so the

lines of the life of Doctor Meyer Isaacson seemed laid in pleasant places. And not a few thought him one of the fortunate of this world.

One morning of June the doctor was returning to Cleveland Square from his early ride in the Park. He was alone. The lively bay horse he rode—an animal that seemed almost as full of nervous vitality as he was—had had a good gallop by the Serpentine, and now trotted gently towards Buckingham Palace, snuffing in the languid air through its sensitive nostrils. The day was going to be hot. This fact inclined the Doctor to idleness, made him suddenly realize the bondage of work. In a few minutes he would be in Cleveland Square; and then, after a bath, a cup of coffee, a swift glance through the *Times* and the *Daily Mail,* there would start the procession that until evening would be passing steadily through his consulting-room.

He sighed, and pulled in his horse to a walk. To-day he was reluctant to encounter that procession.

And yet each day it brought interest into his life, this procession of his patients.

Generally he was a keen man. He had no need to feign an ardour that he really felt. He had a passion for investigation, and his profession enabled him to gratify it. Very modern, as a rule, were those who came to him, one by one, admitted each in turn by his Jewish man-servant; complex, caught fast in the net of civilized life. He liked to sit alone with them in his quiet chamber, to seek out the hidden links which united the physical to the mental man in each, to watch the pull of soul on body, of body on soul. But to-day he recoiled from work. Deep down in his nature, hidden generally beneath his strong activity, there was something that longed to sit in the sunshine and dream away the hours, leaving all fates serenely, or perhaps indifferently, between the hands of God.

"I will take a holiday some day," he said to himself, "a long holiday. I will go far away from here, to the land where I am really at home, where I am in my own place."

As he thought this, he looked up, and his eyes rested upon the brown façade of the King's Palace, upon the gilded railings that separated it from the public way, upon the sentries who were on guard, fresh-faced, alert, staring upon London with their calmly British eyes.

"In my own place," he repeated to himself.

And now his lips and his eyes were smiling. And he saw the great drama of London as something that a schoolboy could understand at a glance.

Was it really idleness he longed for? He did not know why, but abruptly his desire had changed. And he found himself wishing for events, tragic, tremendous, horrible even—anything, if they were unusual, were such as to set the man who was involved in them apart from his fellows. The foreign element in him woke up, called, perhaps, from repose by the unusually languid air, and London seemed meaningless to him, a city where a man of his type could neither dream, nor act, with all the languor, or all the energy, that was within him. And he imagined, as sometimes clever children do, a distant country where all romances unwind their shining coils, where he would find the incentive which he needed to call all his secret powers—the powers whose exercise would make his life complete—into supreme activity.

He gripped his horse with his knees. It understood his desire. It broke into a canter. He passed in front of the garden of Stafford House, turned to the left past St. James's Palace and Marlborough House, and was soon at his own door.

"Please bring up the book with my coffee in twenty minutes, Henry," he said to his servant, as he went in.

In half an hour he was seated in an arm-chair in an upstairs sitting-room, sipping his coffee. The papers lay folded at his elbow. Upon his knee, open, lay the book in which were written down the names of the patients with whom he had made appointments that day.

He looked at them, seeking for one that promised interest. The first patient was a man who would come in on his way to the city. Then followed the names of three women, then the name of a boy. He was coming with his mother, a lady of an anxious mind. The Doctor had a sheaf of letters from her. And so the morning's task was over. He turned a page and came to the afternoon.

"Two o'clock, Mrs. Lesueur; two-thirty, Miss Mendish; three, the Dean of Greystone; three-thirty, Lady Carle; four, Madame de Lys; four-thirty, Mrs. Harringby; five, Sir Henry Grebe; five-thirty, Mrs. Chepstow."

The last name was that of the last patient. Doctor Meyer Isaacson's day's work was over at six, or was supposed to be over. Often, however, he gave a patient more than the fixed half-hour, and so prolonged his labours. But no one was admitted to his house for consultation after the patient whose name was against the time of five-thirty.

And so Mrs. Chepstow would be the last patient he would see that day.

He sat for a moment with the book open on his knee, looking at her name.

It was a name very well known to him, very well known to the English-speaking world in general.

Mrs. Chepstow was a great beauty in decline. Her day of glory had been fairly long, but now it seemed to be over. She was past forty. She said she was thirty-eight, but she was over forty. Goodness, some say, keeps women fresh. Mrs. Chepstow had tried a great many means of keeping fresh, but she had omitted that. The step between æstheticism and asceticism was one which she had never taken, though she had taken many steps, some of them, unfortunately, false ones. She had been a well-born girl, the daughter of aristocratic but impecunious and extravagant parents. Her father, Everard Page, a son of Lord Cheam, had been very much at home in the Bankruptcy Court. Her mother, too, was reckless about money, saying, whenever it was mentioned, "Money is given us to spend, not to hoard." So little did she hoard it, that eventually her husband published a notice in the principal papers, stating that he would not be responsible for her debts. It was a very long time since he had been responsible for his own. Still, there was a certain dignity in the announcement, as of an honest man frankly declaring his position.

Mrs. Chepstow's life was very possibly influenced by her parents' pecuniary troubles. When she was young she learnt to be frightened of poverty. She had known what it was to be "sold up" twice before she was twenty; and this probably led her to prefer the alternative of being sold. At any rate, when she was in her twenty-first year, sold she was to Mr. Wodehouse Chepstow, a rich brewer, to whom she had not even taken a fancy; and as Mrs. Chepstow she made a great fame in London society as a beauty. She was christened Bella Donna. She was photographed, written about, worshipped by important people, until her celebrity spread far over the world, as the celebrity even of a woman who is only beautiful and who does nothing can spread in the era of the paragraph.

And then presently she was the heroine of a great divorce case.

Mr. Chepstow, forgetting that among the duties required of the modern husband is the faculty of turning a blind eye upon the passing fancies of a lovely and a generally admired wife, suddenly proclaimed some ugly truths, and completely ruined Mrs. Chepstow's reputation. He won his case. He got heavy damages out of a well-known married man. The married man's wife was forced to divorce him. And Mrs. Chepstow was socially "done for." Then began the new period of her life, a period utterly different from all that had preceded it.

She was at this time only twenty-six, and in the zenith of her beauty. Every one supposed that the man to whom she owed her ruin would marry her as soon as it was possible. Unfortunately, he died before the decree *nisi* was made absolute. Mrs. Chepstow's future had been committed to the Fates, and they had turned down their thumbs.

Notorious, lovely, now badly off, still young, she was left to shift for herself in the world.

It was then that there came to the surface of her character a trait that was not beautiful. She developed a love of money, a passion for material things. This definite greediness declared itself in her only now that she was poor and solitary. Probably it had always existed in her, but had been hidden. She hid it no longer. She tacitly proclaimed it, and she ordered her life so that it might be satisfied.

And it was satisfied, or at the least for many years appeased. She became the famous, or the infamous, Mrs. Chepstow. She had no child to be good for. Her father was dead. Her mother lived in Brussels with some foreign relations. For her English relations she took no thought. The divorce case had set them all against her. She put on the panoply of steel so often assumed by the woman who has got into trouble. She defied those who were "down upon her." She had made a failure of one life. She resolved that she would make a success of another. And for a long time she was very successful. Men were at her feet, and ministered to her desires. She lived as she seemed to desire to live, magnificently. She was given more than most good women are given, and she seemed to revel in its possession. But though she loved money, her parents' traits were repeated in her. She was a spendthrift, as they had been spendthrifts. She loved money because she loved spending, not hoarding it. And for years she scattered it with both hands.

Then, as she approached forty, the freshness of her beauty began to fade. She had been too well known, and had to endure the fate of those who have long been talked about. Men said of her, " Mrs. Chepstow—oh, she's been going a deuce of a time. She must be well over fifty." Women—good women especially—pronounced her nearer sixty. Almost suddenly, as often happens in such cases as hers, the roseate hue faded from her life and a greyness began to fall over it.

She was seen about with very young men, almost boys. People sneered when they spoke of her. It was said that she was not so well off as she had been. Some shoddy millionaire had put her into a speculation. It had gone wrong, and he had not thought it necessary to pay up her losses. She moved from her house in Park Lane to a flat in Victoria Street, then to a little house in Kensington. Then she gave that up, and took a small place in the country, and motored up and down, to and from town. Then she got sick of that, and went to live in a London hotel. She sold her yacht. She sold a quantity of diamonds.

And people continued to say, "Mrs. Chepstow—oh, she must be well over fifty."

Undoubtedly she was face to face with a very bad period. With every month that passed, loneliness stared at her more fixedly, looked at her in the eyes till she began to feel almost dazed, almost hypnotized. A dulness crept over her.

Forty struck—forty-one—forty-two.

And then, one morning of June, Doctor Meyer Isaacson sat sipping his coffee and looking at her name, written against the time, five-thirty, in his book of consultations.

II

DOCTOR MEYER ISAACSON did not know Mrs. Chepstow personally, but he had seen her occasionally, at supper in smart restaurants, at first nights, riding in the Park. Now, as he looked at her name, he realized that he had not even seen her for a long time, perhaps for a couple of years. He had heard the rumours of her decadence, and taken little heed of them, not being specially interested in her. Nevertheless, this morning, as he shut up his book and got up to go downstairs to his work, he was aware of a desire to hear the clock strike the half-hour after five, and to see Henry opening the door to show Mrs. Chepstow into his consulting-room. A woman who had lived her life and won her renown—or infamy—could scarcely be uninteresting.

As the day wore on, he was several times conscious of a

wish to quicken the passing of its moments, and when Sir Henry Grebe, the penultimate patient, proved to be an elderly *malade imaginaire* of dilatory habit, involved speech, and determined misery, he was obliged firmly to check a rising desire to write a hasty bread-pill prescription and fling him in the direction of Marlborough House. The half-hour chimed, and still Sir Henry explained the strange symptoms by which he was beset—the buzzings in the head, the twitchings in the extremities, the creepings, as of insects with iced legs, about the roots of the hair. His eyes shone with the ardour of the determined valetudinarian closeted with one paid to attend to his complaints.

And Mrs. Chepstow? Had she come? Was she sitting in the next room, looking inattentively at the newest books?

"The most extraordinary matter in my case," continued Sir Henry, with uplifted finger, "is the cold sweat that——"

The doctor interrupted him.

"My advice to you is this——"

"But I haven't explained to you about the cold sweat that——"

"My advice to you is this, Sir Henry. Don't think about yourself; walk for an hour every day before breakfast, eat only two meals a day, morning and evening, take at least eight hours' rest every night, give up lounging about in your club, occupy yourself—with work for others, if possible. I believe that to be the most tonic work there is—and I see no reason why you should not be a centenarian."

"I—a centenarian?"

"Why not? There is nothing the matter with you, unless you think there is."

"Nothing—you say there is nothing the matter with me!"

"I have examined you, and that is my opinion."

The face of the patient flushed with indignation at this insult.

"I came to you to be told what was the matter."

"And I am glad to inform you nothing is the matter—with your body."

"Do you mean to imply that my mind is diseased?"

"No. But you don't give it enough to think about. You only give it yourself. And that isn't nearly enough."

Sir Henry rose, and put a trembling finger into his waistcoat-pocket.

"I believe I owe you——?"

"Nothing. But if you care to put something into the box on my hall table, you will help some poor man to get away to the seaside after an operation, and find out what is the best medicine in the world."

"And now for Mrs. Chepstow!" the Doctor murmured to himself, as the door closed behind the outraged back of an enemy.

He sat still for a minute or two, expecting to see the door open again, the form of a woman framed in the doorway. But no one came. He began to feel restless. He was not accustomed to be kept waiting by his patients, although he often kept them waiting. There was a bell close to his elbow. He touched it, and his man-servant instantly appeared.

" Mrs. Chepstow is down for five-thirty. It is now"—he pulled out his watch—" nearly ten minutes to six. Hasn't she come?"

"No, sir. Two or three people have been, without appointments."

"And you have sent them away, of course? Quite right. Well, I shan't stay in any longer."

He got up from his chair.

"And if Mrs. Chepstow should come, sir?"

"Explain to her that I waited till ten minutes to six and then——" He paused. The hall door-bell was ringing sharply.

"If it is Mrs. Chepstow, shall I admit her now, sir?"

The doctor hesitated, but only for a second.

"Yes," he said.

And he sat down again by his table.

He had been almost looking forward to the arrival of his last patient of that day, but now he felt irritated at being detained. For a moment he had believed his day's work to be over, and in that moment the humour for work had left him. Why had she not been up to time? He tapped his delicate fingers impatiently on the table, and drew down his thick brows over his sparkling eyes. But directly the door moved, his expression of serenity returned, and when a tall woman came in, he was standing up and gravely smiling.

"I'm afraid I am late."

The door shut on Henry.

"You are twenty minutes late."

"I'm so sorry."

The rather dawdling tones of the voice denied the truth of the words, and the busy Doctor was conscious of a slight sensation of hostility.

"Please sit down here," he said, "and tell me why you come to consult me."

Mrs. Chepstow sat down in the chair he showed her. Her movements were rather slow and careless, like the movements of a person who is quite alone and has nothing to do. They suggested to the watching man vistas of empty hours—how different from his own! She settled herself in her chair, leaning back. One of her hands rested on the handle of a parasol she carried. The other held lightly an arm of the chair. Her height was remarkable, and was made the more apparent by her small waist, and by the small size of her beautifully shaped head, which was poised on a long but exquisite neck. Her whole outline announced her gentle breeding. The most lovely woman of the people could never be shaped quite like that. As Doctor Isaacson realised this, he felt a sudden difficulty in connecting with the woman before him her notorious career. Surely pride must be a dweller in a body so expressive of race!

He thought of the very young men, almost boys, with whom Mrs. Chepstow was seen about. Was it possible?

Her eyes met his, and in her face he saw a subtle contradiction of the meaning her form seemed eloquently to indicate.

It was possible.

Almost before he had time to say this to himself, Mrs. Chepstow's face had changed, suddenly accorded more definitely with her body.

"What a clever woman!" the Doctor thought.

With an almost sharp movement he sat forward in his chair, braced up, alert, vital. His irritation was gone with the fatigue engendered by the day's work. Interest in life tingled through his veins. His day was not to be wholly dull. His thought of the morning, when he had looked at the patients' book, was not an error of the mind.

" You came to consult me because——?"

"I don't know that I am ill," Mrs. Chepstow said, very composedly.

"Let us hope not."

"Do you think I look ill?"

"Would you mind turning a little more towards the light?"

She sat still for a minute, then she laughed.

"I have always said that so long as one is with a doctor, *qua* doctor, one must never think of him as a man," she said; "but——"

"Don't think of me as a man."

"Unfortunately, there is something about you which absolutely prevents me from regarding you as a machine. But—never mind!"

She turned to the light, lifted her thin veil, and leaned towards him.

"Do you think I look ill?"

He gazed at her steadily, with a scrutiny that was almost cruel. The face presented to him in the bold light that flowed in through the large window near which their chairs were placed still preserved elements of the beauty of which the world had heard too much. Its shape, like the shape of Mrs. Chepstow's head, was exquisite. The line of the features was not purely Greek, but it recalled things

Greek, profiles in marble seen in calm museums. The outline of a thing can set a sensitive heart beating with the strange, the almost painful longing for an ideal life, with ideal surroundings, ideal loves, ideal realizations. It can call to the imagination that lies drowsing, yet full of life, far down in the secret recesses of the soul. The curve of Mrs. Chepstow's face, the modelling of her low brow, and the undulations of the hair that flowed away from it—although, alas! that hair was obviously, though very perfectly, dyed—had this peculiar power of summons, sent forth silently this subtle call. The curve of a Dryad's face, seen dimly in the green wonder of a magic wood, might well have been like this, or of a nymph's bathing by moonlight in some very secret pool. But a Dryad would not have touched her lips with this vermilion, a nymph have painted beneath her laughing eyes these cloudy shadows, or drawn above them these artfully delicate lines. And the weariness that lay about these cheeks, and at the corners of this mouth, suggested no early world, no goddesses in the springtime of creation, but an existence to distress a moralist, and a lack of pleasure in it to dishearten an honest pagan. The ideality in Mrs. Chepstow's face was contradicted, was set almost at defiance, by something—it was difficult to say exactly what; perhaps by the faint wrinkles about the corners of her large and still luminous blue eyes, by a certain not yet harsh prominence of the cheek-bones, by a slight droop of the lips that hinted at passion linked with cynicism. There was a suggestion of hardness somewhere. Freshness had left this face, but not because of age. There are elderly, even old women who look almost girlish, fragrant with a charm that has its root in innocence of life. Mrs. Chepstow did not certainly look old. Yet there was no youth in her, no sweetness of the girl she once had been. She was not young, nor old, nor definitely middle-aged.

She was definitely a woman who had strung many experiences upon the chain of her life, yet who, in certain aspects, called up the thought of, even the desire for, things ideal, things very far away from all that is sordid, ugly, brutal, and defaced.

The look of pride, or perhaps of self-respect, which Doctor Isaacson had seen born as if in answer to his detrimental thought of her, stayed in this face, which was turned towards the light.

He realized that in this woman there was much will, perhaps much cunning, and that she was a past mistress in the art of reading men.

"Well," she said, after a minute of silence, "what do you make of it?"

She had a very attractive voice, not caressingly but carelessly seductive; a voice that suggested a creature both warm and lazy, that would, perhaps, leave many things to chance, but that might at a moment grip closely, and retain, what chance threw in her way.

"Please tell me your symptoms," the Doctor replied.

"But you tell me first—do I look ill?"

She fixed her eyes steadily upon him.

"What is the real reason why this woman has come to me?"

The thought flashed through the Doctor's mind as his eyes met hers, and he seemed to divine some strange under-reason lurking far down in her shrewd mind, almost to catch a glimpse of it ere it sank away into complete obscurity.

"Certain diseases," he said slowly, "stamp themselves unmistakably upon the faces of those who are suffering from them."

"Is any one of them stamped upon mine?"

"No."

She moved, as if settling herself more comfortably in her chair.

"Shall I put your parasol down?" he asked, stretching out his hand.

"No, thanks. I like holding it."

"I'm afraid you must tell me what are your symptoms."

"I feel a sort of general malaise."

"Is it a physical malaise?"

"Why not?" she said, almost sharply.

She smiled, as if in pity at her own childishness, and added immediately:

"I can't say that I suffer actual physical pain. But without that one may not feel particularly well."

"Perhaps your nervous system is out of order."

"I suppose every day you have silly women coming to you full of complaints but without the ghost of a malady?"

"You must not ask me to condemn my patients. And not only women are silly in that way."

He thought of Sir Henry Grebe, and of his own prescription.

"I had better examine you. Then I can tell you more about yourself."

While he spoke, he felt as if he were being examined by her. Never before had he experienced this curious sensation, almost of self-consciousness, with any patient.

"Oh, no," she said, "I don't want to be examined. I know my heart and my lungs and so on are sound enough."

"At any rate, allow me to feel your pulse."

"And look at my tongue, perhaps!"

She laughed, but she pulled off her glove and extended her hand to him. He put his fingers on her wrist, and looked at his watch. Her skin was cool. Her pulse beat regularly and strongly. From her, a message to his lightly touching fingers, flowed surely determination, self-possession, hardihood, even combativeness. As he felt her pulse he understood the defiance of her life.

"Your pulse is good," he said, dropping her hand.

During the short time he had touched her, he seemed to have learnt a great deal about her.

And she—how much had she learnt about him?

He found himself wondering in a fashion unorthodox in a doctor.

"Mrs. Chepstow," he said, speaking rather brusquely, "I wish you would kindly explain to me exactly why you have come here to-day. If you don't feel ill, why waste your time with a doctor? I am sure you are not a woman to run about seeking what you have."

"You mean health! But—I don't feel as I used to feel. Formerly I was a very strong woman, so strong that I often felt as if I were safe from unhappiness, real unhappiness. For Schopenhauer was right, I suppose, and if one's health is perfect, one rises above what are called misfortunes. And, you know, I have had great misfortunes."

"Yes?"

"You must know that."

"Yes."

"I didn't really mind them—not enormously. Even when I was what I suppose nice people called 'ruined'—after my divorce—I was quite able to enjoy life and its pleasures, eating and drinking, travelling, yachting, riding, motoring, theatre-going, gambling, and all that sort of thing. People who are being universally condemned, or pitied, are often having a quite splendid time, you know."

"Just as people who are universally envied are often miserable."

"Exactly. But of late I have begun to—well, to feel different."

"In what way exactly?"

"To feel that my health is no longer perfect enough to defend me against—I might call it ennui."

"Yes?"

"Or I might call it depression, melancholy, in fact. Now I don't want—I simply will not be the victim of depression, as so many women are. Do you realise how frightfully women—many women—suffer secretly from depression when they—when they begin to find out that they are not going to remain eternally young?"

"I realize it, certainly."

"I will not be the victim of that depression, because it ruins one's appearance and destroys one's power. I am thirty-eight."

Her large blue eyes met the Doctor's eyes steadily.

"Yes?"

"In England nowadays that isn't considered anything. In England, if one has perfect health, one may pass for a charming and attractive woman till one is at least fifty, or even more. But to seem young when one is getting on, one must feel young. Now, I no longer feel young. I am positive feeling young is a question of physical health. I believe almost everything one feels is a question of physical health. Mystics, people who believe in metempsychosis, in the progress upward and immortality of the soul, idealists —they would cry out against me as a rank materialist. But you are a doctor, and know the empire of the body. Am I not right? Isn't almost everything one feels an emanation from one's molecules, or whatever they are called? Isn't it an echo of the chorus of one's atoms?"

"No doubt the state of the body affects the state of the mind."

"How cautious you are!"

A rather contemptuous smile flickered over her too red lips.

"And really you must be in absolute antagonism with the priests, the Christian Scientists, with all the cranks and the self-deceivers who put soul above matter, who pretend that soul is independent of matter. Why, only the other day I was reading about the psychophysical investigations with the pneumograph and the galvanometer, and I'm certain that——" Suddenly she checked herself. "But that's beside the question. I've told you what I mean, what I think, that health triumphs over nearly everything."

"You seem to be very convinced, a very sincere materialist."

"And you?"

"Despite the discoveries of science, I think there are still depths of mystery in man."

"Woman included?"

"Oh, dear, yes! But to return to your condition."

" Ah!"

She glanced at a watch on her wrist.

"Your day of work ends——?"

"At six, as a rule."

"I mustn't keep you. The truth is this. I am losing my zest for life, and because I am losing my zest, I am losing my power over life. I am beginning to feel weary, melancholy, sometimes apprehensive."

"Of what?"

"Middle age, I suppose, and the ending of all things."

"And you want me to prescribe against melancholy?"

"Why not? What is a doctor for? I tell you I am certain these feelings in me come from a bodily condition."

"You think it quite impossible that they may proceed from a condition of the soul?"

"Quite. I believe it all ends here on the day one dies. I feel as certain of that as of my being a woman. And this being my conviction, I think it of paramount importance to have a good time while I am here."

"Naturally."

"Now, a woman's good time depends on a woman's power over others, and that power depends on her thorough-going belief in herself. So long as she is perfectly well, she feels young, and so long as she feels young, she can give the impression that she is young—with the slightest assistance from art. And so long as she can give that impression—of course I am speaking of a woman who is what is called ' attractive '—it is all right with her. She will believe in herself, and she will have a good time. Now, Doctor Isaacson—remember that I consider all confidences made to a physician of your eminence, all that I tell you to-day, as inviolably secret——"

"Of course," he said.

"Lately my belief in myself has been—well, shaken. I attribute this to some failure in my health. So I have come to you. Try to find out if anything in my bodily condition is wrong."

"Very well. But you must allow me to examine you, and I must put to you a number of purely medical questions which you must answer truthfully."

"En avant, monsieur!"

She put her parasol down on the floor beside her.

"I don't believe in subterfuge—with a doctor," she said.

III

Mrs. Chepstow came out of the house in Cleveland Square as the clocks were striking seven, stepped into a taximeter cab, and was hurried off into the busy whirl of St. James's Street, while Doctor Meyer Isaacson went upstairs to his bedroom to rest and dress for dinner. His clothes were already laid out, and he sent his valet away. As soon as the man was gone, the Doctor took off his coat and waistcoat, his collar and tie, sat down in an arm-chair by the open window, leaned his head against a cushion, shut his eyes, and deliberately relaxed all his muscles. Every day, sometimes at one time, sometimes at another, he did this for ten minutes or a quarter of an hour; and in these moments, as he relaxed his muscles, he also relaxed his mind, banishing thoughts by an effort of the will. So often had he done this that generally he did it without difficulty; and though he never fell asleep in daylight, he came out of this short rest-cure refreshed as after two hours of slumber.

But to-day, though he could command his body, his mind was wilful. He could not clear it of the restless thoughts. Indeed, it seemed to him that he became all mind as he sat there, motionless, looking almost like a dead man, with his stretched-out legs, his hanging arms, his dropped jaw. His last patient was fighting against his desire for complete repose, was defying his will and conquering it.

After his examination of Mrs. Chepstow, his series of questions, he had said to her, "There is nothing the matter with you." A very ordinary phrase, but even as he spoke it, something within him cried to him, "You liar!" This woman suffered from no bodily disease. But to say to her, "There is nothing the matter with you," was, nevertheless, to tell her a lie. And he had added the qualifying statement, "that a doctor can do anything for." He could see her face before him now as it had looked for a moment after he had spoken.

Her exquisite hair was dyed a curious colour. Naturally a bright brown, it had been changed by art to a lighter, less warm hue, that was neither flaxen nor golden, but that held a strange pallor, distinctive, though scarcely beautiful. It had the merit of making her eyes look very vivid between the painted shadows and the painted brows, and this fact had been no doubt realized by the artist responsible for it. Apparently Mrs. Chepstow relied upon the fascination of a peculiar, almost anæmic fairness, in the midst of which eyes, lips, and brows stood forcibly out to seize the attention and engross it. There was in this fairness, this blanched delicacy, something almost pathetic, which assisted the completion, in the mind of a not too astute beholder, of the impression already begun to be made by the beautiful shape of the face.

When Doctor Meyer Isaacson had finished speaking, that face had been a still but searching question; and almost immediately a question had come from the red lips.

"Is there absolutely no unhealthy condition of body such as might be expected to produce low spirits? You see how medically I speak!"

"None whatever. You are not even gouty, and three-quarters, at least, of my patients are gouty in some form or other."

Mrs. Chepstow frowned.

"Then what would you advise me to do?" she asked. "Shall I go to a priest? Shall I go to a philosopher? Shall I go to a Christian Science temple? Or do you think a good dose of the 'New Theology' would benefit me?"

She spoke satirically, yet Doctor Isaacson felt as if he heard, far off, faintly behind the satire, the despair of the materialist, against whom, in certain moments, all avenues of hope seem inexorably closed. He looked at Mrs. Chepstow, and there was a dawning of pity in his eyes as he answered:

"How can I advise you?"

"How indeed? And yet—and that's a curious thing—you look as if you could."

"If you are really a convinced materialist, an honest atheist——"

"I am."

"Well, then it would be useless to advise you to seek priests or to go to Christian Science temples. I can only tell you that your complaint is not a complaint of the body."

"Then is it a complaint of the soul? That's a bore, because I don't happen to believe in the soul, and I do believe very much in the body."

"I wonder what exactly you mean when you say you don't believe in the soul."

"I mean that I don't believe there is in human beings anything mysterious which can live unless the body is living, anything that doesn't die simultaneously with the body. Of course there is something that we call mental, that likes and dislikes, loves and hates, and so on."

"And cannot that something be depressed by misfortune?"

"I did not say I had had any misfortune."

"Nor did I say so. Let us put it this way then—cannot that something be depressed?"

"To a certain degree, of course. But keep your body in perfect health, and you ought to be immune from extreme depression. And I believe you are immune. Frankly, Doctor Meyer Isaacson, I don't think you are right. I am sure something is out of order in my body. There must be some pressure somewhere, some obscure derangement of the nerves, something radically wrong."

"Try another doctor. Try a nerve specialist—a hynotist, if you like: Hinton Morris, Scalinger, or Powell Burnham; I fear I cannot help you."

"So it seems."

She got up slowly. And still her movements were careless, but always full of a grace that was very individual.

"Remember," she said, "that I have spoken to you so frankly in your capacity as a physician."

"All I hear in this room I forget when I am out of it."

"Truly?" she said.

"At any rate, I forget to speak of it," he said, rather curtly.

"Good-bye," she rejoined.

She left him with a strange sensation of the hopelessness that comes from greed and acute worldliness, uncombined with any, even subconscious, conception of other possibilities than purely material ones.

What could such a woman have to look forward to at this period of her life?

Doctor Isaacson was thinking about this now. He remained always perfectly motionless in his arm-chair, but he had abandoned the attempt to discipline his mind. He knew that to-day his brain would not repose with his limbs, and he no longer desired his usual rest-cure. He preferred to think—about Mrs. Chepstow.

She had made upon him a powerful impression. He recalled the look in her eyes when she had said that she was thirty-eight, a look that had seemed to command him to believe her. He had not believed her, yet he had no idea what her real age was. Only he knew that it was not thirty-eight. How determined she was not to suffer, to get through life—her one life, as she thought it—without distress! And she was suffering. He divined why. That was not difficult. She was "in low water." The tides of pleasure were failing. And she had nothing to cling to, clever woman though she was.

Why did he think her clever?

He asked himself that question. He was not a man to take cleverness on trust. Mrs. Chepstow had not said anything specially brilliant. In her materialism she was surely short-sighted, if not blind. She had made a mess of her life. And yet he knew that she was a clever woman.

She had been very frank with him.

Why had she been so frank?

More than once he asked himself that. His mind was full of questions to-day, questions to which he could not immediately supply answers. He felt as if in all she had said Mrs. Chepstow had been prompted by some very definite purpose. She had made upon him the impression of a woman full of purpose, and often full of subtlety. He could not rid himself of the conviction that she had had some concealed reason for wishing to make his acquaintance, some reason unconnected with her health. He believed she had wished honestly for his help as a doctor. But surely that was not her only object in coming to Cleveland Square.

The clock on his chimney-piece struck. His time for repose was at an end. He shut his mouth with a snap, contracted his muscles sharply, and sprang up from his chair. Ten minutes later he was in a cold bath, and half an hour later he was dressed for dinner, and going downstairs with the light, quick step of a man in excellent physical condition and capital spirits. The passing depression he had caught from his last patient had vanished away, and he was in the mood to enjoy his well-earned recreation.

He was dining in Charles Street, Berkeley Square, with Lady Somerson, a widow who was persistently hospitable because she could not bear to be alone. To-night she had a large party. When Doctor Isaacson came into the room on the ground floor where Lady Somerson always received her guests before a dinner, he found her dressed in rusty black, with her grey hair done anyhow, managing and directing the conversation of quite a crowd of important and interesting persons, most of whom had got well away from their first youth, but were so important and interesting that they did not care at all what age they were. It was Wednesday night, and the flavour of the party was political; but among the men were two soldiers, and among the women was a well-known beauty, who cared very little for politics. but a great deal for good talk. She was one of those beauties who reign only in faithful London, partly because of London's faithfulness, but partly also because of their excellent digestions, good spirits, and entire lack of pretence. Her name was Mrs. Derringham; her age was forty-eight. She was not "made up." She made no attempt to look any younger than she was. Lively, energetic, without wrinkles, and apparently without vanity, she neither forbade nor encouraged people to think of her years, but attracted them by her splendid figure, her animation, her zest and her readiness to enjoy the passing hour.

Doctor Isaacson knew her well, and as he shook hands with her he thought of Mrs. Chepstow and of the gospel of Materialism. This woman certainly knew how to enjoy the good things of this world; but she had interests that were not selfish: her husband, her children, her charities, her dependents. She had struck roots deep down into the rich and rewarding soil of the humanities. Women like Mrs. Chepstow struck no roots into any soil. Was it any wonder if the days came and the nights when the souls of them were weary? Was it any wonder if the weariness set its mark upon their beauty?

The door opened, and the last guest appeared—a man, tall, broad-chested, and fair, with short yellow hair parted in the middle, a well-shaped head, a blunt, straight nose, a well-defined but not obstinate chin, a sensitive mouth, and big, sincere, even enthusiastic, blue eyes, surmounted by thick blond eyebrows that always looked as if they had just been brushed vigorously upwards. A small, close-growing moustache covered his upper lip. His cheeks and forehead were tanned by the sun. He was thirty-six years old, but looked a great deal younger, because he was fair. His figure was very muscular and upright, with a hollow back and lean flanks. His capable, rather large-fingered, but not clumsy, hands were brown. There was in his face a peculiarly straight and bright look that suggested the North and Northern things, the glitter of stars upon snows, cool summits of mountains swept by pure winds, the scented freshness of pine forests. He had something of the expression, of the build, and of the carriage of a hero from the North. But he was surely a hero from the North who had very recently had his dwelling in the South, and who had taken kindly to it.

When Lady Somerson saw the newcomer, she rushed at

him and blew him up. Then she introduced him to the lady he was to take in to dinner, and, with an alacrity that was almost feverish, gave the signal for her guests to move into the dining-room, disclosed at this moment by two assiduous footmen who briskly pushed back the sliding doors that divided it from the room in which she had received.

"Our hostess does not conceal her feelings," murmured Mrs. Derringham, who was Doctor Isaacson's companion, as they found their places at the long table. "Who is the man whom she has just scolded so vivaciously? I know his face quite well."

"One of the best fellows in the world—Nigel Armine. I have not seen him till to-night since last October. He has been out in Egypt."

At this moment he caught the fair man's eyes, and they exchanged with his a look of friendship.

"Of course! I remember! He looks like a knight-errant. So did his father, poor Harwich. I used to act with Harwich in the early never-mind-whats at Burnham House. One scarcely ever sees Nigel now. I don't think he was ever at all really fond of London and gaieties. Harwich was, of course. Yet even in his face there was a sort of strangeness, of other-worldliness. I used to say he had kitten's eyes. How he believed in women, poor fellow!"

"Don't you believe in women?"

"As a race, no. I believe in a very few individual women. But Harwich believed in women because they were women. That is always a mistake. He believed in them as a good Catholic believes in the Saints. And he was punished for it."

"You mean after Nigel's mother died? That Mrs.—— what was her name?—Mrs. Alstruther?"

"Yes, Mrs. Alstruther. She treated Harwich abominably. Even if she had been free, she would never have married him. He bored her. But he worshipped her, and thought to the end that her husband ill-used her. So absurd, when Paul Alstruther could call neither his soul nor his purse his own. Nigel Armine has his father's look. He, too, is born to believe in women."

She paused; then she added:

"I must say it would be rather nice to be the woman he believed in."

"Tell me something about this Mr. Armine, Doctor Isaacson," said Lady O'Ryan, who was sitting on the Doctor's other side, and had caught part of this conversation. "You know I am always in County Clare, and as ignorant as a violet. Who is he exactly?"

"A younger brother of Harwich's, and the next heir to the title."

"That immensely rich Lord Harwich whose horses have won so many races, and who married Zoe Mulligan, of Chicago, more than ten years ago?"

"Yes. They've never had any children, and Harwich has knocked his health to pieces, so Armine is pretty sure to succeed. But he's fairly well off, I suppose, for a bachelor. When his mother died, she left him her property."

"And what does he do?"

"He was in the army, but resigned his commission when he came into his land."

"Why?"

"To look after his people. He had great ideas about a landlord's duties to his tenants."

"O'Ryan's tenants have enormous ideas about his duties to them."

"That must be trying. Armine lived in the country, and made a great many generous experiments—built model cottages, started rifle ranges, erected libraries, gymnasiums, swimming baths. In fact, he spent his money royally—too royally."

"And were they sick with gratitude?"

"Their thankfulness did not go so far as that. In fact, some of Armine's schemes for making people happy met with a good deal of opposition. Finally there was a tremendous row about a right of way. The tenants were in the wrong, and Armine was so disgusted at their trying to rob him of what was his, after he had showered benefits upon them, that he let his place and hasn't been there since."

"That's so like people, to ignore libraries and village halls, and shriek for the right to get over a certain stile, or go down a muddy path that leads from nothing to nowhere."

"The desire of the star for the moth!"

"You call humanity a star?"

"I think there is a great brightness burning in it; don't you?"

"There seems to be in Mr. Armine, certainly. What an enthusiastic look he has! How could he get wrong with his tenants?"

"It may have been his enthusiasm, his great expectations, his ideality. Perhaps he puzzled his people, asked too much imagination, too much sacred fire from them. And then he has immense ideas about honesty, and the rights of the individual; and, in fact, about a good many things that seldom bother the head of the average man."

"Don't tell me he has developed into a crank," said Mrs. Derringham. "There's something so underbred about crankiness; and the Harwich family have always been essentially aristocrats."

"I shouldn't think Armine was a crank, but I do think he is an idealist. He considers Watts's allegorical pictures the greatest things in Art that have been done since Botticelli enshrined Purity in paint. In modern music Elgar's his man; in modern literature, Tolstoy. He loves those with ideals, even if their ideals are not his. I do not say he is an artist. He is not. His motto is not 'Art for art's sake,' but 'Art for man's sake.'"

"He is a humanitarian?"

"And a great believer."

"In man?"

"In the good that is in man. I often think at the back

of his mind, or heart, he believes that the act of belief is almost an act of creation."

"You mean, for instance, that if you believe in a man's truthfulness you make him a truthful man?"

"Yes."

"Oh, Doctor Isaacson," said Lady O'Ryan, "do introduce Mr. Armine to my husband, and make him believe my husband is a miser instead of a spendthrift. It would be such a mercy to the family. We might begin to pay off the mortgage on the castle."

The conversation took a frivolous turn, and died in laughter.

But towards the end of dinner Mrs. Derringham again spoke of Nigel Armine, asking:

"And what does Mr. Armine do now?"

"He went to Egypt after he let his place, bought some land there, in the Fayyūm, I believe, and has been living on it a good deal. I think he has been making some experiments in farming."

"And does he believe in the truth and honesty of the average donkey-boy?"

"I don't know. But I must confess I have heard him extol the merits of the Bedouins."

At this moment Lady Somerson sprang up, in her usual feverish manner, and the men in a moment were left to themselves. As the sliding doors closed behind Lady Somerson's active back, there was a hesitating movement among them, suggestive of a half-formed desire for rearrangement.

Then Armine came decisively away from his place on the far side of the long table, and joined Meyer Isaacson.

"I'm glad to meet you again, Isaacson," he said, grasping the Doctor's hand.

The Doctor returned his grip with a characteristic clasp, and they sat down side by side, while the other men began talking and lighting cigarettes.

"Have you only just come back?" asked the Doctor.

"I have been back for a week."

"So long! Where are you staying?"

"At the Savoy."

"The Savoy?"

"Are you surprised?"

The Doctor's brilliant eyes were fixed upon Armine with an expression half humorous, half affectionate.

"Any smart hotel would seem the wrong place for you," he said. "I can see you on the snows of the Alps, or your own moors at Etchingham, even at—where is it?"

"Sennoures."

"But at the Savoy, the Ritz, the Carlton—no. Their gilded banality isn't the *cadre* for you at all."

"I'm very happy at the Savoy," Armine replied.

As he spoke, he looked away from Meyer Isaacson across the table to the wall opposite to him. Upon it hung a large reproduction of Watts's picture, "Progress." He gazed at it, and his face became set in a strange calm, as if he had for a moment forgotten the place he was in, the people round about him. Meyer Isaacson watched him with a concentrated interest. There was something in this man— there always had been something—which roused in the Doctor an affection, an admiration, that were mingled with pity and even with a secret fear. Such a nature, the Doctor often thought, must surely be fore-ordained to suffering in a world that holds certainly many who cherish ideals and strive to mount upwards, but a majority that is greedy for the constant gratification of the fleshly appetites, that seldom listens to the dim appeal of the distant voices which sometimes speak, however faintly, to all who dwell on earth.

"What a splendid thing that is!" Armine said, at last, with a sigh. "You know the original?"

"I saw it the other day at the gallery in Compton."

"Progress—advance—going on irresistibly all the time, whether we see it, feel it, or not. How glorious!"

"You are always an optimist?"

"I do believe in the triumph of good. More and more every day I believe in that, the triumph of good in the world, and in the individual. And the more believers there are—true believers—in that triumph, the more surely, the more swiftly, it will be accomplished. You can help, Isaacson."

"By believing?"

"Yes, that's the way to help. But Lord! how few people take it! Suspicion is one of the most destructive agents at work in the world. Suspect a man, and you almost force him to give you cause for suspicion. Suspect a woman, and instantly you give her a push towards deceit. How I hate to hear men say they don't trust women."

"Women say that, too."

"Sex treachery! Despicable! They who say that are traitresses in their own camp."

"You value truth, don't you?"

"Above everything."

"Suppose women truly mistrust other women; are they to pretend the contrary?"

"They can be silent, and try to stamp out an unworthy, a destructive, feeling."

He said nothing for a moment. Then he looked up at Meyer Isaacson and continued:

"Are you going anywhere when you leave here?"

"I've accepted something in Chesham Place. Why?"

"Must you go to it?"

"No."

"Come and have supper with me at the Savoy."

"Supper! My dear Armine! You know nowadays we doctors are preaching, and rightly preaching, less eating and drinking to our patients. I can eat nothing till to-morrow after my morning ride."

"But you can sit at a supper-table, I suppose?"

"Oh, yes, I can do that."

"Come and sit at mine. Let's go away from here together."

"Certainly."

"You shall see whether I am out of place at the Savoy."

IV

At a quarter to eleven that night Meyer Isaacson and Nigel Armine came down the bit of carpet that was unrolled to the edge of the pavement in front of Lady Somerson's door, and got into the former's electric brougham. As it moved off noiselessly, the Doctor said:

"You had a long talk with Mrs. Derringham in the drawing-room."

"Yes," replied Armine, rather curtly.

He relapsed into silence, leaning back in his corner.

"I like her," the Doctor continued, after a pause.

"Do you?"

"And you—don't."

"Why do you say that?"

"Because I feel it; I gather it from the way you said 'yes.'"

Armine moved, and leaned slightly forwards.

"Isn't she rather *mauvaise langue?*" he asked.

"Mrs. Derringham? I certainly don't think her so."

"She's one of the disbelievers in women you spoke of after dinner; one of the traitresses in the woman's camp. Why can't women hang together?"

"They do sometimes."

"Yes, when there's a woman to be hounded down. They hang together when there's a work of destruction on hand. But do they hang together when there's a work of construction to be done?"

"Do you mean a reputation to be built up?"

Armine pulled his moustache. In the electric light Meyer Isaacson could see that his blue eyes were shining.

"Because," Meyer Isaacson continued, "if you do mean that, I should be inclined to say that each of us must build up his or her reputation individually for himself or herself."

"We need help in nearly all our buildings-up, and how often, how damnably often, we don't get it!"

"Was Mrs. Derringham specially down upon some particular woman to-night?"

"Yes, she was."

"Do you care to tell me upon whom?"

"It was Mrs. Chepstow."

"You were talking about Mrs. Chepstow?" Isaacson said slowly. "The famous Mrs. Chepstow?"

"Famous!" said Armine. "I hardly see that Mrs. Chepstow is a famous woman. She is not a writer, a singer, a painter, an actress. She does nothing that I ever heard of. I shouldn't call such a woman famous. I daresay her name is known to lots of people. But this is the age of chatterboxes, and of course——"

At this moment the brougham rolled on to the rubber pavement in front of the Savoy Hotel and stopped before the entrance.

As he was getting out and going into the hall, Meyer Isaacson remembered that the letter Mrs. Chepstow had written to him asking for an appointment had been stamped "Savoy Hotel." She had been staying at the hotel then. Was she staying there now? He had never heard Armine mention her before, but his feminine intuition suddenly connected Armine's words, "I'm very happy at the Savoy," with the invitation to sup there, and the conversation about Mrs. Chepstow just reported to him by his friend. Armine knew Mrs. Chepstow. They were going to meet her in the restaurant to-night. Meyer Isaacson felt sure of it.

They left their coats in the cloak-room and made their way to the restaurant, which as yet was almost empty. The *maître d'hôtel* came forward to Armine, bowing and smiling, and showed them to a table in a corner. Meyer Isaacson saw that it was laid for only two. He was surprised, but he said nothing, and they sat down.

"I really can't eat supper, Armine," he said. "Don't order it for me."

"Have a little soup, at least, and a glass of champagne?"

Without waiting for a reply, he gave an order.

"We might have sat in the hall, but it is more amusing in here. Remember, I haven't been in London—seen the London show—for over eight months. One meets a lot of old friends and acquaintances in places like this."

Meyer Isaacson opened his lips to say that Armine would be far more likely to meet his friends during the season if he went to parties in private houses. America was beginning to stream in, mingled with English country people "up" for a few days, and floating representatives of the nations of the earth. In this heterogeneous crowd he saw no one whom he knew, and Armine had not so far recognized anybody. But he shut his lips without speaking. He realized that Armine had a purpose in coming to the Savoy to-night, in bringing him. For some reason his friend was trying to mask that purpose, but it must almost immediately become apparent. He had only to wait for a few minutes, and doubtless he would know exactly what it was.

A waiter brought the soup and the champagne.

"If any of the patients to whom I have strictly forbidden supper should see me now," said the Doctor, "and if they should divine that I have come straight from a long dinner!—Armine, I am making a heavy sacrifice on friendship's altar."

"You don't see any patients, I hope?"

"Not as yet," the Doctor answered.

Almost before the words were out of his mouth, he saw Mrs. Chepstow at some distance from them, coming in at the door. She came in alone. He looked to see her escort, but, to his surprise, she was not followed by any one. Holding herself very erect, and not glancing to the right or left, she walked down the room escorted by the *maître d'hôtel*, passed close to Armine and the Doctor, went to a small table set in the angle of a screen not far off, and sat down with her profile turned towards them. She said a few words to the *maître d'hôtel*. He spoke to a waiter, then hurried away. Mrs. Chepstow sat very still in her chair, looking down. She had laid a lace fan beside the knives and glasses that shone in the electric light. Her right hand rested lightly on it. She was dressed in black, and wore a diamond comb in her fair, dyed hair, and white gloves. Her strange, colourless complexion looked extraordinarily delicate and pure from where the two friends were sitting. There was something pathetic in its whiteness, and in the quiet attitude of this woman who sat quite alone in the midst of the gay crowd. Many people stared at her, whispered about her, were obviously surprised at her solitude; but she seemed quite unconscious that she was being noticed. And there was a curious simplicity in her unconsciousness, and in her attitude, which made her seem almost girlish from a little distance.

"There's Mrs. Chepstow," said a man at the next table to Armine's, bending over to his companion, a stout and florid specimen from the City. "And absolutely alone, by Jove!"

"Couldn't get even a kid from Sandhurst to-night, I s'pose," returned the other. "I wonder she comes in at all if she can't scrape up an escort. Wonder she has the cheek to do it."

They lowered their voices and leaned nearer to each other. Armine lifted his glass of champagne to his lips, sipped it, and put it down.

"If you do see any patients, you can explain it's all my fault," he said to the Doctor. "I will take the blame. But surely you don't have to follow all your prescriptions?"

His voice was slightly uneven and abstracted, as if he were speaking merely to cover some emotion he was determined to conceal.

"No. But I ought to set an example of reasonable living, I suppose."

They talked for a few minutes about health, with a curious formality, like people who are conscious that they are being critically listened to, or who are, too consciously, listening to themselves. Once or twice Meyer Isaacson glanced across the room to Mrs. Chepstow. She was eating her supper slowly, languidly, and always looking down. Apparently she had not seen him or Armine. Indeed, she did not seem to see any one, but she was rather sadly unconscious of her surroundings. The Doctor found himself pitying her, then denying to himself that she merited compassion. With many others, he wondered at her solitude. To sup thus alone in a crowded restaurant was to advertise her ill success in the life she had chosen, her abandonment by man. Why did she do this? He could not then divine, although afterwards he knew. And he was quietly astonished. Just at first he expected that she would presently be joined by some one who was late. But no one came, and no second place was laid at her table.

Conversation flagged between Armine and him, until the former presently said:

"I want to introduce you to some one to-night."

"Yes? Who is it?"

He asked, but he already knew.

"Mrs. Chepstow."

The Doctor was on the verge of saying that he was already acquainted with her, when Armine added:

"I spoke about you to her, and she told me she had never met you."

"When was that?"

"Four days ago, when I was introduced to her, and talked to her for the first time."

The Doctor did not speak for a minute. Then he said:

"I shall be delighted to be presented to her."

Although he was remarkably truthful with his friends, he was always absolutely discreet in his professional capacity. He did not know whether Mrs. Chepstow would wish the fact of her having consulted him about her health to be spoken of. Therefore he did not mention it. And as Armine knew that four days ago Mrs. Chepstow and he were strangers, in not mentioning it he was obliged to leave his friend under the impression that they were strangers still.

"She is staying in this hotel, and is sitting over there. But of course you know her by sight," said Armine.

"Oh, yes, I have seen her about."

"I think you will like her, if you can clear your mind of any prejudices you may have formed against her."

"Why should I be prejudiced against Mrs. Chepstow?"

"People are. No one has a good word for her. Both women and men speak ill of her."

From the tone of Armine's voice Meyer Isaacson knew that this fact had prejudiced him in Mrs. Chepstow's favour. There are some men who are born to defend lost causes, who instinctively turn towards those from whom others are ostentatiously turning away, moved by some secret chivalry which blinds their reason, or by a passion of simple human pity that dominates their hearts and casts a shadow over the brightness of their intellects. Of these men Nigel Armine was one, and Meyer Isaacson knew it. He was not much surprised, therefore, when Armine continued:

"They see only the surface of things, and judge by what they see. I suppose one ought not to condemn them. But sometimes it's—it's devilish difficult not to condemn cruelty, especially when the cruelty is directed against a woman. Only to-night Mrs. Derringham—and you say she's a good sort of woman——"

"Very much so."

"Well, she said to me, 'For such women as Mrs. Chepstow I have no pity, so don't ask it of me, Mr. Armine.' What a confession, Isaacson!"

"Did she give her reasons?"

"Oh, yes, she tried to. She said the usual thing."

"What was that?"

"She said that Mrs. Chepstow had sold herself body and soul to the Devil for material things; that she was the typical greedy woman."

"And did she indicate exactly what she meant by the typical greedy woman?"

"Yes. I will say for her that she was plain-spoken. She said: 'The woman without ideals, without any feeling for home and all that home means, the one man, children, peace found in unselfishness, rest in work for others; the woman who betrays the reputation of her sex by being absolutely concentrated upon herself, and whose desires only extend to the vulgar satisfactions brought by a preposterous expenditure of money on clothes, jewels, yachts, houses, motors, everything that rouses wonder and admiration in utterly second-rate minds.'"

"There are such women."

"Perhaps there are. But, my dear Isaacson, one has only to look at Mrs. Chepstow—with unprejudiced eyes, mind you—to see that she could never be one of them. Even if I had never spoken to her, I should know that she must have ideals, could never not have them, whatever her life is, or has been. Physiognomy cannot utterly lie. Look at the line of that face. Don't you see what I mean?"

They both gazed for a moment at the lonely woman.

"There is, of course, a certain beauty in Mrs. Chepstow's face," the Doctor said.

"I am not speaking of beauty; I am speaking of ideality, of purity. Don't you see what I mean? Now, be honest."

"Yes, I do."

"Ah!" said Armine.

The exclamation sounded warmly pleased.

"But that look, I think, is a question merely of line, and of the way the hair grows. Do you mean to say that you would rather judge a woman by that than by the actions of her life?"

"No. But I do say that if you examined the life of a woman with a face like that—the real life—you would be certain to find that it had not been devoid of actions such as you would expect, actions illustrating that look of ideality which any one can see. What does Mrs. Derringham really know of Mrs. Chepstow? She is not personally acquainted with her, even. She acknowledged that. She has never spoken to her, and doesn't want to."

"That scarcely surprises me, I confess," the Doctor remarked.

There was a definite dryness in his tone, and Armine noticed it.

"You are prejudiced, I see," he said.

In his voice there was a sound of disappointment.

"I don't exactly know why, but I have always looked upon you as one of the most fair-minded, broad-minded men I have met, Isaacson," he said. "Not as one of those who must always hunt with the hounds."

"The question is, What is prejudice? The facts of a life are facts, and cannot leave one wholly uninfluenced for or against the liver of the life. If I see a man beating a dog because it has licked his hand, I draw the inference that he is cruel. Would you say that I am narrow-minded in doing so? If one does not judge men and women by their actions, by what is one to judge them? Perhaps you will say, 'Don't judge them at all.' But it is impossible not to form opinions on people, and every time one forms an opinion one passes a secret judgment. Isn't it so?"

"I think feeling enters into the matter. Often one gets an immediate impression, before one knows anything about the facts of a life. The facts may seem to give that impression the lie. But is it wrong? I think very often not. I remember once I heard a woman, and a clever woman, say of a man whom she knew intimately, 'They accuse him of such and such an act. Well, if I saw him commit it, I would not believe he had done it!' Absurd, you will say. And yet is it so absurd? In front of the real man may there not be a false man, is there not often a false man, like a mask over a face? And doesn't the false man do things that the real man condemns? I would often rather judge with my heart than with my eyes, Isaacson—yes, I would. That woman said a fine thing when she said that, and she was not absurd, though every one who heard her laughed at her. When one gets what one calls an impression, one's heart is speaking, is saying, 'This is the truth.' And I believe the heart, without reasoning, knows what the truth is."

"And if two people get diametrically different impressions of the same person? What then? That sometimes happens, you know."

"I don't believe you and I could ever get diametrically

different impressions of a person," said Armine, looking at Mrs. Chepstow; "and to-night I can't bother myself about the rest of the world."

"Don't you think hearts can be stupid as well as heads? I do. I think people can be muddle-hearted as well as muddle-headed."

As the Doctor spoke, it seemed to flash upon him that he was passing a judgment upon his friend—this man whom he admired, whom he almost loved.

"I should always trust my heart," said Armine. "But I very often mistrust my head. Won't you have any more champagne?"

"No, thank you."

"What do you say to our joining Mrs. Chepstow? It must be awfully dull for her, supping all alone. We might go and speak to her. If she doesn't ask us to sit down, we can go into the hall and have a cigar."

"Very well."

There was neither alacrity nor reluctance in Meyer Isaacson's voice, but if there had been, Armine would probably not have noticed it. When he was intent on a thing, he saw little but that one thing. Now he paid the bill, tipped the waiter, and got up.

"Come along," he said, "and I will introduce you."

He put his hand for an instant on his friend's arm.

"Clear your mind of prejudice, Isaacson," he said, in a low voice. "You are too good and too clever to be one of the prejudiced crowd. Let your first impression be a true one."

As the doctor went with his friend to Mrs. Chepstow's table, he did not tell him that first impression had been already formed in the consulting-room of the house in Cleveland Square.

V

"MRS. CHEPSTOW!"

At the sound of Nigel Armine's voice Mrs. Chepstow started slightly, like a person recalled abruptly from a reverie, looked up, and smiled.

"You are here! I'm all alone. But I was hungry, so I had to brave the rabble."

"I want to introduce a friend to you. May I?"

"Of course."

Armine moved, and Doctor Isaacson stood by Mrs. Chepstow.

"Doctor Meyer Isaacson, Mrs. Chepstow."

The Doctor scarcely knew whether he had expected Mrs. Chepstow to recognize him, or whether he had anticipated what actually happened—her slight bow and murmured "I'm delighted to meet you." But he did know that he was not really surprised at her treatment of him as an entire stranger. And he was glad that he had said nothing to Armine of her visit to Cleveland Square.

"Aren't you going to sit down and talk to me for a little?" Mrs. Chepstow said. "I'm all alone and horribly dull."

"May we?"

Armine drew up a chair.

"Sit on my other side, Doctor Isaacson. I've heard a great deal about you. You've made perfect cures of most of my enemies."

There was not the least trace of consciousness in her manner, not the faintest suspicion of embarrassment in her look, and, as he sat down, the Doctor found himself admiring the delicate perfection of her deceit, as he had sometimes admired a subtle *nuance* in the performance of some great French actress.

"You ought to hate me then," he said.

"Why? If I don't hate them?"

"Don't you hate your enemies?" asked Armine.

"No; that's a weakness in me. I never could and never shall. Something silly inside of me invariably finds excuses for people, whatever they are or do. I'm always saying to myself, 'They don't understand. If they really knew all the circumstances, they would'nt hate me. Perhaps they'd even pity me.' Absurd! A mistake! I know that. Such feelings stand in the way of success, because they prevent one striking out in one's own defence. And if one doesn't strike out for oneself, nobody will strike out for one."

"I don't think that's quite true," Armine said.

"Oh, yes, it is. If you're pugnacious, people think you're plucky, and they're ready to stand up for you. Whereas, if you forgive easily, you're not easily forgiven."

"If that is so," Armine said, "why don't you change your tactics?"

As he said this, he glanced at Isaacson, and the Doctor understood that he was seeking to display to his friend what he believed to be this woman's character.

"Simply because I can't. I am what I am. I can't change myself, and I can't act in defiance of the little interior voice. I often try to, for I don't pretend in the least to be virtuous; but I have to give in. I know it's weakness. I know the world would laugh at it. But— *que voulez-vous?*—some of us are the slaves of our souls."

The last sentence seemed almost to be blurted out, so honestly was it said. But instantly, as if regretting a sincere indiscretion, she added:

"Doctor Isaacson, what an idiot you must think me!"

"Why, Mrs. Chepstow?"

"For saying that. You, of course, think we are the slaves of our bodies."

"I certainly do not think you an idiot," he could not help saying, with significance.

"Isaacson is not an ordinary doctor," said Armine. "You needn't be afraid of him."

"I don't think I'm afraid of anybody, but one doesn't want to make oneself absurd. And I believe I often am absurd in rating the body too low. What a conversation!"

she added, smiling. "But, as I was all alone in the crowd, I was thinking of all sorts of things. A crowd makes one think tremendously, if one is quite alone. It stimulates the brain, I suppose. So I was thinking a lot of rubbish over my solitary meal."

She looked at the two men apologetically.

"*La femme pense*," she said, and she shrugged her shoulders.

Armine drew his chair a little nearer to her, and this action suddenly made Doctor Isaacson realize the power that still dwelt in this woman, the power to govern certain types of men.

"And the man acts," completed Armine.

"And the woman acts, too, and better than the man," the Doctor thought to himself.

Again his admiration was stirred, this time by the sledge-hammer boldness of Mrs. Chepstow, by her complete though so secret defiance of himself.

"But what were you thinking about?" Armine continued, earnestly. "I noticed how preoccupied you were even when you came into the room."

"Did you? I was thinking about a conversation I had this afternoon. Oddly enough "—she turned slowly towards Meyer Isaacson—"it was with a doctor."

"Indeed?" he said, looking her full in the face.

"Yes."

She turned away, and once more spoke to Armine.

"I went this afternoon to a doctor, Mr. Armine, to consult him about a friend of mine who is ill and obstinate, and we had a most extraordinary talk about the soul and the body. A sort of fight it was. He thought me a typical silly woman. I'm sure of that."

"Why?"

"Because I suppose I took a sentimental view of our subject. We women always instinctively take the sentimental view, you know. My doctor was severely scientific and frightfully sceptical. He thought me an absurd visionary."

"And what did you think him?"

"I'm afraid I thought him a crass materialist. He had doctored the body until he was able to believe only in the body. He referred everything back to the body. Every emotion, according to him, was only caused by the terminal of a nerve vibrating in a cell contained in the grey matter of the brain. I dare say he thinks the most passionate love could be operated for. And as to any one having an immortal soul—well, I did dare, being naturally fearless, just to mention the possibility of my possessing such a thing. But I was really sorry afterwards."

"Tell us why."

"Because it brought upon me such an avalanche of scorn and arguments. I didn't much mind the scorn, but the arguments bored me."

"Did they convince you?"

"Mr. Armine! Now, did you ever know a woman convinced of anything by argument?"

He laughed.

"Then you still believe that you have an immortal soul?"

"More, far more, than ever."

She was laughing, too. But, quite suddenly, the laughter died out of her, and she said, with an earnest face:

"I wouldn't let any one—any one—take some of my beliefs from me."

The tone of her voice was almost fierce in its abrupt doggedness.

"I must have some coffee," she added, with a complete change of tone. "I sleep horribly badly, and that's why I take coffee. Mere perversity! Three black coffees, waiter."

"Not for me!" said Meyer Isaacson.

"You must, for once. I hate doing things alone. There is no pleasure in anything unless some one shares it. At least"—she looked at Armine—"that is what every woman thinks."

"Then how unhappy lots of women must be," he said.

"The lonely women. Ah! no man will ever know how unhappy."

There was a moment of silence. Something in the sound

of Mrs. Chepstow's voice as she said the last words almost compelled a silence.

For the first time since he had been with her that night Meyer Isaacson felt that perhaps he had caught a glimpse of her true self, had drawn near to the essential woman.

The waiter brought their coffee, and Mrs. Chepstow added, with a little laugh:

"Even a meal eaten alone is no pleasure to a woman. To-night, till you came to take pity upon me, I should have been far happier with 'something on a tray' in my own room. But now I feel quite convivial. Isn't the coffee here good?"

Suddenly she looked cheerful, almost gay. Happiness seemed to blossom within her.

"Never mind if you lie awake for once, Doctor Isaacson," she continued, looking across at him. "You will have done a good action; you will have cheered up a human being who had been feeling down on her luck. That talk I had with a doctor had depressed me most horribly, although I told myself that I didn't believe a word he said."

Meyer Isaacson sipped his coffee and said nothing.

"I think one of the wickedest things one can do in the world is to try to take any comforting and genuine belief away from the believer," said Armine, with energy.

"Would you leave people even in their errors?" said the Doctor. "Suppose, for instance, you saw some one—some friend—believing in a person whom you knew to be unworthy, would you make no effort to enlighten him?"

He spoke very quietly—almost carelessly. Mrs. Chepstow fixed her big blue eyes on him and for a moment forgot her coffee.

"Perhaps I should. But you know my theory."

"Oh—to be sure!"

Meyer Isaacson smiled. Mrs. Chepstow looked from one man to the other quickly.

"What theory? Don't make me feel an outsider," she said.

"Mr. Armine thinks—may I, Armine?"

"Of course."

"Thinks that belief in the goodness, the genuineness of people helps them to become good, genuine, so that the unworthy might be made eventually worthy by a trust at first misplaced."

"Mr. Armine is——" She checked herself. "It is a pity the world isn't full of Mr. Armines," she said, softly.

Armine flushed, almost boyishly.

"I wish my doctor knew you, Mr. Armine. If you create by believing, I'm sure he destroys by disbelieving."

As she said the last words, her eyes met Meyer Isaacson's, and he saw in them, or thought he saw, a defiance that was threatening.

The lights winked. Mrs. Chepstow got up.

"They're going to turn us out. Let us anticipate them—by going. It's so dreadful to be turned out. It makes me feel like Eve at the critical moment of her career."

She led the way from the big room. As she passed among the tables, every man, and almost every woman, turned to stare at her as children stare at a show. She seemed quite unconscious of the attention she attracted. But when she bade good night to the two friends in the hall, she said:

"Aren't people horrible sometimes? They seem to think one is—" She checked herself. "I'm a fool!" she said. "Good night. Thank you both for coming. It has done me good."

"Don't mind those brutes!" Armine almost whispered to her, as he held her hand for a moment. "Don't think of them. Think of—the others."

She looked at him in silence, nodded, and went quietly away.

Directly she had gone Meyer Isaacson said to his friend:

"Well, good night, Armine. I am glad you're back. Let us see something of each other."

"Don't go yet. Come to my sitting-room and have a smoke."

"Better not. I have to be up early. I ride at half-past seven."

"I'll ride with you, then."

"To-morrow?"

"Yes, to-morrow."

"But have you got any horses up?"

"No; I'll hire from Simonds. Don't wait for me, but look out for me in the Row. Good night, old chap."

As they grasped hands for a moment, he added:

"Wasn't I right?"

"Right?"

"About her—Mrs. Chepstow? She may have been driven into the Devil's hands, but don't you see, don't you feel, the good in her, struggling up, longing for an opportunity to proclaim itself, to take the reins of her life and guide her to calm, to happiness, to peace? I pity that woman, Isaacson; I pity her."

"Pity her if you like," the Doctor said, with a strong emphasis on the first word, "but——"

He hesitated. Something in his friend's face stopped him from saying more, told him that perhaps it would be much wiser to say nothing more. Opposition drives some natures blindly forward. Such natures should not be opposed.

"I pity Mrs. Chepstow, too," he concluded. "Poor woman!"

And in saying that he spoke the truth. But his pity for her was not of the kind that is akin to love.

The black coffee Mrs. Chepstow had persuaded Meyer Isaacson to take kept him awake that night. Like some evil potion, it banished sleep and peopled the night with a rushing crowd of thoughts. Presently he did not even try to sleep. He gave himself to the crowd with a sort of half-angry joy.

In the afternoon he had been secretly puzzled by Mrs. Chepstow. He had wondered what under-reason she had for seeking an interview with him. Now he surely knew that reason. Unless he was wrong, unless he misunderstood her completely, she had come to make a curiously audacious *coup*. She had seen Nigel Armine, she had read his strange nature rightly; she had divined that in him there was a man who, unlike most men, instinctively loved to go against the stream, who instinctively turned towards that which most men turned from. She had seen in him the born espouser of lost causes.

She was a lost cause. Armine was her opportunity.

Armine had talked to her four days ago of Meyer Isaacson. The Doctor guessed how, knowing the generous enthusiasm of his friend. And she, a clever woman, made distrustful by misfortune, had come to Cleveland Square, led by feminine instinct, to spy out this land of which she had heard so much. The Doctor's sensation of being examined, while he sat with Mrs. Chepstow in his consulting-room, had been well-founded. The patient had been reading the Doctor, swiftly, accurately. And she had acted promptly upon the knowledge of him so rapidly acquired. She had "given herself away" to him; she had shown herself to him as she was. Why? To shut his mouth in the future. The revelation, such as it was, had been made to him as a physician, under the guise of described symptoms. She had told him the exact truth of herself in his consulting-room, in order that he might not tell others—tell Nigel Armine—what that truth was.

Her complete reliance upon her own capacity for reading character surprised and almost delighted the Doctor. For there was something within him which loved strength and audacity, which could appreciate them artistically at their full value. She had given a further and a fuller illustration of her audacity that evening in the restaurant.

Now, in the night, he could see her white face, the look in her brilliant eyes above the painted shadows, as she told to Nigel the series of lies about the interview in Cleveland Square, putting herself in the Doctor's place, him in her own. She had enjoyed doing that, enjoyed it intellectually. And she had forced the Doctor to dance to her piping. He had been obliged to join her in her deceit—almost to back her up in it.

He knew now why she had been alone at her table, why she had advertised her ill success in the life she had chosen, her present abandonment by men. This had been done to strike at Armine's peculiar temperament. It was a very clever stroke.

But it was a burning of her boats.

Meyer Isaacson frowned in the night.

A woman like Mrs. Chepstow does not burn her boats for nothing. How much did she expect to gain by that sacrifice of improper pride, a pride almost dearer than life to a woman of her type? The *quid pro quo*—what was it to be?

He feared for Nigel, as he lay awake while the night drew on towards dawn.

VI

Mrs. Chepstow's sitting-room at the Savoy was decorated with pink and green in pale hues which suited well her present scheme of colour. In it there was a little rosewood piano. Upon that piano's music-desk, on the following day, stood a copy of Elgar's "Dream of Gerontius," open at the following words:

"Proficiscere, anima Christiana, de hoc mundo! Go forth upon thy journey, Christian soul! Go from this world!"

Scattered about the room were *The Nineteenth Century and After*, *The Quarterly Review*, the *Times*, and several books; among them Goethe's "Faust," Maspero's "Manual of Egyptian Archæology," "A Companion to Greek Studies," Guy de Maupassant's "Fort Comme la Mort," D'Annunzio's "Trionfo della Morte," and Hawthorne's "Scarlet Letter." There was also a volume of Emerson's "Essays." In a little basket under the writing-table lay the last number of *The Winning Post*, carefully destroyed. There were a few pink roses in a vase. In a cage some canary-birds were singing. The furniture had been pulled about by a clever hand until the room had lost something of its look of a room in a smart hotel.

The windows were wide open on to the balcony. They dominated the Thames Embankment, and a light breeze from the water stirred the white and green curtains that framed them.

Into this pretty and peacefully cheerful chamber Nigel Armine was shown by a waiter at five o'clock precisely, and left with the promise that Mrs. Chepstow should be informed of his arrival.

When the door had closed behind the German waiter's back, Nigel stood for a moment looking around him. This was the first visit he had paid to Mrs. Chepstow. He sought for traces of her personality in this room in which she lived. He thought it looked unusually cosy for a room in an hotel, although he did not discover, as Isaacson would have discovered in a moment, that the furniture had been deftly disarranged. His eyes roved quickly: no photographs, no embroideries, one or two extra cushions, birds, a few perfect roses, a few beautifully bound books, the windows widely opened to let the air stream in. And there was an open piano! He went over to it and bent down.

"Proficiscere, anima Christiana, de hoc mundo! Go forth upon thy journey, Christian soul! Go from this world!"

So she loved "Gerontius," that intimate musical expression of the wonder and the strangeness of the Soul! He did not remember he had told her that he loved it. He stood gazing at the score. The light wind came in from the river far down below, and the curtains made a faint sound as they moved. The canaries chirped intermittently. But Nigel heard the voice of a priest by the side of one who was dying. And as he looked at the chords supporting the notes on which the priest bade the soul of the man return to its Maker, he seemed to hear them, as he had heard them, played by a great orchestra; to feel the mysterious, the terrible, yet beautiful act of dissolution.

He started. He had launched himself into space with the soul. Now, abruptly, he was tethered to earth in the body. Had he not heard the murmur of a dress announcing the coming of its wearer? He looked towards the second door of the room, which opened probably into a bedroom. It was shut, and remained shut. He came away from the piano. What books was she fond of reading! Emerson—optimism in boxing-gloves; Maspero—she was interested, then, in things Egyptian. "Faust"—De Maupassant—D'Annunzio—Hawthorne, "The Scarlet Letter." He took this last book, which was small and bound in white, into his hand. He had known it once. He had read it long ago. Now he opened it, glanced quickly through its pages. Hester Prynne, Arthur Dimmesdale—suddenly he remembered the story, the sin of the flesh, the scarlet letter that branded the sin upon the woman's breast while the man went unpunished.

And Mrs. Chepstow had it, bound in white.

"Are you judging my character by my books?"

A warm and careless voice spoke behind him. She had come in and was standing close to him, dressed in white, with a black hat, and holding a white parasol in her hand. In the sunshine she looked even fairer than by night. Her pale but gleaming hair was covered by a thin veil, which she kept down as she greeted Nigel.

"Not judging," he said, as he held her hand for a moment. "Guessing, perhaps, or guessing at."

"Which is it? 'The Scarlet Letter'! I got it a year ago. I read it. And when I had read it, I sent it to be bound in white."

"Why was that?"

" 'Though your sin shall be as scarlet,' " she quoted.

He was silent, looking at her.

"Let us have tea."

As she spoke, she went, with her slow and careless walk which Isaacson had noticed, towards the fireplace, and touched the electric bell. Then she sat down on a sofa close to the cage of the canary-birds, and with her back to the light.

"I suppose you are fearfully busy with engagements," she continued, as he came to sit down near her. "Most people are, at this time of year. One ought to be truly grateful for even five minutes of anybody's time. I remember, ages ago, when I was one of the busy ones, I used to expect almost servile thankfulness for any little minute I doled out. How things change!"

She did not sigh, but laughed, and, without giving him time to speak, added:

"Which of my other books did you look at?"

"I saw you had Maspero."

"Oh, I got that simply because I had met you. It turned my mind towards Egypt, which I have never seen, although I've yachted all over the place. Last night, after we had said good night, I couldn't sleep; so I sat here and read Maspero for a while, and thought of your Egyptian life. I didn't mean to be impertinent. One has to think of something."

"Impertinent!"

Her tone, though light, had surely been coloured with apology.

"Well, people are so funny—now. I remember the time when lots of them were foolish in the opposite way. If I thought of them, they seemed to take it as an honour. But then I wasn't thirty-eight, and I was in society."

The German waiter came in with tea. When he had arranged it and gone out, Nigel said, with a certain diffidence:

"I wonder you don't live in the country."

"I know what you mean. But you're wrong. One feels even more out of it there."

She gave him his cup gently, with a movement that implied care for his comfort, almost a thoughtful, happy service.

"The Rector is embarrassed, his wife appalled. The Doctor's 'lady,' much as she longs for one's guineas, tries to stop him even from attending one's dying bed. The Squire, though secretly interested to fervour, is of course a respectable man. He is a 'stay' to country morality, and his wife is a pair of stays. The neighbours respond in their dozens to the *mot d'ordre*, and there one is *plantée*, like a lonely white moon encircled by a halo of angry fire. Dear acquaintance, I've tried it. Egypt—Omaha—anything would be better. What are you eating? Have one of these little cakes. They really are good. I ordered them specially for you and our small festivity."

She was smiling as she handed him the plate.

"I should think Egypt would be better!" exclaimed Nigel, with a strength and a vehemence that contrasted almost startlingly with her light, half-laughing tone. "Why don't you go there? Why don't you try the free life?"

"Live among the tribes, like Lady Hester Stanhope in the Lebanon? I'm afraid I could never train myself to wear a turban. Besides, Egypt is fearfully civilized now. Every one goes there. I should be cut all up the Nile."

The brutality of her frankness startled and almost pained him. For a moment, in it he seemed to discern a lack of taste.

"You are right," she said; and suddenly the lightness died away altogether from her voice. "But how is one not to get blunted? And even long ago I always hated pretence. Women are generally pretending. And they are wise. I have never been wise. If I were wise, I should not let you see my lonely, stupid, undignified situation."

Suddenly she turned so that the light from the window fell full upon her, and lifted her veil up over the brim of her hat.

"Nor my face, upon which, of course, must be written all sorts of worries and sorrows. But I couldn't pretend at eighteen, nor can I at thirty-eight. No wonder so many men—the kind of men you meet at your club, at the Marlborough, or the Bachelors', or the Travellers'—call me an 'ass of a woman.' I am an ass of a woman, a little—little—ass."

In saying the very last words all the severity slipped away out of her voice, and as she smiled again and moved her head, emphasizing humorously her own reproach to herself, she looked almost a girl.

"The 'little' applies to my mind, of course, not to my body; or perhaps I ought to say to my soul, instead of to my body."

"No, 'little' would be the wrong adjective for your soul," Nigel said.

Mrs. Chepstow looked touched, and turned once more away from the light, after Nigel had noticed that she looked touched.

"Have you seen your friend, Doctor Isaacson, to-day?" she said, seeming to make an effort in changing the conversation. "I like that man, though usually I dislike Jews because of their love for money. I like him, and somehow I feel as if he had liked me the other night, as if he had felt kindly towards me."

"Isaacson is a splendid fellow. I haven't seen him again. He has been called away by a case. We were to have ridden together this morning, but he sent to say it was impossible. He has gone into the country."

"Will he be away long?"

"I don't know. I hope not. I want him here badly."

"Oh?"

"I mean that he's congenial to me in many ways, and that congenial spirits are rare."

"You must have troops of friends. You are a man's man."

"I don't know. What is a man's man?"

"A man like you."

"And a woman's man?" he asked, drawing his chair a little towards her.

"Every man's man is a woman's man."

"You say you cannot pretend. Cannot you flatter?"

"I can pretend to that extent, and sometimes do. But why should I flatter you? I don't believe you care a bit about it. You love a kindly truth. Who doesn't? I've just told you a kindly truth."

"I should like to tell you some kindly truths," he said.

"I'm afraid there are not many you, or any one else, could tell. I dare say there are one or two, though, for I believe there is in every one of us a little bit—almost infinitesimal, perhaps—of ineradicable good, a tiny flame which no amount of drenching can ever extinguish."

"I know it."

"Oh, but it does want cherishing—cherishing—cherishing all the time, the tiny flame of ineradicable good."

She took his cup quickly, and began to pour out some more tea for him, like one ashamed of an outburst and striving to cover it up by action.

"Bring Doctor Isaacson to see me one day—if he'll come," she said, in a changed, cool voice, the non-committal voice of the trained woman of the world.

He felt that the real woman had for an instant risen to the surface, and had sunk again into the depths of her; that she was almost ashamed of this real, good woman. And he longed to tell her so, to say to her, "Don't be ashamed. Let me see the real woman, the good woman. That is the woman I seek when I am near you." But he did not dare to strike a blow on her reserve.

"I will bring Isaacson," he said, quietly. "I want him to know you really. Why are you smiling?"

"But—I am not smiling!"

Nor was she; and, seeing her quiet gravity and wonder, he was surprised that he had imagined it.

"I must tell you," she said, "that though I took such a fancy to Doctor Isaacson, I don't think he is like you; I don't think he is a psychologist."

"You think me a psychologist?" said Nigel, in very honest surprise.

"Yes, and I'll tell you why, if you'll promise not to be offended."

"Please—please do."

"I think one reads character as much with the eyes of the heart as with the eyes of the brain. You use two pairs of eyes in your reading. But I am not sure that Doctor Isaacson does."

"Why did you ask me not to be offended? You meant to put it differently. And you would have been right.

Isaacson is a brilliant man, and I am not. But he has as much heart as I, although he has so much more brain than I. And the stronger each is, the better for a man."

"But the brain—oh, it has such a tendency to overshadow, to browbeat the heart. In its strength it so often grows arrogant. The *juste milieu*—I think you have it. Be content, and never let your brain cry out for more, lest your heart should have to put up with less."

"You think too well of me," he said; "much too well."

She leaned forward over the tea-table and looked at him closely, with the peculiar scrutiny of one so strongly concentrated upon the matter in hand as to be absolutely unself-conscious.

"I wonder if I do," she said; and he felt as if she were trying to drag the very heart out of him and to see how it was beating. "I wonder if I do."

She relaxed her muscles, which had been tense, and leaned back, letting her right hand, which for a moment had grasped the edge of the table, drop down on to her lap.

"It may be so. I do think well of you. That is certain. And I'm afraid I think very often badly of men. And yet I do try to judge fairly, and not only to put on the black cap because of my own unfortunate experiences. There are such splendid men—but there are such utter brutes. You must know that. And yet I doubt if a man ever knows how good, or how bad, another man can be. Perhaps one must be a woman thoroughly to know a man—man, the beast and the angel."

"I dare say that is true."

He spoke almost with conviction. For all the time he had been with her he had been companioned by a strange, unusual feeling of being understood, of having the better part of him rightly appraised, and even too greatly appreciated. And this feeling had warmed his mind and heart almost as a generous wine warms the body.

"I'm sure it is true."

He put down his cup. Suddenly there had come to

him the desire to go away, to be alone. He saw the curtains moving gently by the windows, and heard the distant, softened sound of the voices and the traffic of the city. And he thought of the river, and the sunset, and the barges swinging on the hurrying tide, and of the multitudes of eddies in the water. Like those eddies were the thoughts within his mind, the feelings within his heart. Were they not being driven onwards by the current of time, onwards towards the spacious sea of action? Abruptly his heart was invaded by a longing for largeness, a longing that was essential in his nature, but that sometimes lay quiescent, for largeness of view, such as the Bedouin has upon the desert that he loves and he belongs to; largeness of emotion, largeness of action. Largeness was manliness—largeness of thinking and largeness of living. Not the drawing-room of the world, but the desert of the world, with its exquisite oases, was the right place for a man. Yet here he was in a drawing-room. At this moment he longed to go out from it. But he longed also to catch this woman by the hand and draw her out with him. And he remembered how Browning, the poet, had loved a woman who lay always in a shrouded room, too ill to look on the sunshine or breathe the wide airs of the world; and how he carried her away and took her to the peaks of the Apennines. The mere thought of such a change in a life was like a cry of joy.

"What is it?" said Mrs. Chepstow, surprised at the sudden radiance in Nigel's face, seeing before her for the first time a man she could not read, but a man whose physique now forcibly appealed to her—seemed to become splendid under some inward influence, as a half-naked athlete's does when he slowly fills his lungs, clenches his fists, and hardens all his muscles. "What is it?"

But he did not tell her. He could not tell her. And he got up to go away. As he passed the piano, he looked again at the score of "The Dream of Gerontius."

"Are you fond of that?" he asked her.

"What? Oh—'Gerontius'"

She let her eyes rest for a brief instant on his face.

"I love it. It carries me away—as the soul is carried away by the angel. 'This child of clay to me was given'—do you remember?"

"Yes."

He bade her good-bye. The last thing he looked at in her room was "The Scarlet Letter," bound in white, lying upon her table. And he glanced from it to her before he went out and shut the door.

Just outside in the corridor he met a neatly dressed French girl, whose eyes were very red. She had evidently been crying long and bitterly. She carried over her arm the skirt of a gown, and she went into the room which communicated with Mrs. Chepstow's sitting-room.

"Poor girl!" thought Nigel. "I wonder what's the matter with her."

He went on down the corridor to the lift, descended, and made his way to the Thames Embankment.

When the door shut behind him, Mrs. Chepstow remained standing for a minute near the piano, waiting, like one expectant of a departing guest's return. But Nigel did not come back to say any forgotten, final word. Presently she realized that she was safely alone, and she went to the piano, sat down, and struck the chords which supported the notes on which the priest dismissed the soul. But she only played them for a moment. Then, taking the music off the stand and throwing it on the floor, she began to play a Spanish dance, lascivious, alluring, as full of the body as the music of Elgar is full of the soul. And she played it very well, as well, almost, as a hot-blooded girl of Seville could have danced it. As she drew near the end, she heard a sound in the adjoining room, and she stopped abruptly and called out:

"Henriette!"

There was no reply.

"Henriette!" Mrs. Chepstow called again.

The door of the bedroom opened, and the French girl with red eyes appeared.

"Why don't you answer when I speak to you? How long have you been there?"

"Two or three minutes, madame," said the girl, in a low voice.

"Did you meet any one in the corridor?"

"Yes, madame, a gentleman."

"Coming from here?"

"Yes, madame."

"Did he see you?"

"Naturally, madame."

"I mean—to notice you?"

"I think he did, madame."

"And did he see you go into my room—with those eyes?"

"Yes, madame."

An angry frown contracted Mrs. Chepstow's forehead, and her face suddenly became hard and looked almost old.

"Heavens!" she exclaimed. "If there is a stupid thing to be done, you are sure to—— Go away! go away!"

The maid retreated quickly, and shut the door.

"Idiot!" Mrs. Chepstow muttered.

She knew the value of a last impression.

She went out on to her balcony and looked down to the Embankment, idly watching the traffic, the people walking by.

Although she did not know it, Nigel was among them. He was strolling by the river. He was looking at the sunset. And he was thinking of the poet Browning, and of the woman whom love took from the shrouded chamber and set on the mountain peaks.

VII

ALTHOUGH Nigel Armine was an enthusiast, and what many people called an "original," he was also a man of the world. He knew the trend of the world's opinion, he realized clearly how the world regarded any actions that were not worldly. The fact that often he did not care did not mean that he did not know. He was no ignorant citizen, and in his acquaintance with Mrs. Chepstow his worldly knowledge did not forsake him. Clearly he understood how the average London man—the man he met at his clubs, at Ranelagh, at Hurlingham—would sum up any friendship between Mrs. Chepstow and himself.

"Mrs. Chepstow's hooked poor old Armine!"

Something like that would be the verdict.

Were they friends? Could they ever be friends?

Nigel had met Mrs. Chepstow by chance in the vestibule of the Savoy. He had been with a racing man whom he scarcely knew, but who happened to know her well. This man had introduced them to each other carelessly, and hurried away to "square things up with his bookie." Thus casually and crudely their acquaintance was begun. How was it to continue? Or—was it to continue?

Nigel was a strong man in the flower of his life. He was not a saint. And he was begining to wonder. And Isaacson, who was again in town, was beginning to wonder, too.

During the season the Doctor was very busy. Many Americans and foreigners desired to consult him. He adhered to his rule, and never admitted a patient to his house after half-past five had struck, yet his work was seldom over before the hour of seven. He could not see Nigel often, because he could not see any one often; but he had seen him more than once, more than once he had heard gossip about him, and he realized, partly through knowledge, and partly through instinct, his situation with Mrs. Chepstow. Nigel longed to be frank with Isaacson, yet told him very little, held back by some strange reserve, subtly inculcated, perhaps, by the woman. Other men told Isaacson far too much, drawing evil inferences with the happy laughter of the beast and not of the angel.

And the Doctor drew his own conclusion.

From the very first, he had realized that the acquaintance between this socially ruined, no longer young, yet still fascinating woman, and this young, enthusiastic man would be no slight, ephemeral thing. The woman had willed it otherwise. And perhaps the almost ungovernable root-qualities of Nigel had willed it otherwise, too, although he did not know that. Enthusiasm plies a whip that starts steeds in a mad gallop it is not easy to arrest. Even the vigorous force that started them may be unable to pull them up.

Where exactly was Nigel going?

Smiling and sneering men in the clubs said, to a crude liaison. They said more. They said the liaison was a fact, and marvelled that a fellow like Armine should be willing to be "a bad last." Isaacson knew the untruth of this gossip. There was no liaison. But would there ever be one? Did Mrs. Chepstow intend that there should be one? Or had her intention from the beginning been quite otherwise?

Isaacson did not know in detail what Nigel's past had been. He imagined it, from the man's point of view, to have been unusually pure. But he did not suppose it stainless. His keen eyes of a physician read the ardour of Nigel's temperament. He made no mistake about his man. Nigel ought to have married. That he had never done so was due to a sorrow in early life, the death of a girl whom he had loved. Isaacson knew nothing of this, and sometimes he had wondered why no woman captured this nature so full of impulse and of sympathy, so full of just those qualities which make good women happy. If Mrs. Chepstow should capture it, the irony of life would be in flood.

Would she win the love as well as the pity and the chivalry of Nigel, which she already had? Would she awaken the flesh of this man as well as the spirit, and through spirit and flesh would she attain his soul?

And then?

Isaacson's sincerity was sorely tested by his friendship at this period. Original though he was, and full of the sensitive nature's distaste for marching with the mob, he was ranged with the mob against Nigel in this affair of Mrs. Chepstow. Yet Nigel claimed him as an ally, a kindred spirit. He was not explicit, but in their fugitive intercourse he was perpetually implying. It was "You and I," and the rest of the world shut out. Pity was working within him, chivalry was working, the generosity of his soul, but also its fighting obstinacy. There was something in Nigel which loved to have its back against the wall. He wanted to put Isaacson into the same pugnacious position, facing the overwhelming odds. But the overwhelming odds were on the same side as the Doctor. On the whole, Isaacson was not sorry that he had so few hours to spare. For he did not know what to do. Professional secrecy debarred him from telling Nigel what Mrs. Chepstow had said of herself. What others said of her would never set Nigel against her, but would always incline him towards her.

So far Mrs. Chepstow and he were acquaintances. But already the moment had come when Nigel was beginning to want of her more than mere acquaintanceship, and, because of this driving want of more, to ask himself whether he should require less. His knowledge of the world might, or might not, have told him that with Mrs. Chepstow an unembarrassed friendship would be difficult. That would have been theory. Practice already taught him that the difficulty would probably prove insurmountable even by his enthusiasm and courage. Were they friends? Could they ever be friends?

Even while he asked himself the question, a voice within him answered, "No."

Women who have led certain lives lose the faculty for friendship, if they ever possessed it. Events have taught them, what instinct seems to teach many women, to look on men as more physical even than they are. And such women show their outlook perpetually, in word, in look, in action, and in the indefinable *nuances* of manner which make a person's atmosphere. This outlook affects men, both shames them and excites them, acting on god and brute. Neither shamed god nor brute with lifted head is in the mood for friendship.

Mrs. Chepstow had this instinctive outlook on male creation, and not even her delicate gifts as a *comédienne* could entirely disguise it.

At last Nigel reached a crisis of restlessness and uncertainty, which warned him that he must drift and delay no longer, but make up his mind quite definitely what course he was going to take. He was not a man who could live comfortably in indecision. He hated it, indeed, as an attribute of weakness.

He must "have it out" with himself.

It was now July. The season would soon be over. And his acquaintance with Mrs. Chepstow? Would that be over too? It might come to an end quite naturally. He would go into the country, presently to Scotland for the shooting. And she—where would she go? This question set him thinking, as often in these last days—thinking about her loneliness, a condition exaggerated and underlined by her to make an impression on him. She did not seem to dwell upon it. She was far too clever for that. But somehow it was always cropping up. When he paid her a visit, she was scarcely ever out. And if she was in, she was invariably alone. Sometimes she wore a hat and said she had just come in. Sometimes, when he left her, she would say she was going out. But always the impression created was of a very lonely woman, with no engagements and apparently no friends, who passed the long summer days in solitude, playing—generally "Gerontius"—upon the little rosewood piano, or reading "The Scarlet Letter," or some sad or high-minded book. There was no pose apparent in all this. Indeed, sometimes Mrs. Chepstow seemed slightly confused, almost ashamed, at being so unoccupied, so unclaimed by any society or any bright engagements. And more than once Nigel suspected her of telling him white lies when she spoke of dining out with "people" in the evening, or of joining a "party" for the play. For he noticed that when she made such statements it was generally after some remark, some little incident, which had indicated his pity. And he divined the pride of a wellbred woman stirring within her, the desire to conceal or to make the least of her unfortunate situation. Far from posing to gain his pity, he believed her to be "playing up," if possible, to avoid it. And this belief, not unnaturally, rendered it far more keen. So he fell in with her intention.

Once or twice when, in mental colloquies, he played, as he supposed, the part of the ordinary man of the world arguing out the question with the impulsive, chivalrous man, he said, and insisted strongly, that a woman such as Mrs. Chepstow, justifiably famous for beauty and scandalously famous for very different reasons, if she sought to deceive—and of course the man of the world thought such women compact of deception—would try to increase her attraction by representing herself as courted, desired, fêted, run after by men. Such women always did that. Never would she wish it to be known that she was undesired, that she was abandoned. Men want what other men want. But who wants the unwanted? The fact that Mrs. Chepstow allowed him to see and to realize her solitude, so simply and so completely, proved to Nigel her almost unwise unworldliness. The man of the world, so sceptical, was convinced. And as to the enthusiast—he bowed down.

Nigel made the mistake of judging Mrs. Chepstow's capacity by the measure of his own shrewdness, which in such a direction was not great. What seemed the inevitable procedure of such a woman to Nigel's amount of worldly cleverness, seemed the procedure to be avoided to Mrs. Chepstow's amount of the same blessing. She seldom took the obvious route in deception, as Isaacson had realized almost from the first moment when he knew her. She paid people the compliment of crediting them with astuteness, and thought it advisable to be not only more clever than they were stupid, but more clever than they were clever.

And so Nigel's pity grew; and now, when he was "having it out" with himself, he felt that when the season was over Mrs. Chepstow must miss him, not because she had picked him out as a man specially attractive to her, but simply because he had brought the human element into a very lonely life. In their last conversation he had spoken of the end of the season, of the exodus that would follow it.

"Oh—yes, of course," she had said, rather vaguely.

"Where are you going?"

She had sat for a moment in silence, and he had believed he followed the movement of her thought. He had felt certain that she was considering whether she would tell him a lie, recount some happy plan invented at the moment to deceive him. Feeling this certainty, he had looked at her, and his eyes had asked her to tell him the truth. And he had believed that she yielded to them, when at length she said:

"I haven't any special plans. I dare say I shall stay on quietly here."

She had not given him an opportunity of making a rejoinder, but had at once turned the conversation to some quite different topic. And again he had divined pride working busily within her.

She must miss him.

She must miss any one who occasionally stepped in to break her solitude. Sometimes he had wondered at this solitude's completeness. He wondered again now. Everybody had their friends, their intimates, whether delightful or preposterous. Who were hers? Of course the average woman had "dropped" her long ago. But there are other women in London besides the average woman. There are brilliant women of Bohemia, there are clever women even belonging to society who "take their own way," and know precisely whom they choose, whoever interests or attracts them. And—there are friends, faithful through changes, misfortunes, even disasters. Where were Mrs. Chepstow's? He did not dare to ask.

He recalled his first visit to her, not with any maudlin sentimentality, but with a quiet earnestness: the empty room looking to the river, the open piano and the music upon it, the few roses, and the books. He recalled "The Scarlet Letter" bound in white, and her partial quotation from the Bible in explanation of its binding. Abruptly she had stopped, perhaps suddenly conscious of the application to herself. At tea she had said of the cakes that were so good, "I ordered them specially for you and our little festivity." There was a great simplicity in the words, and in her voice when she had said them. In her loneliness, a cup of tea drunk with him was a "festivity." He imagined her sitting alone in that room in August, when the town is parched, dried up, and half deserted. How would she pass her days?

He compared his life with hers, or rather with a life he imagined as hers. And never before had he realized the brightness, even the brilliance, of his life, with its multitudinous changes and activities, its work—the glorious sweating with the brown labourers in the sand flats at the edge of the Fayyūm—its sport, its friendships, its strenuous and its quiet hours, so dearly valued because they were rather rare. It was a good life. It was almost a grand life. London now, Scotland presently; then the late autumn, the train, the sight of the sea, the cry of the siren, the throbbing of the engines, and presently—Egypt! And then the winter of sunshine, and the songs of his workmen, his smiling fellahin, and the reclaiming of the desert.

The reclaiming of the desert!

Nigel was alone in his bedroom in the Savoy. It was late at night. He was in pajamas, smoking a cigar by the open window. He looked down to the red carpet on which his bare feet were set in their red babouches, and suddenly he realized the beauty of what he was doing in the Fayyūm. He had never really thought of it before in this way—of the reclaiming of the desert; but now that he did think of it, he was glad, and his heart bounded, looking forward in affection to the winter.

And her winter? What would that be like?

What an immense difference one honest, believing, and therefore inspiring affection must make in a lonely life! Only one—that is enough. And the desert is reclaimed.

He saw the brakes of sugar-cane waving, the tall doura swaying in the breeze, where only the sands had been. And his brown cheeks glowed, as a hot wave of blood went through them.

Progress! He loved to think of it. It was his passion. That grand old Watts's picture, with its glow, its sacred glow of colour, in which was genius! Each one must do his part.

And in that great hotel, how many were working consciously for the cause?

Excitement woke in him. He thought of the rows and rows of numbered doors in the huge building, and within, beyond each number, a mind to think, a heart to feel, a soul to prompt, a body to act. And beyond his number—himself! What was he doing? What was he going to do? He got up and walked about his room, still smoking his cigar. His babouches shuffled over the carpet. He kicked them off, and went on walking, with bare, brown feet. Often in the Fayyūm he had gone barefoot, like his labourers. What was he going to do to help on the slow turning of the mighty wheel of progress? He must not be a mere talker, a mere raver about grand things, while accomplishing nothing to bring them about. He despised those windy talkers who never act. He must not be one of them. That night, when he sat down "to have it out" with himself, he had done so for his own sake. He had been an egoist, had been thinking, perhaps not solely but certainly chiefly, of himself. But in these lonely moments men are generally essentially themselves. Nigel was not essentially an egoist. And soon himself had been almost forgotten. He had been thinking far more of Mrs. Chepstow than of himself. And now he thought of her again in connection with this turning of the great wheel of progress. At first he thought of her alone in this connection, then of her and of himself.

It is difficult to do anything quite alone, anything wholly worth the doing. That was what he was thinking. Nearly always some other intrudes, blessedly intrudes, to give conscious, or unconscious, help. A man puts his shoulder to the wheel, and in front of him he sees another shoulder. And the sight gives him courage.

The thought of strenuous activity made him think of Mrs. Chepstow's almost absolute inactivity. He saw her sitting, always sitting, in her room, while life flowed on outside. He saw her pale face. That her face was carefully made pale by art did not occur to him. And then again he thought of Mrs. Browning and of the mountain peaks.

What was he going to do?

He made a strong mental effort, as he would have expressed it, to "get himself in hand." Now, then, he must think it out. And he must "hold up" his enthusiasm, and just be calm and reasonable, and even calculating.

He thought of the girl whom he had loved long ago and who had died. Since her death he had put aside love as a passion. Now and then—not often—a sort of travesty of love had come to him, the spectre of the real. It is difficult for a young, strong man in the pride of his life never to have any dealing either with love or with its spectre. But Isaacson was right. Nigel's life had been much purer than are most men's lives. Often he had fought against himself, and his own natural inclination, because of his great respect for love. Not always had he conquered. But the fights had strengthened the muscles of his will, and each fall had shown him more clearly the sadness, almost the horror, imprinted on the haggard features of the spectre of the real.

Mrs. Chepstow for years had been looking upon, had been living with, that spectre, if what was said of her was true.

And Nigel did not deceive himself on this point. He did not sentimentally exalt a courtesan into an angel, as boys so often do. Mrs. Chepstow had certainly lived very wrongly, in a way to excite disgust, perhaps, as well as pity. Yet within her were delicacy, simplicity, the pride of breeding, even a curious reserve. She had still a love of fine things. She cared for things ethereal. He thought of his first visit to her, the open piano, " Proficiscere, anima Christiana," " The Scarlet Letter," and her quotation. What had she been thinking while she played Elgar's curiously unearthly music, while she read Hawthorne's pitiful book? She had been using art, no doubt, as so many use it, as a means of escape from life. And her escape had been not into filth or violence, not into the salons of wit, or into the alcoves where secrets are unveiled, but into the airy spaces with the angel, into the forest with Hester and little Pearl.

Why could they not continue friends?

His body spoke in answer, and he laid the blame for the answer entirely on himself. He condemned himself at that moment, was angry with himself, cursed himself. And he cursed himself, not because he was morbid, but because he was healthy-minded, and believed that his evil inclinations had been aroused by his knowledge of Mrs. Chepstow's past. And that fact was a beast, was something to be stamped on. He would never allow himself comfortably to be that sort of man. Yet he was, it seemed, enough that sort of man to make friendship with Mrs. Chepstow difficult, perhaps impossible. If love had led him to such an inclination, he would, being no prude, have understood it as a perfectly natural and perfectly healthy thing. But he did not love Mrs. Chepstow. He would never love, really love, again. For years he had said that to himself, and had believed it. He said it again now. And even if he could renew that strange power, to love, he could not love a woman who was not pure. He felt certain of that. He thought of the dead girl and of Mrs. Chepstow. But to-night he could not recall the dead girl's figure, face, look, exactly. Mrs. Chepstow's he could, of course, recall. He had seen her that very day. And the girl he had loved had been dead for many years. She lived in his memory now rather as a symbol of purity and beauty than as a human being.

Mrs. Chepstow, of course, would never find a man sincerely to love her now.

And yet why not? Suddenly Nigel checked himself, as he generally did when he found himself swiftly subscribing to the general opinion of the great mass of men. Why not? The shoulder to the wheel; it was nearly always the shoulder of love—love of an idea, love of a woman, love of humanity, love of work, love of God. All the men he knew, or very nearly all, would laugh at the idea of Mrs. Chepstow being sincerely loved. But the fact that they would laugh could have no effect on a manly heart or a manly spirit.

He felt almost angry with her for the loneliness and the immobility which pained his chivalry and struck at his sense of pity. If he could think of her as going away, too, as wandering, in Switzerland, in Italy, in some lovely place, he would feel all right. But always he saw her seated in that room, alone, deserted, playing the piano, reading, with no prospect of company, of change. Mrs. Chepstow had acted her part well. She had stamped a lonely image upon the retina of Nigel's imagination.

He was still walking about his room in bare feet. But his cigar had gone out, though it was still between his lips. The hour was very late. He heard a distant clock strike two. And just after he had listened to its chime, followed by other chimes in near and distant places of the city, the night idea of a strong and young man came to him.

If he could not be friends with Mrs. Chepstow, could he be—the other thing to her?

He put up his hand to his lips, took away the cigar, and flung it out of the window violently. And this physical violence was the echo of his mental violence. She might allow such a thing. Often, if half of what was said of her was true, she had entered into a similar relation with other men. He would not believe that "often." He put it differently. She had certainly entered into a similar relation with some men—perhaps with two or three, multiplied by scandal—in the past. Would she enter into it with him, if he asked her? And would he ever ask her?

He threw himself down again in his arm-chair, and stared at his bare feet planted firmly on the floor. But he saw, not his feet, but the ugly spectre of love, that hideous, damnable ghost, that most pretentious of all pretensions. She had lived with the ghost till she had become pale like a ghost. In the picture of "Progress," which he loved, there was a glow, a glory of light, raying out to a far horizon. It would be putting a shoulder to the wheel to set a glow in the cheeks of a woman, not a glow of shame but of joy. And to be—and then Nigel used to himself that expression of the laughing men in the clubs—"a bad last!" No, that sort of thing was intolerable.

Suddenly the ghost faded away, and he saw his brown feet. They made him think at once of the sun, of work, of the good, real, glowing life.

No, no; none of those intolerable beastlinesses for him. That thought, that imagination, it was utterly, finally done with. He drew a long breath, and stretched up his arms, till the loose sleeves of his night-suit fell down, exposing the strong, brown limbs. And as he had looked at his feet, he looked at them, then felt them, thumped them, and rejoiced in the glory of health. But the health of mind and heart was essential to the complete health of the body. He felt suddenly strong—strong for more than one, as surely a man should be—strong for himself, and his woman, for her who belongs to him, who trusts him, who has blotted out— it comes to that with a woman who loves—all other men for him.

Was he really condemned to an eternal solitude because of the girl who had died so many years ago? For his life was a solitude, as every loveless life is, however brilliant and strenuous. He realized that, and there came to him a thought that was natural and selfish. It was this: How good it must be to be exclusively loved by a woman, and how a woman, whom men and the world have abandoned, must love the man who comes, like a knight through the forest, and carries her away, and takes her into his life, and gives her back self-respect, and a place among women, and, above all, the feeling that of all feelings a woman holds dearest, "Somebody wants me." It must be good to be loved as such a woman would love. His generosity, which instinctively went out to abandoned things, walked hand in hand with man's eternal, indestructible selfishness that night, as he thought of Mrs. Chepstow for the first time as married again to some man who cared not for the world's opinion, or who cared for it so much as to revel in defying it.

How would she love such a man?

He began to wonder about that part of her nature dedicated to, designed for, love.

With him she was always perfectly simple, and seemed extremely frank. But he felt now that in her simplicity she had always been reserved, almost strangely reserved for such a woman. Perhaps that reserve had been her answer to his plainly shown respect. Just because of her position, he had been even more respectful to her than he was to other women, following in this a dictate of his temperament. What would she be like in the unreserve of a great love?

And now a fire was kindled in Nigel, and began to burn up fiercely. He felt, very consciously and definitely, the fascination of this woman. Of course, he had always been more or less subject to it. Isaacson had known that when he saw Nigel draw his chair nearer to hers at the supper-table in the Savoy. But he had been subject to it without ever saying to himself, "I am in subjection." He had never supposed that he was in subjection. The abrupt consciousness of how it was with him excited him tremendously. After the long interval of years, was he to feel again the powerful fever, and for a woman how different from the woman he had loved? She stood, in her young purity, at one end of the chain of years, and Mrs. Chepstow —did she really stand at the other?

BELLA DONNA 77

He seemed to see these two looking at each other across the space that was set by Time, and for a moment his face contracted. But he had changed while traversing that space. Then he was an eager boy, in the joy of his bounding youth. Now he was a vigorous man. And during the interval that separated boy from man had come up in him his strong love of humanity, his passion for the development of the good that lies everywhere, like the ore in gold-bearing earth. That love had perhaps been given to him to combine the two loves, the altruistic love, and the love for a woman bringing its quick return.

The two faces of women surely softened as they gazed now upon each other.

Such loves in combination might crown his life with splendour. Nigel thought that, with the enthusiasm which was his birthright, which set him so often apart from other men. And, moving beneath such a splendour, how absolutely he could defy the world's opinion! Its laughter would be music, its sneering word only the signal to a smile.

But—he must think—he must think——

He sprang up, pulled up his loose sleeves to his shoulders, tucked them together, and with bared arms leaned out to the night, holding his hands against his cheeks.

VIII

Mrs. Chepstow had said to Nigel, "Bring Doctor Isaacson—if he'll come." He had never gone, though Nigel had told him of her words, had told him more than once. Without seeming deliberately to avoid the visit, he had deliberately avoided it. He never had an hour to spare in the day, and Nigel knew it. But he might have gone on a Sunday. It happened that, at present, on Sundays he was always out of town.

He had said to himself, "*Cui bono?*"

He had the sensitive nature's dislike of mingling intimately in the affairs of others, and moreover he felt instinctively that if he tried to play a true friend's part to Nigel, he might lose Nigel as a friend. His clear insight would be antagonistic to Nigel's blind enthusiasm, his calm worldly knowledge would seem only frigid cruelty to Nigel's generosity and eagerness in pity. And, besides, Isaacson had a strong personal repulsion from Mrs. Chepstow, a repulsion almost physical.

The part of him that was Jewish understood the part of her that was greedy far too well. And he disliked, while he secretly acknowledged, his own Jewishness. He seldom showed this dislike, even subtly, to the world and never showed it crudely, as do many of Jewish blood, by a strange and hideous anti-Semitism. But it was always alive within him, always in conflict with something belonging to his nature's artistic side, a world-feeling to which race-feeling seemed stupid and very small. The triumphs of art aroused this world-feeling within him, and in his love of art he believed that he touched his highest point. As Isaacson's mental unconventionality put him *en rapport* with Nigel, his Jewishness, very differently, put him *en rapport* with her. There is a communion of repulsion as well as a communion of affection. Isaacson knew that Mrs. Chepstow and he could be linked by their dislike. His instinct was to avoid her, not to let this link be formed. Subsequent circumstances made him ask himself whether men do not often call things towards them with the voices of their fears.

The season was waning fast, was nearly at an end, when one night, very late, Nigel called in Cleveland Square. Isaacson had just come back from dining with the Dean of Waynfleet when the bell rang. He feared a professional summons, and was relieved when a sleepy servant asked if he would see Mr. Armine. They met in a small, upstairs room where Isaacson sat at night, a room lined with books, cosy, but perhaps a little oppressive. As Nigel came in quickly with a light coat over his arm and a crush hat in his hand, a clock on the mantelpiece struck one.

"I caught sight of you just now in St. James's Street in your motor, or I wouldn't have come so late," Nigel said. "Were you going straight to bed? Tell me the truth. If you were, I'll be off."

"I don't think I was. I've been dining out, and should have had to read something. That's why you kept your coat?"

"To demonstrate my good intention. Well!"

He put the coat and hat on a chair.

"Will you have anything?"

"No, thanks."

Nigel sat down in an arm-chair.

"I've seen so little of you, Isaacson. And I'm going away to-morrow."

"You've had enough of it?"

"More than enough."

Isaacson was sitting by a table on which lay a number of books. Now and then he touched one with his long and sallow fingers, lifted its cover, then let it drop mechanically.

"You are coming back in the autumn?"

"For some days, in passing through. I'm going to Egypt again."

"I envy you—I envy you."

As he looked at Nigel's Northern fairness, and thought of his own darkness, it seemed to him that he should be going to the sun, Nigel remaining in the lands where the light is pale. Perhaps a somewhat similar thought occurred to Nigel, for he said:

"You ought to go there some day. You'd be in your right place there. Have you ever been?"

"Never. I've often wanted to go."

"Why don't you go?"

Isaacson's mind asked that question, and his Jewishness replied. He made money in London. Every day he spent out of London was a loss of so much money.

"Some day," Nigel continued, "you must take a holiday and see Egypt."

"This winter?" said Isaacson.

He lifted the cover of a book. His dark, shining, almost too intelligent eyes looked at Nigel, and looked away.

"Not this winter," he added, quietly.

"But—why not this winter?"

Nigel spoke with a slight embarrassment.

"I couldn't get away. I have too much work. You'll be in the Fayyūm?"

Nigel was staring at the Oriental carpet. His strong hands lay palm downwards on the arms of his chair, pressing them hard.

"I shall go there," he replied.

"And live under the tent? I met a man last night who knows you, an Egyptian army man on leave, Verreker. He told me you were reclaiming quite a lot of desert."

"I should like to reclaim far more than I ever can. It's a good task."

"Hard work?"

"Deuced hard. That's why I like it."

"I know; man's love of taming the proud spirit."

"Is it that? I don't think I bother much about what prompts me to a thing. But—I say, Isaacson, sometimes it seems to me that you have a devilish long sight into things, an almost uncanny long sight."

He leaned forward.

"But in you I don't mind it."

"I don't say I acknowledge it. But why should you mind it in any one?"

Nigel quoted some words of Mrs. Chepstow, but Isaacson did not know he quoted.

"Hasn't the brain a tendency to overshadow, to browbeat the heart?" he said. "Isn't it often arrogant in its strength?"

"One must let both have an innings," said Isaacson, smiling at the slang which suited him so little and suited Nigel so well.

"Yes, and I believe you do. That's why—but to go on with what we were saying. You've got a long sight into things. Now, living generally, as you do, here in London, don't you think that men and women living in crowds often get off the line of truth and kindness? Don't you think that being all together, backed up, as it were, by each other—as a soldier is by his regiment when going into battle—they often become hard, brutal, almost get the blood-lust into them at times?"

Isaacson did not reply for a moment.

"Perhaps sometimes they do," he answered at last.

"And don't you think they require sacrifices?"

"Do you mean human sacrifices?"

"Yes."

"Perhaps—sometimes."

"Why have you never been to call on Mrs. Chepstow?"

Again the sallow fingers began to play with the book-covers, passing from one to another, but always slowly and gently.

"I haven't much time for seeing any one, except my patients, and the people I meet in society."

"And of course you never meet Mrs. Chepstow in society."

"Well—no, one doesn't."

"She would have liked a visit from you, and she's very much alone."

"Is she?"

"Are you stopping on much longer in London?"

"Till the twelfth or fifteenth of August."

"She is stopping on, too."

"Mrs. Chepstow! In the dog-days!"

"She doesn't seem to have anywhere special to go to."

"Oh!"

Isaacson opened a book, and laid his hand upon a page. It happened to be a book on poisons and their treatment. He smoothed the page down mechanically and kept his hand there.

"I say, Isaacson, you couldn't have the blood-lust?"

"I hope not. I think not."

"I believe you hate it as I do, hate and loathe it with all your soul. But I've always felt that you think for yourself, and don't care a rap what the world is thinking. I've looked in to-night to say good-bye, and to ask you, if you can get the time, just to give an eye to—to Mrs.

Chepstow now and again. I know she would value a visit from you, and she really is infernally lonely. If you go, she won't bore you. She's a clever woman, and cares for things you care for. Will you look in on her now and then?"

Isaacson lifted his hand from the book.

"I will call upon her," he said.

"Good!"

"But are you sure she wishes it?"

"Quite sure—for she told me so."

The simplicity of this answer made Isaacson's mind smile and something else in him sigh.

"I have to go into the country," Nigel said. "I've got to see Harwich and Zoe, my sister-in-law you know, and my married sister——"

A sudden look of distress came into his eyes. He got up. The look of distress persisted.

"Good-night, Isaacson, old fellow!"

He grasped the Doctor's hand firmly, and his hand was warm and strong.

"Good-night. I like to feel I know one man who thinks so entirely for himself as you do. For—I know you do. Good-bye."

The look of distress had vanished, and his sincere eyes seemed to shine again with courage and with strength.

"Good-bye."

When he was gone, Isaacson stood by the mantel-piece for nearly five minutes, thinking and motionless. The sound of the little clock striking roused him. He lifted his head, looked around him, and was just going to switch off the light, when he noticed the open book on his table. He went to shut it up.

"It must be ever remembered that digitalin is a cumulative poison, and that the same dose, harmless if taken once, yet frequently repeated becomes deadly; this peculiarity is shared by all poisons affecting the heart."

He stood looking at the page.

"This peculiarity is shared by all poisons affecting the heart."

He moved his head as if in assent. Then he closed the book slowly and switched off the light.

On the August Bank Holiday, one of the most dreadful days of London's year, he set out to call on Mrs. Chepstow.

A stagnant heat pervaded London. There were but few people walking. Few vehicles drove by. Here and there small groups of persons, oddly dressed, and looking vacant in their rapture, stared, round-eyed, on the town. Londoners were in the country, staring, round-eyed, on fields and woods. The policemen looked dull and heavy, as if never again would any one be criminal, and as if they had come to know it. Bits of paper blew aimlessly about, wafted by a little, feverish breeze, which rose in spasms and died away. An old man, with a head that was strangely bald, stared out from a club window, rubbed his enquiring nose, looked back into the room behind him and then stared out again. An organ played "The Manola," resuscitated from a silence of many years.

London was at its summer saddest.

Could Mrs. Chepstow be in it? Soon Isaacson knew. In the entrance hall of the Savoy, where large and lonely porters were dozing, he learnt that she was at home. So be it. He stepped into the lift, and presently followed a servant to her door. The servant tapped. There was no answer. He tapped again more loudly, while Isaacson waited behind him.

"Come in!" called out a voice.

The servant opened the door, announcing:

"Doctor Meyer Isaacson."

Mrs. Chepstow had perhaps been sitting on her balcony, for when Isaacson went in she was in the opening of a window space, standing close to a writing-table, which had its drawers facing the window. Behind her, on the balcony, there was a small arm-chair.

"Doctor Meyer Isaacson!" she said, with an intonation of surprise.

The servant went out and shut the door.

"How quite amazing!"

"But—why, Mrs. Chepstow?"

He had taken and dropped her hand. As he touched her, he remembered holding her wrist in his consulting-room. The sensation she had communicated to him then she communicated again, this time perhaps more strongly.

"Why? It is Bank Holiday! And you never come to see me. By the way, how clever of you to divine that I should be in on such a day of universal going out."

"Even men have their intuitions."

"Don't I know it, to my cost? But to-day I can only bless man's intuition. Where will you sit?"

"Anywhere."

"Here, then."

He sat down on the sofa, and she in a chair, facing the light. She was without a hat. Isaacson wondered what she had been doing all the day, and why she was in London. That she had her definite reason he knew, as a woman knows when another woman is wearing a last year's gown. As their eyes met, he felt strongly the repulsion he concealed. Yet he realized that Mrs. Chepstow was looking less faded, younger, more beautiful than when last he had been with her. She was very simply dressed. It seemed to him that the colour of her hair was changed, was a little brighter. But of this he was not sure. He was sure, however, that a warmth, as of hope, subtly pervaded her whole person. And she had seemed hard, cold, and almost hopeless on the day of her visit to him.

A woman lives in the thoughts of men about her. At this moment Mrs. Chepstow lived in Isaacson's thought that she looked younger, less faded, and more beautiful. Her vanity was awake. His thought of her had suddenly increased her value in her own eyes, made her think she could attract him. She had scarcely tried to attract him the first time that she had met him. But now he saw her go to her armoury to select the suitable weapon with which to strike him. And he began to understand why she had calmly faced the light. Never could such a man as Nigel get so near to Mrs. Chepstow as Doctor Meyer Isaacson, even though Nigel should love her and Isaacson learn to hate her. At that moment Isaacson did not hate her, but he almost hated his divination of her, the "Kabbala," he carried within him and successfully applied to her.

"What has kept you in this dreary city, Doctor Isaacson," she said. "I thought I was absolutely alone in it."

"People are still thinking they are ill."

"And you are still telling them they are not?"

"That depends!"

"I believe you have adopted that idea, that no one is ill, as a curative method. And really there may be something in it. I fancied I was ill. You told me I was well. Since that day something—your influence, I suppose—seems to have made me well. I think I believe in you—as a doctor."

"Why spoil everything by concluding with a reservation?"

"Oh, but your career is you!"

"You think I have sunk my humanity in ambition?"

"Well, you are in town on Bank Holiday!"

"In town to call on you!"

"You were so sure of finding me on such a day?"

She sent him a look which mocked him.

"But, seriously," she continued, "does not the passion for science in you dominate every other passion? For science—and what science brings you?"

With a sure hand she had touched his weak point. He had the passion to acquire, and through his science of medicine he acquired.

"You cannot expect me to allow that I am dominated by anything," he answered. "A man will seldom make a confession of slavery even to himself, if he really is a man."

"Oh, you really are a man, but you have in you something of the woman."

"How do you know that?"

"I don't know it; I feel it."

"Feeling is woman's knowledge."

"And what is man's?"

"Do women think he has any?"

"Some men have knowledge—dangerous men, like you."

"In what way am I dangerous?"

"If I tell you, you will be more so. I should be foolish to lead you to your weapons."

"You want no leading to yours."

It was, perhaps, almost an impertinence; but he felt she would not think it so, and in this he accurately appraised her taste, or lack of taste. Delicacy, reverence, were not really what she wanted of any man. Nigel might pray to a pale Madonna; Isaacson dealt with a definitely blunted woman of the world. And in his intercourse with people, unless indeed he loved them, he generally spoke to their characters, did not hold converse with his own, like a man who talks to himself in an unlighted room.

She smiled.

"Few women do, if they have any."

"Is any woman without them?"

"Yes, one."

"Name her."

"The absolutely good woman."

For a moment he was silent, struck to silence by the fierceness of her cynicism, a fierceness which had leapt suddenly out of her as a drawn sword leaps from its sheath.

"I don't acknowledge that, Mrs. Chepstow," he said—and at this moment perhaps he was the man talking to himself in the dark, as Nigel often was.

"Of course not. No man would."

"Why not?"

"Men seldom name, even to themselves, the weapons by which they are conquered. But women know what those weapons are."

"The Madame Marneffes, but not the Baroness Hulots."

"A Baroness Hulot never counts."

"Is it really clever of you to generalize about men? Don't you differentiate among us at all?"

He spoke entirely without pique, of which he was quite unconscious.

"I do differentiate," she replied. "But only sometimes, not always. There are broad facts which apply to men, however different they may be from one another. There are certain things which all men feel, and feel in much the same way."

"Nigel Armine and I, for instance?"

A sudden light—was it a light of malice?—flashed in her brilliant eyes.

"Yes, even Mr. Armine and you."

"I shall not ask you what they are."

"Perhaps the part of you which is woman has informed you."

Before she said "woman" she had paused. He felt that the word she had thought of, and had wished to use, was "Jewish." Her knowledge of him, while he disliked it because he disliked her, stirred up the part of him which was mental into an activity which he enjoyed. And the enjoyment, which she felt, increased her sense of her own value. Conversation ran easily between them. He discovered, what he had already half suspected, that, though not strictly intellectual—often another name for boring— she was far more than merely shrewd. But her mentality seemed to him hard as bronze. And as bronze reflects the light, her mentality seemed to reflect all the cold lights in her nature. But he forgot the stagnant town, the bald-headed man at the club window, the organ and "The Manola." Despite her generalizing on men, with its unexpressed avowal of her deep-seated belief in physical weapons, she had chosen aright in her armoury. His brain had to acknowledge it. There again was the link between them. When at last he got up to go, she said:

"I suppose you will soon be leaving London?"

"I expect to get away on the fifteenth. Are you staying on?"

"I dare say I shall. You wonder what I do here?"

"Yes."

"I am out a great deal on my balcony. When you came I was there."

She made a movement towards it.

"Would you like to see my view?"

"Thank you."

As he followed her through the window space, he was suddenly very conscious of the physical charm that clung about her. All her movements were expressive, seemed very specially hers. They were like an integral part of a character—her character. They had almost the individuality of an expression in the eyes. And in her character, in her individuality, mingled with much he hated was there not something that charmed? He asked himself the question as he stood near her on the balcony. And now, escaped from her room, even at this height there came upon him again the hot sluggishness of London. The sun was shining brightly, the air was warm and still, the view was large and unimpeded; but he felt a strange, almost tropical dreariness that seemed to him more dreadful than any dreariness of winter.

"Do you spend much of your time here?" he said.

"A great deal. I sit here and read a book. You don't like it?"

She turned her bright eyes, with their dilated pupils, slowly away from his, and looked down over the river.

"I do. But there's a frightful dreariness in London on such a day as this. Surely you feel it?"

"No. I don't feel such things this summer."

In saying the words her voice had altered. There was a note of triumph in it. Or so Isaacson thought. And that warmth, as of hope, in her had surely strengthened, altering her whole appearance.

"One has one's inner resources," she added, quietly, but with a thrill in her voice.

She turned to him again. Her tall figure—she was taller than he by at least three inches—was beautiful in its commanding, yet not vulgar, self-possession. Her thin and narrow hands held the balcony railing rather tightly.

Her long neck took a delicate curve when she turned her head towards him. And nothing that time had left of beauty to her escaped his eyes. He had eyes that were very just.

"Did you think I had none?"

Suddenly he resolved to speak to her more plainly. Till this moment she had kept their conversation at a certain level of pretence. But now her eyes defied him, and he replied to their defiance.

"Do you forget how much I know of you?" he said.

"Do you mean—of the rumours about me?"

"I mean what you told me of yourself."

"When was that? Oh, do you mean in your consulting-room? And you believe all a woman tells you?"

She smiled at him satirically.

"I believe what you told me that day in my consulting-room, as thoroughly as I disbelieve what you told me, and Mr. Armine, the night we met you at supper."

"And what are your grounds for your belief and disbelief?"

"Suppose I said my instinct?"

"I should answer, by all means trust it, if you like. Only do not expect every one to trust it, too."

Her last words sounded almost like a half-laughing menace.

"Why should I want others to trust it?" he asked, quietly.

"I leave your instinct to tell you that, my dear Doctor," she answered gently, with a smile.

"Well," he said, "I must say good-bye. I must leave you to your inner resources. You haven't told me what they are."

"Can't you imagine?"

"Spiritual, I suppose!"

"You've guessed it—clever man!"

"And your gospel of Materialism, which you preached to me so powerfully, gambling, yachting, racing, motoring, theatre-going, eating and drinking, in the 'for to-morrow we die' mood: those pleasures of the typical worldly life of to-day which you said you delighted in? You have replaced them all satisfactorily with 'inner resources'?"

"With inner resources."

Her smiling eyes did not shrink from his. He thought they looked hard as two blue and shining jewels under their painted brows.

"Good-bye—and come again."

While Isaacson walked slowly down the corridor, Mrs. Chepstow opened her writing-table drawer, and took from it a packet of letters which she had put there when the servant first knocked to announce the visitor.

The letters were all from Nigel.

IX

Isaacson did not visit Mrs. Chepstow again before he left London for his annual holiday. More than once he thought of going. Something within him wanted to go, something that was perhaps intellectually curious. But something else rebelled. He felt that his finer side was completely, ignored by her. Why should he care what she saw in him or what she thought about it? He asked himself the question. And when he answered it, he was obliged to acknowledge that she had made upon his nature a definite impression. This impression was unfavorable, but it was too distinct. Its distinctness gave a measure of her power. He was aware that, much as he disliked Mrs. Chepstow, much as he even shrank from her, with a sort of sensitive loathing, if he saw her very often he might come to wish to see her. Never had he felt like this towards any other woman. Does not hatred contain attraction? By the light of his dislike of Mrs. Chepstow, Isaacson saw clearly why she attracted Nigel. But during those August days, in the interior combat, his Jewishness conquered his intellectual curiosity, and he did not go again to the Savoy.

His holiday was spent abroad on the Lake of Como, and

quite alone. Each year he made a "retreat," which he needed after the labours of the year, labours which obliged him to be perpetually with people. He fished in the green lake, sketched in the lovely garden of the almost deserted hotel, and passed every day some hours in scientific study.

This summer he was reading about the effects of certain little-known poisons. He spent strange hours with them. He had much imagination, and they became to him like living things, these agents of destruction. Sometimes, after long periods passed with them, he would raise his head from his books, or the paper on which he was taking notes, and, seeing the still green waters of the lake, the tall and delicate green mountains lifting their spires into the blue, he would return from his journey along the ways of terror, and, dazed, like a tired traveller, he would stare at the face of beauty. Or when he worked by night, after hours during which the swift action of the brain had rendered him deaf to the sounds without, suddenly he would become aware of the chime of bells, of bells in the quiet waters and on the dreaming shores. And he would lift his head and listen, till the strangeness of night, and of the world with its frightful crimes and soft enchantments, stirred and enthralled his soul. And he compared his two lives, this by the quiet lake, alone, filled with research and dreams, and that in the roar of London, with people streaming through his room. And he seemed to himself two men, perhaps more than two.

Soon the four weeks by the lake were gone. Then followed two weeks of travel—Milan, Munich, Berlin, Paris. And then he was home again.

He had heard nothing of Nigel, nothing of Mrs. Chepstow.

September died away in the brown arms of October, and at last a letter came from Nigel. It was written from Stacke House, a shooting-lodge in Scotland, and spoke of his speedy return to the South.

"I am shooting with Harwich," he wrote, "but must soon be thinking about my return to Egypt. I didn't write to you before, though I wanted to thank you for your visit to Mrs. Chepstow. You can't think how she appreciated it. She was delighted by your brilliant talk and sense of humour, but still more delighted by your cordiality and kindness. Of late she hasn't had very much of the latter commodity, and she was quite bowled over. By Jove, Isaacson, if men realized what a little true kindness means to those who are down on their luck, they'd have to 'fork out,' if only to get the return of warm affection. But they don't realize.

"I sometimes think the truest thing said since the Creation is that 'They know not what they do.' Add, 'and what they leave undone,' and you have an explanation of most of the world's miseries. Good-bye, old chap. I shall come to Cleveland Square directly I get to London. Thank you for that visit. Yours ever, Nigel Armine."

Nigel's enthusiasm seemed almost visibly to exhale from the paper as Isaacson held the letter in his hands. "Your cordiality and kindness." So that had struck Mrs. Chepstow—the cordiality and kindness of his, Isaacson's, manner! Of course she and Nigel were in correspondence. Isaacson remembered the occasional notes almost of triumph in her demeanour. She had had letters from Nigel during his absence from London. His letters—the hope in her face. Isaacson saw her on the balcony looking out over the river. Had she not looked out as the human soul looks out upon a prospect of release? In the remembrance of them her expression and her attitude became charged with more definite meaning. And he surely grasped that meaning, which he had wondered about before.

Yet Nigel said nothing. And all this time he had been away from Mrs. Chepstow. Such an absence was strange, and seemed unlike him, quite foreign to his enthusiastic temperament, if Isaacson's surmise was correct. But perhaps it was not correct. That well-spring of human kindness which bubbled up in Nigel, might it not, perhaps, deceive?

"Feeling is woman's knowledge." Isaacson had said that. Now mentally he added, "And sometimes it is man's." He felt too much about Nigel, but he strove to put his feeling away.

Presently he would know. Till then it was useless to debate. And he had very much to do.

Not till nearly the end of October did Nigel return to London. The leaves were falling in battalions from the trees. The autumn winds had come, and with them the autumn rain, that washes sadly away the last sweet traces of summer. Everywhere, through country and town, brooded that grievous atmosphere of finale which in England seldom or never fails to cloud the waning year.

The depression that is characteristic of this season sent many people to doctors. Day after day Isaacson sat in his consulting-room, prescribing rather for the minds of men than for their bodies, living rather with their misunderstood souls than with their physical symptoms. And this year his patients reacted on him far more than usual. He felt almost as if by removing he received their ills, as if their apprehensions were communicated to his mind, as germs are communicated to the body, and as if they stayed to do evil. He told himself that his holiday had not rested him enough. But he never thought for a moment of diminishing his work. Success swept him ever onward to more exertion. As his power grew, his appetite for it grew. And he enjoyed his increasing fortune.

At last Nigel rang at his door. Isaacson could not see him, but sent out word to make an appointment for the evening. They were to meet at eight at an orchestral concert in Queen's Hall.

Isaacson was a little late in keeping this engagement. He came in quickly and softly between two movements of Tschaikowsky's "Pathetic Symphony," found Nigel in his stall, and, with a word, sat down beside him. The conductor raised his baton. The next movement began.

In the music there was a throbbing like the throbbing of a heart, that persisted and persisted with a beautiful yet terrible monotony. Often Isaacson had listened to this symphony, been overwhelmed by the two effects of this monotony, an effect of loveliness and an effect of terror that were inextricably combined. To-night, either because he was very tired or for some other reason, the mystery of the sadness of this music, which floats through all its triumph, appealed to him more than usual, and in a strangely poignant way. The monotonous pulsation was like the pulse of life, that life in which he and the man beside him were for a time involved, from which presently they would be released, whether with or against their wills. The pulse of life! Suddenly from the general his mind passed to the particular. He thought of a woman's pulse, strong, regular, inexorable. He seemed to feel it beneath his fingers, the pulse of Mrs. Chepstow. And he knew that he had thought of her because Nigel Armine was thinking of her, that he connected her with this music because Nigel was doing the same. This secretly irritated Isaacson. He strove to detach his mind from this thought of Mrs. Chepstow. But his effort was in vain. Her pulse was beneath his fingers, and with every stroke of it he felt more keenly the mystery and cruelty of life. When the movement was finished, he did not speak a word. Nor did he look at Nigel. Even when the last note of the symphony seemed to fade and fall downwards into an abyss of misery and blackness, he did not speak or move. He felt crushed and overwhelmed, like one beaten and bruised.

"Isaacson!"

"Yes?"

He turned a little in his seat.

"Grand music! But it's all wrong."

"Why?"

"Wrong in its lesson."

The artist in Isaacson could not conceal a shudder.

"I don't look for a lesson; I don't want a lesson in it."

"But the composer forces it on one—a lesson of despair. Give it all up! No use to make your effort. The Immanent Will broods over you. You must go down in the end. That music is a great lie. It's splendid, it's superb, but it's a lie."

"Shall we go out? We've got ten minutes."

They made their way to the corridor and strolled slowly up and down, passing and repassing others who were discussing the music.

"Such music puts my back up," Nigel continued, with energy; "makes me feel I won't give in to it."

Isaacson could not help smiling.

"I can't look at Art from the moral plane."

"But surely Art often makes you think either morally or immorally. Surely it gives you impulses which connect themselves with life, with people."

Isaacson looked at him.

"I don't deny it. But these impulses are like the shadowy spectres of the Brocken, mere outlines which presently, very soon, dissolve into the darkness. Though great music is full of form, it often creates chaos in those who hear it."

"Then that music should call up in you a chaos of despair."

"It does."

"It makes me want to fight."

"What?"

"All the evil and the sorrow of the world. I hate despair."

Isaacson glanced at him again, and noticed how strong he was looking, and how joyous.

"Scotland has done you good," he said. "You look splendid to-night."

Secretly he gave a special meaning to the ordinary expression. To-night there was a splendour in his friend which seemed to be created by an inner strength radiating outward, informing, and expressing itself in his figure and his features.

"I'm looking forward to the winter."

Isaacson thought of the note of triumph in Mrs. Chepstow's voice when she said to him, "I don't feel such things this summer." Surely Nigel now echoed that note.

An electric bell sounded. They returned to the concert-room.

They stayed till the concert was over, and then walked

away down Regent Street, which was moist and dreary, full of mist and of ugly noises.

"When do you start for Egypt?" said Meyer Isaacson.

"In about ten days, I think. Do you wish you were going there?"

"I cannot possibly escape."

"But do you wish to?"

For a moment Isaacson did not answer.

"I do and I don't," he said, after the pause. "Work holds one strangely, because, if one is worth anything as a worker, its grip is on the soul. Part of me wants to escape, often wants to escape."

He remembered a morning ride, his desire of his "own place."

"The whole of me wants to escape," Nigel replied.

He looked about him. People were seeking "pleasure" in the darkness. He saw them standing at street corners, watchfully staring lest they should miss the form of joy. Cabs containing couples rolled by, disappeared towards north and south, disappeared into the darkness.

"I want to get into the light."

"Well, there it is before us."

Isaacson pointed to the brilliant illumination of Piccadilly Circus.

"I want to get into the real light, the light of the sun, and I want every one else to get into it too."

"You carry your moral enthusiasm into all the details of your life," exclaimed Isaacson. "Would you carry the world to Egypt?"

Nigel took his arm.

"It seems so selfish to go alone."

"Are you going alone?"

The question was forced from Isaacson. His mind had held it all the evening, and now irresistibly expelled it into words.

Nigel's strong fingers closed more tightly on his arm.

"I don't want to go alone."

"I would far rather be alone than not have the exactly

right companion—some one who could think and feel with me, and in the sort of way I feel. Any other companionship is destructive."

Isaacson spoke with less than his usual self-possession, and there were traces of heat in his manner.

"Don't you agree with me?" he added, as Nigel did not speak.

"People can learn to feel alike."

"You mean that when two natures come together, the stronger eventually dominates the weaker. I should not like to be dominated, nor should I like to dominate. I love mutual independence combined with perfect sympathy."

Even while he was speaking, he was struck by his own exigence, and laughed, almost ironically.

"But where to find it!" he exclaimed. "Those are right who put up with less. But you—I think you want more than I do, in a way."

He added that lessening clause, remembering, quite simply, how much more brilliant he was than Nigel.

"I like to give to people who don't expect it," Nigel said. "How hateful the Circus is!"

"Shall we take a cab to Cleveland Square?"

"Yes—I'll come in for a little."

When they were in the house, Nigel said:

"I want to thank you for your visit to Mrs. Chepstow."

He spoke abruptly, as a man does who has been for some time intending to say a thing, and who suddenly, but not without some difficulty, obeys his resolution.

"Why on earth should you thank me?"

"Because I asked you to go."

"Is Mrs. Chepstow still in London?"

"Yes. I saw her to-day. She talks of coming to Egypt for the winter."

"Cairo, I suppose?"

'I think she is sick of towns."

"Then no doubt she'll go up the Nile."

There was a barrier between them. Both men felt it acutely.

"If she goes—it is not quite certain—I shall look after her," said Nigel.

Meyer Isaacson said nothing; and, after a silence that was awkward, Nigel changed the conversation, and not long after went away. When he was gone, Isaacson returned to his sitting-room upstairs and lit a nargeeleh pipe. He had turned out all the electric burners except one, and as he sat alone there in the small room, so dimly lighted, holding the long, snake-like pipe-stem in his thin, artistic hands, he looked like an Eastern Jew. With a fez upon his head, Europe would have dropped from him. Even his expression seemed to have become wholly Eastern, in its sombre, glittering intelligence, and in the patience of its craft.

"I shall look after her."

Said about a woman like Mrs. Chepstow by a man of Nigel's youth, and strength, and temperament, that could only mean one of two things, a liaison or a marriage. Which did it mean? Isaacson tried to infer from Nigel's tone and manner. His friend had seemed embarrassed, had certainly been embarrassed. But that might have been caused by something in his, Isaacson's, look or manner. Though Nigel was enthusiastic and determined, he was not insensitive to what was passing in the mind of one he admired and liked. He perhaps felt Isaacson's want of sympathy, even direct hostility. On the other hand, he might have been embarrassed by a sense of some obscure self-betrayal. Often men talk of uplifting others just before they fall down themselves. Was he going to embark on a liaison with this woman whom he pitied? And was he ashamed of the deed in advance?

A marriage would be such madness! Yet something in Isaacson at this moment almost wished that Nigel contemplated marriage—his secret admiration of the virtue in his friend. Such an act would be of a piece with Nigel's character, whereas a liaison—and yet Nigel was no saint.

Isaacson thought what the world would say, and suddenly he knew the reality of his affection for Nigel. The idea of the gossip pained, almost shocked him; of the gossip and bitter truths. A liaison would bring forth almost disgusted and wholly ironical laughter at the animal passions of man, as blatantly shown by Nigel. And a marriage? Well, the verdict on that would be, "Cracky!"

Isaacson's brain could not dispute the fact that there would be justice in that verdict. Yet who does not secretly love the fighter for lost causes?

"I shall look after her."

The expression fitted best the cruder, more sordid method of gaining possession of this woman. And men seem made for falling.

The nargeeleh was finished, but still Isaacson sat there. Whatever happened, he would never protest to Nigel. The *feu sacré* in the man would burn up protest. Isaacson knew that—in a way loved to know it. Yet what tears lay behind—the tears for what is inevitable, and what can only be sad! And he seemed to hear again the symphony which he had heard that night with Nigel, the unyielding pulse of life, beautiful, terrible, in its monotony; to hear its persistent throbbing, like the beating of a sad heart—which cannot cease to beat.

Upon the window suddenly there came a gust of wild autumn rain. He got up and went to bed.

X

VERY seldom did Meyer Isaacson allow his heart to fight against the dictates of his brain; more seldom still did he, presiding over the battle, like some heathen god of mythology, give his conscious help to the heart. But all men at times betray themselves, and some betrayals, if scarcely clever, are not without nobility. Such a betrayal led him upon the following day to send a note to Mrs. Chepstow, asking for an appointment. "May I see you alone?" he wrote.

In the evening came an answer:

"DEAR DOCTOR:

"I thought you had quite forgotten me. I have a pleasant recollection of your visit in the summer. Indeed, it made me understand for the first time that even a Bank Holiday need not be a day of wrath and mourning. Do repeat your visit. And as I know you are always so busy telling people how perfectly healthy they are, come next Sunday to tea at five. I shall keep out the clamouring crowd, so that we may discuss any high matter that occurs to us.
"Yours sincerely,
"RUBY CHEPSTOW."

It was Wednesday when Isaacson read, and re-read, this note. He regretted the days that must intervene before the Sunday came. For he feared to repent his betrayal. And the note did not banish this fear. More than once he did repent. Then he and Nigel met and again he gave conscious help to his heart. He did not speak to Nigel of the projected visit, and Nigel did not say anything more about Mrs. Chepstow. Isaacson wondered at this reserve, which seemed to him unnatural in Nigel. More than once he found himself thinking that Nigel regretted what he had said about the possibility of Mrs. Chepstow visiting Egypt. But of this he could not be sure. On Sunday, at a few minutes past five, he arrived at the Savoy, and was taken to Mrs. Chepstow's room.

The autumn darkness had closed over London, and when he came into the room, which was empty, the curtains were drawn, the light shone, a fire was blazing on the hearth. Not far from it was placed a tea-table, close to a big sofa which stood out at right angles from the wall.

There were quantities of white carnations in vases on the mantel-piece, on the writing-table, and on the top of the rosewood piano. The piano was shut, and no "Gerontius" was visible.

Meyer Isaacson stood for a moment looking round, feeling the atmosphere of this room, or at least trying to feel it. In the summer had it not seemed a little lonely, a little dreary, a chamber to escape from, despite its comfort and pretty colours? Now it was bright, cosy, even hopeful. Yes, he breathed a hopeful atmosphere.

A door clicked. Mrs. Chepstow came in.

She wore a rose-coloured dress, cut very high at the throat, with tight sleeves that came partly over her hands, emphasizing their attractive delicacy. The dress was very plainly made and seemed moulded to her beautiful figure. She had no hat on, but Isaacson had never before been so much struck by her height. As she came in, she looked immensely tall. And there was some marked change in her appearance. For an instant he did not know what it was. Then he saw that she had given to her cheeks an ethereal flush of red. This altered her extraordinarily. It made her look younger, more brilliant, but also much less refined. She smiled gaily as she took his hand. She enveloped him at once with a definite cheerfulness which came to him as a shock. As she held his hand, she touched the bell. Then she drew him down on the sofa, with a sort of coaxing cordiality.

"This shall be better than Bank Holiday," she said. "I know you pitied me then. You wondered how I could bear it. Now I've shut out the river. I'm glad you never came again till I could have the lights and the fire. I love the English winters, don't you, because one has to do such delicious things to keep all thought of them out. Now, in the hot places abroad, that people are always raving about, all the year round one can never have a room like this, an hour like this by a clear fire, with thick curtains drawn—and a friend."

As she said the last three words, her voice had a really beautiful sound in it, and a sound that was surely beautiful because of some moral quality it contained or suggested. More than a whole essay of Emerson's did this mere sound suggest friendship. The leaves of the book of this woman's attractions were being turned one by one for Isaacson. And of all her attractions her voice perhaps was the greatest.

The waiter came in with tea. When he had gone, the Doctor could speak.

But he scarcely knew what to say. Very seldom was his self-possession disturbed. To-day he felt at a disadvantage. The depression, perhaps chiefly physical, which had lately been brooding over him, and which had become acute at the concert, deepened about him to-day, made him feel morally small. Mrs. Chepstow's cheerfulness seemed like height. For a moment in all ways she towered above him, and even her bodily height seemed like a mental triumph, or a triumph of her will over his.

"But this is only autumn," he said.

"We can pretend it is winter."

She gave him his cup of tea, with the same gesture that had charmed Nigel on the day when he first visited her. Then she handed him a plate with little bits of lemon on it.

"I've found out your tastes, you see. I know you never take milk."

He was obliged to feel grateful. Yet something in him longed to refuse the lemon, the something that never ceased from denouncing her. He uttered the right banality:

"How good of you to bother about me!"

"But you bother about me, and on your only free day! Don't you think I am grateful to you?"

There was no mockery in her voice. To-day her irony was concealed, but, like a carefully-covered fire, he knew it was burning still. And because it was covered he resented it. He resented this comedy they were playing, the insincerity into which she was smilingly leading him. She could not imagine that she deceived him. She was far too clever for that. Then what was the good of it all?—that she had put him, that she kept him, at a disadvantage.

She handed him the muffins. She ministered to him as if she wanted to pet him. Again he had to feel grateful. Even in acute dislike men must be conscious of real charm in a woman. And Isaacson did not know how to ignore anything that was beautiful. Had the Devil come to him —with a grace, he must have thought, " How graceful is the Devil!" Now he was charmed by her gesture. Nevertheless, being a man of will, and, in the main, a man who was very sincere, he called up his hard resolutions, and said:

"No, I don't think you are grateful. I don't think you are the woman to be grateful without a cause."

"Or with one," he mentally added.

"But here is the cause!"

She touched his sleeve. And suddenly, with that touch, all her charm for him vanished, and he was angry with her for daring to treat him like those boys by whom she had been surrounded, for daring to think that she could play upon the worst in him.

"I'm afraid you are mistaken," he said. "I am no cause for your gratitude."

She looked more cordial and natural even than before.

"But I think you are. For you don't really like me, and yet you come to see me. That is unselfishness."

"Only supposing what you say were true, and that you did like me."

"I do like you."

She said it quite simply, without emphasis. And even to him it sounded true.

" Some day perhaps you will know it."

"But—I do not believe it."

He had recovered from the stroke of her greatest weapon, her voice.

"That does not matter. What is matters, not what some one thinks is, or is not."

"Yes," he said. "What is matters. I have come here, not to pay a formal call, or even a friendly visit, but, perhaps, to commit an impertinence."

She smilingly moved her head, and handed him her cigarette-case.

"No, you would never do that."

He hesitated to take a cigarette—and now her bright eyes frankly mocked him, and said, "A cigarette commits you to nothing!" Certainly she knew how to make him feel almost like an absurd and awkward boy; or was it his feeling of overwork, of physical depression, that was disarming him to-day?

"Thank you."

He lighted a cigarette, and she lighted another, still with a happy air.

"How do you know that?" he asked.

"I feel it."

With a little laugh, she reminded him of his saying about women.

"You are wrong. I am going to do it," he said.

"But—do you really think it an impertinence?"

He was beset by his sensitive dislike to mix in other people's affairs, but almost angrily he overcame it.

"I don't know. You may. Mrs. Chepstow, you were raving just now about the delights of the English winter——"

"Shut out!" she interpolated.

"Then why should you avoid them?"

"And who says I am going to?"

"Are not you going to Egypt?"

She settled herself in the angle of the sofa.

"Would it be the wrong climate for me, Doctor Isaacson?"

She put an emphasis on "Doctor."

" I am not talking as a doctor."

"Then as a friend—or as an enemy?"

"As a friend—of his."

"Of whom?"

"Of Nigel Armine."

" Because he is working in the Fayyūm, may not I go up the Nile?"

"If you were on the Nile, Armine would not be in the Fayyūm."

"You are anxious about his reclaiming of the desert? Have you put money into his land scheme?"

"You think I only care for money?" he said, nettled, despite himself, at the sound of knowledge in her voice. "What do you know of me?"

"And you—of me?"

She still spoke lightly, smilingly. But he thought of the inexorable beating of that pulse of life—of life, and the will to live as her philosophy desired.

"I don't wish to speak of any knowledge I may have of you. But—leave Armine in the Fayyūm."

"Did he say I was going to Egypt?"

"He only spoke of it once. Then he said you might go."

"Anything else?"

"He said that if you did go he would look after you."

She sat looking at him in silence.

"And—why not?" she said at last, as he said nothing more.

"Others have—looked after you."

Her face did not change.

"Doesn't he know it?" she said.

"And he isn't like—others."

"I know what he is like."

When she said that, Isaacson hated her, hated her for her woman's power of understanding, and, through her understanding, of governing men.

"What does he mean by—looking after you?" he said.

And now, almost without knowing it, he spoke sternly, and his dark face was full of condemnation.

"What did you mean when you said that 'others' have done it?"

"Then it is that!"

Isaacson had not meant to speak the words, but they escaped from his lips. No passing light in her eyes betrayed that she had caught the reflection of the thought that lay behind them.

"Men! Men!" his mind was saying. "And—even Armine!"

"You are afraid for the Fayyūm?" she said.

"Oh, Mrs. Chepstow!" he began, with a sudden vehemence that suggested the unchaining of a nature. Then he stopped. Behind his silence there was a flood of words —words to describe her temperament and Armine's, her mode of life and Armine's, what she deserved—and he; words that would have painted for Mrs. Chepstow not only the good in Isaacson's friend, but also the secret good in Isaacson, shown in his love of it, his desire to keep it out of the mud. And it was just this secret good that prevented Isaacson from speaking. He could not bear to show it to this woman. Instinctively she knew, appreciated, what was, perhaps, not high-minded in him. Let her be content with that knowledge. He would not make her the gift of his goodness.

And—to do so would be useless.

"Yes?" she said.

She sat up on the sofa. She was looking lightly curious.

"If you do go to the Nile, let me wish you a happy winter."

He was once more the self-possessed Doctor so many women liked.

"If I go, I shall know how to make him happy," she replied, echoing his cool manner, despite her more earnest words.

He got up. Again he hated her for her knowledge of men. He hated her so much that he longed to be away from her. Why should she be allowed to take a life like Armine's into her soiled hands, even if she could make him happy for a time, being a mistress of deception?

"Good-bye."

He just touched her hand.

"Good-bye. I am grateful. You know why."

Again she sent him that cordial smile. He left her standing up by the hearth. The glow from the flames played over her rose-coloured gown. Her beautiful head was turned towards the door to watch him go. In one hand she held her cigarette. Its tiny wreath of smoke curled lightly about her, mounting up in the warm, bright room. Her figure, the shape of her head, her eyes—they looked really lovely. She was still the "Bella Donna" men had talked about so long. But as he went out, he saw the tiny wrinkles near her eyes, the slight hardness about her cheekbones, the cynical droop at the corners of her mouth.

Armine did not see them. He could not make Armine see them. Armine saw only the beauties she possessed. His concentration on them made for blindness.

And yet even he had his ugliness. For now Isaacson believed in the liaison between him and Mrs. Chepstow.

Only eight days later, after Mrs. Chepstow and Nigel had sailed for Alexandria, did he learn that they were married.

XI

IMMEDIATELY after their marriage at a registrar's office, Nigel and his wife, with a maid, and a great many trunks of varying shapes and sizes, travelled to Naples and embarked on the *Hohenzollern* for Egypt, where Nigel had rented for the winter the Villa Androud, on the bank of the Nile near Luxor.

Nigel was happy, but he was not wholly free from anxiety, although he was careful to keep that anxiety from his wife, and desired even sometimes to deny that it existed to himself. In making this marriage he had obeyed the cry of two voices within him, the voice of the senses and the voice of the soul. He did not know which had sounded most clearly; he did not know which inclination had prevailed over him most strongly, the longing for a personal joy, or the pitiful desire to shed happiness and peace on a darkened and soiled existence. The future perhaps would tell him. Meanwhile he put before him one worthy aim, to be the perfect husband.

Although the month was November, and the rush for the Nile had not begun, the *Hohenzollern* was crowded with passengers, and when the Armines came into the dining-room for lunch, as the vessel was leaving Naples, every place was already taken.

"Give us a table upstairs alone," said Nigel to the head-steward, putting something into his hand. "We shall like that ever so much better."

He had caught sight of a number of staring English

faces, on some of which there seemed to be more than the dawning of a recognition of Mrs. Armine.

As if mechanically the rosy Prussian retained the something, and replied, with a strong German accent:

"I must give you the table at the top of the staircase, sir, but I cannot promise that you will be alone. If there are any more to come, they will have to sit with you."

"Anyhow, put us there."

"Pray that we have this to ourselves for the voyage, Ruby," said Nigel, a moment later, as they sat side by side on a white settee close to the open door which led out on to the deck at the top of the main companion.

As he finished speaking, a steward appeared, quickly conducting to their table a tall and broad young man, who made them a formal bow, and composedly sat down opposite to them.

He was remarkably well dressed in clothes which must have been cut by an English tailor, and which he wore with a carelessness almost English, but also with an easy grace that was utterly foreign. Thin, with mighty shoulders and an exceptionally deep chest, it was obvious that his strength must be enormous. His neck looked as powerful as a bull's, and his rather small head was poised upon it with a sort of triumphant boldness. His hair was black and curly, his forehead very broad, his nose short, straight, and determined, with wide and ardent nostrils. Under a small but dense moustache his lips were thick and rather pouting. His chin, thrust slightly forward in a manner almost aggressive, showed the dusk of close-shaven hair. The tint of his skin, though dark, was clear—had even something of delicacy. His hands, broad, brown, and muscular, had very strong-looking fingers which narrowed slightly at the tips. His eyes were large and black, were set in his head with an almost singular straightness, and were surmounted by brows which, depressed towards the nose, sloped upwards towards the temples. These brows gave to the eyes beneath them, even to the whole face, a curiously distinctive look of open resolution, which was seizing, and attractive or unattractive according to the temperament of the beholder.

He took up the *carte du jour,* studied it at length and with obvious care, then gave an order in excellent French, which the steward hastened away to carry out. This done, he twisted his moustaches and looked calmly at his companions, not curiously, but rather as if he regarded them with a polite indifference, and merely because they were near him. Mrs. Armine seemed quite unaware of his scrutiny, but Nigel spoke to him almost immediately, making some remark about the ship in English. The stranger answered in the same language, but with a strong foreign accent. He seemed quite willing to talk. He apologized for interrupting their tête-à-tête, but said he had no choice, as the saloon was completely full. They declared they were quite ready for company, Nigel with his usual sympathetic geniality, Mrs. Armine with a sort of graceful formality beneath which—or so her husband fancied—there was just a suspicion of reluctance. He guessed that she would have much preferred a private table, but when he said so to her, as they were taking their coffee on deck, she answered:

"No, what does it matter? We shall so soon be in our own house. Tell me about the villa, Nigel, and Luxor. You know I have never seen it."

With little more than a word she had deftly flicked the intruding stranger out of their lives, she had concentrated herself on Nigel. He felt that all her force, like a strong and ardent stream, was flowing into the new channel which he had cut for her. He obeyed her. He told her about Egypt. And as he talked, and watched her listening, he began to feel thoroughly for the first time the vital change in his life, and something within him rejoiced, that was surely his manhood singing.

The voyage passed swiftly by, attended by perfect weather, calm, radiant, blue—weather that releases humanity from any bonds of depression into a joyous world. Yet for the Armines it was not without an unpleasant incident.

Among the pasengers were a Lord and Lady Hayman, whom Nigel Armine knew, and whom Mrs. Armine had known in the days when London had loved her. It was impossible not to meet them, equally impossible not to perceive their cold confusion at each encounter, shown by a sudden interest in empty seas and unpopulated horizons. That they mistook the situation was so evident to Nigel that one day he managed to confront Lord Hayman in the smoke-room and to have it out with him.

"Congratulate you, I'm sure, congratulate you!" murmured that gentleman, whose practical brown eyes became suddenly wells full of ironical amazement. " Tell my wife at once. Knew nothing at all about it."

He got away, with a moribund cigar between his teeth, and no doubt informed Lady Hayman, who thereafter bowed to Nigel, but with a reluctant muscular movement that adequately expressed an inward moral surprise mingled with condemnation. Mrs. Armine seemed totally undisturbed by these demonstrations, her only comment upon the lady being that it was really strange that "in these days" any one could be found to wear magenta and red together, especially any one with a complexion like Lady Hayman's. And her astonishment at the triple combination of colours seemed so simple, so sincere, that it had to be believed in as merely an emanation from an artistic temperament. It was probable that the Haymans told other English on the *Hohenzollern* the news of Nigel's marriage, for several of the faces that had stared from the luncheon-tables continued to stare on the deck, but with a slightly different expression; the sheer, dull curiosity being exchanged for that half-satirical interest with which the average person of British blood regards a newly-married couple.

This contemplation of them made Nigel secretly angry, and awoke in him a great and peculiar tenderness for his wife, founded on a suddenly more acute understanding of the brutality of the ostracism, combined with notoriety, which she had endured in recent years. Now at last she had some one to protect her. His heart enfolded her with ample wings. But he longed to be free from this crowd, from which on a ship they could not escape, and they spoke to no one during the voyage except to their companion at meals.

With him they were soon on the intimate terms of shipboard—terms that commit one to nothing in the future when land is reached. Although he was dressed like an Englishman, and on deck wore a straw hat with the word " Scott " inside it, he soon let them know that his name was Mahmoud Baroudi, that his native place was Alexandria, that he was of mixed Greek and Egyptian blood, and that he was a man of great energy and will, interested in many schemes, pulling the strings of many enterprises.

He spoke always with a certain polite but bold indifference, as if he cared very little what impression he made on others; and all the information that he gave about himself was dropped out in a careless, casual way that seemed expressive of his character. The high rank, the great riches of his father he rather implied than definitely mentioned. Only when he talked of his occupations was he more definite, more strongly personal. Nigel gathered that he was essentially a man of affairs, had nothing in common with the typical lazy Eastern, who loves to sit in the sun, to suffer the will of Allah, and to fill the years with dreams; that he was cool, clear-headed, and full of the marked commercial ability characteristic of the modern Greek. Whether this aptitude was combined with the sinuous cunning that is essentially Oriental Nigel did not know. He certainly could not perceive it. All that Baroudi said was said with clearness, and a sort of acute precision, whether he discussed the land question, the irrigation works on the Nile, the great boom of 1906, in which such gigantic fortunes were made, or the cotton and sugar industries, in both of which he was interested. The impression he conveyed to Nigel was that he was born to " get on " in whatever he undertook, and that in almost any form of activity he could be a fine ally, or an equally fine opponent. That he was fond of sport was soon apparent. He spoke with an enthusiasm that was always mingled with a certain serene *insouciance* of the horses he had bred and of the races he had won in Alexandria and Cairo, of yachting, of big-game shooting up the Nile beyond Khartum in the country of the Shillouks, and of duck, pigeon, and jackal shooting in the Fayyūm and on the sacred Lake of Kurun.

Nigel found him an excellent fellow, the most sympathetic and energetic man of Eastern blood whom he had ever encountered. Mrs. Armine spoke of him more temperately; he did not seem to interest her, and Nigel was confirmed by her lack of appreciation in an idea that had already occurred to him. He believed that Baroudi was a man who did not care for women, except, no doubt, as the occasional and servile distractions of an unoccupied hour in the harem. He was always very polite to Mrs. Armine, but when he talked he soon, as if almost instinctively, addressed himself to Nigel; and once or twice, when Mrs. Armine left them alone together over their coffee and cigars, he seemed to Nigel to become another man, to expand almost into geniality, to be not merely self-possessed —that faculty never failed him—but to be more happily at his ease, more racy, more ready for intimacy. Probably he was governed by the Oriental's conception of woman as an inferior sex, and was unable to be quite at home in the complete equality and ease of the English relation with women.

When the *Hohenzollern* sighted Alexandria, Baroudi went below for a moment. He reappeared wearing the fez. They bade each other good-bye in the harbour, with the usual vague hopes of a further meeting that do duty on such occasions, and that generally end in nothing.

Mrs. Armine seemed glad to be rid of him and to be alone with her husband.

"Don't let us stay in Cairo," she said. "I want to go up the river. I want to be in the Villa Androud."

After one night at Shepheard's they started for Luxor,

or rather for Keneh, where they got out in the early morning to visit the temple of Denderah, taking a later train which brought them to Luxor towards evening, just as the gold of the sunset was beginning to steal into the sky and to cover the river with glory.

Mrs. Armine was fatigued by the journey, and by the long day at Denderah, which had secretly depressed her. She looked out of the window of their compartment at the green plains of doura, at the almost naked brown men bending rhythmically by the shadûfs, at the children passing on donkeys, and the women standing at gaze with corners of their dingy garments held fast between their teeth; and she felt as if she still saw the dark courts of Hathor's dwelling, as if she still heard the cries of the enormous bats that inhabit them. When the train stopped, she got up slowly, and let Nigel help her down to the platform.

"Is the villa far away?" she said, looking round on the crowd of staring Egyptians.

"No, I want you to walk to it. Do you mind?"

His eyes demanded a "no," and she gave it him with a good grace that ought to have been written down to her credit by the pen of the recording angel. They set out to walk to the villa. As they went through the little town, Nigel pointed out the various "objects of interest": the antiquity shops, where may be purchased rings, necklaces, and amulets, blue and green "servants of the dead," scarabs, winged discs, and mummy-cases; the mosque, a Coptic church, cafés, the garden of the Hôtel de Luxor. He greeted several friends of humble origin: the black barber who called himself "Mr. White"; Ahri Achmed, the Folly of Luxor, who danced and gibbered at Mrs. Armine and cried out a welcome in many languages; Hassan, the one-eyed pipe-player; and Hamza, the praying donkey-boy, who in winter stole all the millionaires from his protesting comrades and in summer sat with the dervishes in the deep shadows of the mosques.

"You seem to be as much at home here as in London," said Mrs. Armine, in a voice that was rather vague.

"Ten times more, Ruby. And so will you be soon. I love a little place."

"Yes?"

After a pause she added:

"Are there many villas here?"

"Only two on the bank of the Nile. One belongs to a Dutchman. Our villa is the other."

"Only two—and one belongs to a Dutchman!" she thought.

And she wondered about their winter.

"When I've settled you in, I must run off to the Fayyûm to see how the work is going, and rig up something for you. I want to take you there soon, but it's really in the wilds, and I didn't like to straight away. Besides I was afraid you might be dull and unhappy without any of your comforts. And I do want you to be happy."

There was an anxiety that was almost wistful in his voice.

"I do want you to like Egypt," he added, like an eager boy.

"I am sure I shall like it, Nigel. There's no Casino, I suppose?"

"Good heavens, no! What should one do with a Casino here?"

"Oh, they sometimes have one, even in places like this. A friend of mine who went to Biskra told me there was one there."

"Look at that, Ruby! That's better than any Casino—don't you think?"

They had turned to the left and come to the river bank.

All the Nile was flooded with gold, in which there were eddies of pale mauve and distant flushes of a red that resembled the red on the wing of a flamingo. The clear and radiant sky was drowned in a quivering radiance of gold, that was like a thing alive and sensitively palpitating. The far-off palms, the lofty river banks that framed the Nile's upper reaches, the birds that flew south, following the direction of the breeze, the bats that wheeled about the great columns of the temple, the boats that with widespread lateen sails went southward with the birds, were like motionless and moving jewels of black against the vibrant gold. And the crenellated mountains of Libya, beyond Thebes and the tombs of the Kings, stood like spectral sentinels at their posts till the pageant should be over.

"Isn't it wonderful, Ruby?"

"Yes," she said. "Quite wonderful."

She honestly thought it superb, but the dust in her hair and in her skirts, the lassitude that seemed to hang, almost like spiders' webs about wood, about the body which contained her tired spirit, restrained her enthusiasm from being a match for his. Perhaps she knew this and wished to come up with him, for she added, throwing a warm sound into her voice:

"It is exquisite. It is the most magical thing I have ever seen."

She touched her veil, as she spoke, and put up her hand to her hair behind. Two Frenchmen, talking with sonorous voices, were just then passing them on the road.

"I didn't know any sunset could be so marvellous."

She was still touching her hair, and now she felt clothed in dust; and, with the ardour of a fastidious woman who has not seen the inside of a dressing-room for twenty-four hours, she longed to be rid both of the sunset and of the man.

"Where is the villa, Nigel?"

"Not ten minutes away."

The spirit groaned within her, and she went resolutely forward, passing the Winter Palace Hotel.

"What a huge hotel—but it isn't open!" she said.

"It will be almost directly. We turn to the right down here."

Some large rats were playing on the uneven stones close to the river; from a little shed close by there came the dull puffing of an engine.

"Where on earth are we going, Nigel? This is only a donkey track."

"It's all right. Just wait a minute. There's the Dutchman's castle, and we are just beyond it. Am I walking too fast for you, Ruby?"

"No, no."

She hurried on. Her whole body was clamouring for warm water with a certain essence dissolved in it, for a change of stockings and shoes, for a tea-gown, for a sofa with a tea-table beside it, for a hundred and one things his manhood did not dream of.

"Here it is at last!" he said.

A tall and amiable-looking boy in a flowing gold-coloured robe suddenly appeared before them, holding open a wooden gate, through which they passed into a garden.

"Hulloh, Ibrahim!" cried Nigel.

"Hulloh, my gentleman!" returned the boy, inclining his body towards Mrs. Armine and touching his fez with his hand. "I am Ibrahim Ahmed, my lady, the special servant called a dragoman of my Lord Arminigel. I can read the hieroglyphs, and I am always young and cheerful."

He took Nigel's right hand, kissed it and placed it against his forehead rapidly three times in succession, smiled, and looked sideways on the ground.

"I am always young and cheerful," he repeated, softly and dreamily. He picked a red rose from a bush, placed it between his white teeth, and turned to conduct them to the white house that stood in the midst of the garden perhaps a hundred yards away.

"What a nice boy!" said Mrs. Armine.

"He's been my dragoman before. This is our little domain."

Mrs. Armine saw a flat expanse of brown and sun-dried earth, completely devoid of grass, and divided roughly into sunken beds containing small orange-trees, mimosas, rose-bushes, poinsettias, and geraniums. It was bounded on three sides by earthen walls and on the fourth side by the Nile.

"Is it not beautiful, mees?" said Ibrahim.

Mrs. Armine began to laugh.

"He takes me for a *vieille fille!*" she said. "Is it a compliment, Nigel? Ibrahim,"—she touched the boy's robe—"won't you give me that rose?"

"My lady, I will give you all what you want."

Already she had fascinated him. As she took the rose, which he offered with a salaam, she began to look quite gay.

"All what you want you must have," continued Ibrahim, gravely.

"Ibrahim reads my thoughts like a true Eastern!" said Nigel.

"What I want now is a bath," remarked Mrs. Armine, smelling the rose.

"Directly we have had one more look at the Nile from our own garden," exclaimed Nigel.

But she had stopped before the house.

"I can't take my bath in the Nile. Good-bye, Nigel!"

Before he could say a word she had crossed a little terrace, disappeared through a French window, and vanished into the villa.

Ibrahim smiled, hung his head, and then murmured in a deep contralto voice:

"The wife of my Lord Arminigel, she does not want Ibrahim any more, she does not want the Nile, she wants to be all alone."

He shook his head, which drooped on his long and gentle brown neck, sighed, and repeated dreamily:

"She wants to be all alone."

"We'll leave her alone for a little and go and look at the gold."

Meanwhile within the house Mrs. Armine was calling impatiently for her maid.

"For mercy's sake, undress me. I am a mass of dust, and looking perfectly dreadful. Is the bath ready?" she asked, as the girl, who had come running, showed her into a good-sized bedroom.

The maid, who was not the red-eyed maid Nigel had met

at the Savoy, shrugged up her small shoulders, and extended her little, greedy hands.

"It is ready, madame; but the water—oh, *là, là!*"

"What's the matter. What do you mean?"

"The water is the colour of madame's morning chocolate."

"Oh!" said Mrs. Armine, almost with a sound of despair.

She sank into a chair, taking in with a glance every detail of the chamber, which had been furnished and arranged by a rich and consumptive Frenchman who had lived there with his mistress and had recently died at Cairo.

"Bring me the mirror from my dressing-case, and get me out of this gown."

Marie hastened to fetch the mirror, into which, after unpinning and removing her hat and veil, Mrs. Armine looked long and earnestly.

"There are no women servants, madame."

. . . . . .

"All the servants here are men, madame, and all are as black as boots."

"Shut the door into monsieur's room, and don't chatter so much. My head is simply splitting."

. . . . . .

"What are you doing? One would think you had never seen a corset before. Don't fumble! If you fumble, I shall pack you off to Paris by the first train to-morrow morning. Now where's the bath?"

Marie, wrinkling up her nose, which looked like a note of interrogation, led the way into the bathroom, and pointed to the water with a grimace.

"*Voilà*, madame!"

"*Mon Dieu!*" said Mrs. Armine.

She stared at the water, and repeated her exclamation.

"That makes pity to think that madame——"

"Have you put in the *eau de paradis?*"

"But certainly, madame."

"Very well then—ugh!"

She shuddered with disgust as the rich brown water of the Nile came up to her breast, to her chin.

"And to think that it looked golden," she murmured, "when we were standing on the bank!"

XII

Soon after half-past eight that evening, when darkness lay over the Nile and over the small garden of the villa, a tall Nubian servant, dressed in white with a scarlet girdle, spread two prayer rugs on the terrace before the French windows of the drawing-room, and placed upon them a coffee-table and two arm-chairs. At first he put the chairs a good way apart, and looked at them very gravely. Then he set them quite close together, and relaxed into a smile. And before he had finished smiling, over the parquet floor behind him there came the light rustle of a dress. The Nubian servant turned round and gazed at Mrs. Armine, who had stopped beside a table and was looking about the room; a white-and-yellow room, gaily but rather sparsely furnished, that harmonized well with the fair beauty which moved the black man's soul.

He thought her very wonderful. The pallor of her face, the delicate lustre of her hair, quite overcame his temperament, and when she caught sight of him and smiled, and observed the contrast between the snowy white of his turban, his scarlet girdle and babouches, and the black lustre of his skin, with eyes that frankly admired, he compared her secretly to the little moon that lights up the Eastern night. He went softly to fetch the coffee, while she stepped out on to the terrace.

At first she stood quite still, and stared at the bit of garden which revealed itself in the darkness; at the dry earth, the untrimmed, wild-looking rose-bushes, and the little mimosa-trees, vague almost as pretty shadows. A thin, dark-brown dog, with pale yellow eyes, slunk in from the night and stood near her, trembling and furtively watching her. She had not seen it yet, for now she was gazing up at the sky, which was peopled with myriads of stars, those piercingly bright stars which look down from African skies. The brown dog trembled and blinked, keeping his yellow eyes upon her, looked self-consciously down sideways, then looked at her again.

From the hidden river there came a distant song of boatmen, one of those vehement and yet sad songs of the Nile that the Nubian waterman loves.

"Sh—sh—sh!"

Mrs. Armine had caught sight of the dog. She hissed at him angrily, and made a threatening gesture with her hands, which sent him slinking back to the darkness.

"What is it, Ruby?" called out a strong voice from above.

She started.

"Oh, are you there, Nigel?"

"Yes. What's the matter?"

"It was only a dreadful-looking dog. What are you doing up there?"

"I was looking at the stars. Aren't they wonderful to-night?"

There was in his voice a sound of warm yet almost childlike enthusiasm, with which she was becoming very familiar.

"Yes, marvellous. Oh, there's the dog again! Sh—sh—sh!"

"I'll come down and drive it away."

In a moment he was with her.

"Where is the little beast?"

"It's gone again. I frightened it. Oh, you've brought me a cloak, you thoughtful person."

She turned for him to put it round her, and as he began to do so, as he touched her arms and shoulders, his eyes shone and his brown cheeks slightly reddened. Then his expression changed; he seemed to repress, to beat back something; he drew her down into a chair, and quietly sat down by her. The Nubian came with coffee, and went softly away, smiling.

Mrs. Armine poured out the coffee, and Nigel lit his cigar.

"Turkish coffee for my lord and master!" she said, pushing a cup towards him over the little table. "I think I must learn how to make it."

He was gazing at her as he stretched out his hand to take it.

"Do you feel at home here, Ruby?" he asked her.

"It's such a very short time, you dear enquirer," she answered. "Remember I haven't closed an eye here yet. But I'm sure I shall feel at home. And what about you?"

"I scarcely know what I feel."

He sipped the coffee slowly.

"It's such a tremendous change," he continued. "And I've been alone so long. Of course, I've got lots of friends, but still I've often felt very lonely, as you have, Ruby, haven't you?"

"I've seldom felt anything else," she replied.

"But to-night——?"

"Oh, to-night—everything's different to-night. I wonder——"

She paused. She was leaning back in her chair, with her head against a cushion, looking at him with a slight, half-ironical smile in her eyes and at the corners of her lips.

"I wonder," she continued, "what Meyer Isaacson will think."

"Of our marriage?"

"Yes. Do you suppose it will surprise him?"

"I—no, I hardly think it will.'

"You didn't hint it to him, did you?"

"I said nothing about any marriage, but he knew something of my feeling for you."

"All the same, I think he'll be surprised. When shall we get the first post from England telling us the opinion of the dear, kind, generous-hearted world?"

"Ruby, who cares what any one thinks or says?"

"Men often don't credit us with it, but we women, as a rule, are horribly sensitive, more sensitive than you can imagine. I—how I wish that some day your people would try to like me!"

He took one of her hands in his.

"Why shouldn't they? Why shouldn't they? But this winter we'll keep to ourselves, learn to know each other, learn to trust each other, learn to—to love each other in the very best and finest way. Ruby, I took this villa because I thought you would like it, that it would not be so bad as our first home. But presently I want you to come with me to Sennoures. When we've had our fortnight's honeymoon here, I'll go off for a few nights, and look into the work, and arrange something for you. I'll get a first-rate tent from Cairo. I want you in camp with me. And it's farther away there, wilder, less civilized; one gets right down to Nature. When I was in London, before I asked you to marry me, I thought of you at Sennoures. My camp used to be pitched near water, and at night, when the men slept covered up in their rugs and bits of sacking, and the camels lay in a line, with their faces towards the men's tent, eating, I used to come out alone and listen to the frogs singing. It's like the note of a flute, and they keep it up all night, the beggars. You shall come out beside that water, and you shall hear it with me. It's odd how a little thing like that stirs up one's imagination. Why, even just thinking of that flute of the Egyptian Pan in the night——" He broke off with a sound that was not quite a laugh, but that held laughter and something else. "We've got, please God, a grand winter ahead of us, Ruby," he finished. "And far away from the world."

"Far—far away from the world!"

She repeated his words rather slowly.

"I must have some more coffee," she added, with a change of tone.

"Take care. You mayn't be able to sleep."

"Nigel—do you want me to sleep to-night?"

He looked at her, but he did not answer.

"Even if I don't sleep I must have it. Besides I always sit up late."

"But to-night you're tired."

"Never mind. I must have the coffee."

She poured it out and drank it.

"I believe you live very much in the present," he said.

"Well—you live very much in the future."

"Do I? What makes you think so?"

"My instinct informs me of the fact, and of other facts about you."

"You'll make me feel as if I were made of glass if you don't take care."

"Live a little more in the present. Live in the present to-night."

There was a sound of insistence in her voice, a look of insistence in her bright blue eyes which shone out from their painted shadows, a feeling of insistence in the thin and warm white hand which now she laid upon his. "Don't worry about the future."

He smiled.

"I wasn't worrying. I was looking forward."

"Why? We are here to-night, Nigel, to live as if we had only to-night to live. You talk of Sennoures. But who knows whether we shall ever see Sennoures, ever hear the Egyptian Pan by the water? I don't. You don't. But we do know we are here to-night by the Nile."

With all her force, but secretly, she was trying to destroy in him the spiritual aspiration which was essential in his nature, through which she had won him as her husband, but which now could only irritate and confuse her, and stand in the way of her desires, keeping the path against them.

"Yes," he said, drawing in his breath. "We are here to-night by the Nile, and we hear the boatmen singing."

The distant singers had been silent for some minutes; now their voices were heard again, and sounded nearer to the garden, as if they were on some vessel that was drifting down the river under the brilliant stars. So much nearer was the music that Mrs. Armine could hear a word cried out by a solo voice, "Al-lah! Al-lah! Al-lah!" The voice was accompanied by a deep and monotonous murmur. The singer was beating a *daraboukkeh* held loosely between his knees. The chorus of nasal voices joined in with the rough and artless vehemence which had in it something that was sad, and something that, though pitiless, seemed at moments to thrill with yearning, like the cruelty of the world, which is mingled with the eternal longing for the healing of its wounds.

"We hear the boatmen singing," he repeated, "about Allah, and always Allah, Allah, the God of the Nile, and of us two on the Nile."

"Sh—sh! There's that dog again! I do wish——"

She had begun to speak with an abrupt and almost fierce nervous irritation, but she recovered herself immediately.

"Couldn't the gardener keep him out?" she said, quietly.

"Perhaps he belongs to the gardener. I'll go and see. I won't be a minute."

He sprang up and followed the dog, which crept away into the garden, looking around with its desolate, yellow eyes to see if danger were near it.

Allah—Allah—Allah in the night!

Mrs. Armine did not know that this song of the boatmen of Nubia was presently, in later days she did not dream of, to become almost an integral part of her existence on the Nile; but although she did not know this, she listened to it with an attention that was strained and almost painful.

"Al-lah—Al-lah——"

"And probably there is no God," she thought. "How can there be? I am sure there is none."

Abruptly Meyer Isaacson seemed to come before her in the darkness, looking into her eyes as he had looked in his consulting-room when she had put up her veil and turned her face towards the light. She shut her eyes. Why should she think about him now? Why should she call him up before her?

She heard a slight rustle near her, and she started and opened her eyes. By one of the French windows the dragoman Ibrahim was standing, perfectly still now, and looking steadily at her. He held a flower between his teeth, and when he saw that she had seen him, he came gracefully forward, smiling and almost hanging his head, as if in half-roguish deprecation.

"What did you say your name was?" Mrs. Armine asked him.

He took the flower from his teeth, handed it to her, then took her hand, kissed it, bent his forehead quite low, and pressed her hand against it.

"Ibrahim Ahmed, my lady."

She looked at his gold-coloured robe, at his European jacket, at the green and gold fringed handkerchief which he had wound about his tarbush, and which covered his throat and fell down upon his breast.

"Very pretty," she said, approvingly. "But I don't like the jacket. It looks too English."

"It is a present from London, my lady."

"Al-lah——"

Always the sailors' song seemed growing louder, more vehement, more insistent, like a strange fanaticism ever increasing in the bosom of the night.

"Where are those people singing, Ibrahim?" said Mrs. Armine.

She put his flower in the front of her gown, opening her cloak to do so.

"They seem to get nearer and nearer. Are they coming down the river?"

"I s'pose they are in a felucca, my lady. They are Noobian peoples. They always make that song. It is a pretty song."

He gently moved his head, following the rhythm of the

music. Between the green and gold folds of his silken handkerchief his gentle brown eyes always regarded her.

"Nubian people!" she said. "But Luxor isn't in Nubia."

"Noobia is up by Aswân. The obelisks come from there. I will show you the obelisks to-morrow, my lady. There is no dragoman who understands all 'bout obelisks like Ibrahim."

"I am sure there isn't. But"—those voices of the singing sailors were beginning almost to obsess her—"are all the boatmen Nubians then?"

"Nao!" he replied, with a sudden cockney accent.

"But these that are singing?"

"I say they are Noobian peoples, my lady. They are Mahmoud Baroudi's Noobian peoples."

"Baroudi's sailors!" said Mrs. Armine.

She sat up straight in her chair.

"But Mahmoud Baroudi isn't here, at Luxor?"

Ibrahim's soft eyes had become suddenly sharp and bright.

"Do you know Mahmoud Baroudi, my lady?"

"We met him on the ship coming from Naples."

"Very big—big as Rameses the Second, the statue of the King hisself what you see before you at the Ramesseum—eyes large as mine, and hair over them what goes like that!"

He put up his brown hands and suddenly sketched Baroudi's curiously shaped eyebrows.

Mrs. Armine nodded. Ibrahim stretched out his arm towards the Nile.

"Those are his Noobian peoples. They come from his dahabeeyah. It is at Luxor, waiting for him. They have nuthin' to do, and so they make the fantasia to-night."

"He is coming here to Luxor?"

Ibrahim nodded his head calmly.

"He is comin' here to Luxor, my lady, very nice man, very good man. He is as big as Rameses the Second, and he is as rich as the Khedive. He has money—as much as that."

He threw out his arms, as if trying to indicate the proportions of a great world or of an enormous ocean.

"Here comes my gentleman!" he added, suddenly dropping his arms.

Nigel returned from the darkness of the garden.

" Hulloh, Ibrahim!"

"Hulloh, my gentleman!"

"Keeping your mistress company while I was gone? That is right."

Ibrahim smiled, and sauntered away, going towards the bank of the Nile. His golden robe faded among the little trunks of the orange-trees.

"It was the gardener's dog," said Nigel, letting himself down into his chair with a sigh of satisfaction. I've made him feed the poor brute. It was nearly starving. That's why it came to us."

"I see."

"Al-lah!" he murmured, saying the word like an Eastern man.

He looked into her eyes.

"The first word you hear in the night from Egypt, Ruby, Egypt's night greeting to you. I have heard that song up the river in Nubia often, but—oh, it's so different now!"

During her long experience in a life that had been complex and full of changes, Mrs. Armine had heard the sound of love many times in the voices of men. But she had never heard till this moment Nigel's full sound of love. There was something in it that she did not know how to reply to, though she had the instinct of the great courtesan to make the full and perfect reply to the desires of the man with whom she had schemed to ally herself. She owed this reply to him, but she owed it how much more to something within herself! But there existed within him a hunger for which she had no food. Why did he show this hunger to her? Already its demonstration had tried her temper, but to-night, for the first time, she felt her whole being set on edge by it. Nevertheless, she was determined he should not see this, and she answered very quietly:

"I am hearing this song for the first time with you, so I shall always associate it with you."

He drew a little nearer to her. And she understood and could reply to the demand which prompted that movement.

"We must drink Nile water together, Ruby, Nile water —in all the different ways. I'll take you to the tombs of the Kings, and to the Colossi when the sun is setting. And when the moon comes, we'll go to Karnak. I believe you'll love it all as I do. One can never tell, of course, for another. But—but do you think you'll love it all with me?"

Mingled with the ardour and the desire there was a hint in his voice of anxiety, of the self-doubt which, in certain types of natures, is the accompaniment of love.

"I know I shall love it all—with you," she said.

She let her hand fall into his, and as his hand closed upon it she was physically moved. There was in Nigel something that attracted her physically, that attracted her at certain moments very strongly. In the life that was to come she must sweep away all interference with that.

"And some day," he said, "some day I shall take you to see night fall over the Sphinx, the most wonderful thing in Egypt and perhaps in the whole world. We can do that on our way to or from the Fayyūm when we have to pass through Cairo, as soon as I've arranged something for you."

"You think of everything, Nigel."

"Do you like to be thought for?"

"No woman ever lived that did not."

She softly pressed his hand. Then she lifted it and held it on her knee.

Presently she saw him look up at the stars, and she felt sure that he was connecting her with them, was thinking of her as something almost ideal, or, if not that, as something that might in time become almost ideal.

"I am not a star," she said.

He did not make any answer.

"Nigel, never be so absurd as to think of me as a star!"

He suddenly looked around at her.

"What do you say, Ruby?"

"Nothing."

"But I heard you speak."

"It must have been the sailors singing. I was looking up at the stars. How wonderful they are!"

As she spoke, she moved very slightly, letting her cloak fall open so that her long throat was exposed.

"And how beautifully warm it is!"

He looked at her throat, and sighed, seemed to hesitate, and then bent suddenly down as if he were going to kiss it.

"Al-lah!"

Almost fiercely the nasal voice of the singing boatman who gave out the solo part of the song of the Nile came over the garden from the river, and the throbbing of the *daraboukkeh* sounded loudly in their ears. Nigel lifted his head without kissing her.

"Those boatmen are close to the garden!" he said.

Mrs. Armine wrapped her cloak suddenly round her.

"Would you like to go down to the river and see them?" he added.

"Yes, let us go. I must see them," she said.

She got up from her chair with a quick but graceful movement that was full of fiery impetus, and her eyes were shining almost fiercely, as if they gave a reply to the fierce voices of the boatmen.

Nigel drew her arm through his, and they went down the little sandy path past the motionless orange-trees till they came to the bank of the Nile. Ibrahim was standing there, peeping out whimsically from his fringed and tasselled wrappings, and smoking a cigarette.

"Where are the boatmen, Ibrahim?" said Nigel.

"Here they come, my gentleman!"

Upon the wide and moving darkness of the river, a great highway of the night leading to far-off African lands, hugging the shore by a tufted darkness of trees, there came a felucca that gleamed with lanterns. The oars sounded in the water, mingling with the voices of the men, whose vague, uncertain forms, some crouched, some standing up, some leaning over the river, that was dyed with streaks of light into which the shining drops fell back from the lifted blades, were half revealed to the watchers above them in the garden.

"Here come the Noobian peoples!"

"I wonder what they are doing here," said Nigel, "and why they come up the river to-night. Whose people can they be?"

Ibrahim opened his lips to explain, but Mrs. Armine looked at him, and he shut them without a word.

"Hush!" she whispered. "I want to listen."

This was like a serenade of the East designed to give her a welcome to Egypt, like the voice of this great, black Africa speaking to her alone out of the night, speaking with a fierce insistence, daring her not to listen to it, not to accept its barbaric summons. A sort of animal romance was stirred within her, and she began to feel strongly excited. She heard no longer the name of Allah, or, if she heard it, she connected it no longer with the Christian's conception of a God, with Nigel's conception of a God, but perhaps with strange idols in dusky temples where are mingled crimes and worship. Her imagination suddenly rose up, gathered its energies, and ran wild.

The boat stayed opposite the garden.

"It must be meant for me, it is meant for me!" she thought.

At that moment she knew quite certainly that this boat had come to the garden because she lived in the garden, that it paused so that she might be sure that the music was directed to her, was meant for no one but her. It was not for her and Nigel. Nigel had nothing to do with it. He did not understand its meaning.

At last the boat moved on, the flickering spears of light on the water travelled on and turned away, the voices floated away under the stars till the night enfolded them, the light and the music were taken and kept by the sleepless mystery of Egypt.

"Shall we go into the villa, Ruby?" said Nigel, almost diffidently, yet with a thrill in his voice.

She did not answer for a moment, then she said.

"Yes, I suppose it is time to go to bed."

Nigel drew her arm again through his, and they went away towards the house, while Ibrahim looked after them, smiling.

XIII

"RUBY," said Nigel, a fortnight later, coming into his wife's bedroom after the morning walk on the river bank which invariably succeeded his plunge into the Nile, "whom do you think I've just met in Luxor?"

He was holding a packet of letters and papers in his hand. The post had just arrived.

Mrs. Armine, wrapped in a long white gown which did not define her figure, with her shining hair coiled loosely at the back of her neck, was sitting before the toilet-table, and looked round over her shoulder.

"Some one we both know, Nigel?" she asked.

He nodded.

"Not the magenta and red together, then?"

"The Haymans—no, though I believe they are here at the Winter Palace."

"God bless them!" she murmured, with a slight contraction of her forehead. "Is it a man or a woman?"

"A man."

"A man!" She turned right round, with a sharp movement, holding the arms of her chair tightly. "Not Meyer Isaacson?"

"Isaacson! Good heavens! He never takes a holiday except in August. Dear old chap! No, this is some one not specially interesting, but not bad; only Baroudi."

Mrs. Armine's hands dropped from the arms of the chair, as she turned towards the glass.

"Baroudi!" she said, as if the name meant nothing to her. "Why do you string one up for nothing, Nigel?"

She took up a powder-puff.

"Do you mean the man on the *Hohenzollern?* What has he to do with us?"

Nigel crossed the room, and sat down on a chair by the side of the toilet-table, facing his wife and holding in his lap the bundle of letters and papers.

"Are you disappointed, Ruby?"

"No, because we don't need any one. But you roused my expectation, and then played a cold douche upon it, you tiresome person!"

There was a sort of muffled crossness in her voice, but as she passed the powder-puff over her face her eyes and her lips were smiling. Nigel leaned his arm upon the table.

"Ruby," he said.

"Well—what is it?"

She stopped powdering.

"I wish you wouldn't do—all that."

"All what?"

"All those things to your face. You are beautiful. I wish you would leave your face alone."

"I do, practically. I only try to save it a little from the sun. You wouldn't have me look like the wife of one of what Ibrahim calls 'the fellaheen peoples,' would you?"

"I want you to look as natural and simple as you always are with me. I don't mean that you are simple in mind, of course. I am speaking of your manner."

"My dear Nigel, who is affected nowadays? But I really mustn't look like the fellaheen peoples. Ibrahim would be shocked."

Nevertheless, she put the powder-puff down.

"You don't trust your own beauty, Ruby," he said.

She sat back and looked at him very gravely, as if his remark had made a strong impression upon her. Then she looked into the mirror, then she looked again at him.

"You think I should be wise to trust it as much as that?"

"Of course you would."

He laid his hand on hers.

"You are blossoming here in Egypt, but you hardly let one know it when you put things on your face."

She gazed again into the glass in silence.

"Any letters for me?" she said, at last.

"I haven't looked yet. I walked with Baroudi on the bank. He's joined his dahabeeyah, and is going up to Armant to see to his affairs in the sugar business up there."

"Oh!"

"I believe he only stays till to-morrow or Wednesday. He invited me to go over to his boat and have a look at it this afternoon."

"Are you going?"

"I told him I'd let him know. Shall I go?"

"Don't you want to?"

"I should like to see the boat, but—you see, he's half an Oriental, and perhaps he didn't think it was the proper thing to do, but——"

"He didn't invite me. Why should he? Go, Nigel. You want a man's society sometimes. You mustn't always sit in my pocket. And besides, you're just off to the Fayyûm. I must get accustomed to an occasional lonely hour."

He pressed his hand on hers.

"I shall soon come back. And soon you shall come with me there."

"I love this place," she said. "Are there any letters for me?"

He untied the string of the packet, looked over the contents, and handed her three or four.

"And now run away and read yours," she said. "When you're in my room I can do nothing. You take up all my attention. I'll come down in a few minutes."

He gave her a kiss and obeyed her.

When he was in the little drawing-room, he threw the papers carelessly on a table without taking off their wrappers. He had scarcely looked at a paper since he had been in Egypt; he had had other things to do, things that had engrossed him mind and body. Like many men who are informed by a vital enthusiasm, Nigel sometimes lived for a time in blinkers, which shut out from his view completely the world to right and left of him. He could be an almost terribly concentrated man. And since he had been in Egypt he had been concentrated on his wife, and on his own life in relation to her. The affairs of the nations had not troubled him. He had read his letters, and little besides. Now he took those which had come that morning, and went out upon the terrace to run through them in the sunshine.

Bills, a communication from his agent at Etchingham, a note from his man of affairs in Cairo, and—hullo!—a letter from his brother, Harwich!

That did not promise him much pleasure. Already he had received several family letters scarcely rejoicing in his marriage. They had not bothered him as much as he had formerly feared they would. He did not expect his relations, or the world, to look at things with his eyes, to think of Ruby with gentleness or even forgiveness for her past. He knew his world too well to make preposterous mental demands upon it. But Harwich had already expressed himself with his usual freedom. There seemed no particular reason why he should write so soon again.

Nigel tore open the letter, read it quickly, re-read it, then laid it down upon his knees, pulled his linen hat over his eyes, and sat for a long while quite motionless, thinking.

His brother's letter informed him that his sister-in-law, Zoe, Harwich's wife, had given birth to twin children—sons—and that they were "stunningly well—hip, hip, hooray!"

Harwich's boisterous joy was very natural, and might be supposed to spring from paternal feelings that did him honour, but there was a note of triumph in his exultation which Nigel understood, and which made him thoughtful now. Harwich was glorying in the fact that Nigel and Nigel's wife were cut out of the succession—that, so far as one could see, Mrs. Armine would now never be Lady Harwich.

For himself Nigel did not care at all. Harwich was ten years older than he was, but he had never thought about succeeding him, had never wished to succeed him, and when he had married Ruby he had known that his sister-in-law was going to have a child. He had known this, but he had not told it to Ruby. He had not concealed it; simply, it had not occurred to him to tell her. Now the tone of Harwich's letter was making him wonder, "Will she mind?"

Presently he heard her coming into the room behind him, crossing it, stepping out upon the terrace.

"Nigel! Are you asleep?"

"Asleep!" he said. "At this hour!"

For once there was an unnatural sound in his voice, a note of carelessness that was forced. He jumped up from his chair, scattering his letters on the ground.

"You haven't read your letters all this time!"

"Not yet; not all of them, at least," he said, bending to pick them up. "I've been reading one from my brother, Harwich."

"From Lord Harwich?" She sent a sharp look to him. "Is it bad news? Is Lord Harwich ill?"

"No, Ruby."

"Then what's the matter?"

"The matter? Nothing! On the contrary, it's a piece of good news."

In spite of himself almost, his eyes were staring at her with an expresion of scrutiny that was fierce, because of the anxiety within him.

"Poor old Harwich has had to wait so long, and now at last he's got what he's wanted."

"What's that?"

"A child—that is, children—twins."

There was a moment of silence. Then Mrs. Armine said, with a smile:

"So that's it!"

"Yes, that's it, Ruby."

"Girls? Boys? Girl and boy?"

"Boys, both of them."

"When you write, congratulate him for me. And now read the rest of your letters. I'm going to take a stroll in the garden."

As she spoke, she put up her parasol and sauntered

away towards the Nile, stopping now and then to look at a flower or tree, to take a rose in her hand, smell it, then let it go with a careless gesture.

"Does she really mind? Damn it, does she mind?"

There had been no cloud on her face, no involuntary movement of dismay, yet in her apparently unruffled calm there had been a reticence that somehow had chilled him. She was so clever in reading people that surely she must have felt the anxiety in his heart, the eager desire to be reassured. If she had only responded to it frankly, if she had only come up to him, touched his hand, said, "Dear old boy, what does it matter? You don't suppose I've ever bothered about being the future Lady Harwich?"—something of that kind, all his doubts would have been swept away. But she had taken it too coolly, almost, had dismissed it too abruptly. Perhaps that was his fault, though, for he had been reserved with her, had not said to her all he was thinking, or indeed anything he was thinking.

"Ruby! I say, Ruby!"

Following a strong impulse, he hastened after her, and came up with her on the bank of the Nile.

"Look!" she said.

"What? Oh, Baroudi's dahabeeyah tied up over there! Yes, I knew that. It's to get out of the noise of Luxor. Ruby, you—you don't mind about Harwich and the boys?"

"Mind?" she said.

Her voice was suddenly almost angry, and an expression that was hard came into her brilliant eyes.

"Mind? What do you mean, Nigel?"

"Well, you see it makes a lot of difference in my position from the worldly point of view."

"And you think I care about that! I knew you did. I knew exactly what you were thinking on the terrace!"

There was a wounded sound in her voice. Then she added, with a sort of terribly bitter quietness:

"But—what else could you, or anyone, think?"

"Ruby!" he exclaimed.

He tried to seize her hand, but she would not let him.

"No, Nigel! don't touch me now. I—I shall hate you if you touch me now."

Her face was distorted with passion, and the tears stood in her eyes.

"I don't blame you a bit," she said. "I should be a fool to expect anyone, even you, to believe in me after all that— all that has happened. But—it is hard, sometimes it is frightfully hard, to bear all this disbelief that one can have any good in one."

She turned hurriedly away.

"Ruby!" he said, with a passion of tenderness.

"No, no! Leave me alone for a little. I tell you I must be alone!" she exclaimed, as he followed her.

He stopped on the garden path and watched her go into the house.

"Beast, brute that I am!" he said to himself.

He clenched his hands. At that moment he hated himself; he longed to strike himself down—himself, and all men with himself—to lay them even with the ground— cynics, unbelievers, agents destructive of all that was good and noble.

Mrs. Armine went straight up to her room, locked the door against her maid, and gave way to a violent storm of passion, which had been determined by Nigel's impulse to be frank, following on his news of Harwich. With the shrewd cleverness that scarcely ever deserted her, she had forced her temper into the service of deception. When she knew she had lost her self-control, that she must show how indignant she was, she had linked her anger to a cause with which it had nothing to do, a cause that would stir all his tenderness for her. At the moment when she was hating him, she was teaching him to love her, and deliberately teaching him. But now that she was alone, all that was deliberate deserted her, and, disregarding even the effect grief and anger unrestrained must have upon her appearance, she gave way, and gave way completely.

She did not come down to lunch, but towards tea-time she reappeared in the garden, looking calm, but pathetically tired, with soft and wistful eyes.

"When are you starting for the dahabeeyah?" she asked, as Nigel came anxiously, repentantly forward to meet her.

"I don't think I'll go at all. I don't want to go. I'll stay here and have tea with you."

"No, you mustn't do that. I shall like to have tea alone to-day."

She spoke very gently, but her manner, her eyes, and every word rebuked him.

"Then I'll go," he said, "if you prefer it."

He looked down.

"Baroudi's men have come already to take me over."

"I heard them singing, up in my bedroom. Run along! Don't keep him waiting."

With the final words she seemed to make an effort, to try to assume the playful, half-patronizing manner of a pretty woman of the world to a man supposed to adore her; but she allowed her lips to tremble so that he might see she was playing a part. He did not dare to say that he saw, and he went down to the bank of the Nile, got into the felucca that was waiting, and was rowed out into the river.

As soon as he had gone, Mrs. Armine called Ibrahim to come and put a chair and a table for her in the shadow of the wall, close to the stone promontory that was thrust out into the Nile to keep its current from eating away the earth embankment of the garden.

"I am going to have tea here, Ibrahim," she said. "Tell Hassan to bring it directly the sun begins to set."

"Yes, suttinly," replied the always young and cheerful. "And shall Ibrahim come back and stay with you?"

She shook her head, looking kindly at the boy, who had quickly learnt to adore her, as had all the Nubians in the villa.

"Not to-day, Ibrahim. To-day I want to be alone."

He inclined his long, thin body, and answered gravely:

"All what you want you must have, my lady."

"Don't call me 'my lady' to-day!" she exclaimed, with a sudden sharpness.

Ibrahim looked amazed and hurt.

"Never mind, Ibrahim!"—she touched her forehead—"I've got a bad head to-day, and it makes me cross about nothing."

He thrust one hand into his gold-coloured skirt, and produced a glass bottle full of some very cheap perfume from Europe.

"This will cure you, my la— mees. Rub it on your head. It is a bootiful stink. It stinks lovely indeed!"

She accepted it with a grateful smile, and he went pensively to order the tea; letting his head droop towards his left shoulder, and looking rather like a faithful dog that, quite unexpectedly, is not wanted by his mistress. Mrs. Armine sat still, frowning.

She could hear the Nubians of Baroudi singing as they bent to their mighty oars; not the song of Allah with which they had greeted her on her arrival, obedient perhaps to some message sent from Alexandria by their master, but a low and mysterious chaunt that was almost like a murmur from some spirit of the Nile, and that seemed strangely expressive of a sadness of the sun, as if even in the core of the golden glory there lurked a canker, like the canker of uncertainty that lies in the heart of all human joy.

The day was beginning to decline; the boatmen's voices died away; Hassan, in obedience to Ibrahim's order, brought out tea to his mistress in the garden. When he had finished arranging it, he stood near her for a moment, looking across the water to Baroudi's big white dahabeeyah, which was tied up against the bank a little way down the river. In his eyes there were yellow lights.

"What are you doing, Hassan?" asked Mrs. Armine.

The tall Nubian turned towards her.

"Mahmoud Baroudi is rich!" he said. "Mahmoud Baroudi is rich!"

He looked again at the dahabeeyah; then he came to the little table, moved a plate, touched and smoothed the table-cloth, and went quietly away.

Mrs. Armine sipped her tea and looked, still frowning,

at the river, which began to lose its brown colour slowly, to gleam at first with pallid gold, then with a gold that shone like fire. The eddies beyond the breakwater were a light and delicate mauve and looked nervously alive. A strange radiance that was both ethereal and voluptuous, that seemed to combine elements both spiritual and material, was falling over this world, clothing it in a sparkling veil of beauty. And as the gold on the river deepened in hue, it spread swiftly upon the water, it travelled down towards Luxor, it crept from the western bank to the eastern bank of the Nile, from the dahabeeyah of Baroudi almost to the feet of Mrs. Armine.

"Mahmoud Baroudi is rich! Mahmoud Baroudi is rich!"

Why had Hassan said that? What had it to do with her? She looked across at Baroudi's great white boat, which now was turning into a black jewel on the gold of the moving river, and she felt as if, like some magician who understood her nature, he was trying to comfort her to-day by showering gold towards her. It was an absurd fancy, at which, in a moment, she was smiling bitterly enough.

She almost hated Nigel to-day. When she had left him in the garden before luncheon, she had quite hated him for his unworldliness, combined with a sort of boyish simplicity and wistfulness. Of course he had known, he must have known, that Zoe Harwich was going to have a child; he must have known it when he was shooting with his brother in the autumn. And he had never said a word of it to her. And now he was cut out of the succession. He might never have succeeded his brother; but there had been a great chance that he would, that some day she would be reigning as Lady Harwich. That thought had swayed her towards him, had had very much to do with the part she had played in London which had won her Nigel as a husband. If what was now a fact had been a fact a few weeks ago, would she ever have schemed to marry him, would such an alliance have been "worth her while"?

How Lady Hayman and all her tribe, a tribe which once had petted and entertained the beautiful Mrs. Chepstow, had dubbed her "Bella Donna," how they must be rejoicing to-day! She could almost hear what they were saying as she sat in the sunset by the Nile. "What a mercy that woman has overreached herself!" "How furious she must be, now Harwich has got sons!" "What a delicious slap in the face for her after catching that foolish Nigel Armine!" Hundreds of women were smiling over her discomfiture at this moment, and probably also hundreds of men. For no one would give her credit for having married Nigel for himself, for having honestly fallen in love with him and acted "squarely" towards him. And, of course, she had not fallen in love with him. He was not, indeed, the type of man with whom a nature and a temperament like hers could fall in love. She had liked him before she married him, he had even had for her a certain physical attraction; but already that physical attraction—really the passing fancy of a capricious and a too-experienced woman—had lost its savour, and for a reason that, had he known it, would have cut Nigel to the heart.

She could not bear his love of an ideal, his instinct to search for hidden good in men and women, but especially in herself, his secret desire for moral progress. She knew that these traits existed in him, and therefore was able to hate them; but she was incapable of really understanding them, clever woman though she was. Her cleverness was of that type which comprehends vice more completely than virtue, and although she could apprehend virtue, as she had proved by her conduct in London which had led to her capture of Nigel, she could never learn really to understand its loveliness, or to bask happily in its warmth and light. Morally she seemed to be impotent. And the great gulf which must for ever divide her husband from her was his absolute disbelief that any human being can be morally impotent. He must for ever misunderstand her, because his power to read character was less acute than his power to love. And she, in her inmost chamber of the soul, though she might play a part to deceive, though she might seldom be, however often appearing to be, truly her natural self, had the desire, active surely or latent in the souls of all human creatures, to be understood, to be known as she actually was.

Nigel had been aware that Zoe Harwich was going to have a child, and he had never let her know it.

She repeated that fact over and over in her mind as she sat and looked at the sunset. Ever since the morning she had been repeating it over and over. Even her violent outburst of temper had not stilled the insistent voice which in reiteration never wearied. In the first moments of her bitterness and anger, the voice had added, "Nigel shall pay me for this." It did not add this now, perhaps because into her fierceness had glided a weariness. She was paying for her passion. Perhaps Nigel would have to pay for that payment too. He was going away to the Fayyûm in two or three days. How she wished he was going to-night, that she need not be with him to-night, need not play the good woman, or the woman with developing goodness in her, to-night, now that she was weary from having been angry!

The tea had become almost black from standing. She poured out another cupful, and began to drink it without putting in milk or sugar. It tasted acrid, astringent, almost fierce, on her palate; it lifted the weariness from her, seemed to draw back curtains from a determined figure which slipped out naked into the light, the truth of herself untired and unashamed.

Nigel would have to reckon with that some day.

The gold was fading from the river now, the water was becoming like liquid silver, then, in a moment, like liquid steel. On the dahabeeyah, which began to look as if it were a long way off and were receding from her, shone a red and a blue light. Still the vehement voices of the brown fellahîn at work by the shadûf rose unwearied along the Nile. During the last days Mrs. Armine's ears had grown accustomed to these voices, so accustomed to them that it was already becoming difficult to her to realize that but a short time ago she had never heard them, never felt their curious influence, their driving power, which, mingled with other powers of sun and air, flogs the souls of men and women into desire of ungentle joys and of sometimes cruel pleasures. And now, with the fading away of the daylight, those powerful, savage, and sad voices gained in meaning, seemed no more to be issuing from the throats of toiling and sweating Egyptians, but to be issuing from the throat of this land of ruins and gold, where the green runs flush with the sand, and the lark sings in the morning, where the jackal whines by night.

For a long time Mrs. Armine listened, sitting absolutely still. Then suddenly she moved, got up, and went swiftly towards the house. Nigel was coming back. Mingling with the voices of the shadûf men she heard the voices of Baroudi's Nubians.

When she had reached the house, she went up at once to her bedroom, shut the door, and stood by the open window that gave on to a balcony which faced towards the Nile. The voices of the shadûf men had now suddenly died away. With the rapid falling of night the singers' time for repose had come; they had slipped on their purple garments, and were walking to their villages. Those other voices drew nearer and nearer, murmuring deeply, rather than actually singing, their fatalistic chaunt which set the time for the oars.

Darkness came. The voices ceased.

Mrs. Armine leaned forward, with one hand on the window-frame. Her white teeth showed on her lower lip.

In the garden she heard two voices talking, and moving towards the house.

. . . . . .

"Marie! Marie!"

Her maid came running.

"*V'là*, madame? What does madame want?"

"I am going to change my gown."

"Madame is going to dress for the evening?"

"No. I don't dine for two hours."

"Then madame——"

"Don't talk so much. Get me out a white gown, that white linen gown I got at Paquin's and have never worn yet. And put me out——"

She gave some directions about stockings and shoes, and went in to her dressing-room, where she stood before the mirror, carefully examining her face. Then she took off the hat she was wearing.

"Lock the bedroom door and the door into monsieur's room!" she called, in a moment.

"*Bien*, madame!"

"*Mon Dieu!*" muttered the maid, as she went to turn the keys, "is she going mad? What has she? There is no one here, there is no one coming, and all this *tohu-bohu!*"

"Get out the white hat with the white picotees!"

"Ah, *mon Dieu!*"

"Do you hear? The white——"

"I hear, I hear, madame! Oh, *là, là, là!*"

"Make haste!"

"*Bien*, madame, *très bien!*"

The girl ran for the hat, and Mrs. Armine, who had lighted all the candles, sat down before the glass. She remembered Nigel's desire expressed to her that day that she would give up "doing things" to her face. Well, she would respond to it in this way!

Very carefully and cleverly she began to whiten her face, to touch up her eyes and her narrow, definite eyebrows.

"All is ready, madame!"

Marie was standing at the dresing-room door; she started and swung round on her heels as there came a knock at the door of the bedroom, the creak of the handle turning.

"Be quiet!"

Mrs. Armine had caught her arm. The girl stood still, staring and marvelling, while her mistress went noiselessly

BELLA DONNA 145

into the bedroom and sat down on the far side of the bed, leaning backwards till her head was near the pillows, which she took care not to touch.

"Ruby! Ruby!"

"What is it? Who's there? Who's there?"

The voice that replied sounded both languid and surprised.

"I—Nigel!"

Mrs. Armine sat up.

"What is it, Nigel? I'm lying down."

"Oh, I'm—I'm sorry if I've disturbed you, but—you're not ill?"

"No, only resting. What is it, Nigel?"

"I've brought Baroudi over to see you and the villa, and to dine with us to-night."

"Oh—very well."

"You don't mind, Ruby?"

The voice outside the door was suddenly very low.

"Go down and entertain him, and I'll come almost directly."

The handle creaked, as he let it go, but for a moment there was no sound of retreating footsteps.

"Look here, Ruby, if——"

"Go down! I'll come directly."

Footsteps went towards the stairs.

"Get me into my gown! Wait—change my stockings first."

Marie knelt down quickly on the floor. As she bent her head, she was smiling.

She began to understand.

XIV

WHEN Mrs. Armine came into the little drawing-room, it was empty, but she smelt cigars, and heard the murmur of voices outside near the terrace. The men were evidently walking up and down enjoying the soft air of the evening. She did not go out immediately, but stood and listened to the voices.

Ah, they were talking about the Fayyūm—doubtless discussing some question of sowing, planting, of the cultivation of land!

This evening her face seemed to retain in its skin an effect of her outburst of passion, a sensation of dryness and harshness, as if it were unduly stretched over the flesh and had lost its normal elasticity. Just before she came out of her bedroom, Marie, with a sort of reluctant admiration, had exclaimed, *"Madame est exquise ce soir!"* She wondered if it were true, and as the voices without grew softer for a moment, more distant, she went to stand again before a mirror, and to ask herself that question.

She had chosen to put on a walking-dress instead of a tea-gown, because she believed that in it she would look younger, her splendid figure being still one of her greatest advantages. Yes, her figure was superb, and this gown showed it off superbly. The long quiet of her very dull life in London while she had known Nigel, followed by her comparative repose in the splendid climate of Egypt, had done wonders for her appearance. Certainly to-night, despite any ravages made by her injudicious yielding to anger, she looked years younger than she had looked in Isaacson's consulting-room. The wrinkles about her eyes showed scarcely at all, or—not at all. And she was marvellously fair.

Orientals delight in fairness, and always suppose Occidentals to be years younger than they really are, if they have succeeded in retaining any of the charms of youth.

Marie was not far wrong.

She turned to step out upon the terrace.

"Ah, Mahmoud Baroudi!" she said, with a sort of lazy but charming indifference, as the two men came to meet her. "So you have come up the river to look after—what is it? your something—your sugar?"

"My sugar; exactly, madame," he replied gravely, bowing over her hand. "I hope you will forgive my intrusion. Your husband kindly insisted on bringing me over—and in flannels."

His apology was extremely composed, but Nigel was looking a little excited, a little anxious, was begging forgiveness with his eyes for all the trouble of the morning. She was not going to seem to give it him yet; a man on the tenter-hooks was a man in the perfectly right place. So she was suave, and avoided his glance without seeming to avoid it. They strolled about a little, talking lightly of nothing particular; then she said, speaking for the first time directly to her husband,

"Nigel, don't you think you'd better just go and tell Hassan we shall be three at dinner, and have a little talk to the cook? Your Arabic will have more effect upon the servants than my English. Mahmoud Baroudi and I will sit on the terrace till you come back."

"Right you are!" he said.

And he went off at once, leaving them together.

As soon as he was gone, Mrs. Armine sat down on a basket chair. For a moment she said nothing. In the silence her face changed. The almost lazy naturalness and simplicity faded gradually out of it, revealing the alert and seductive woman of the world. Even her body seemed to change, to become more sensitive, more conscious, under the eyes of Baroudi; and all the woman in her, who till now, save for a few subtle and fleeting indications of life, had lain almost quiescent, rose suddenly and signalled boldly to attract the attention of this man, who sat down a little way from her, and gazed at her in silence with an Oriental directness and composure.

Although they had talked upon shipboard, this was the first time they had been *en tête-à-tête*.

To-night Mrs. Armine's eyes told Baroudi plainly that she admired him, told him more—that she wished him to know it; and he accepted her admiration, and now made a bold return. For soon the change in her was matched by the change in him. The open resolution of his face, which on the ship had often attracted Nigel, was now mingled with a something sharp, as of cunning, with a ruthlessness she could understand and appreciate. As she looked at him in the gathering darkness of the night, she realized that housed within him, no doubt with many companions, there was certainly a brigand, without any fear, without much pity. And she compared this brigand with Nigel.

"How do you find Egypt, madame? Do you like my country?"

He leaned a little forward as at last he broke their silence, and the movement, and his present attitude, drew her attention to the breadth of his mighty shoulders and to the arresting poise of his head, a poise that, had it been only a shade less bold, would have been almost touchingly gallant.

"Have you seen all the interesting things in Thebes and Karnak?"

"Yes. We've been quite good tourists. We've been to the Colossi, the tombs, the temples. We've dined by moonlight on the top of the Pylon at Karnak. We've seen sunset from Deir-al-Bahari."

"And sunrise?"

"From nowhere. I prefer to sleep in the morning."

"And do you care about all these things, tombs, temples, mummies—madame? Have you enjoyed your Egyptian life?"

She paused before answering the question. As a fact, she had often enjoyed her expeditions with Nigel in the bright and shimmering gaiety of the exquisite climate of Luxor; the picnic lunches out in the open, or within the walls of some mighty ruin; the smart canters on the straight brown paths between the waving green prairies or crops, above which the larks sang and the wild pigeons flew up to form the only cloud in the triumph of gold and of blue; the long climbs upward into the mountains along the tiger-coloured ways, where the sun had made his empire since the beginning of the world; the descents when day was declining, when the fellahîn went homewards under the black velvet of the palm-trees, and the dust stirred by their brown and naked feet rose up in spirals towards the almost livid light of the afterglow. And she had enjoyed the dinner at Karnak in the pale beams of a baby moon. For she still had the power to enjoy, and much of the physical energy of the average Englishwoman, who is at home in the open air and quite at her ease in the saddle. And Egypt was for her a complete novelty, and a novelty bringing health, and a feeling almost of youth.

Nevertheless, she paused before replying.

Secretly, during all these days she was now considering, she had been as one who walks in a triumph. She had been exulting in the *coup* she had made just when her life seemed turning to greyness, exulting in the blow she had struck against a society which had despised her and cast her out. Exultation had coloured her days. Now suddenly, unexpectedly, she knew she had been living in a fool's paradise, into which Nigel had led her. And this knowledge fell, like a great shadow, over all the days in Egypt behind her, blotting out their sunshine, their gaiety, their glow.

"Pretty well," she said, at last. "Do you care about such things?"

He shrugged his mighty shoulders.

"Madame, I am not a tourist. What should I do in the temples among the bats, and in the tombs where one can almost smell the dead people? You must not come to us Egyptians for all that. You must go to the old English maidens—is that it?—maidens who wear helmets on their grey hair done so"—he put up his brown hands, and pretended to twist up a tiny top-knot at the back of his head—"and who stroke the heads of the dragomans sitting there at their feet, what they call their 'tootsicums,' and telling them thousands of lies. Or you must go to the thin antiquaries, with the red noses and the heads without any hair, who dig for mummies while their wives—ah, well I must not say that! But we Egyptians, we have other things to do than to go and stare at the Sphinx. We have always seen it. We know it is there, that it is not going to run away. So we prefer to enjoy our lives while we can, and not to trouble about it. Do you blame us?"

"No," she said. "I never blame any one for enjoying life."

There was in his look and manner, even in his attitude, a something that was almost like a carelessly veiled insolence. In a European she would perhaps have resented it. In him not only did she not resent it, but she was attracted by it. For it seemed to belong as of right to his great strength, his bold and direct good looks, which sprang to the eyes, his youth, and his Eastern blood. Such a man must feel often insolent, however carefully he might hide it. Why should he not show some grains of his truth to her?

"Nor for any way of enjoying life, madame?" he said.

And he leaned still a little more forward, put up one big hand to his cheek, let it drop down to his splendid throat, and kept the fingers inside his soft turn-down collar while he looked into her eyes.

"I didn't say that."

"Would you care much what way it was if it gave the enjoyment?"

"Would you?"

"I! Certainly not. But—I am not like Mr. Armeen."

He slightly mispronounced the name.

"Mr. Armine?" she said. "What about him?"

"Would he not think that some things one might do and many things one must not do? All the Englishmen are like that. Oh, dear, if one does the thing they think wrong! Oh, dear! Oh, Law!"

He took away his hand from his throat, held it up, then slapped it down upon his knee.

"My word!" he added, smiling, and always searching her eyes with his. "It is worse than to eat pig by daylight in Ramadan would seem to an Egyptian."

"Do you dislike the English?"

"What must I say?"

"Say the truth."

"If it is the English ladies, I think them lovely."

"And the Englishmen?"

"Oh, they are all—good fellers."

He threw into the last two words an indescribable sound of half-laughing contempt.

"They are all—good fellers. Don't you think so?"

"But what does that mean?"

"Splendid chaps, madame!"

He sat up straight, and threw out his chest and thumped it.

"Beef, plum pudding, fine fellers, rulers!"

"You mustn't laugh at my countrymen."

"Laugh—never! But—may I smile, just at one corner?"

He showed his rows of little, straight, white teeth, which looked strong enough to bite through a bar of iron.

"The Englishman rules us in Egypt. He keeps saying we are ruling, and he keeps on ruling us. And all the time he rules us, he despises us, madame. He thinks us silly children. But sometimes we smile at him, though of course he never smiles at us, for fear a smile from him should make us think we are not so far below him. It is very wrong of us, but somehow Allah permits us to smile. And then"—again he leaned forward, and his chair creaked in the darkness—"there are some Englishwomen who like to see us smile, some who even smile with us behind the Englishman's back."

He spoke calmly, with a certain subtle irony, but quite without any hint of bitterness, and in speaking the last words he slightly lowered his voice.

"Is it very wrong of them, madame? What do you say? Do you condemn them?"

She did not answer, but her mobile, painted lips quivered, as if she were trying to repress a smile and were not quite succeeding.

"If they smile, if they smile—isn't that a shame, madame?"

He was smiling into her eyes.

"It is a great shame," she said. "I despise deceitful women."

"And yet who does not deceive? Everybody—except the splendid fellers!"

He threw back his head and laughed, while she looked at his magnificent throat.

"You never talked like this on the *Hohenzollern*," she said.

"Madame, I was never alone with you. How could I talk like this? I should not have been properly understood."

Not only in his eyes, but also in this assumption of a certain comradeship and sympathy from which Nigel and Nigel's kind were necessarily excluded, there was a definite insolence that seemed to strike upon and challenge Mrs. Armine, like a glove flung in her face. Would she perhaps have resented it even yesterday? She could not tell. To-night she was ready to welcome it, for to-night she almost hated Nigel. But, apart from her personal anger, Baroudi made an impression upon her that was definite and strong. She felt, she ever seemed to perceive with her eyes, the love of brigandage in him—and had she not been a brigand? There were some ruined men who could have answered that question. And in this man there was a great fund of force and of energy. He threw out an extraordinary atmosphere of physical strength, in which seemed involved a strength that was mental, like dancing motes in a beam of light. Mrs. Armine was a resolute woman, as Meyer Isaacson had at once divined. She felt that here was a human being who could be even more resolute than herself, more persistent, more unyielding, and quite as subtle, quite as cool. Though he was an Eastern man and she was a Western woman, how should each not understand much of the other's character? And as to him—Orientals are readers of brains, if not of souls.

She felt a great sense of relief, as if a balm were laid at evening upon the morning's wound.

"Ruby!"

Baroudi leaned back quietly, looking calm and strong and practical. And this time Mrs. Armine noticed that the basket chair did not creak beneath his movement.

BELLA DONNA 153

"Is it all right about the dinner, Nigel?"

"I hope so," he said. "But Baroudi mustn't suppose we've got a *chef* like his."

"I'll leave you for a little while," she said, getting up. "Dinner at a quarter past eight."

"Thank you, madame."

He was standing up.

"You pardon my flannels?"

"I like men in flannels, don't I, Nigel?"

She spoke carelessly, almost absently, and went slowly into the house. Again she had subtly cast around her a gentle atmosphere of rebuke.

On the table in the drawing-room were lying, still in their wrappers, the papers which had come by the morning's post. She took one up, as she passed, and carried it upstairs with her; and when she was in her bedroom she opened it, and glanced quickly through the social news. Ah! there was a paragraph about Lady Harwich!

"The birth of twin sons to the Countess of Harwich has given much satisfaction in social circles, as both Lord and Lady Harwich are universally popular and esteemed. It is said that the baptism of the infants will take place in the Chapel Royal of St. James's Palace, and that His Majesty the King will be one of the sponsors. Until this happy event, the next heir to the title and the immense estates that go with it was the Honourable Nigel Armine, who recently married the well-known Mrs. Chepstow, and who is ten years younger than Lord Harwich."

Somehow, now that she saw the fact stated in print, Mrs. Armine felt suddenly more conscious both of the triumph of Lady Harwich and of the Harwich, which was the social, faction generally, and of what seemed her own defeat. What a comfortable smile there must be just now upon the lips of the smart world, upon the lips of numbers of women not a bit better than she was! And Nigel had "let her in" for it all. Her lips tightened ominously as she remembered the cool American eyes of Lady Harwich, which had often glanced at her with the knowing contempt of the lively but innocent woman, which stirs the devil in women who are not innocent, and who are known not to be innocent.

She put down the paper; she went to the window and looked out. From the garden there rose to her nostrils the delicate scent of some hidden flower that gave its best gift to the darkness. In the distance, to her right, there was a pattern of coloured fire relieved against the dimness, that was not blackness, of the world. That was Baroudi's dahabeeyah.

Women were smiling in London, were rejoicing in her misfortune. As she looked at the lines of lamps, they seemed to her lines of satirical eyes, then, presently, lines of eyes that were watching her and were reading the truth of her nature.

She called Marie, and again she changed her gown.

While she was doing so, Nigel came up once more, taking Baroudi to a bedroom, and presently tried the door between her bedroom and his.

"Can't come in!" she called out, lightly.

"You're not changing your dress?"

"I couldn't dine in linen."

"But we are both——"

"Men—and I'm a woman, and I can't dine in linen. I should feel like a sheet or a pillow-case. Run away, Nigel!"

She heard him washing his hands, and presently she heard him go away. She knew very well that the lightness in her voice had whipped him, and that he was "feeling badly."

When the small gong sounded for dinner, she went downstairs, dressed in a pale yellow gown with a high bodice in which a bunch of purple flowers was fastened. She wore no jewels and no ornament in her hair.

As she came into the room, for a moment Nigel had the impression that she was a stranger coming in. Why was that? His mind repeated the question, and he gazed at her with intensity, seeking the reason of his impression. She was looking strangely, abnormally fair. Had she again, despite the conversation of the morning, "done something" to her face? Was its whiteness whiter than usual? Or were her lips a little redder? Or—he did not know what she had done, whether, indeed, she had done anything—but he felt troubled, ill at ease. He felt a longing to be alone with Ruby, to make her forgive him for having hurt her in the morning. He hated the barrier between them, and he felt that he had created it by his disbelief in her. Women are always more sensitive than men, and who is more sensitive than the emerging Magdalen, encompassed by disbelief, by irony, by wonder? He felt that in the morning he had been radically false to himself, that by his lapse from a high ideal of conduct he had struck a heavy blow upon a trembling virtue which had been gathering its courage to venture forth into the light.

During the dinner, almost everything, every look, tone, gesture, attitude, that was expressive of Ruby, confirmed him in self-rebuke. She was certainly changed. The rather weary and wistful woman who had stayed alone in the garden when he went to the dahabeeyah had given place to a woman more resolute, brilliant, animated—a woman who could hold her own, who could be daring, almost defiant, and a woman who could pain him in return, perhaps, for the pain he had inflicted on her. The dinner was quite good. Their Nubian cook had been trained in a big hotel, and Mrs. Armine had nothing to apologize for. Baroudi politely praised the cooking. Yet she felt that behind his praise there lurked immeasurable reservations, and she remembered the time when her *chef* was the most famous in London, a marvel who had been bribed by a millionaire lover of hers to leave the service of a royalty to bring his gift to her. She mentioned this fact to Baroudi. It was a vulgar thing to do, and at heart she was not vulgar; but she was prompted by two desires. She felt in her guest the Oriental's curious and almost romantic admiration of riches, and wished to draw this admiration towards herself; and she wanted to inflict some more punishment on Nigel.

"You seem to be something of an epicure, Mahmoud

Baroudi," she said. "I suppose you have heard of Armand Carrier?"

"The best *chef* in Europe, madame? How should I not have heard of him among my friends of Paris?"

"He was in my service for five years."

There was a pause. Nigel suddenly turned red. Baroudi moved his large eyes slowly from Mrs. Armine to him, and at length observed calmly:

"I felicitate you both. You must have had a treasure. But why did you let him go?"

He addressed the question to Nigel.

"He was not in my service," said Nigel, with a sudden, very English stiffness that was almost like haughtiness. "It was long before we were married."

"Oh—I see. But what a pity! Then you did not have the benefit of eating his marvellous *plats*."

"No. I don't care about that sort of thing."

"Really!"

They talked of other matters, but Nigel had lost all his *bonhomie*, and seemed unable to recover it.

Baroudi, like a good Mohammedan, declined to drink any wine, but when the fruit was brought, Mrs. Armine got up.

"I'll leave you for a little while," she said. "You'll find me on the terrace. Although Mahmoud Baroudi drinks nothing, I am sure he likes men's talk better than woman's chatter."

Baroudi politely but rather perfunctorily denied this.

"But what do you say," he added, "to coming as my guest to take a cup of coffee and a liqueur at the Winter Palace Hotel? To-night there is the first performance of a Hungarian band which I introduced last winter to Egypt, and which—I am told; I am not, perhaps, a judge of your Western music—plays remarkably. What do you say? Would it please you, madame?"

"Yes, do let us go. Shan't we go?"

She turned to Nigel.

"Of course," he said, "if you like. But can you walk in that dress?"

She nodded.

"It's perfectly dry outside. I'll come down in a moment."

She was away for nearly ten; then she returned, wrapped up in a marvellous ermine coat, and wearing on her head a yellow toque with a high aigrette at one side.

"I'm ready now," she said.

"What a beautiful coat!" Nigel said.

He had not seen it before. He gently smoothed it with his brown fingers. Then he looked at her, took them away, and stepped back rather abruptly.

When they arrived at the great hotel the band was already playing in the hall, and a number of people, scattered about in little detached groups, were listening to it and drinking Turkish coffee. It was very early in the season. The rush up the Nile had not begun, and travellers had not yet cemented their travelling acquaintanceships. People looked at each other rather vaguely, or definitely ignored each other, with profiles and backs which said quite plainly: "We won't have anything to do with you until we know more about you." The entrance of the party from the Villa Androud created a strong diversion. As soon as Baroudi was perceived by the attendants, there was a soft and gliding movement to serve him. The tall Nubians in white and scarlet smiled, salaamed, and showed their pleasure and their desire for his notice. The German hall porter hastened forward, with a pink smile upon his countenance; the *chef d'orchestre,* a real Hungarian, began to play at him with fervour; and a black gentleman in gold and scarlet, who looked like a Prince of the East, but who was really earning his living in connection with the lift to the first floor, bounded to show them to a table.

Baroudi accepted all these attentions with a magnificent indifference that had in it nothing of assumption. They sat down, he ordered coffee and liqueurs, and they listened to the music, which was genuinely good, and had the peculiar fervent and yet melancholy flavour which music receives from the bows of Hungarian fiddlers. Nigel was smoking. He seemed profoundly attentive, did not attempt any conversation, and kept his eyes on the ground. Mrs. Armine seemed listening attentively, too, but she had not been sitting for five minutes before she had seen and summed up every group in her neighborhood; had defined the nationalities, criticized the gowns and faces of the women, and made up her mind as to the characters of the men who accompanied them, and as to the family or amorous ties uniting them to each other and the men.

And she had done more than this: she had measured the amount of interest, of curiosity, of admiration, of envy, of condemnation which she herself excited with the almost unerring scales of the clever woman who has lived for years both in the great and the half worlds.

Quite near them, not level with their table, but a little behind it on the right, within easy range of her eyes, Lord and Lady Hayman were sitting, with another English couple, a Sir John and Lady Murchison, smart, gambling, racing, pleasure-loving people, who seemed to be everywhere at the same time, and never to miss any function of importance where their "set"' put in an appearance. Lady Murchison was a pretty and vindictive blonde—the sort of woman who looks as if she would bite you if you did not let her have her way. She was smiling cruelly now, and murmuring to Lady Hayman, a naturally large, but powerfully compressed personage, with a too-sanguine complexion insufficiently corrected by powder, and a too-autocratic temperament insufficiently corrected by Lord Hayman.

All these people—Mrs. Armine knew it "in her bones" —had just been reading the *Morning Post*. Here in Egypt they stood for "London." She saw London's verdict, "Serve her right," in their cool smiles, their moments of direct attention to herself—an attention hard, insolent, frigid as steel—in the curious glances of pity combined with a sort of animal, almost school-boy, amusement, which the two men sent towards Nigel.

She looked from "London" to "Egypt," represented by Baroudi. In marrying Nigel she had longed to set her heel upon the London which had despised her; she had hoped some day to set the heel of Lady Harwich upon more than one woman whom she had known before she was cast out. Secretly she had reckoned upon that, as upon something that was certain, something for which she had only to wait. Lord Harwich was worn out, and he was a wildly reckless man, always having accidents, always breaking his bones. She would only have to wait.

And now—twin boys, and all London smiling!

Again she looked at Baroudi. The fervent and melancholy music was rising towards a climax. It caught hold of her now, had her in a grip, swept her onwards. When it ceased, she felt as if she had been carried away from "London," and from those old ambitions and hopes for ever.

Baroudi's great eyes were upon her, and seemed to read her thoughts; and now for the first time she felt uneasy under their resolute gaze, felt the desire, almost the necessity to escape from it and to be unwatched.

"Have you had enough of the music, Nigel?" she said to her husband, as the musicians lifted their chins from their instruments, and let their arms drop down.

He started.

"What, Ruby? By Jove, they do play well!"

There was a look in his eyes almost as of one coming back from a long and dark journey underground into the light of day. That music had taken him back to the side of the girl whom he had loved, and who had died so long ago. Now he looked at the woman who was living, and to whom the great power to love which was within him was being directed, on whom it was being concentrated.

"Do you mind if we go home?" she said.

"You have had enough of it already?"

"No, not that; but—I'm tired," she said.

As she spoke, skilfully, without appearing to do so, she led him to look towards the little group of the Murchisons and the Haymans; led him to pity her for their observation, and to take that as the cause of her wish to go. Perhaps it was partly the cause, but not wholly, and not as she made him believe it.

"I'll take you home at once," Nigel said, tenderly.

When they were outside Baroudi bade them good-bye, and invited them to tea on the *Loulia*—so his dahabeeyah was called—on the following day.

"In the evening I may start for Armant," he said. "Will it bore you to come, madame?"

He spoke politely, but rather perfunctorily, and she answered with much the same tone.

"Thanks, I shall be delighted. Good-night. The music was delicious."

His tall figure went away in the dark.

When he had left them there was a silence. Nigel made a movement as if he were going to take her hand, and draw her arm within the circle of his; but he did not do it, and they walked on side by side by the river, not touching each other, not speaking. And so, presently, they came to the villa, and to the terrace before the drawing-room. Then Nigel spoke at last.

"Are—you are going in at once, Ruby?" he said.

"Yes."

"I—will you call from your window presently?"

"Why?"

"When I may come up. After this morning I must talk to you before we sleep."

She looked at him, then looked down, resting her white chin on the warm white fur of the ermine.

"I'll call," she said.

As she went away he looked after her, and thought how almost strangely tall she looked in the long white coat. He paced up and down as he waited, listening for the sound of her voice. After what seemed to him a very long time he heard it at last.

"Nigel! You can come up now—if you like."

He went upstairs at once to her room, and found her

sitting in an arm-chair near the window, which led on to the balcony, and which was wide open to the night. She was in a loose and, to him, a mysterious white and flowing garment, with sleeves that fell away from her arms like wings. Her hair was coiled low at the back of her neck.

The room was lit by two candles, which burned upon a small writing-table, and by the wan and delicate moonlight that seemed to creep in stealthily, yet obstinately, from the silently-breathing Egypt in whose warm breast they were. He stood for a moment; then he sat down on a little sofa, not close to her, but near her.

"Ruby," he said.

"Well, Nigel?"

"This has been the first unhappy day for me since we've been married."

"Unhappy!"

"Yes, because of the cloud between us."

She said nothing, and he resumed:

"It's made me know something, though, Ruby; it's made me know how much I care—for you."

He leaned forward, and, as he did so, her mind went to Baroudi, and she remembered exactly the look of his shoulders and of his throat when he was leaning towards her.

"I don't think I really knew it before. I'm sure I didn't know it. What made me understand it was the way I felt when I found I had hurt you, had done you a wrong for a moment. Ruby, my own feeling has punished me so much that I don't think you can want to punish me any more."

"I punish you!" she said. "But what wrong have you done me? And how could I punish you?"

"I did you a wrong this morning by thinking for a moment——" He stopped; he found he could not put it quite clearly into words. "Over Harwich and the boys," he concluded.

"Oh, that! That didn't matter!" she said.

She spoke coldly, but she was feeling more excited,

more emotional, than she had felt for a very long time, than she had known that she could feel.

"It mattered very much. But I don't think I really thought it."

"Yes, you did!" she said, sharply.

He sat straight up, like a man very much startled.

"You did think it. Don't try to get out of it, Nigel."

"Ruby, I'm not trying. Why, haven't I said——"

But she interrupted him.

"You did think, what every one thinks, that I'm a greedy, soulless woman, and that I even married you"—she laid a fierce emphasis on the pronoun—"out of the wretched, pettifogging ambition some day to be Lady Harwich. You did think it, Nigel. You did think it!"

"For one moment," he said.

He got up from the sofa, and stood by the window. He felt like a man in a moral crisis, and that what he said at this moment, and how he said it, with how much deep sincerity and how much warmth of heart, might, even must, determine the trend of the future.

"For one moment I did just wonder whether perhaps when you married me you had thought I might some day be Lord Harwich."

"Of course."

"Al-lah——"

Through the open window came faintly the nasal cry of the Nubian sailor beginning the song of the Nile upon the lower deck of the *Loulia*. With it there entered the very dim throbbing of the beaten *daraboukkeh*, sounding almost like some strange and perpetual ground-swell of the night, that flood of shadowy mystery and beauty in which they and the world were drowned. The distant music added to her sense of excitement and to his.

"Ruby—try to see—I think it was partly a humble feeling that made me wonder—a difficulty in believing you had cared very much for me."

"Why should you, or any one, think I have it in me to care?"

"I thought so in London, I think so here, I have always thought so—always. If others have—have disbelieved in you ever, I haven't been like them. You doubt it?"

He moved a step forward, and stood looking down on her.

"But I could prove it."

"Oh—how?"

"Meyer Isaacson knows it."

He did not refer to his marrying her as a proof already given, for that might have meant something else than belief in the hidden unworldliness of her, and in her hidden desire for that which was good and beautiful.

"And don't you—don't you know it, even after this morning?"

"After this morning—I don't want to hurt you—but after this morning you will have to prove it to me, thoroughly prove it, or else I shall not believe it."

The solo voice of the Nubian sailor was lost in the chorus of voices which came floating over the Nile.

"I don't want to be cold," she continued, "and I don't want to be unkind, but one can't help certain things. I have been driven, forced, into scepticism about men. I don't want to go back into my life, I don't want to trot out the old 'more sinned against than sinning' *cliché*. I don't mean to play the winey-piney woman. I never have done that, and I believe I've got a little grit in me to prevent me ever doing it. But such a thing as happened this morning must breed doubts and suspicions in a woman who has had the experience I have had. I might very easily tell you a lie, Nigel. I might very easily fall into your arms and say I've forgotten all about it, and I'll never think of it again, and all that sort of thing. It would be the simplest thing in the world for me to act a part to you. But you've been good to me when I was lonely, and you've cared for me enough to marry me, and—well, I won't. I'll tell you the truth. It's this: I can't help knowing you did doubt me, and I'm not really a bit surprised, and I don't know that I'd any right to be hurt; but whether I had any right or not, I was hurt, and it will take a little time to make me feel quite safe with you—quite safe—as one can only feel when the little bit of sincerity in one is believed in and trusted."

She spoke quietly, but he felt excitement behind her apparent calm. In her voice there was an inflexible sound, that seemed to tell him very clearly it meant what it was saying.

Always across the Nile came the song of the Nubian sailors.

"I'm not surprised that you feel like that," he said.

He stood for a moment considering, then he sat down once more, and began to speak with a resolution that seemed to be prompted by passion.

"Ruby, to-day I think I was false to myself, because to-day I was false to my real, my deep-down belief in you. In London I did think you cared for me as a man, not perhaps specially because I'd attracted you by my personality, but because I felt how others misunderstood you. It seemed to me—it seems to me now—that I could answer to a desire in you to which no one else ever tried, ever wished to answer. The others seemed to think you only wanted the things that don't really count—lots of money, luxury, jewels, clothes—you know what I mean. I felt that your real desire was—well, I must put it plainly—to be loved and not lusted after, to be asked for something, not only to be given things. I felt that, I seemed to know it. Wasn't I right?"

"To-night—I don't know," she said.

Her ears were full of the music that wailed and throbbed in the breast of the night.

"Can't you forgive that one going back on myself after all these days and—and nights together? Haven't I proved anything to you in them?"

"You have seemed to, perhaps. But men so often seem, and aren't. And I did think you knew why I had married you."

"Tell me why you married me."

"Not to-night."

"Long ago," he said, and now he spoke slowly, and with a deep earnestness which suddenly caught the whole of her attention, "Long ago I loved a girl, Ruby. She was very young, knew very little of the world, and nothing at all of its beastlinesses. I think I loved her partly because she knew so little, she was so very pure. One could see—see in her eyes that they had never looked, even from a distance, on mud, on anything black. She loved me. She died. And, after that, she became my ideal."

He looked at her, slowly lifting his head a little. There was a light in his eyes which for a moment half frightened, half fascinated her, so nakedly genuine was it—genuine as a flame which burns straight in an absolutely windless place.

"In my thoughts I always kept her apart from all other women—always—for years and years, until one night in London, after I knew you. That night—I don't know how it was, or why—I seemed to see her and you standing together, looking at each other; I seemed to know that in you both—I don't know how to tell it exactly"—he stopped, looked down, like one thinking deeply, like one absorbed in thought—"that in you both, mixed with quantities of different things, there was one thing—a beautiful thing—that was the same. She—she seemed that night to tell me that you had something I had loved in her, that it was covered up out of sight, that you were afraid to show it, that nobody believed you had it within you. She seemed to tell me that I might teach you to trust me and show it to me. That night I think I began to love you. I didn't know I should ever tell this to any one, even to you. Do you think I could tell it if I distrusted you as much as you seem to think?"

"Give me a glass of Apollinaris, will you, Nigel?" she said. "It's over there beside the bed."

"Apollinaris!"

He stared at her as if confused by this sudden diversion.

" Over there!"

She pointed. The long sleeve, like a wing, fell away from her soft, white arm.

"Oh—all right."

He went to get it. She sat still, looking out through the open window to the moonlight that lay on the white stone of the balcony floor. She heard the chink of glass, the thin gurgle of liquid falling. Then he came back and stood beside her.

"Here it is, Ruby."

The enthusiasm had gone out of his voice, and the curious light had gone out of his eyes.

"Thank you."

She took it, put it to her lips, and drank. Then she set the glass down on the writing-table.

"We're at the beginning of things, Nigel," she said. "That's the truth. We can't jump into a mutual perfection of relationship at once. I've got very few illusions, and I dare say I'm absurdly sensitive about certain matters, much more sensitive than even you can imagine. The fact is I've—I've been trodden on for a long while. A man can't know what a woman—a lady—who's been thoroughly 'in it' feels when she's put outside, and kept outside, and—trodden on. It sends her running to throw her arms round the neck of the Devil. That may be abominable, but it's the fact. And, when she tries to come back from the Devil—well, she's a mass of nerves, and ready to start at a shadow. I saw a shadow to-day in the garden——"

"I know, I know!"

"You remember the night we dined on the Pylon at Karnak? After dinner you tried to show me the ruins by moonlight, and wherever we went a black-robed watchman followed us, or a black-robed watchman glided from behind a pillar, or an obelisk, or a crumbling wall, and faced us, and at last we took to flight. Well, that's what life is like to certain women; that's what life has been for a long time to me. Whenever I've tried to look at anything beautiful quietly, I've been followed or faced by a black-robed watchman, staring at me suspiciously. And to-day you seemed to be one when you asked me that about Harwich."

She took up the glass and drank some more of the water. When she put it down he was kneeling beside her. He put his arms around her.

"I won't be that again."

A very faint perfume from her hair came to him, now that he was so close to her.

"I don't want to be that ever."

He held her, and, while he held her, he listened to the Nubian sailors and to the word that was nearly always upon their tireless lips.

"Al-lah—Al-lah—Al-lah!"

God was there in the night, by the great, mysterious Nile, that flows from such far-off sources in the wild places of the earth; God was attending to them—to him and Ruby. He had the simple faith almost of a child in a God who knew each thing that he thought, each thing that he did. Thousands of men have this faith, and thousands of men conceal it as they might conceal a sin. They fear their own simplicity.

The purpose of God, was it not very plain before him? He thought now that it was. What he had to do was to restore this woman's confidence in the goodness that exists by having a firm faith in the goodness existing in her, by not letting that faith be shaken, as he had let it be shaken that day.

He hated himself for having wounded her, and as he hated himself his strong arms closed more firmly round her, trying to communicate physically to her the resolution he was forming.

And the Nubian sailors went on singing.

To him that night they sang of God.

To her they sang of Mahmoud Baroudi.

XV

"What is the meaning of that Arabic writing, Mahmoud Baroudi?" said Mrs. Armine on the following afternoon, as she stood with him and her husband upon the lower deck of the *Loulia,* at the foot of the two steps which led down to the big door dividing the lines of living-rooms from the quarters of the Nubian sailors. The door was white, with mouldings of gold, and the inscription above it was in golden characters.

"It looks so significant that I must know what it means," she added.

"It is taken from the Koran, madame."

"And it means?"

He fixed his great eyes upon her.

"'The fate of every man have we bound about his neck.'"

"'The fate of every man have we bound about his neck,'" she repeated, slowly. "So that is the motto for the *Loulia!*"

She was standing quite still, staring up at the cabalistic signs beneath which she was going to pass.

"Do you dislike it, madame?"

"No, it's strong, but—well, it leaves no loophole for escape, and it rather suggests a prison."

"We are in the prison of our lives, and we are in the prison of ourselves," he answered, calmly.

She dropped her eyes from the words.

"Yes?" she said, looking at him like one who asks for more.

"Prison!" said Nigel, behind her. "I hate that word. You're wrong, Baroudi. Life is a fine freedom, if we choose it to be so, and we can act in it according to our own free-will. Our fate is not bound about our necks. It is only we ourselves who can bind it there."

"All that is not at all in my belief," returned Baroudi, inflexibly. "Here are cabins for servants."

He led them into a passage, and pointed to little doors on the right and left.

"And here is my room for working and arranging all I have to do. I believe you English call it a 'den.'"

He opened a door that faced them at the end of the passage, and preceded them into his "den." The effect of this chamber was that it was a "double room," for an exquisite screen of mashrebeeyeh work, in the centre of which was a small round arch, divided it into two compartments. On each side of this arch, facing the entrance door, were divans covered with embroideries and heaped with enormous cushions. Prayer-rugs covered the floor, prayer-rugs of very varied patterns and colours, on which yellows, greens, mauves, pinks, reds, purples, and browns dwelt in perfect accord; on which vases were seen with trees, lamps with flowers, strange and conventional buildings with ships, with chains, with pedestals, with baskets of fruit, mingled together, apparently at haphazard, yet forming a blend that was restful. By the windows there were lattices of mashrebeeyeh work, which could be opened and closed at will. At present they were open. Beneath them were fitted book-cases containing rows of books, in English and French, many of them works on agriculture, on building, on mining, on the sugar and cotton industries in various parts of the world. There was a large writing-table of lacquer-work, on which stood a movable electric lamp without a shade, in the midst of a rummage of pamphlets and papers. Near it were a coffee-table and two deep arm-chairs. From the ceiling, which was divided into compartments painted in dark red and blue, hung a heavy lamp by a chain of gilded silver. A stick of incense burned in a gilded holder. The dining-room, on the other side of the screen, was fitted with divans running round the walls, and contained a large table and a number of chairs with curved backs. The table was covered with a long and exquisitely embroidered Indian cloth, of which the prevailing colour was a brilliant orange-red, that glowed and had a sheen which was almost fiery. In the centre of this table stood a tawdry Japanese vase, worth, perhaps, five or six shillings. A lovely bracket of carved wood fixed to the wall held a cheap cuckoo-clock from Switzerland.

Mrs. Armine looked around in silence, with eyes that missed no detail. The clock whirred, a minute door flew open, the cuckoo appeared, and the two notes that are the cry of the English spring went thinly out to the Nile. Then the cuckoo disappeared, and the little door shut sharply.

Mrs. Armine smiled.

"You bought that?" she asked.

"Yes, madame. Everything here was bought by me, and arranged according to my poor judgment."

He opened the door, and led them into a long passage with a shining parquetted floor.

"Here are the bedrooms, madame."

He pushed back two or three doors, showing beautiful little cabins, evidently furnished from Paris, with bedsteads, mosquito-curtains, long mirrors, small arm-chairs in white, and green and rose-colour; walls painted ivory-white; and delicate, pretty, but rather frivolous, curtains and portières, with patterns of flowers tied up with ribands, and flying and perching birds. All the toilet arrangements were perfect, and each room had a recess in which was a large enamelled bath.

"That is my bedroom, madame," said Baroudi, pointing to a door which he did not open. "It is the largest on the boat. And here is my room for sitting alone. When I want to be disturbed by no one, when I want to smoke the keef, to eat the hashish, or just to sit by myself and forget my affairs, and dream quietly for a little, I shut myself in here."

An embroidered curtain, the ground of which was orange colour, covered with silks of various hues, faced them at the end of the corridor. Baroudi pulled aside this curtain, pushed back a sliding door of wood that was almost black, and said:

' Will you go in first, madame?"

BELLA DONNA

Mrs. Armine stepped in, wtih an almost cautious slowness.

She found herself in a large saloon, which took in the whole width of the stern of the dahabeeyah. The end of this saloon widened out and was crescent-shaped, and contained a low dais with curving divans, divided by two sliding doors which were now pushed back in their recesses, giving access to a big balcony that looked out over the Nile and that was protected by an awning. The wooden ceiling was cut up into lozenges of black and gold, and was edged by minute inscriptions from the Koran, in gold on a black ground. All the windows had lattices of mashrebeeyeh work fitted to them, and all these lattices were closed. Against the walls, which were as dark in colour as the mashrebeeyeh work, there were a number of carved brackets, on which were placed various extremely common things—cheap and gaudy vases from Naples and Paris, two more Swiss cuckoo-clocks, a third clock with a blue and white china face—and a back that looked as if were made of brass, a musical-box, and a grotesque monster, like a dragon with a dog's head, in rough yellow and blue earthenware. There were no chairs in the room, though there were some made of basket-work on the balcony, but all the lower part of the wall space was filled with broad divans. In the centre of the floor there was a sunken receptacle of marble, containing earth, in which dwarf palms were growing, and a faskeeyeh, or little fountain, which threw up a minute jet of water, upon which airily rose and fell a gilded ball about the size of a pea. All over the floor were strewn exquisite rugs. The room was pervaded by a faint but heavy perfume, which had upon the senses an almost narcotic effect.

"What a strange room!" said Mrs. Armine.

She had stood quite still near the door. Now she walked forward, followed by the two men, until she had passed the faskeeyeh and had reached the foot of the dais. There she turned round, with her back to the light that came in through the narrow doorways leading to the balcony.

Baroudi had shut the door by which they had come in, and had pulled over it a heavy orange-coloured curtain, which she now saw for the first time. Although lovely in itself both in colour and material, fiercely lovely, like the skin of some savage beast, it did not blend with the rest of the room, with the dim hues of the superb embroideries and prayer-rugs, with the dark wood of the lattices that covered the windows. Like the cheap clocks on the exquisite brackets, and the vulgar ornaments from Naples and Paris, it seemed to reveal a certain childishness in this man, a bad taste that was naïve in its crudity, but daring in its determination to be gratified. Oddly, almost violently, this curtain, these clocks and vases, the musical-box, even the tiny gilded ball that rose and fell in the fountain, displayed a part of him strangely different from that which had selected the almost miraculously beautiful rugs, and the embroideries on the divans. Exquisite taste was married with a commonness that was glaring.

Mrs. Armine wished she could see his bedroom.

"I wish—" she began, and stopped.

"Yes, madame?" said Baroudi.

"What is it, Ruby?" asked Nigel.

"You'll laugh at me. But I wish you would both go out upon the balcony, shut the doors, and leave me for a minute shut up alone in here. I think I should feel as if I were in the heart of an Eastern house."

"In a harîm, do you mean?" asked Nigel.

"That—perhaps. Do go."

Baroudi smiled, showing his rows of tiny teeth.

"Come, Mr. Armeen!" he said.

He stepped out on to the balcony, followed by Nigel, and pulled out from the recess the first of the sliding doors.

"You really wish the other, too?" he asked, looking in upon Mrs. Armine. "You will be quite in the dark."

"Shut it!" she said, in a low voice.

He pulled out the second door. Gently it slid across the oblong of sunlight, blotting out the figures of the two men from her sight. Baroudi had said that she would be quite in the dark. That was not absolutely true. How and from where she could not determine, a very faint suggestion—it was hardly more than that—of light stole in to show the darkness to her. She went to the divan on the starboard side of the vessel, felt for some cushions, piled them together, and lay down, carefully, so as not to disarrange her hat. The divan was soft and yielding. It held and caressed her body, almost as if it were an affectionate living thing that knew of her present desire. The cushions supported her arm as she lay sideways—listening, and keeping perfectly still.

She had some imagination, although she was not a highly or a very sensitively imaginative woman, and now she left her imagination at play. It took her with it into the heart of an Eastern house which was possessed by an Eastern master. Where was the house, in what strange land of sunshine? She did not know or care to know. And indeed, it mattered little to her—an Eastern woman whose life was usually bounded by a grille.

For she imagined herself an Eastern woman, subject to the laws and the immutable customs of the unchanging East, and she was in the harîm of a rich Oriental, to whom she belonged body and soul, and who adored her, but as the man of the East adores the woman who is both his mistress and his slave. For years she had ruled men, and trodden them under her feet. She had lived for that— the ruling of men by her beauty and her clever determination. Now she imagined herself no longer possessing but entirely possessed; no longer commanding, but utterly obedient. What a new experience that would be! All the capricious womanhood of her seemed to be alert and tingling at the mere thought of it. Instead of having slaves, to be herself a slave!

She moved a little on the divan. The heavy perfume that pervaded the room seemed to be creeping about her with an intention—to bring her under its influence. She heard the very faint and liquid murmur of the faskeeyeh, where the tiny gilded ball was rising, poising, sinking, governed by the aspiring and subsiding water. That, too, was a slave—a slave in the Eastern house of Baroudi.

Slowly she closed her eyes, in the Eastern house of Baroudi.

Here Baroudi lay, as she was lying, and smoked the keef, and ate the hashish, and dreamed.

He would never be the slave of a woman. She felt sure of that. But he might make a woman his slave. At moments, when he looked at her, he had the eyes of a slave-owner. But he might adore a slave with a cruel adoration. She felt cruelty in him, and it attracted her, it lured her, it responded to something in her nature which understood and respected cruelty, and which secretly despised gentleness. In his love he would be cruel. Never would he be quite at the feet of the woman. His eyes had told her that, had told it to her with insolence.

The gilded ball in the faskeeyeh, the slave covered with jewels in the harîm.

She stretched out her arms along the cushions; she stretched out her limbs along the divan, her long limbs that were still graceful and supple.

How old did Baroudi think her?

Arabs never know their ages. A man, a soldier whom she had known, had told her that once, had told her that Arabs of sixty declare themselves to be twenty-five, not from vanity, but merely because they never reckon the years. Baroudi would probably never think of her as Englishmen thought of her, would never "bother about" her age. She had seen no criticism of that kind in his eyes when they stared at her. Probably he believed her to be quite young, if he thought of her age at all. More probably he did not think about the matter.

She was in the Eastern house of Baroudi.

When she and Nigel had left London for Egypt she had imagined herself one day, if not governing London—the "London" that had once almost worshipped her beauty—at least spurning it as Lady Harwich. She had wrapped herself in that desire, that dream. All her thoughts had been connected with London, with people there. Some day

Lord Harwich would die or get himself killed. Zoe Harwich would sink reluctantly into "Zoe, Lady Harwich," and she, once the notorious Mrs. Chepstow, would be mistress of Harwich House, Park Lane; of Illington Park, near Ascot; of Goldney Chase in Derbyshire; of Thirlton Castle in Scotland; and of innumerable shooting-lodges, to say nothing of houses at Brighton and Newmarket. Society might not receive her, but society would have to envy her. And perhaps—in the end—for are not all things possible in the social world of to-day?—perhaps in the end she would impose herself, she would be accepted again because of her great position. She had felt that her cleverness and her force of will made even that possible. Harwich's letter had swept the dream away, and now, the first shock of her new knowledge passed, though not the anger, the almost burning sense of wrong that had followed immediately upon it, she was characteristically readjusting her point of view upon her future. She had schemed for a certain thing; she had taken the first great step towards the realization of her scheme; and then she had suddenly come upon catastrophe. And now her thoughts began to turn away from London. The London thoughts were dying with the London hopes. "All that is useless now." That was what her mind was saying, bitterly, but also with decision. Schooled by a life filled with varying experiences, Mrs. Armine had learnt one lesson very thoroughly—she had learnt to cut her losses. How was she going to cut this loss?

She was in the Eastern house of Baroudi.

Only a few hours ago she had looked out upon Egypt and things Egyptian almost as a traveller looks upon a world through which he is rushing in a train, a world presented to him for a brief moment, but with whose inhabitants he will never have anything to do, in whose life he will never take part. She had to be in Egypt for a while, but all her desires and hopes and intentions were centred in London. There her destiny would be played out, there and in the land of which London was the beating heart.

Now she must centre her desires, her hopes, her intentions elsewhere, if she centred them anywhere. She must centre them upon Nigel, must centre them in the Fayyūm, in the making of crops to grow where only sand had been, both in the Fayyūm and in another place, or she must centre them——

She smelt the heavy perfume; she smoothed the silken pillows with her long fingers; she stretched her body on the soft divan; she listened to the liquid whisper of the faskeeyeh.

There were many sorts of lives in the world. She had had many experiences, but how many experiences she had never had! No longer did she feel herself to be a traveller rushing onward through a land of which she would never know, or care to know, anything. The train was slackening speed. She saw the land more clearly. Details came into view, making their strange and ardent appeal. The train would presently stop. And she would step out of it, would face the new surroundings, would face the novel life.

Suddenly she distended her nostrils to inhale the perfume more strongly, her hands closed upon the silken cushions with a grip that was almost angry, and something within her, the something that tries to command from its secret place, scourged her imagination to force it to more violent efforts—in the Eastern house of Baroudi.

"Ruby! Ruby!"

One of the sliding doors was pushed back, the sunlight came in, tempered by the shade thrown by the awning, and she saw the little ball dancing in the faskeeyeh, and her husband looking inquiringly upon her, framed in the oblong of the doorway.

"What on earth are you doing?"

"Nothing!" she said, sitting up with a brusque movement.

He laughed.

"I believe you were taking a nap."

She got up.

"To tell the truth, I was almost asleep."

She stood up, put her hands to her hat, to her hair, and

with a slight but very intelligent movement sent the skirt of her gown into place.

"Let me out," she said.

Nigel drew back, and she stepped out upon the balcony, where Baroudi was leaning upon the railing, looking over the sunlit Nile. He turned round slowly and very calmly to meet her, moving with the almost measured ease of the very supple and strong man, drew forward a basket chair, arranged a cushion for her politely, but rather carelessly, and not at all cleverly, and said, as she sat down:

"You like the heart of my Eastern house?"

"How do you manage the fountain?" she asked.

He embarked upon a clear and technical explanation, but when he had said a very few words, she stopped him.

"Please don't! You are spoiling my whole impression. I oughtn't to have asked."

"Baroudi is a very practical man," said Nigel. "I only wish I had him as my overseer in the Fayyūm."

"If I can ever give you advice I shall be very glad," said Baroudi. "I know all about agriculture in my country."

Mrs. Armine leaned back, and looked at the broad river, upon which there were many native boats creeping southward with outspread sails, at the columns of the great Temple of Luxor standing up boldly upon the eastern bank, at the cloud of palm-trees northward beyond the village, at the far-off reaches of water, at the bare and precipitous hills that keep the deserts of Libya. At all these features of the landscape she looked with eyes that seemed to be new.

"Talk about agriculture to my husband, Mahmoud Baroudi," she said. "Forget I am here, both of you."

"But——"

"*Pas de compliments!* This is my first visit to a dahabeeyah. Your Nile is making me dream. If only the sailors were singing!"

"They shall sing."

He went up a few steps, and looked over the upper

deck; then he called out some guttural words. Almost instantly the throb of the *daraboukkeh* was audible, and then a nasal cry: "Al-lah!"

"And now—talk about agriculture!"

Baroudi turned away to Nigel, and began to talk to him in a low voice, while Mrs. Armine sat quite still, always watching the Nile, and always listening to the sailors singing. Presently tea was brought, but even then she preserved, smiling, her soft but complete detachment.

"Go on talking," she said. "You don't know how happy I am."

She looked at her husband, and added:

"I am drinking Nile water to-day."

Into his face there came a strong look of joy, which stirred irony in the deeps of her nature. He did not say anything to her, but in a moment he renewed his conversation with Baroudi, energetically, vivaciously, with an ardour which she had deliberately given him, partly out of malice, but partly also to gain for herself a longer lease of tranquillity. For she had spoken the truth. She was drinking Nile water to-day, and she wanted to drink more deeply.

The river was like a dream, she thought. The great boats, with their lateen sails and their grave groups of silent brown men, crept noiselessly by like the vessels that pass in a dream. Against the sides of the *Loulia* she heard the Nile water whispering softly, whispering surely to her. From the near bank, mingling with the loud and nasal song of the Nubian sailors, rose the fierce and almost tragic songs of the fellahîn working the shadûfs. How many kinds of lives there were in the world!

The blow that had fallen upon Mrs. Armine had made her unusually thoughtful, unusually introspective, unusually sensitive to all influences from without; had left her vibrating like a musical instrument that had been powerfully struck by a ruthless hand. The gust of fury that had shaken her had stirred her to a fierce and powerful life, had roused up all her secret energies of temper, of will, of desire, all her greed to get the best out of life, to wring dry, as it were, of their golden juices every one of the fleeting years. "To-morrow we die." Those who believe that, as she believed it, desire to live as no believer in a prolonged future in other worlds can ever desire to live— here, for the little day—and never had she felt that hungry wish more than she felt it now. Through her dream she felt it, almost as a victim of ardent pain feels that pain, without suffering under it, after an injection of morphia. If she could not have the life to which she had looked forward of triumph in England, she must have in its place some other life that suited her special temperament, some other life that would answer to the call within her for material satisfactions, for strong bodily pleasures, for the joys of the pagan, the unbeliever, who is determined to "make the most of" the short span of human life on earth.

How could she now have that other life with Nigel? He would never be Lord Harwich. He would never be anything but Nigel Armine, a man of moderate means interested in Egyptian agriculture, with a badly let property in England, and a strip of desert in the Fayyūm. He would never be anything except that—and her husband, the man who had "let her in." She did not mentally add to the tiny catalogue—"and the man who loved her."

For a long while she sat quite still, leaning her head on the cushion, hearing the singing and crying voices, the perpetual whisper of the water against the *Loulia's* sides, watching the gleaming Nile and the vessels that crept upon it going towards the south; and now, for the first time, there woke in her a desire to follow them up the river, to sail, too, into the golden south. Instead of the longing to return to and reign in England, came the desire to push England out of her life, almost to kick it away scornfully and have done with it for ever. Since she could never reign in England, she felt that she hated England.

"In the summer? Oh, I always spend the summer in England."

Nigel was speaking cheerfully. She began to attend to

his conversation with Baroudi, but she still looked out to the Nile, and did not change her position. They were really talking about agriculture, and apparently with enthusiasm. Nigel was giving details of his efforts in the Fayyūm. Now they discussed sand-ploughs. It seemed an unpromising subject, but they fell upon it with ardour, and found it strangely fruitful. Even Baroudi seemed to be deeply interested in sand-ploughs. Mrs. Armine forgot the Nile. She was not at all interested in sand-ploughs, but she was interested in this other practical side of Baroudi, which was now being displayed to her. Very soon she knew that of all these details connected with land, its cultivation, the amount of profit it could be made to yield in a given time, the eventual probabilities of profit in a more distant future, he was a master. And Nigel was talking to him, was listening to him, as a pupil talks and listens to a master. The greedy side of Mrs. Armine was very practical, as Meyer Isaacson had realized, and therefore she was fitted to appreciate at its full value the practical side of Baroudi. She felt that here was a man who knew very well how and where to tap the streams whose waters are made of gold, and, as romance seduces many women, so, secretly, this powerful money-making aptitude seduced her temperament, or an important part of it. She was fascinated by this aptitude, but presently she was still more fascinated by the subtle use that he was making of it.

He was deliberately rousing up Nigel's ambitions connected with labour, was deliberately stinging him to activity, deliberately prompting him to a sort of manly shame at the thought of his present life of repose. But he was doing it with an apparent carelessness that was deceptive and very subtle; he was doing it by talking about himself, and his own energy, and his own success, not conceitedly, but simply, and in connection with Nigel's plans and schemes and desires.

Why was he doing this? Did he want to send Nigel to spend the winter in the Fayyūm? And did he know that Nigel intended to "rig up something" in the Fayyūm for her?

She began to wonder, to wonder intensely, why Baroudi was stirring up Nigel's enthusiasm for work. It seemed as if, for the moment, the two men had entirely forgotten that she was there, had forgotten that in the world there was such a phenomenon as woman. She had a pleasant sensation of listening securely at a key-hole. Usually she desired to attract to herself the attention of every man who was near her. To-day she wished that the conversation between her husband and Baroudi might be indefinitely prolonged; for a strange sense of well-being, of calmness, indeed of panacea, was beginning to steal at last upon her, after the excitement, the bitter anger that had upset her spirit. It seemed to her as if in that moment of utter repose in the darkness of the chamber near the fountain a hypnotic hand had been laid upon her, as if it had not yet been removed. Really she was already captured by the dahabeeyah spell, although she did not know it. A dahabeeyah is the home of dreams, and of a deeply quiet physical well-being. Mrs. Armine was a very sensuous woman, and sensitive to all sensuous impressions; so now, while her husband talked eagerly, enthusiastically, of the life of activity and work, she received from the Nile its curious gift of bodily indolence and stillness. Her body never moved, never wished to move, in the deep and cushioned chair, was almost like a body morphia-stricken; but her mind was alert, and judging the capacities of these two men. And still it was seeking secretly the answer to a "Why?" when Nigel at length exclaimed:

"Anyhow, I meant to get off by the train to-morrow night. And you? When are you starting up the river?"

"I have a tug. I go away to-night."

"To Armant?"

"To Armant for some days. Then I go farther up the river. I have interests near Kom Ombos. I shall be away some time, and then drop down to Assiout. I have nothing more to do here."

"Interests in Assiout, too?"

"Oh, yes; at Assiout I have a great many. And just

beyond here I have some—a little way up the river on the western bank."

"Lands?"

"I have orange-gardens there."

"I wonder you can manage to look after it all—sugar, cotton, quarries, house property, works, factories. Phew! it almost makes one's head spin. And you see into everything yourself!"

"Where the master's eye does not look, the servant's is turned away. Do you not find it so in the Fayyūm?"

"I shall know in two or three days."

Nigel suddenly looked round at his wife.

"I hear you," she said, slowly. "You had forgotten all about me, but I was listening to you."

She moved, and sat straight up, putting her hands on the broad cushioned arms of the chair.

"I was receiving a lesson," she added.

"A lesson, Ruby?" said Nigel.

"A lesson in humility."

Both men tried to make her explain exactly what she meant, but she would not satisfy their curiosity.

"You have brains enough to guess," was all she said. "We must be going, Nigel. Look! it is nearly sunset. Soon the river will be turning golden."

As she said the last word, she looked at Baroudi, and her voice seemed to linger on the word as on a word beloved.

"Won't you stay and see the sunset from here, madame?" he said.

"I am sure you have lots to do. I have been listening to some purpose, and I know you are a man of affairs, and can have very little time for social nonsense, such as occupies the thoughts of women. I feel almost guilty at having taken up even one of your hours."

Nigel thought there was in her voice a faint sound as if she were secretly aggrieved.

Baroudi made a polite rejoinder, in his curiously careless and calmly detached way, but he did not press them again to stay any longer, and Nigel felt certain that he had many things to do—preparations, perhaps, to make for his departure that evening. He was decidedly not a "woman's man," but was a keen and pertinacious man of affairs, who liked the activities of life and knew how to deal with men.

He bade them good-bye on the deck of the sailors.

Just before she stepped down into the waiting felucca, Mrs. Armine, as if moved by an impulse she could not resist, turned her head and gazed at the strange Arabic letters of gold that were carved above the doorway through which she had once more passed.

"The fate of every man have we bound about his neck."

Baroudi followed her eyes, and a smile, that had no brightness in it, flickered over his full lips, then died, leaving behind it an impassible serenity.

That night, just when the moon was coming, the *Loulia*, gleaming with many lights, passed the garden of the Villa Androud, and soon was lost in the night, going towards the south.

On the following evening, by the express that went to Cairo, Nigel started for the Fayyüm.

XVI

THE *Loulia* gone from the reach of the river which was visible from the garden of the Villa Androud; Nigel gone from the house which was surrounded by that garden; a complete solitude, a complete emptiness of golden days stretching out before Mrs. Armine! When she woke to that little bit of truth, fitted in to the puzzle of the truths of her life, she looked into vacancy, and asked of herself some questions.

Presently she came down to the drawing-room, dressed in a thin coat and skirt that were suitable for riding, for walking, for sitting among ruins, for gardening, for any active occupation. Yet she had no plan in her head; only she was absolutely free to-day, and if it occurred to her to want to do anything, why, she was completely ready for the doing of it. Meanwhile she sat down on the terrace, and she looked about the garden.

No one was to be seen in it from where she was sitting. The Egyptian gardener was at work, or at rest in some hidden place, and all the garden was at peace.

It was a golden day, almost incredibly clear and radiant, quivering with brightness and life, and surely with ecstasy. She was set free, in a passionate wonder of gold. That was the first fact of which she was sharply conscious. By this time Nigel must be in Cairo; by the evening he would be in that fabled Fayyūm of which she had heard so much, which had become to her almost as a moral symbol. In the Fayyūm fluted the Egyptian Pan by the water; in the Fayyūm, as in an ample and fruitful bosom, dwelt untrammelled Nature, loosed from all shackles of civilization. And there, perhaps to-morrow, Nigel would begin making his eager preparations for her reception and housing—his ardent preparations for the taking of her "right down to Nature," as he had once phrased it to her. She touched her whitened cheek with her carefully manicured fingers, and she wondered, not without irony, at the strange chances of human life. What imp had taken her by the hand to lead her to a tent in the Fayyūm, in which she would dwell with a man full of an almost sacred moral enthusiasm? She would surely be more at home lying on embroideries and heaped-up cushions, with her nostrils full of a faint but heavy perfume of the East, and her ears of the murmur of dancing waters, and her mind, or spirit, or soul, or whatever it was, in contact with another "whatever it was," unlit, unheated, by fires that might possibly scorch her, but that could never purify her.

What a marvellous golden day it was! This morning she felt the beneficent influence of the exquisite climate in a much more intimate way than she had ever felt it before. Why was that? Because of Nigel's absence, or because of some other reason? Although she asked herself the question, she did not seek for an answer; the weather was subtly showering into her an exquisite indifference—the golden peace of "never mind!" In the Eastern house of Baroudi, as she squeezed the silken cushions with her fingers, something within her had said, "I must squeeze dry of their golden juices every one of the fleeting years." In this day there were some drops of the golden juices—some drops that she must squeeze out, that her thirsty lips must drink. For the years were fleeting away, and then there would come the black, eternal nothingness. She must turn all her attention towards the joys that might still be hers in the short time that was left her for joy—the short time, for she was a woman, and over forty.

A tent in the Fayyūm with Nigel! Nobody else but Nigel! Days and days in complete isolation with Nigel! With the man who had "let her in"! And life, not stealing, but clamorously rushing away from her!

She thought of this, she faced it; the soul of her condemned it as a fate almost ludicrously unsuited to her. And yet she was undisturbed in the depths of her, although, perhaps, the surface was ruffled. For the weather would not be gainsaid, the climate would have its way; the blue, and the gold, and the warmth, combining with the knowledge of freedom, could not be conquered by any thought that was black, or by any fear. It seemed to her for a moment as if she were almost struggling to be angry, to be unhappy, and as if the struggle were vain.

She was quite free in this world of gold. What was she going to do with her freedom?

In the golden stillness of the garden she heard the faint rustle of a robe, and she looked round and saw Ibrahim coming slowly towards her, smiling, with his curly head drooping a little to the left side. Behind both his ears there were roses, and he held a rose in his hand with an unlighted cigarette.

"What are we going to do to-day, Ibrahim?" said Mrs. Armine, lazily.

Ibrahim came up and stood beside her, looking down in his very gentle and individual way. He smoothed the front of his djelabieh, lifted his rose, smelt it, and said in his low contralto voice:

"We are goin' across the river, my lady."

"Are we?"

"We are goin' to take our lunchin'; we are goin' to be out all day."

"Oh! And what about tea?"

"We are goin' to take it with us in that bottle that looks all made of silver."

"Silver and—gold," she murmured, looking into the radiant distance where Thebes lay cradled in the arms of the sun-god.

"And when are we going, Ibrahim?"

He looked at her, and his soft, pale brown lips stretched themselves and showed his dazzling teeth.

"When you are ready, my lady."

She looked up into his face. Ibrahim was twenty, but he was completely a boy, despite his great height and his tried capacities as a dragoman. Everything in him suggested rather the boy than the young man. His long and slim and flexible body, his long brown neck, his small head, covered with black hair which curled thickly, the expression in his generally smiling eyes, even his quiet gestures, his dreamy poses, his gait, his way of sitting down and of getting up, all conveyed, or seemed to convey, to those about him the fact that he was a boy. And there was something very attractive in this very definite youngness of his. Somehow it inspired confidence.

"I suppose I am ready now."

Mrs. Armine spoke slowly, always looking up at Ibrahim.

"But is there a felucca to take us over?" she added.

"In four five minutes, my lady."

"Call to me from here when it is ready. I leave all the lunch and tea arrangements to you."

"All what you want you must have, my lady."

Was that a formula of Ibrahim's? To-day he seemed to speak the words with a conviction that was not usual, with some curious under-meaning. How much of a boy was he really? As Mrs. Armine went upstairs she was wondering about him.

Nigel had said to her, "You are blossoming here." And he had said to her, "You are beautiful, but you do not trust your own beauty." And that was true, perhaps. To-day she would be quite alone with Ibrahim and the Egyptians; she would be in perfect freedom, and downstairs upon the terrace the idea had come to her to fill up the time that must elapse before the felucca arrived in "undoing" her face. She went into her bedroom, and shut and locked the door.

"The felucca is here suttinly, my lady!"

Ibrahim called from the terrace some ten minutes later; then he came round to the front of the house, and cried out the words again.

"I shall be down in a moment."

Another ten minutes went by, and then Mrs. Armine appeared. She had an ivory fly-whisk in her hand, and a white veil was drawn over her face.

"Is everything ready, Ibrahim?"

"Everythin'."

They went to the felucca and crossed the river.

At a point where there was a stretch of flat sandy soil on the western shore, Hamza, the praying donkey-boy, was calmly waiting with two large and splendidly groomed donkeys. Mrs. Armine stepped out of the felucca, helped by Ibrahim, and the felucca at once put off, and began to return across the Nile. The boatmen sang in deep and almost tragic voices as they plied the enormous oars. Their voices faded away on the gleaming waste of water.

Mrs. Armine had stood close to the river listening to them. When the long diminuendo was drawn back into a monotonous murmur which she could scarcely hear, she turned round with a sigh; and she had a strange feeling that a last link which had held her to civilization had snapped, and that she was now suddenly grasped by the dry, hot hands of Egypt. As she turned she faced Hamza, who stood immediately before her, motionless as a statue, with his huge, almond-shaped eyes fixed unsmilingly upon her.

"May your day be happy!"

He uttered softly and gravely the Arabic greeting. Mrs. Armine thanked him in English.

Why did she suddenly to-day feel that she lay in the hot breast of Egypt? Why did she for the first time really feel the intimate spell of this land—feel it in the warmth that caressed her, in the softness of the sand that lay beneath her feet, in the little wind that passed like a butterfly, and in the words of Hamza, in his pose, in his look, in his silence? Why? Was it because she was no longer companioned by Nigel?

On the day of her arrival Nigel had pointed out Hamza to her. Now and then she had seen him casually, but till to-day she had never looked at him carefully, with woman's eyes that discern and appraise.

Hamza was of a perfectly different type from Ibrahim's. He was excessively slight, almost fragile, with little bones, delicate hands and feet, small shoulders, a narrow head, and a face that was like the face of a beautiful bronze, grave, still, enigmatic, almost inhuman in its complete repose and watchfulness—a face that seemed to take all and to give absolutely nothing. As Mrs. Armine looked at him she remembered the descriptive phrase that set him apart from all the people of Luxor. He was "the praying donkey-boy."

Why had Ibrahim engaged him for their expedition to-day? She had never had him in her service before.

In a low voice she asked Ibrahim the question.

"He is a very good donkey-boy, but he is not for my lord Arminigel."

Mrs. Armine wondered why, but she asked nothing more. To-day she felt herself in the hands of Egypt, and of Egypt Ibrahim and Hamza were part. If she were to enjoy to-day to the utmost, she felt that she must be passive. And something within her seemed to tell her that in all that Ibrahim was doing he was guided by some very definite purpose.

He helped her on to her donkey. Upon the beast he was

BELLA DONNA

going to ride were slung two ample panniers. The fragile-looking Hamza, whose body was almost as strong and as flexible as mail, would run beside them—to eternity, if need be—on naked feet.

"Where are we going, Ibrahim?"

"We are goin' this way, my lady."

He gave a loud, an almost gasping, sigh. Instantly his donkey started forward, followed by Mrs. Armine's. The broad river was left behind; they set their course toward the arid mountains of Libya. Ibrahim kept always in front to lead the way. He had pushed his tarbush to the back of his curly head, and as he rode he leaned backwards from his beast, sticking out his long legs, from which the wrinkling socks slipped down, showing his dark brown skin. He began to sing to himself in a low and monotonous voice, occasionally interrupting his song to utter the loud sigh that urged the donkey on. Hamza ran lightly beside Mrs. Armine. He was dressed in white, and wore a white turban. In his right hand he grasped a long piece of sugar-cane. As he ran, holding himself quite straight, his face never changed its expression, his eyes were always fixed upon the mountains of Libya.

Upon the broad, flat lands that lay between the Nile and the ruins of Thebes the young crops shed a sharp green that looked like a wash of paint. Here and there the miniature forests of doura stood up almost still in the sunshine. Above the sturdy brakes of the sugar-cane the crested hoopoes flew, and the larks sang, fluttering their little wings as if in an almost hysterical ecstasy. Although the time was winter, and the Christians' Christmas was not far off, the soft airs seemed to be whispering all the sweet messages of the ardent spring that smiles over Eastern lands. This was a world of young rapture, not careless, but softly intense with joy. All things animate and inanimate were surely singing a love-song, effortless because it flowed from the very core of a heart that had never known sorrow.

"You are blossoming here!"

Nigel had said that to Mrs. Armine, and she thought of his words now, and she felt that to-day they were true. Where was she going? She did not care. She was going under this singing sky, over this singing land, through this singing sunshine. That was surely enough. Once or twice she looked at Hamza, and, because he never looked at her, presently she spoke to him, making some remark about the weather in English. He turned his head, fixed his unyielding eyes upon her, said "Yes," and glanced away. She asked him a question which demanded "No " for an answer. This time he said "Yes," but without looking at her. Like a living bronze he ran on, lightly, swiftly, severely, towards the tiger-coloured mountains. And something in Hamza now made Mrs. Armine wonder where they were going. Already she had seen the ruins on the western shore of the Nile; she was familiar with Medinat-Habu, with Deir-al-Bahari, with Kurna, with the Ramesseum, with the tombs of the Kings and of the Queens. They had landed at a point that lay to the south of Thebes, and now seemed to be making for Medinat-Habu.

"Where are we going, Hamza?" she asked.

"Yes," he replied.

And he ran on, holding the piece of sugar-cane, like some hieratic figure holding a torch in a procession. Ibrahim stopped his song to sigh, and struck his donkey lightly under the right ear, causing it to turn sharply to the left. In the distance Mrs. Armine saw the great temple of Medinat-Habu, but it was not their destination. They were leaving it on their right. And now Ibrahim struck his donkey again, and they went on rapidly towards the Libyan mountains. The heat increased as the day wore on towards noon, but she did not mind it—indeed, she had the desire that it might increase. She saw the drops of perspiration standing on the face of the living bronze who ran beside her. Ibrahim ceased from singing. Had the approach of the golden noontide laid a spell upon his lips?

They went on, and on, and on.

· · · · ·

BELLA DONNA   191

"This is the lunchin'-place, my lady."

At last Ibrahim pulled up his donkey, and slid off, drawing his djelabieh together with his brown hands.

"Ss—ss—ss—ss!"

Hamza hissed, and Mrs. Armine's donkey stopped abruptly. She got down. She was, or felt as if she was, in the very heart of the mountains, in a fiery place of beetling yellow, and brownish and reddish yellow, precipices and heaped up rocks that looked like strangely-shaped flames solidified by some cruel and mysterious process. The ground felt hot to her feet as she stood still and looked about her. Her first impression was one of strong excitement. This empty place excited her as a loud, fierce, savage noise excites. The look of it was like noise. For a moment she stood, and though she was really only gazing, she felt as if she were listening—listening to hardness, to heat, to gleam, that were crying out to her.

Hamza took down the panniers after laying his wand of sugar-cane upon the burning ground.

"Why have you brought me here?"

The question was in Mrs. Armine's mind, but she did not speak it. She put up her hands, lifted her veil, and let the sun fall upon her "undone" face, but only for an instant. Then she let her veil down again, and said to Ibrahim:

"You must find me some shade, Ibrahim."

"My lady, you come with me!"

He walked on up the tiny, ascending track, that was like a yellow riband which had been let down from the sun, and she followed him round a rock that was thrust out as if to bar the way, and on to a flat ledge over which the mountain leaned. A long and broad shadow fell here, and the natural wall behind the ledge was scooped out into a shape that suggested repose. As she came upon this ledge, and confronted this shadow, Mrs. Armine uttered a cry of surprise. For against the rock there lay a pile of heaped-up cushions, and over a part of the ledge was spread a superb carpet. In this hot and savage and desolate place it so startled that it almost alarmed her to come abruptly on these things, which forcibly suggested luxury and people, and she glanced sharply round, again lifting her veil. But she saw only gleaming yellow and amber and red rocks, and shining tresses of sand among them, and precipices that looked almost like still cascades of fire. And again she seemed to hear hardness, and heat, and gleam that were crying out to her.

"This is the lunchin'-place, my lady."

Ibrahim was looking at the ground where the carpet was spread.

"But—whom do these things belong to?"

"Suttinly they are for you."

"They were put here for me?"

"Suttinly."

Always he looked like a gentle and amiable boy. Mrs. Armine stared at him searchingly for a moment, then, swayed by a sudden impulse, she went to the edge of the great rock that hid Hamza and the donkeys from them, and looked round it to the path by which she had come. On it Hamza was kneeling with his forehead against the ground. He lifted himself up, and with his eyes fast shut he murmured, murmured his prayers. Then he bent again, and laid his forehead once more against the ground. Mrs. Armine drew back. She did not know exactly why, but she felt for an instant chilled in the burning sunshine.

"Hamza is praying," she said to Ibrahim, who stood calmly by the carpet.

"Suttinly!" he replied. "When Hamza stop, him pray. Hamza is very good donkey-boy."

Mrs. Armine asked no more questions. She sat down on the carpet and leaned against the cushions. Now she was protected from the fierce glare of the sun, and, almost as from a box at a theater, she could comfortably survey the burning pageant that Nature gave to her eyes. Ibrahim went to and fro in his golden robe over the yellow ground, bringing her food and water with lemon-juice in it, and, when all was carefully and deftly arranged, he said:

"Is there anythin' more, my lady?"

Mrs. Armine shook her head.

"No, Ibrahim. I have everything I want; I am very comfortable here."

"All what you want you must have to-day, my lady."

He looked at her and went away, and was hidden by the rock. It seemed to her that a curious expression, that was unboyish and sharp with meaning, had dawned and died in his eyes.

Slowly she ate a little food, and she sipped the lemon and water.

Ibrahim did not return, nor did she hear his voice or the voice of Hamza. She knew, of course, that the two Egyptians were near her, behind the rock; nevertheless, presently, since she could not see or hear them, she began to feel as if she were entirely alone in the mountains. She drew down one of the cushions from the rock behind her, and laid and kept her hand upon it. And the sensation the silk gave to her fingers seemed to take her again into the Eastern house of Baroudi. She finished her meal, she put down upon the carpet the empty glass, and, shutting her eyes, she went on feeling the cushions. And as she felt them she seemed to see again Hamza, with his beautiful and severe face, praying upon the yellow ground.

Hamza, Ibrahim, Baroudi. They were all of Eastern blood, they were all of the same faith, of the faith from the bosom of which emanated the words which were written upon the *Loulia:*

"The fate of every man have we bound about his neck."

Of every man! And what of the fate of woman? What of her fate?

She opened her eyes, and saw Baroudi standing near her, leaning against a rock and looking steadily at her.

For an instant she did not know whether she was startled or not. She seemed to be aware of two selves, the conscious self and the subconscious self, to know that they were in a sharp conflict of sensation. And because of this conflict she could not say, to herself even, that the sum total of her was this or that. For the conscious self had surely never expected to see Baroudi here; and the subconscious self had surely known quite well that he would come into this hard and yellow place of fire to be alone with her.

"Thank you so much for the carpet and the cushions."

The subconscious self had gained the victory. No, she was not surprised. Baroudi moved from the rock, and, without smiling, came slowly up to her over the shining ground that looked metal in the fierce radiance of the sun. He wore a suit of white linen, white shoes, and the tarbush.

"*Puisque votre mari n'y est plus, parlons Français,*" he said.

"*Comme vous voulez,*" she replied.

She did not ask him why he preferred to speak in French. Very few whys stood just then between her and this man whom she scarcely knew. They went on talking in French. At first Baroudi continued to stand in the sun, and she looked up at him with composure from her place of shadow.

"Armant is in this direction?" she said.

"I do not say that, but it is not so far as the Fayyûm."

"I know so little of Egypt. You must forgive my ignorance."

"You will know more of my country, much more than other Englishwomen—some day."

He spoke with an almost brutal composure and self-possession, and she noticed that he no longer closed his sentences with the word "madame." His great eyes, as they looked steadily down to her, were as direct, as cruelly direct, in their gaze as the eyes of a bird of prey. They pierced her defences, but to-day did not permit her, in return, to pierce his, to penetrate, even a little way, into his territory of thought, of feeling. She remembered the eyes of Meyer Isaacson. They, too, were almost cruelly penetrating; but whereas they distinctly showed his mind at work, the eyes of Baroudi now seemed to hide what his mind was doing while they stared at the working of hers.

And this combination of refusal and robbery, blatantly selfish and egoistic, conveyed to her spirit an extraordinary sense of his power. For years she had dominated men. This man could dominate her. He knew it. He had always known it, from the first moment when his eyes rested on hers. Was it that which was Greek or that which was Egyptian in him which already overcame her? the keenly practical and energetic or the mysterious and fatalistic? As yet she could not tell. Perhaps he had a double lure for the two sides of her nature.

"Do you think so?" she said. "I doubt it. I'm not sure that I shall spend another winter in Egypt."

His eyes became more sombre, looked suddenly as if even their material weight must have increased.

"That is known, but not to you," he said.

"And not to you!" she said, with a sudden sharpness, very womanly and modern.

With a quick and supple movement he was beside her, stretching his length upon the ground in the shadow of the mountain. He turned slightly to one side, raising himself up a little on one strong arm, and keeping in that position without any apparent effort.

"Please don't try the old hypnotic fakir tricks upon me, Baroudi," she added, pushing up the cushions against the rock behind her. "I know quantities of hysterical European women make fools of themselves out here, but I am not hysterical, I assure you."

"No, you are practical, as I am, and something else— as I am."

He bent back his head a little. The movement showed her his splendid throat, which seemed to announce all the concentrated strength that was in him—a strength both calm and fiery, not unlike that of the rocks, like petrified flames which hemmed them in.

"Something else? What is it?"

"Why do women so often ask questions to which they know the answers? Here is Ibrahim with our coffee."

At this moment, indeed, Ibrahim came slowly from

behind the rocky barrier, carrying coffee-cups, sugar, and a steaming brass coffee-pot on a tray. Without speaking a word, he placed the tray gently upon the ground, filled the cups, handed them to Mrs. Armine and Baroudi, and went quietly away. He had not looked at Mrs. Armine.

And she had thought of Ibrahim as just a gentle and amiable boy!

Could all these people read her mind and follow the track of her distastes and desires, even the dragomans and the donkey-boys? For an instant she felt as if the stalwart Englishmen, the governing race, whom she knew so well, were only children—short-sighted and frigid children—that these really submissive Egyptians, Baroudi, Ibrahim, and the praying Hamza, were crafty and hot-blooded men with a divinatory power.

"Your coffee," said Baroudi, handing to her a cup.

She drank a little, put down the cup, and said:

"The first night we were at the Villa Androud your Nubian sailors came up the Nile and sang just underneath the garden. Why did they do that?"

"Because they are my men, and had my orders to sing to you."

"And Ibrahim—and Hamza?" she asked.

"They had my orders to bring you here."

"Yes," she said.

She was silent for an instant.

"Yes; of course they had your orders."

As she spoke a hot wave of intimate satisfaction seemed to run all over her. From Alexandria this man had greeted her on the first evening of her new life beside the Nile. He had greeted her then, and now he had surely insulted her. He acknowledged calmly that he had treated her as a chattel.

She loved that.

He had greeted her on that first evening with a song about Allah. Her mind, moving quickly from thought to thought, now alighted upon that remembrance, and immediately she recollected Hamza and his prayer, and she wondered how strong was the belief in Allah of the ruthless being beside her.

"They sang a song about Allah," she said, slowly. "Allah was the only word I could understand."

Baroudi raised himself up a little more, and, staring into her face, he opened his lips, and, in a loud and melancholy voice, sang the violent, syncopated tune the Nubian boatmen love. The hot yellow rocks around them seemed to act as a sounding-board to his voice. Its power was surely unnatural, and, combined with his now expressionless face, made upon her an effect that was painful. Nevertheless, it allured her. When he was silent, she murmured:

"Yes, it was that."

He said nothing, and his absolute silence following upon his violent singing strengthened the grip of his strangeness upon her. Only a little while ago she had felt, had even known, that she and Baroudi understood one another as Nigel and she could never understand one another. Now suddenly she felt a mystery in Baroudi far deeper, far more impenetrable, than any mystery that dwelt in Nigel. This mystery seemed to her to be connected with his belief in an all-powerful God, in some Being outside of the world, presiding over its destinies, ordering all the fates which it contained. And whereas the belief of her husband, which she divined and was often sharply conscious of, moved her to a feeling of irony such as may be felt by a naturally sardonic person when hearing the naïve revelations of a child, the faith of Baroudi fascinated her, and moved her almost to a sensation of awe. It was like a fire which burnt her, and like an iron door which shut against her.

Yet he had never spoken of it; he did not speak of it now. But he had sung the song of Nubia.

"Did you tell Ibrahim that he was to choose Hamza as my donkey-boy to-day?" she said.

She was still preoccupied, still she seemed to see Hamza running beside her towards the mountains, praying among the rocks.

"Yes."

"Why?"

"Hamza is a very good donkey-boy."

In that moment Mrs. Armine began to feel afraid of Hamza, even afraid of his prayers. That was strangely absurd, she knew, because she believed in nothing. Baroudi now let himself sink down a little, and rested his cheek upon his hand. Somewhere he had learnt the secret of European postures. There had been depths of strangeness in his singing. There was a depth of strangeness in his demeanour. He had greeted her from the Nile by night when he was far away in Alexandria; he had ordered Ibrahim and Hamza to bring her into this solitary place, and now he lay beside her with his strong body at rest, and his mind, apparently, lost in some vagrant reverie, not heeding her, not making any effort to please her, not even —so it seemed to her now—thinking about her. Why was she not piqued, indignant? Why was she even actually charmed by his indifference?

She did not ask herself why. Perhaps she was catching from him a mood that had never before been hers.

For a long time they remained thus side by side, quite motionless, quite silent. And that period of stillness was to Mrs. Armine the most strange period she had ever passed through in a life that had been full of events. In that stillness she was being subdued, in that stillness moulded, in that stillness drawn away. What was active, and how was it active? What spoke in the stillness? No echoes replied with their charmed voices among the gleaming rocks of the Libyan mountains. Nevertheless, something had lifted up a voice and had cried aloud. And an answer had come that had been no echo.

In repose there is renewal. When they spoke again the almost avid desire to make the most of the years that remained to her had grown much stronger in Mrs. Armine, and there had been born within her one of those curious beliefs which, it seems, come only to women—the belief that there was reserved for her a revenge upon a fate, the fate that had taken from her the possibility of having all that she had married Nigel to obtain, and the belief that she would achieve that revenge by means of the man who lay beside her.

XVII

THAT evening, when Mrs. Armine stepped out of the felucca at the foot of the garden of the Villa Androud, she did not wait for Ibrahim to help her up the bank, but hurried away alone, crossed the garden and the terrace, went to her bedroom, shut and locked the door, lit the candles on either side of the long mirror that stood in the dressing-room, pushed up her veil, and anxiously looked at her "undone" face in the glass.

Had her action been very unwise? Several times that day, while with Baroudi, she had felt something that was almost like panic invade her at the thought of what she had done. Now, quite alone and safe, she asked herself whether she had been a fool to obey Nigel's injunction and to trust her own beauty.

She gazed; she took off her hat and she gazed again, hard, critically, almost cruelly.

There came a sharp knock against the door.

"Who is it?"

"*C'est moi, madame!*"

Mrs. Armine went to the door and opened it.

"Come here, Marie!" she said, almost roughly, "and tell me the truth. I don't want any flattering or any palavering from you. Do you think I look younger, better looking, with something on my face, or like this?"

She put her face close to the light of the candles and stood quite still. Marie examined her with sharp attention.

"Madame has got to look much younger here," she said, at length. "Madame has changed very much since we have been in Egypt. I do not know, but I think, perhaps, here madame can go without anything, unless, of course, she is going to be with Frenchmen. But if madame is much in the sun, at night she should be careful to put——"

And the maid ran on, happy in a subject that appealed to her whole nature.

Mrs. Armine dined alone and quickly. It was past nine o'clock when she finished, and went out to sit on the terrace, and to smoke her cigarette and drink her coffee. In returning from the mountains she had scarcely spoken to Ibrahim, and had not spoken to Hamza except to wish him good-night upon the bank of the Nile. She remembered now the expression in his almond-shaped eyes when he had returned her salutation—an unfathomable expression of ruthless understanding that stripped her nature bare of all disguises, and seemed to leave it as it was for all the men of this land to see.

Ibrahim's eyes never could look like Hamza's. And yet between Ibrahim and Hamza what essential difference was there!

Suddenly she said to herself: "Why should I bother my head about these people, a servant and a donkey-boy?"

In England she would never have cared in the least what the people in her service thought about her. But out here things seemed to be different. And Ibrahim and Hamza had brought her to the place where Baroudi had been waiting to meet her. They were in Baroudi's pay. That was the crude fact. She considered it now as she sat alone, sipping the Turkish coffee that Hassan had carried out to her, and smoking her cigarette. She said to herself that she ought to be angry, but she knew that she was not angry. She knew that she was pleased that Ibrahim and Hamza had been bought by Baroudi. Easterns are born with an appetite for intrigue, with a love of walking in hidden ways and creeping along devious paths. Why should those by whom she happened to be surrounded discard their natures?

And then she thought of Nigel.

How much more at her ease she was with Baroudi than she could ever be with Nigel! What Nigel desired she could never give him. She might seem to give it, but the bread would be really a stone, even if he were deceived.

And he would be deceived. But what Baroudi desired she could give. It seemed to her to-night indeed that she was born to give just what he desired. She made no mistake about herself. And he could give to her exactly what she wanted. So she thought now. For, since the long day in the mountains, her old ambition seemed to have died, to have been slain, and, with its death, had suddenly grown more fierce within her the governing love, or governing greed, for material things—for money, jewels, lovely bibelots, for all that is summed up in the one word *luxe*. And Baroudi was immensely rich, and would grow continually richer. She knew how to weigh a man in the balance, and though, even for her, there was mystery in him, she could form a perfectly right judgment of his practical capacity, of his power of acquirement.

But he could give her more than *luxe,* much more than *luxe*.

And as she acknowledged that to herself, there came into Mrs. Armine's heart a new inhabitant.

That inhabitant was fear.

She knew that in Baroudi she had found a man by whom she could be governed, by whom, perhaps, she could be destroyed, because in him she had found a man whom she could love, in no high, eternal way—she was not capable of loving any man like that—but with the dangerous force, the jealous physical passion and desire, the almost bitter concentration, that seem to come to life in a certain type of woman only when youth is left behind.

She knew that, and she was afraid as she had never been afraid before.

That night she slept very little. Two or three times, as she lay awake in the dark, she heard distant voices singing somewhere on the Nile, and she turned upon the bed, and she longed to be out in the night, nearer to the voices. They seemed to be there for her, to be calling her, and they brought back to her memory the sound of Baroudi's voice, when he raised himself up, stared into her face, and sang the song about Allah, the song of the Nubian boatmen.

And then she saw him before her in the darkness with a painful clearness, as if he were lit up by the burning rays of the sun. Why had she met this man immediately after she had taken the vital step into another marriage? For years she had been free, free as only the social outcast can be who is forcibly driven out into an almost terrible liberty, and through all those years of freedom she had used men without really loving any man. And then, at last, she had once more bound herself, she had taken what seemed to be a decisive step towards an ultimate respectability, perhaps an ultimate social position, and no sooner had she done this than chance threw in her way a man who could grip her, rouse her, appeal to all the chief wants in her nature. Those words in the Koran, were they not true for her? Her fate had surely been bound about her neck. By whom? If she asked Baroudi she knew what he would tell her. Strangely, even his faith fascinated her, although at Nigel's faith she secretly laughed; for in Baroudi's faith there seemed to be a strength that was hard, that was fierce and cruel. Even in his religion she felt him to be a brigand, trying to seize with greedy hands upon the promises and the joys of another world. He was determined not to be denied anything that he really desired.

She turned again on her pillows, and she put her arms outside the sheet, then she put her hands up to her face and felt that her cheeks were burning. And she remembered how, long ago, when she was a young married woman, one night she had lain awake and had felt her burning cheeks with her hands.

That was soon after she had met the man for whom she had been divorced, the man who had ruined her social life. Does life return upon its steps? She remembered the violent joys of that secret love which had ultimately been thrown down in the dust for all the world to stare at. Was she to know such joys again? Was it possible that she could know them, had she the capacity to know them after all she had passed through?

She knew she had that capacity, and with her fear was

mingled a sense of triumph; for she felt that with the years the capacity within her for that which to her was joy had not diminished, but increased. And this sense of increase gave her a vital sense of youth. Even Nigel had said, "You are blossoming here!" Even he, whom she had so easily and so completely deceived, had seen that truth of her clearly.

And when he came back from the Fayyûm to stay again with her, or, more probably, to fetch her away?

The voices that had come to her from far away on the Nile were hushed. The night at last had imposed herself on the singers, and they had sunk down to sleep under the mantle of her silence. But Mrs. Armine still lay awake, felt as if the cessation of the singing had made her less capable of sleeping.

When Nigel came to fetch her away to the tent in the Fayyûm, what then?

She would not think about that, but she would obey her temperament. She had two weeks of freedom before her, she who had had so many years of freedom. She had only two weeks. Then she would use them, enjoy them to the uttermost. She would think of nothing but the moment. She would squeeze, squeeze out the golden juices that these moments contained which lay immediately before her. The tent in the Fayyûm—perhaps she would never see it, would never come out in the night with Nigel to hear the Egyptian Pan by the water. But—she would surely hear Baroudi sing again to-morrow, she would surely, to-morrow, watch him while he sang.

She put her arms inside the bed, and feverishly drew the sheet up underneath her chin. She must sleep, or to-morrow her face would show that she had not slept. And Baroudi stared at her while he sang.

Again she was seized by fear.

XVIII

LATE the next morning there awoke with Mrs. Armine a woman who for a time had lain in a quiescence almost like that of death, a woman who years ago had risked ruin for a passion more physical than ideal, who, when ruin actually overtook her, had let the ugly side of her nature run free with a loose rein, defiant of the world.

Only when she awoke to that new day did she fully realize the long effort she had been making, and how it had tired and irritated her nerves and her temperament. She had won her husband by playing a part, and ever since she had won him she had gone on playing a part. And this acting had not hitherto seemed to her very difficult, although there had been moments when she had longed fiercely to show herself as she was. But now that she had spent some hours with a man who read her rightly, and who desired of her no moral beauty, no strivings after virtue, no bitter regret for any actions of the past, she realized the weight of the yoke she had been bearing, and she was filled with an almost angry desire for compensation.

She felt as if destiny were heavily in her debt, and she was resolved that the debt should be paid to the uttermost farthing.

Freed from the restraint of her husband's presence, and from the burden of his perpetual though very secret search for the moral rewards she could never give him, her whole nature seemed violently to rebound. During the days that immediately followed she sometimes felt more completely, more crudely, herself than she had ever felt before, and she was often conscious of the curious, almost savage, relief that the West sometimes feels when brought into close touch with the warm and the subtle barbarity of the East, of the East that asks no questions, that has omitted "Why?" from its dictionary.

Baroudi was as totally devoid of ordinary scruples as the average well-bred Englishman is full of them. He had, no doubt, a code of his own to guide his conduct towards his co-religionists, but this code seemed wholly inoperative when he was brought into relation with those of another race and faith.

And Mrs. Armine was a woman, and therefore, in his eyes, on a lower plane than himself.

Among the attractions which he possessed for Mrs. Armine, certainly not the least was his lack of respect for women as women. It is usually accepted as true of all women that, however low one of them has fallen, she preserves for ever within her a secret longing to be respected by man. Whether Mrs. Armine shared this secret longing or not, one thing is certain: her husband had respect for her, and she wore his respect like a chain; Baroudi had not respect for her, and she wore his lack of respect like a flower.

When she had visited the *Loulia*, reading, as women often do, the character of a man in the things by which he has deliberately surrounded himself, Mrs. Armine had grasped at once certain realities of him which, in his intercourse with her, he was at no pains to conceal. Mingled with his penetration, his easy subtlety, his hard lack of scruple, his boldness that was smooth, and polished, and cool as bronze, there went a naïve crudity, a simplicity like that of a school-boy, an uncivilized ingenuousness which was startling, and yet attractive, in its unexpectedness. The man who had bought the cuckoo-clocks and the cheap vases, who had set the gilded ball dancing upon the water of the faskeeyeh, who had broken the dim harmony of the colours in his resting-place by the introduction of that orange hue which seemed to reflect certain fierce lights within his nature, walked hand-in-hand with the shrewd money-maker, the determined pleasure-seeker, the sensual dreamer, the acute diplomatist. The combination was piquant, though not very unusual in the countries of the sun. It appealed to Mrs. Armine's wayward love of novelty, it made her feel that despite her wide experience of life in relation to men there still remained *terra incognita* on which she might set her feet. And though she did not care particularly for children, and had never longed to have a child of her own, she knew she would love occasionally to play with the child enclosed in this man, to pet it, to laugh at it, to feel superior to it, to feel tender over it, as the hardest woman can feel tender over that which wakes in her woman's dual capacity for passion and for motherliness. She both feared Baroudi and smiled, almost laughed, at him; she both wondered at and saw through him. At one moment he was transparent as glass to her view, at another he confronted her like rock surrounded by the blackness of an impenetrable night. And he never cared whether she was looking through the glass or whether she was staring, baffled, at the rock.

Never, for one moment, did he seem to be self-conscious when he was with her, did he seem to be anxious about, or even attentive to, what she was thinking of him. And the completeness of his egoism called from her egoism respect, as she was forced to realize that he possessed certain of her own qualities, but exaggerated, made portentous, brilliant, mysterious, by something in his temperament which had been left out of hers, something perhaps racial which must be for ever denied to her.

Each day Hamza, the praying donkey-boy, awaited her at some point fixed beforehand on the western side of the river, and Ibrahim escorted her there in the felucca, smiling gently like an altruistic child, and holding a rose between his teeth.

Far up the river the *Loulia* was moored, between Baroudi's orange-gardens and Armant, and each day he dropped down the Nile in his white boat to meet the European woman, bringing only one attendant with him, a huge Nubian called Aïyoub. The tourists who come to Luxor seldom go far from certain fixed points. Their days are spent either floating upon the river within sight of the village and of Thebes, among the temples and tombs on the western bank, or at Karnak, the temple of Luxor, in the antiquity shops, or in the shade of the palm-groves immediately around the brown houses of Karnak and the minarets of Luxor. Go to the north beyond Kurna, to the south beyond Madinat-Habu, or to the east to the edge of the mountains that fringe the Arabian desert, and a man is beyond their ken and the clamour of their gossip. Baroudi and Mrs. Armine met in the territory to the south, once again among the mountains, then in the plain, presently under the flickering shade of orange-trees neatly planted in serried rows and accurately espaced.

When she started in the morning from the river-bank below the garden, Mrs. Armine did not ask where she was going of Ibrahim; when she got upon her donkey did not put any question to Hamza. She just gave herself without a word into the hands of these two, let them take her, as on that first day of her freedom, where they had been told, where they had been paid to take her. As on that first day of her freedom! Soon she was to ask herself whether part of the creed of Islâm was not true for those beyond its borders, whether, till the sounding of the trumpet by the angel Asrâfil, each living being was not confined in the prison of the fate predestined for it. But, able to be short-sighted sometimes, although already in the dark moments of the night far-sighted and afraid, she had now often the sensation of an untrammelled liberty, realizing the spaces that lay between her and the Fayyûm, seeing no longer the eyes that asked gifts of her, hearing no longer the voice that pleaded for graces in her, that she could never make, could never display, though she might pretend to display them.

And so she sometimes hugged to her breast the spectre of perfect liberty in the radiant, unclouded mornings when Ibrahim came to tell her it was time to start, and she heard the low chaunt of the boatmen in the felucca. If her fate were being bound about her neck, there were moments when she did not fully realize it, when she was informed by a light and a heady sensation of strength and of youth, when she thought of the woman who had sat one day in Meyer Isaacson's consulting-room as of a weary stranger with whom she had no more to do.

But though Mrs. Armine had moments of exultation in these days, which she often told herself were her days of liberty, she had also many moments of apprehension, of depression, of wonder about the future, moments that were more frequent as she began more fully to realize the truth of her nature now fiercely revealing itself.

She had never supposed that within her there still remained so strong a capacity for feeling. She had never supposed it possible that she could really care for a man again—care, that is, with ardour, with the force that brings in its train uneasiness and the cruel desire to monopolize, to assert oneself, to take possession, not because of feminine vanity or feminine greed, but because of something lodged far deeper among the very springs of the temperament. She had never imagined that, at this probably midmost epoch of her life, there could be within her such a resurrection as that which soon she began to be anxiously aware of. The weariness, the almost stagnant calm that had, not seldom, beset her—they sank down suddenly like things falling into a measureless gulf. Body and mind bristled with an alertness that was not free from fever.

She said to herself sometimes, trying to play false even with herself, that the blame, or at least the responsibility, for this change must be laid on the shoulders of Egypt.

And then she looked, perhaps, at the mighty shoulders of Baroudi. And he saw the look, and understood her better than she just then chose to say to herself that she understood herself.

And yet for many years she had not been a woman who had tried to play tricks with her own soul. This man was to have an effect not only upon the physical part of her, but also upon that in her which would not respond to tender attempts at influencing it towards goodness or any lofty morality, but which existed, a vital spark, incorporeal, the strange and wonderful thing in the cage of her ardent flesh.

And Mahmoud Baroudi? Was there any drama being acted behind the strong, but enigmatic, exterior which he offered to the examination of the world and of this woman?

Mrs. Armine sometimes wondered, and could not determine. She knew really little of him, for though he seemed often to be very carelessly displaying himself exactly as he was, at the close of each interview she went back to the villa with a mind not yet emptied of questions. She was often strangely at ease with him because he did not ask from her that which she could not give, and therefore she could be herself when with him. But the Eastern man does not pour confidences into the ear of the Western woman, nor are the workings of his mind like the workings of the mind of a Western man. Never till now had Mrs. Armine known a secret intimacy, or any intimacy, like this, procured by bribery, and surely hastening to a swift and decisive ending.

Upon the *Hohenzollern* Baroudi must have laid his plans to see her as he was seeing her now. He did not tell her so, but she knew it. Had she not known it upon shipboard? In their exchange of glances how much had been said and answered?

Despite her life of knowledge, she said to herself now that she did not know. And there was much in Baroudi's mind, even in connection with herself, that she could not possibly know.

Something about him, nevertheless, she was able to find out.

Baroudi's father was a rich Turco-Egyptian. His mother had been a beautiful Greek girl, who had embraced Islâm when his father fell in love with her and proposed to marry her. She assumed the burko, and vanished from the world into the harîm. And in the harîm she had eventually died, leaving this only son behind her.

The Turco-Egyptians are as a rule more virile, more active, more dominant, and perhaps more greedy than are the pure-bred Egyptians. In the days before the English protectorate they held many important positions among the ruling classes of Egypt. They lined their pockets well, plundering those in their power with the ruthlessness characteristic of the Oriental character. The English came and put a stop to their nefarious money-making. And even to-day love of the Englishman is far less common than hatred in the heart of a Turco-Egyptian. In the Turco-Egyptian nature there is, nevertheless, not seldom something that is more nearly akin to the typical Englishman's nature than could be found in the pure-bred Egyptian. And possibly because he sometimes sees in the Englishman what—but for certain Oriental characteristics that hold him back—he might almost become himself, the Turco-Egyptian often nourishes a peculiar venom against him. Men may hate because of ignorance, but they may hate also because of understanding.

Baroudi had been brought up in an atmosphere of Anglophobia. His father, though very rich, had lost place and power through the English. He had once had the upper hand with many of his countrymen. He had the upper hand no longer, would never have it again. The opportunity to plunder had been quietly taken from him by the men who wore the helmet instead of the tarbush, and who, while acknowledging that there is no god but God, deny that Mohammed was the Prophet of God. He hated the English, and he taught his half-Greek son to hate them, but never noisily or ostentatiously. And Baroudi learnt the lesson of his father quickly and very thoroughly. He grew up hating the English, and yet, paradoxically, developing a nature in which were certain characteristics, certain aptitudes, certain affections shared by the English.

He was no lethargic Eastern, unpractical, though deviously subtle, taking no thought for the morrow, uselessly imaginative, submissive, ready to cringe genuinely to authority, then turn and kick the man below him. He was no stagnant pool with only the iridescent lights of corruption upon it. Almost in the English sense he was thoroughly manly. He had the true instinct for sport, the true ability of the thorough sportsman. He was active. He had within him the faculty to command, to administrate, to organize. He had, like the Englishman, the assiduity that brings a work undertaken to a successful close. He had will as well as cunning, persistence as well as penetration. From his father he had inherited instincts of a conquering race—therefore akin to English instincts; from his mother, who had sprung from the lower classes, that extraordinary acquisitive faculty, that almost limitless energy, regardless of hardship, in the pursuit of gain which is characteristic of the modern Greek in Egypt.

But he had also within him a secret fanaticism that was very old, a fatalism, obscure, and cruel, and strange, a lack of scruple that would have revolted almost any Englishman who could have understood it, an occasional childishness, rather Egyptian than Turco-Egyptian, and a quick and instinctive subtlety that came from no sunless land.

He prayed, and was a sensualist. He fasted, and loved luxury. He could control his appetites, and fling self-control to the winds. But in all that he did and left undone there was the diligent spirit at work of the man who can persevere, in renunciation even as in pursuit. And that presence of the diligent spirit made him a strong man.

That he was a strong man, with a strength not merely physical, Mrs. Armine swiftly realized. He told her of his father and mother, but he did not tell her of the atmosphere in which he had been brought up. He told her of his father's large fortune and wide lands, of his own schemes, what they had brought him, what they would probably bring him in the future; of certain marvellous *coups* which he had made by selling bits of land he had possessed in the environs of Cairo when the building craze was at its height during the "boom" of 1906. But he did not tell her of a governing factor in his life—his secret hatred of the English, originally implanted in him by his father, and nourished by certain incidents that had occurred in his own experience. He did not tell her, in more ample detail, what he had already hinted at on the evening when Nigel had brought him to the villa, how certain Egyptians love to gratify not merely their vanity and their sensuality, but also their secret loathing of their masters, by betraying those masters in the most cruel way when the opportunity is offered to them. He did not tell her that since he had been almost a boy—quite a boy according to English ideas—he, like a good many of his smart, semi-cultured, self-possessed, and physically attractive young contemporaries, had gloried in his triumphs among the Occidental women who come in crowds to spend the winters in Cairo and upon the Nile, had gloried still more in the thought that with every triumph he struck a blow at the Western man who thought him a child, unfit to rule, who ruled him for his own benefit, and who very quietly despised him.

Perhaps he feared lest Mrs. Armine might guess at a bitter truth of his nature, and shrink from him, despite the powerful attraction he possessed for her, despite her own freedom from scruple, her own ironic and even cruel outlook upon the average man.

In any case he was silent, and she almost forgot the shadow of his truth, which had risen out of the depths and stood before her on the terraces of the Villa Androud. Had she remembered it now, it might have rendered her uneasy, but it could not have recalled her from the path down which she was just beginning to go. For her life had blunted her, had coarsened her nature. She had followed too many ignoble impulses, has succumbed too often to whim, to be the happy slave of delicacy, or to allow any sense of patriotism to keep her hand in virtue's.

She told herself that when Baroudi's eyes had spoken to her on the *Hohenzollern* they had spoken in reply to the summons of her beauty, and for no other reason. What else could such a woman think? And yet there were moments when feminine intuition sought for another reason, and, not finding it, went hungry.

Baroudi had no need to seek for more reasons in her than jumped to his eyes. Ever since he had been sixteen he had been accustomed to the effect that his assurance, combined with his remarkable physique, had upon Western women.

And so each day Ibrahim and Hamza brought this Western woman to the place he had appointed, and always he was there before her.

Baroudi loved secrecy, and Mrs. Armine had nothing to fear at present from indiscretion of his. And she had no fear of that kind in connection with him.

But there were envious eyes in the villa—eyes which watched her go each morning, which greeted her on her return at sundown with a searching light of curiosity. For years she had not been obliged to care what her maid thought about her. But now she had to care. Obligations swarm in the wake of marriage. Marie knew nothing, had really no special reason to suspect anything, but, because of her mistress's personality, suspected all that a sharp French girl with a knowledge of Paris can suspect. And while Mrs. Armine trusted in the wickedness of Ibrahim and Hamza, she did not trust in the wickedness of Marie.

The *Loulia* had vanished from Luxor with its master. Mrs. Armine, left alone for a little while, naturally spent her time, like all other travellers upon the Nile, in sight-seeing. She lunched out, as almost every one else did. There was no cause for Marie to be suspicious.

Yes, there was a cause—what Mrs. Armine was, and was actually doing. Truth often manifests itself, how no one can say, not even she who sees it. Mrs. Armine knew this at evening when she saw her maid's eyes, and she wished she had brought with her an unintelligent English maid.

And then, from the Fayyūm, a shadow fell over her— the shadow of her husband.

Eight days after her meeting with Baroudi among the flame-coloured rocks she was taken by Ibrahim and Hamza to the orange-gardens up the river which Baroudi had mentioned to Nigel. They lay on the western bank of the Nile, between Luxor and Armant, and at a considerable distance from Luxor. But it chanced that the wind was fair, and blew with an unusual briskness from the north.

The sailors set the great lateen sails of the felucca, which bellied out like things leaping into life. The greenish-brown water curled and whispered about the prow, and the minarets of Luxor seemed to retreat swiftly from Mrs. Armine's eyes, as if hastening from her with the desire to be lost among the palm-trees. As the boat drew on and on, and reach after reach of the river was left behind, she began to wonder about this expedition.

"Where are we going?" she asked of Ibrahim.

"To a noo place," he answered, composedly. "To a very pretty place, a very nice place."

"We must not go too far," she said, rather doubtfully. "I must not be very late in getting back."

She was thinking at the moment angrily of Marie. If only Marie were not in the Villa Androud! She had no fear of the Nubian servants. They were all devoted to her. Already she had begun to consider them as her—not Nigel's —black slaves. But that horrid little intelligent, untrustworthy French girl——

"I have tell the French mees we are goin' to see a temple in the mountains—a temple that is wonderful indeed, all full of Rameses. I have tell her we may be late."

Mrs. Armine looked sharply into the boy's gentle, shining eyes.

"Yes; but we must be back in good time," she said.

And her whole nature, accustomed to the liberty that lies outside the pale, chafed against this small obligation. Suddenly she came to a resolve. She would get rid of Marie—send her back to Europe. How was she to manage without a maid? She could not imagine, and at this moment she did not care. She would get rid of Marie and—— Suddenly a smile came to her lips.

"Why do you larf?" asked Ibrahim.

"Because it is so fine, because I'm happy," she said.

Really she had smiled at the thought of her explanation to Nigel: "I don't want a maid here. I want to learn to be simple, to do things for myself. And how could I take her to the Fayyūm?"

BELLA DONNA

Nigel would be delighted.

And the Fayyūm without a maid? But she turned her mind resolutely away from that thought. She would live for the day—this day on the Nile. She leaned over the gunwale of the boat, and she gazed towards the south across the great flood that was shining in the gold of the sunshine. And as she gazed the boat went about, and presently drew in towards the shore. And upon the top of a high brown bank, where naked brown men were bending and singing by a shadûf, she saw the long ears of a waiting donkey, and then a straight white robe, and a silhouette like a silhouette of bronze, and a wand pointing towards the sun.

Hamza was waiting for her, was waiting—like a Fate.

XIX

Mrs. Armine rode slowly along the river-bank. Hamza did not turn the head of the donkey towards the Libyan mountains. The tombs and the temples of Thebes were far away. She wondered where she was being taken, but she did not ask again. She enjoyed this new sensation of being governed from a distance, and she remembered her effort of the imagination when she was shut up in the scented darkness of the *Loulia*. She had imagined herself a slave, as Eastern wives are slaves. Now she glanced at Ibrahim and Hamza, and she thought of the eunuchs who often accompany Eastern women of the highest rank when they go out veiled into the world. And she touched her floating veil and smiled, as she played with her vagrant thoughts.

This Egyptian life was sharp with the spice of novelty.

Before her, at a short distance, she saw a great green dusk of trees spreading from the river-bank inland, sharply defined, with no ragged edges—a dusk that had been planned by man, not left to Nature's dealings. This was not a feathery dusk of palm-trees. She looked steadily, and knew.

"Mahmoud Baroudi's orange-gardens!" she said to Ibrahim.

"Suttinly!" he replied.

He looked towards them, and added, after a pause:

"They are most beautiful, indeed."

Then he spoke quickly in Arabic to Hamza. Hamza replied with volubility. When he talked with his own people he seemed to become another being. His almost cruel calm of a bronze vanished. His face lit up with expression. A various life broke from him, like a stream suddenly released. But if Mrs. Armine spoke to him, instantly his rigid calm returned. He answered "Yes," and his almond-shaped eyes became impenetrable.

"What are they really?" she thought now, as she heard them talking.

She could not tell, but at least there was in this air a scent of spices, a sharp and aromatic savour. And she had been—perhaps would be again—a reckless woman. She loved the aromatic savour. It made her feel as if, despite her many experiences, she had lived till now perpetually in a groove; as if she had known far less of life than she had hitherto supposed.

They gained the edge of the orange-grove, passed between it and the Nile, and came presently to a broad earth-track, which led to the right. Along this they went, and reached a house that stood in the very midst of the grove, in a delicious solitude, a very delicate calm. From about it on every hand stretched away the precisely ordered rows of small, umbrageous, already fruit-bearing trees, not tall, with narrow stems, forked branches, shining leaves, among which the round balls, some green, some in the way of becoming gold, a few already gold, hung in masses that looked artificial because so curiously decorative. The breeze that had filled the sails of the felucca had either died down or was the possession of the river. For here stillness reigned. In a warm silence the fruit was ripening to bring gold to the pockets of Baroudi. The wrinkled earth beneath the trees was a dark grey in the shade, a warmer hue, in which pale brown and an earthy yellow were mingled, where the sunlight lay upon it.

Mrs. Armine got down before the house, which was painted a very faint pink, through which white seemed trying to break. It had only one storey. A door of palm-wood in the façade was approached by two short flights of steps, descending on the right and left of a small terrace. At this door Baroudi now appeared, dressed in a suit of flannel, wearing the tarbush, and holding in his hand a great palm-leaf fan. Hamza led away the donkey, going round to the back of the house. Ibrahim followed him. Mrs. Armine went slowly up the steps and joined Baroudi on the terrace.

He did not speak, and she stood by his side in silence for a moment, looking into the orange-grove. The world seemed planted with the beautiful little trees, the almost meretricious, carefully nurtured, and pampered belles of their tribe. And their aspect of artificiality, completely—indeed, quite wonderfully—effective, gave a thrill of pleasure to something within her. They were like trees that were perfectly dressed. Since the day when she first met Baroudi in the mountains she had resumed her practice of making up her face. Marie might be wrong, although Baroudi was not a Frenchman. To-day Mrs. Armine was very glad that she had not trusted completely to Nature. In the midst of these orange-trees she felt in place, and now she lifted her veil and she spoke to Baroudi.

"What do you call this? Has it a name?"

"It is the Villa Nuit d'Or. I use the word 'villa' in the Italian sense."

"Oh, of course. Night of gold. Why night?"

"The trees make a sort of darkness round the house."

"The gold I understand."

"Yes, you understand gold."

He stared at her and smiled.

"You understand it as well as I do, but perhaps in a different way," he said.

"I suppose we understand most things in different ways."

They spoke in French. They always spoke French

together now. And Mrs. Armine preferred this. Somehow she did not care so much for this man translated into English. She wished she could communicate with him in Arabic, but she was too lazy to try to learn.

"Don't you think so?" she added.

"I think my way of understanding you is better than Mr. Armeen's way," he answered, calmly.

He lit a cigarette.

"What is your way of understanding me, I do not know," he added.

"Do I understand you at all?" she said. "Do you wish me to understand you?"

Suddenly she seemed to be confronted by the rock, and a sharp irritation invaded her. It was followed by a feeling colder and very determined. The long day was before her. She was in a very perfect isolation with this man. She was a woman who had for years made it her business to understand men. By understanding them—for what is beauty without any handmaid of brains?—she had gained fortunes, and squandered them. By understanding them, when a critical moment had come in her life, she had secured for herself a husband. It was absurd that a man, who was at least half child—she thought of the cuckoo-clocks, the gilded dancing-ball—should baffle her. If only she called upon her powers, she must be able to turn him inside out like one of her long gloves. She would do it to-day. And before he had replied to her question she had left it.

"Who cares for such things on the Nile?" she said.

She laughed.

"At least, what Western woman can care? I do not. I am too drunk with your sun."

She sent him a look.

"Is it to be in—or out?" she asked. "The house or the orange-gardens?"

"Which you wish."

But his movement was outwards, and she seconded it with hers.

As they went down the steps the loud voice of a shadûf man came to them from some distant place by the Nile, reminding her of the great river which seemed ever to be flowing through her Egyptian life, reminding her of the narrowness of Upper Egypt, a corridor between the mountains of Libya and of the Arabian desert. She stood still at the bottom of the steps to listen. There was a pause. Then the fierce voice was lifted again, came to them violently through the ordered alleys of lovely little trees. The first time she had ever seen the man with whom she had been divorced was at the opera in London. She remembered now that the opera on that night of fate had been "Aîda," with its cries of the East, with its scenes beside the Nile. And for a moment it seemed to her that the hidden Egyptian who was working the shadûf was calling to them from a stage, that this garden of oranges was only a wonderful *décor*. But the illusion was too perfect for the stage. Reality broke in with its rough, tremendous touch that cannot be gainsaid, and she walked on in something that had a strangeness of truth—that naked wonder, and sometimes terror—more strange than that to be found in the most compelling art.

And yet she was walking in the Villa Nuit d'Or, a name evidently given to his property by the child of the gilded ball, a name that might be in place, surely, on the most stagey stage. She knew that, felt it, smiled at it—and yet mentally caressed the name, caressed the thing in Baroudi which had sought and found it appropriate.

"What hundreds and hundreds of orange-trees! We are losing ourselves in them," she said.

The little house was lost to sight in the trees.

"Where are we going?" she added.

"Wait a moment and you will see."

He walked on slowly, with his easy, determined gait, which, in its lightness, denoted a strength that had been trained.

"Now to the right."

He was walking on her left. She obeyed his direction, and, turning towards the Nile, saw before her a high arbour made of bamboo and encircled by a hedge of wild geranium. Its opening was towards the Nile, and when she entered it she perceived, far off, at the end of a long alley of orange-trees, the uneven line of the bank. Just where she saw it the ground had crumbled, the line wavered, and was depressed, and though the water was not visible the high lateen sails of the native boats, going southward in the sun, showed themselves to her strangely behind the fretwork of the leaves. At her approach a hoopoo rose and flew away above the trees. Somewhere a lark was singing.

In the arbour was spread an exquisite prayer-rug, and for her there was a low chair, with a cushion before it for her feet. On a table was Turkish coffee. In silver boxes were cigarettes, matches, soft sweetmeats shrouded in powdered sugar, through which they showed rose-colour, amber, and emerald green. At the edge of the table, close to the place where the chair was set, there was a pretty case of gilded silver, the top of which was made of looking-glass. She took it up at once.

"What is in this?" she said.

He opened the case, and showed her gravely a powder-puff, powder, kohl, with a tiny blunt instrument of ivory used in Egypt for its appliance, a glass bottle of rose-water, paste of henna, of smoke-black with oil and quick-lime, and other preparations commonly used in the East for the decoration of women. She examined them curiously and minutely, then looked up at him and smiled, thinking of Nigel's gentle but ardent protest. Yes, she could be strangely at home with Baroudi. But—now to turn inside out that long glove.

She sat down and put her feet on the cushion. Baroudi was instantly cross-legged on the rug. Dressed as he was, in European clothes, he ought to have looked awkward, even ridiculous. She said so to herself as she gazed down on him; and she knew that he was in the perfectly right posture, comfortable, at his ease, even—somehow—graceful. And, as she knew it, she felt the mystery of his body of the East as sometimes she had felt the mystery of his mind.

"Will you take coffee after your ride?" he said.

"Yes. Don't get up. I will pour it out, and give you yours."

She did so, with the smiling grace that had affected Nigel, had even affected Meyer Isaacson. She put up her veil, lifted the gilded case, looked at herself in the mirror steadily, critically, took the powder-puff and deftly used it. She knew instinctively that Baroudi liked to see her do this. When she was satisfied with her appearance she put the case down.

"It is charming," she said, touching it as it lay near her cup.

"It is for you."

"I will take it away this evening."

She wished there was a big diamond, or a big emerald, set in it somewhere. She had had to sell most of her finest jewels when the bad time had come in England.

"I must have a cigarette."

The coffee, the cigarette—they were both delicious. The warmth of the atmosphere was like satin about her body. She heard a little soft sound. An orange had dropped from a branch into the scarlet tangle of the geraniums.

"Why don't you talk to me?" she said to Baroudi.

But she said it with a lazy indifference. Was her purpose beginning to weaken in this morning made for dreaming, in this luxury of isolation with the silent man who always watched her?

"Why should I talk to you? I am not like those who make a noise always whether they have words within them that need to be spoken or not. What do you wish me to say to you?" he answered.

"Well——"

She took up the palm-leaf fan which he had laid upon the table.

"Let me see!"

How should she get at him? What method was the best? Somehow she did not feel inclined to be subtle with him. As she had powdered her face before him so she could calmly have applied the kohl to her eyelids, and so she could now be crude in speech with him. What a rest, what an almost sensuous joy that was! And she had only just realized it, suddenly, very thoroughly.

"What are you like?" she said. "I want to know."

She moved the fan gently, very languidly, to and fro.

"But you can tell me, because you can see me all the time, and I cannot see myself unless I take the glass," he said.

"Not outside, Baroudi, inside."

She spoke rather as if to a child.

"The man who shows all that is in him to a woman is not a clever man."

"But clever men often do that, without knowing they are doing it."

"You are thinking of your Englishmen," he said, but apparently without sarcasm.

She remembered their first conversation alone.

"The fine fellers—the rulers!" she said.

He did not answer her smile.

"Your Englishmen show what they are. They do not care to hide anything. If any one does not like all they are, so much the worse for him. Let him have a kick and no piastre. And to the women they are the same—no! that is not true."

He checked himself.

"No; to the men they are men who are ready to kick, but to the women they are boys. A woman takes a boy by the ear"—he put his left hand over his head and took hold of his right ear by the top—"so, and leads him where she pleases. So the woman leads the Englishman. But we are not like that."

She gazed at the brown hand that held the ear. How unnatural that action had seemed to her! Yet to him it was perfectly natural. Surely in everything he was the opposite of all that she was accustomed to. He took his hand away from his ear.

"How much have you been out of Egypt?" she asked him.

"Not very much. I have been three times to Naples in the hot weather. My father had a villa at Posilipo. I have been with my father to Vichy. I have been four times to Paris. I have been to Constantinople, and I have travelled in Syria."

"Did you go to Palestine?"

"Jerusalem—no. That is for Copts!"

He spoke with disdain. Then he added, with a sort of calm pride and a certain accession of dignity:

"I have been, of course, to Mecca."

"The real man—is he to be found in his religion?"

The thought came to her, and again she—she of all women! How strange that was!—felt the fascination of his faith.

"To Mecca!" she said.

Men passed through deserts to reach the holy places. Nigel one evening had told her something of that journey, and she had felt rather bored. Now she looked at a pilgrim who had gone with the Sacred Carpet, and she was bored no longer.

"Hamza—is he your servant?" she asked, with an apparent irrelevance, that was not really irrelevance.

"He is a donkey-boy at Luxor."

"Yes. He used not to be my donkey-boy. He has only been my donkey-boy since—since my husband has gone. They say in Luxor he is really a dervish."

"They say many things in Luxor."

"They call him the praying donkey-boy. Has he too been to Mecca?"

His face slightly changed. The eyes narrowed, the sloping brows came down. But after a short pause he answered:

"He went to Mecca with me. I paid for him to go."

She did not know much of Mohammedans, but she knew enough to be aware that Hamza was not likely to forget that benefit. And Baroudi had chosen Hamza to be her donkey-boy. She felt as if the hands of Islam were laid upon her.

"Hamza must be very grateful to you!" she said, slowly.

Baroudi made no reply. She looked away over the wild geraniums, down the alley between the trees to the hollow in the river-bank, and she saw a lateen sail glide by, and vanish behind the trees, going towards the south. In a moment another came, then a third, a fourth. The fourth was orange-coloured. For an instant she followed its course beyond the leaves of the orange-trees. How many boats were going southwards!

"All the boats are going southwards to-day," she said.

"The breeze is from the north," he answered, prosaically.

"I want to go further up the Nile."

"If you go, you should take a dahabeeyah."

"Like the *Loulia*. But I am sure there is not a second *Loulia* on the Nile."

"Do you think you would like to live for a time upon my *Loulia*?"

She nodded, without speaking.

More lateen sails went by, like wings. The effect of them was bizarre, seen thus from a distance and without the bodies to which they were attached. They became mysterious, and Mrs. Armine was conscious of their mystery. With Baroudi she felt strangeness, mystery, romance, things she had either as a rule ignored or openly jeered at during many years of her life. Did she feel them because he did? The question could not be answered till she knew more of what he felt.

"Perhaps it will be so. Perhaps you will live upon the *Loulia*," he said.

"How could I? And when?"

"We do in our lives many things we have said to ourselves we never shall do. And we often do them just at the times when we have thought they will be impossible to do."

"But you make plans beforehand."

"Do I?"

"Yes. Have you made a plan about the *Loulia*?"

She felt now that he had, and she felt that, like a fly in a web, she was enmeshed in his plan.

Another orange-coloured sail! Would she ever sail to the south in the *Loulia?*

"Will you not taste this jelly made of rose-leaves?"

Without touching the ground with his hands, he rose to his feet and stood by the table.

"Yes. Give me a little, but only a little."

He drew from one of his pockets a small silver knife, and, with a gentle but strong precision, thrust it into the rose-coloured sweetmeat and carefully detached a piece. Then he took the piece in his brown fingers and handed it to Mrs. Armine—who had been watching him with a deep attention, the attention a woman gives only to all the actions, however slight, of a man whose body makes a tremendous appeal to hers. She took it from him and put it into her mouth.

As she ate it, she shut her eyes.

"And now tell me—have you made a plan about the *Loulia?*" she said.

His face, as he looked at her, was a refusal to reply, and so it was not a denial.

"Live for the day as it comes," he said, "and do not think about to-morrow."

"That is my philosophy. But when you are thinking about to-morrow?"

Again she thought of Hamza, and she seemed to see those two, Baroudi and Hamza, starting together on the great pilgrimage. From it, perhaps made more believing or more fanatical, they had returned—to step into her life.

"Do you know," she said, "that either you, or something in Egypt, is—is——"

"What?" he asked, with apparent indifference.

"Is having an absurd effect upon me."

She laughed, with difficulty, frowned, sighed, while he steadily watched her. At that moment something within her was struggling, like a little, anxious, active creature, striving fiercely, minute though it was, to escape out of a trap. It seemed to her that it was the introduction of Hamza into her life by Baroudi that was furtively distressing her.

"I always do live for the day as it comes," she continued. "In English there's a saying, 'Eat, drink, and be merry, for to-morrow——'"

"To-morrow?"

"'To-morrow we die.'"

"Are you frightened of death?" he said.

There was an open contempt in his voice.

"You aren't?"

A light that she had never seen in them before shone in his eyes. Only from the torches of fatalism does such a light sometimes beacon out, showing an edge of the soul. It was gone almost before she had time to see it.

"Among men I may talk of such things," he said, "but not with women. Do you like the leaves of the roses?"

He held his knife ready above the sweetmeat.

"No; I don't want any more. I don't like it very much. The taste of it is rather sickly. Sit down, Baroudi."

She made a gesture towards the floor. He obeyed it, and squatted down. She had meant to "get at" this man. Well, she had accidentally got at something in him. He was apparently of the type of those Moslems who are ready to rush upon cold steel in order to attain a sensual Paradise.

Her languor, her dreaming mood in the bright silence of this garden of oranges on the edge of the Nile—they were leaving her now. The shadûf man cried again, and again she remembered a night of her youth, again she remembered "Aîda," and the uprising of her nature. She had been punished for that uprising—she did not believe by a God, who educates, but by the world, which despises. Could she be punished again? It was strange that though for years she had defied the world's opinion, since she had married again she had again begun, almost without being aware of it, to tend secretly towards desire of conciliating it. Perhaps that was ungovernable tradition returning to its work within her. To-day she felt, in her middle life, something of what she had felt then in her youth. When she had met for the first time at the opera the man for whom afterwards she had ruined herself, his fierce attraction had fallen upon her like a great blow struck by a determined hand. It had not stunned her to stupidity; it had roused her to feverish life. Now, after years, she was struck another blow, and again the feverish life leaped up within her. But between the two blows what great stretches of experience, and all the lost good opinion of the world! In the deep silence of the orange-garden just then premonition whispered to her. She longed for the renewed cry of the fellah to drown that sinister voice, but when it came, distant, yet loud, down the alley between the trees, it seemed to her like premonition's voice, suddenly raised in menace against her. And she seemed to hear behind it, and very far away, the world which had been her world once more crying shame upon her. Then for a moment she was afraid of herself, as if she stood away from her own evil, and looked at it, and saw, with a wonder mingled with horror, how capable it was.

Would she again set out to earn a punishment?

But how could she be punished again? The world had surely done its worst, and so lost its power over her. The arm that had wielded the lash had wielded it surely to the limit of strength. There could be nothing more to be afraid of.

And then—Nigel stood before the eyes of her mind.

In the exquisite peace of this garden at the edge of the Nile a storm was surging up within her. And Baroudi sat there at her feet, impassive, immobile, with his still, luminous eyes always steadily regarding her.

"My husband will soon be coming back!" she said, abruptly.

"And I shall soon be going up the river to Armant, and from Armant to Esneh, and from Esneh to Kom Ombos and Aswàn."

She felt as if she heard life escaping from her into the

regions of the south, and a coldness of dread encompassed her.

"There is a girl at Aswàn who is like the full moon," murmured Baroudi.

She realized his absolute liberty, and a heat as of fire swept over the cold. But she only said, with a smile:

"Why don't you sail for Aswàn to-night?"

"There is time," he answered. "She will not leave Aswàn until I choose for her to go."

"And are there full moons at Armant, and Esneh, and Kom Ombos?"

She seemed to be lightly laughing at him.

"At Esneh—no; at Kom Ombos—no."

"And Armant?"

A sharpness had crept into her lazy voice.

"There are French at Armant, and where the French come the little women come."

She remembered the pretty little rooms on the *Loulia*. He possessed a floating house—a floating freedom. At that moment she hated the dahabeeyah. She wished it would strike on a rock in the Nile and go to pieces. But he would be floating up the river into the golden south, while she travelled northwards to a tent in the Fayyūm! She could hardly keep her body still in her chair. She picked up one of the silver boxes, and tightened her fingers round it.

"Will you take a little more of the rose-leaf jelly?" he asked.

"No, no."

She dropped the box. It made a dry sound as it struck the table.

"I must stay at Armant some days. I have to look after my sugar interests there."

"Oh—sugar!" she exclaimed. "My husband may think you do nothing but look after your affairs, but you mustn't suppose a woman——"

"A woman—what?"

"I knew from the first you loved pleasure."

She took up the fan again.

"From the first? When was that?"

"On the *Hohenzollern*, of course."

"And I—I knew—I knew——"

He paused, smiling at her.

"What did you know?"

"Oh, I can understand something of women—when they permit me. And on the *Hohenzollern* you permitted me. Did you not?"

"I never spoke to you alone."

"It was not necessary. It was not at all necessary."

"Of course, I know that."

She was burning—her whole body was burning—with retrospective jealousy, and as she looked at him the flame seemed to be fanned, to give out more heat, to scorch her, sear her, more terribly. A man like this, an Eastern, utterly untrammelled, with no public opinion—and at this moment England, in her thought of it, seemed full of public opinion; Puritan England—to condemn him or restrain him, in this climate what must his life have been? And what would his life be? Something in her shrieked out against his freedom. She felt within her a pain that was almost intolerable; the pain of a no longer young, but forcible, woman, who was still brimful of life, and who was fiercely and physically jealous of a young man over whom she had no rights at all. Ah, if only she were twenty years younger! But—even now! She leaned her arms carelessly on the table, and managed to glance into the lid of the *boîte de beauté* which he had given her. The expression in the eyes that looked into hers from the lid startled her. Where was her experience? She was ashamed of herself. Crudity was all very well with this man, but—there were limits. She must not pass them without meaning to do so, without knowing she was doing so. And she had not lived her life since her divorce without discovering that the greatest *faux pas* a jealous woman can take is to show her jealousy. Husbands of other women had proved that to her up to the hilt, when she had been their refuge.

"Of course! You know much of men."

He spoke with a quiet assurance as of one in complete possession of her past. For the first time the question, "Has he heard of the famous Mrs. Chepstow? Does he—*know?*" flashed through her mind. It was possible. For he had been in Europe, to Paris. And he could read English, and perhaps had read many English papers.

"Did you ever hear of some one called 'Bella Donna'?" she said, slowly.

Her voice sounded careless, but her eyes were watching him closely.

"Bella Donna! But any beautiful woman may be that."

"Did you ever hear of Mrs. Chepstow?"

"No."

He stared at her, then added:

"Who is it. Does she come to Cairo in the winter?"

She felt certain he had not heard, and was not sure that she was glad. Her sort of fame might perhaps have attracted him. She wondered and longed to know. She longed to ask him many questions about his thoughts of women. But of course he would not tell her the truth. And men hate to be questioned by women.

"Does she come to Cairo?" he repeated.

"She was there once."

"You are Bella Donna," he said.

"You had to say that."

"Yes, but it is true. You are Bella Donna, but you are not donna onesta."

She did not resent the remark, which was made with an almost naïve gravity and directness. She was quite sure that Baroudi would never appreciate a woman because she was honest. Again she longed to hint at her notoriety, at the evil reputation she had acquired, which yet was a sort of fame.

"In—in Europe they often call me Bella Donna," she said.

"In Europe?"

"In England—London."

"They are right I shall call you Bella Donna here, beside the Nile."

He said it negligently, but something in her rejoiced. Nevertheless, she said, she could not help saying:

"And the full moon?"

"What about her?"

"Is she Bella Donna?"

He half closed his eyes and looked down.

"I don't ask you if she is *donna onesta.*"

He replied: "She is sixteen, and she is a dancing-girl."

"I understand,' she said, with an effort.

She shut her lips tightly and was silent, thinking of Nigel's return, of her departure with him to the Fayyûm, while this man, on his luxurious floating home, went on towards the south. She had resolved to live for the day. But when does any jealous woman live for the day? Jealousy hurls itself into the past and into the future, demanding of the one what was and of the other what will be. And—the canvas of a tent would enfold her, would make her prison walls! Why, why had she tied herself? A month ago, and she was utterly free. She could have gone to the south on the *Loulia.* Her whole body tingled, revolting against the yoke with which her will had burdened it. But when she spoke again her voice was lazy and calm?"

"I suppose you won't stay on the Nile for ever?"

Again her fingers closed mechanically on one of the boxes.

"But no! I shall have to go back to Assiut, and then to Cairo and Alexandria, the Delta, too."

"And the Fayyûm? Haven't you property there? Isn't it one of the richest districts in Egypt?"

He looked at her and smiled, slightly pouting his thick lips.

"Even if I could go to the Fayyûm, I don't think it would be much good," he answered.

He had no scruple in stripping her bare of subterfuge.

"I meant that your advice on Egyptian agriculture might be valuable to my husband," she retorted, with composure.

Something in his glance, in his tone, seemed suddenly to brace her, to restore her.

"Ah! that is true. Mr. Armeen would take my advice. In some ways he is not so very English."

"Then it would be kind to come to the Fayyūm and to give him the benefit of your advice."

He leaned towards her, and said:

"Bella Donna is not so very subtle!"

"You think subtlety so necessary?" she asked, with a light tinge of irony. "I really don't see why."

His eyes narrowed till they were only slits through which gleamed a yellowish light.

"When is your French maid going?" he asked.

She moved, and sat looking at him for a minute without replying. Had he read her thought of the morning?

"My maid!" she said at length. "What do you mean? Why should she go?"

"When is she going?" he repeated.

The brigand had suddenly reappeared in him.

"What an absurd idea! I can't possibly get on without a maid."

She still acted a careless surprise. An obscure voice within her—a voice that she scarcely recognized, whispered to her, "Resist!"

"When is she going?" he said once more, as if he had not heard her.

The man who was working by the shadûf cried out no more. No more did Mrs. Armine see, at the end of the long and narrow alley, behind the fretwork of shining, pointed leaves, the lateen sails go by. And the withdrawal of the crying voices and of the gliding sails seemed to leave this orange-garden at the very end of the world. The golden peace of the noon wrapped it as in a garment, the hem of which was wrought in geranium-red, in shining green, and in yellow turning to gold. But in this peace she was conscious of the need to struggle if she would dwell in safety. Soft seemed this garment that was falling gently about her. But was it not really deadly as a shirt of

Nessus, the poison of which would penetrate her limbs, would creep into her very soul?

It was, perhaps, a little thing, this question of the going, or not, of her maid, but she felt that if she resisted his will in this matter she would win a decisive battle, obtain security from a danger impending, whereas if she yielded in this she would be yielding the whole of her will to his.

"I won't yield!" she said to herself.

And then she looked at the brigand beside her, and something within her, that seemed to be the core of her womanhood, longed intensely to yield.

She had wished to get rid of Marie. Quite without prompting she had decided that very morning to send Marie away. Then how unreasonable it would be to refuse to do it just because he, too, wished the girl to go!

"Why do you want her to go?" she asked slowly, with her eyes upon him. "How can it matter to you whether my maid goes or stays?"

He only looked at her, opened his eyes widely, and laughed. He took another cigarette, lit it, and laughed again quietly, but with surely a real enjoyment of her pretence of ignorance, of her transparent hypocrisy. Nevertheless, she persisted.

"I can't see what such a thing can possibly have to do with you, or why it should interest you at all."

"I will find you a better maid."

"Hamza—perhaps?" she said.

"And why not Hamza?"

He looked at her, and was silent. And again she felt a sensation of fear. There was something deadly about the praying donkey-boy.

"When is that girl going?"

Mrs. Armine opened her lips to say, "She is not going at all." They said:

"I intend to get rid of her within the next few days. I always intended to get rid of her."

"Yes?"

"She isn't really a good maid. She doesn't understand my ways."

"Or she understands them too well," said Baroudi calmly. "When she is gone, I shall burn the alum upon the coals and give it to be eaten by a dog that is black. That girl has the evil eye."

XX

In the lodge in the garden of oranges, when the noontide was past and the land lay in the very centre of the gaze of the sun, Baroudi offered to Mrs. Armine an Egyptian dinner, or El-Ghada, served on a round tray of shining gold, which was set upon a low stool cased with tortoiseshell and ornamented with many small squares of mother-of-pearl. When she and Baroudi came into the room where they were to eat, the tray was already in its place, set out with white silk napkins, with rounds of yellow bread, and with limes cut into slices. The walls were hung with silks of shimmering green, and dull gold, and deep and sultry red. Upon the floor were strewn some more of the marvellous rugs, of which Baroudi seemed to have an unlimited supply. Round the room was the usual deep divan. Incense burned in a corner. Through a large window space, from which the hanging shutters were partially pushed back, Mrs. Armine saw a vista of motionless orange-trees.

She sat down on a pile of silken cushions which had been laid for her on the rugs. As she arranged her skirt and settled herself, from an earthen drum just outside the house and an arghool there came a crude sound of native music, to which almost immediately added itself a high and quavering voice, singing:

"*Doos ya' lellee! Doos ya' lellee!*"

At the same moment Aïyoub came into the room, without noise, and handed to Baroudi, who was sitting opposite to Mrs. Armine, with his left knee touching the rug and his right knee raised with his napkin laid over it, a basin of hammered brass with a cover, and a brass jug. Baroudi held forth his hands, and Aïyoub poured water upon them, which disappeared into the basin through holes pierced in the cover. Then, making a cup of his hands turned upwards, Baroudi received more water into it, conveyed it to his mouth, rinsed his mouth elaborately, and spat out the water upon the cover of the basin. Aïyoub carried away the basin and jug, Baroudi dried his hands on his napkin, and then muttered a word. It was "Bi-smi-llah!" but Mrs. Armine did not know that. She sat quite still, for a moment unseen, unthought of; she listened to the quavering voice, to the beaten drum and arghool, she smelt the incense, and she felt like one at a doorway peering in at an unknown world.

Almost immediately Aïyoub came back, and they began the meal, which was perpetually accompanied by the music. Aïyoub offered a red soup, a Kaw-ur-meh—meat stewed in a rich gravy with little onions—leaves of the vine containing a delicious sort of forcemeat, cucumbers in milk, some small birds pierced with silver skewers, spinach, and fried wheat flour mingled with honey. She was given a knife and fork and a spoon, all made of silver, and the plates were of silver, which did not harmonize well with the golden tray. Baroudi used only his fingers and pieces of bread in eating.

Mrs. Armine was hungry, and ate heartily. She knew nothing about Eastern cooking, but she was a gourmet, and realized that Baroudi's cook was an accomplished artist in his own line. During the meal she was offered nothing to drink, but directly it was over Aïyoub brought to her a beautiful cup of gold or gilded silver—she did not know which—and poured into it with ceremonial solemnity a small quantity of some liquid.

"What is it?" she asked Baroudi.

"Drink!" he replied.

She lifted the cup to her lips and drank a draught of water.

"Oh!" she said, with an intonation of surprised disappointment.

"*Lish rub el Moyeh en Nil awadeh!*" he said.

"What does that mean?"

" 'Who drinks Nile water must return.' "

She smiled, lifted the cup again to her lips, and drank the last drop of water.

"Nile water! I understand."

"And now you will have some sherbet."

He spoke to Aïyoub in Arabic. Aïyoub took away the cup, brought a tall, delicate glass, and having thrown over his right arm an elaborately embroidered napkin, poured into it from a narrow vase of china a liquid the colour of which was a soft and velvety green.

"Is this really sherbet?" Mrs. Armine asked.

"Sherbet made of violets."

"How is it made?"

"By crushing the flowers of violets, making them into a preserve with sugar, and boiling them for a long time.

Aïyoub stayed by her while she drank, and when she had finished he offered her the embroidered napkin. She touched it with her lips.

"Do you like it?"

"It is very strange. But everything here is strange."

Aïyoub brought once more to his master the basin with the cover and the jug, and Baroudi washed his hands and rinsed his mouth as at the beginning of the meal. After this ceremony he again muttered a word or words, rose to his feet, took Mrs. Armine's left hand with his right, and led her to the divan. Aïyoub brought coffee, lifted the golden tray from its stool, set the coffee on a smaller tray upon the stool close to the divan, and went out, carrying the golden tray very carefully. As he vanished, the music outside ceased with an abruptness, a lack of finality, that were startling to an European. The almost thrilling silence that succeeded was broken by a bird singing somewhere among the orange-trees. It was answered by another bird.

"They are singing the praises of God," said Baroudi, in a deep and slow voice, and as if he were speaking to himself.

"Those birds!"

She gazed at him in wonder. He looked at her with sombre eyes.

"You do not know these things."

Suddenly she felt like an ignorant and stupid child, like one unworthy of knowledge.

He sipped his coffee. He was now sitting in European fashion beside her on the divan, and his posture made it more difficult for her to accept his strange mentality; for he looked like a tremendously robust, yet very lithe and extremely handsome and determined young man, who might belong to a race of Southern Europe. Even with the tarbush upon his head his appearance was not unmistakably Eastern.

And this man, evidently quite seriously, talked to her about the birds singing to each other the praises of God.

"You ought to be differently dressed," she said.

"How?"

"In Egyptian clothes, not English flannels."

"Some day you shall see me like that," he said, reassuringly. "I often wear the kuftàn at night upon the *Loulia.*"

"At night upon the *Loulia!* Then how on earth can I see you in it?"

She spoke with a sudden sharp irritation. To-day her marriage with Nigel seemed to her like a sword suspended above her, which would presently descend upon her, striking her to earth with all her capacity for happiness unused.

"You will see me with the drawers of linen, the sudeyree, the kuftàn, the gibbeh—or, as says my father, jubbeh—and the turban on my head. Only you must wait a little. But women do not like to wait for a pleasure. They are always in a hurry."

The cool egoism with which he accepted and commented on her admiration roused in her, not anger, but a sort of almost wondering respect. It seemed part of his strength. He lifted his eyebrows, threw back his head, showing his magnificent throat, and with the gesture that she had noticed in the garden of the Villa Androud thrust two fingers inside his low, soft collar, and kept them there while he added:

"They are like children, and must be treated as children. But they can be very clever, too, when they want to trick. I know that. They can be as cunning as foxes, and as light-footed and swift as gazelles. But all that they do and all that they are is just for men. Women are made for men, and they know it so well that it is only about men that they think. I tell you that."

"No doubt it is true," she said, smilingly accepting his assertions.

"Women will run even after the Chinese shadow of a man if they are not shut close behind the grilles."

Mrs. Armine laughed outright.

"And so you Easterns generally keep them there."

"Well, and are we not wise? Are we not much wiser than the Mr. Armeens of Europe?"

His unexpected introduction of Nigel's name gave her a little shock, and the bad taste of it for an instant distressed even her tarnished breeding. But the sensation vanished directly as she remembered his Eastern birth.

"And you?" she said. "Would you never trust a woman?"

"Never," he calmly returned. "All women are alike. If they see the Chinese shadow, they must run after it. They cannot help themselves."

"You seem to forget that men are for ever running after the Chinese shadows of women," she retorted.

She thought of her own life, of how she had been worshipped and pursued, not *pour le bon motif*, but still——"

She would like him to know about all that.

"Men do that to please women, as to please a child you give it a sand lizard tied to a string. Put the string into its hand and the child is happy. So it is with a woman. Only she wants not the string, but the edge of a kuftàn."

It seemed to Mrs. Armine, as she listened to Baroudi, that she was permanently deposed from the place she had for long been accustomed to occupy. He tacitly demanded and accepted her admiration instead of giving her his. And yet—he had serenaded her on the Nile that first evening of her coming. He had bought Hamza and Ibrahim. He had desired and tried to effect the swift departure of Nigel. He had decreed that Marie must go. And the Nile water—with how much intention he had given it her to drink! And he had plans for the future. They seemed gathering about her silently, softly, like clouds changing the aspect of her world.

She had not turned that glove inside out yet.

She felt that she must alter her tactics, assert herself more strongly, escape from the modest position he seemed to be deliberately placing her in. Where was her pride, even of a courtesan?

She lifted her coffee-cup, emptied it, put it down, and began to pull on one of her long white gloves. Baroudi went on calmly smoking. She picked up the second glove. He sharply clapped his hands. Aïyoub entered, Baroudi spoke to him in Nubian, and he swiftly disappeared. Mrs. Armine pulled on the second glove.

"Now I must go home," she said.

She moved to get up, but her movement was arrested by the furtive entrance of a thin man clad in what looked to her like a bit of sacking, with naked arms, chest, legs, and feet, and a narrow, pointed head, completely shaved in front and garnished at the back with a mane of greasy black hair, which fell down upon his shoulders. In his hand, which was almost black, he held a short stick of palm-wood, and with an air of extravagant mystery, mingled with cunning, he crept round the room close to the walls, alternately whistling and clucking, bending his head, as if peering at the floor, then lifting it to gaze up at the ceiling. He had shot a keen glance at Mrs. Armine as he came in, but he seemed at once to forget her, and to be wholly intent upon his inexplicable occupation.

After moving several times in this manner round the room, he stopped short, almost like a dog pointing, then drew from inside his coarse garment a wrinkled receptacle of discoloured leather with a widely-opened mouth, cried out some words in a loud, fierce voice, leaped upwards, and succeeded in striking the ceiling with his stick.

A long serpent fell down into the bag.

Mrs. Armine uttered a cry of surprise, but not of alarm. She was not afraid of snakes. The darweesh went creeping about as before, presently called out some more words, and struck at the wall. A second serpent fell into the bag, or seemed to fall into it, from some concealed place among the silken draperies. Again he crept about, called, struck, and received another reptile. Then a little dark-eyed boy ran in, salaaming, and the darweesh and the boy, to the accompaniment of wild music played outside, went through a performance of snake-charming and jugglery familiar enough in the East, yet, it seems, eternally interesting to Easterns, and fascinating to many travellers. When it was over the little boy salaamed and ran out, but the music, which was whining and intense, still went on, and the darweesh advanced, holding his bag of snakes, and stood still before Mrs. Armine. For the first time he fixed his cunning and ferocious eyes, which were suffused with blood, steadily upon her, as if he desired to hypnotize her, or to inspire her with deadly fear. She returned his gaze steadily and calmly, and held out her hand towards the bag, indicating by a gesture that she wished to handle the serpents. The darweesh, still staring at her, and very slowly, put the bag close to her, holding it under her breast. A curious musty smell, like the scent of something terribly old, came to her nostrils. She hesitated for a moment, then deliberately pulled off her gloves, put them on the divan, stood up, and plunged her right hand into the bag, at the same time shutting her eyes. She shut them to enjoy with the utmost keenness a sensation entirely new.

Her hand encountered a dry and writhing life, closed upon it firmly but gently, drew it out and towards her. Then she opened her eyes, and saw that she had taken from the dark a serpent that was black with markings of a dull orange colour. It twisted itself in her hand, as if trying to escape, but as she held it firmly it presently became quieter, lifted itself, reared up its flat head, and seemed to regard her with its feverish and guilty eyes, which were like the eyes of something consciously criminal that must always be unrepentant. She looked at those eyes, and she felt a strong sympathy for the creature, and no sense of fear at all. Slowly she brought it nearer to her, nearer, nearer, till it wavered out from her hand and attained her body.

The darweesh always stood before her, but the expression in his eyes had changed, was no longer hypnotic and terrible, but rather deeply observant. Baroudi sat quite still upon the divan. He looked from Mrs. Armine to the serpent, then looked again at her. And she, feeling these two men absolutely concentrated upon her, was happy and at ease. Swiftly the serpent wound itself about her, and, clinging to her waist, thrust forth the upper part of its body towards the darweesh, shooting out its ribbon of a tongue, which quivered like something frail in a draught of wind. It lowered and raised itself several times, rhythmically, as if in an effort to obey the whining music and to indulge in a dancing movement. Then, as a long shrill note was held, it again reared itself up, till its head was level with Mrs. Armine's ear, and remained there quivering, and turning itself slowly from side to side with a flexibility that was abominable and sickening. The music ceased. There was a moment's pause. Then, with a fierce movement that seemed expressive of a jealousy which could no longer be contained, the darweesh seized the snake about two inches below its head, and tore it away from Mrs. Armine. The terrible look had returned to his face with an added fire that beaconed a revengeful intention. Pressing his thumb hard upon the reptile's back, he seemed to fall into a frenzy. He several times growled on a deep note, bowed back and forth, tossing his mane of greasy hair over his face and away from it, depressed his body, then violently drew it up to its full height, while his bare feet executed a sort of crude dance. Then, wrought up apparently to a pitch of fanatical fury, he bent his head, opened his mouth, from which came beads of foam, and bit off the serpent's head. Casting away its body, which still seemed writhing with life, he made a sound of munching, working his jaws extravagantly, shot forth his head towards Mrs. Armine, gaped to show her his mouth was empty, lifted his bag from the floor and rushed noiselessly from the room. She stood looking at the headless body of the reptile which lay on the rug at her feet.

"Take it away!" she said to Baroudi.

He picked it up, went to the window, and threw it out into the orange-garden. Then he came back and stood beside her.

"Horrible brute!" she said.

She spoke angrily. When the darweesh had attacked the serpent she had felt herself attacked, and the killing of it had seemed to her an outrage committed upon herself. Even now that he was gone and the headless body was flung away, she could not rid herself of this sensation. She was full of an intimate sense of fury that longed to be assuaged.

"How could you let the brute do that?" she exclaimed, turning upon Baroudi. "How could you sit there and allow such a hateful thing?"

"But he came here to do it. He is one of the Saadeeyeh."

"He was going to do it even if I hadn't taken the serpent?"

"Of course."

"I don't believe that. He did it because he was angry with the serpent for not hurting me, for letting me take it."

"As you please," he said. "What does it matter?"

She glanced at him, and sat down. The expression in his eyes soothed her, the new look that she could read. Had it been called up by her courage with the serpent? She wondered if, by her impulsive action, she had grasped something in him which till now had seemed to elude her. Nevertheless, although her mood was changing, the sense of personal outrage had not completely died out of her.

"There really are other serpent eaters?" she asked.

"Of course. Saadees."

"And that man is one? But he hated my taking the serpent."

"But I did not hate it."

"No."

More strongly she felt that she had grasped something in him which had eluded her till now.

"Sit there for a minute quietly," he said, with a gentleness that, though far less boyish, recalled to her mind the smiling gentleness of Ibrahim. "And I will give you a new pleasure, and all your anger will go from you as the waves go from the Nile when the breeze has died away."

"What is it?"

His eyes were full of a sort of happy cunning like a child's.

"Sit there and you will know."

He went out of the room, and came back in a moment carrying a good-sized box carefully wrapped in silver paper. She began to think that he was going to give her another present, perhaps some wonderful jewel. But he undid the silver paper cautiously, opened a red-leather case, and displayed a musical box. After placing it tenderly upon the coffee-table, he bent down and set it going. There was a click, a slight buzzing, and then upon Mrs. Armine's enraptured ears there fell the strains of an old air from a forgotten opera of Auber's, "Come o'er the Moonlit Sea!"

The change from the Saadee's atmosphere of savage fanaticism to this mild and tinkling insipidity threw Mrs. Armine's nerves off their balance.

"Oh, Baroudi!" she said.

Her lips began to tremble. She turned away her head. The effort not to betray her almost hysterical amusement, which was combined with an intense desire to pet this great, robust child, almost suffocated her. There was a click. The music stopped.

"Wait a moment!" she heard him say.

And his voice sounded grave, like an intensely appreciative child's.

Click! "Parigi, O Cara!"

Mrs. Armine governed herself, drew breath, and once more turned towards Baroudi. On his strong, bold face there was the delighted expression of a boy. She looked, looked at him, and all her half-tender amusement died away, and again, as in the Villa Androud, she was encompassed by fear. The immense contrasts in this man, combined with his superb physique, made him to her irresistibly fascinating. In him there was a complete novelty to appeal to her jaded appetites, rendered capricious and uneasy by years of so-called pleasure. A few minutes ago, when he had spoken of death, he had been a mysterious and cruel fatalist. Now he was a deliciously absurd child, but a child with the frame of a splendid man.

The musical box clicked. "Salve Dimora."

"Do you feel better?" he asked her.

She nodded.

"I bought it in Naples."

He lifted the box in his strong brown hands, and held it nearer to her. Nothing in his face betrayed any suspicion that she could be amused in an ironical sense. It was obvious that he supposed her to be as happily impressed as he was.

"You hear it better now."

She nodded again. Then:

"Hold it close to my ear," she said, in a whisper, keeping her eyes upon him.

He obeyed. Once his hand touched her ear, and she felt its warm dryness, and she sighed.

"Salve Dimora" ceased.

"Another!" she said.

And she said, "Another!" and "Another!" until the box's repertoire was finished, and then she made him turn on once more, "Come o'er the Moonlit Sea!"

Her gloves lay on the divan beside her, and she did not draw them on again. She did not even pick them up till the heat of the sun's rays was declining, and the musical box had long been silent.

"I must go," she said at last.

She put her hands up to her disordered hair.

"Indeed I must."

She looked at her watch and started up.

"It's horribly late. Where is Ibrahim?"

Ibrahim's smiling face was seen at the window.

"The donkey, Ibrahim! I want the donkey at once!"

"All what you want you must have."

He nodded his head, as if agreeing passively with himself, and looked on the ground.

"Hamza he ready. Hamza very good donkey-boy."

"That's right. I am coming," she said.

Ibrahim saluted, still smiling, and disappeared. Mrs. Armine walked to the window and looked out.

It was already the time of sunset, and the unearthly radiance of the magical hour in this land of atmospheric magic began to fall upon the little isolated house, upon the great garden of oranges by which it was encircled. The dry earth of the alleys glowed gently; the narrow trunks of the trees became delicately mysterious; the leaves and the treasure they guarded seemed, in their perfect stillness, to be full of secret promises. Still the birds that dwelled among them were singing to each other softly the praises of God.

Mrs. Armine looked out, listened to the birds, while the sun went down in the west she could not see. And now Magrib was over, and the first time of the Moslem's prayer was come.

She wished she need not go, wished it so keenly, so fiercely, that she was startled by her own desire almost as if it had been a spectre rising suddenly to confront her. She longed to remain in this lodge in the wilderness, to be overtaken by the night of the African stars in the Villa of the Night of Gold. Now she heard again the far-away voice of the fellah by the shadûf, warning her surely to go. Or was it not, perhaps, telling her to stay? It was strange how that old, dead passion, which had metamorphosed her life, returned to her mind in this land. In its shackles at first she had struggled. But at last she had abandoned herself, she had become its prisoner. She had become its slave. Then she was young. She was able to realize how far more terrible must be the fate of such a slave who is young no longer. Again the fellah cried to her from the Nile, and now it seemed to her that his voice was certainly warning her that she must withdraw herself, while yet there was time, from the hands of El-Islâm—while yet there was time!

She had been so concentrated upon herself and her own fears and desires that, though part of her had been surely thinking of Baroudi, part of her had forgotten his existence near her. As a factor in her life she had been, perhaps, considering him, but not as a man in the room behind her. The outside world, with its garden of dreaming trees, its gleaming and dying lights, its voices of birds, and more distant voice from the Nile, had subtly possessed her, though it had not given her peace. For when passion, even of no high and ideal kind, begins to stir in a nature, it rouses not only the bodily powers, but powers more strange and remote—powers perhaps seldom used, or for long quite disregarded; faculties connected with beauty that is not of man; with odours, with lights, and with voices that have no yearning for man, but that man takes to his inner sanctuary, as his special possession, in those moments when he is most completely alive.

But now into this outer world came an intruder to break a spell, yet to heighten for the watcher at the window fascination and terror. As the fellah's voice died away, and Mrs. Armine moved, with an intention surely of flight from dangerous and inexorable hands, Hamza appeared at a short distance from her among the orange-trees. He spread a garment upon the earth, folded his hands before him, then placed them upon his thighs, inclined himself, and prayed. And as he made his first inclination of humble worship in the little room behind her Mrs. Armine heard a low murmuring, almost like the sound of bees in sultry weather. She turned, and saw Baroudi praying, on a prayer-rug with a niche woven in it, which was duly set towards Mecca.

She, the unbeliever, was encompassed by prayer. And something within her told her that the moment for flight already lay behind her, that she had let it go by unheeded, that the hands which already had touched her would not relax their grasp until—what?

She did not answer that question.

But when the fellah cried out once more in the distance, it seemed to her that she heard a savage triumph in his voice.

XXI

A WEEK later Mrs. Arminè received a telegram from Cairo:

"Starting to-night, arrive to-morrow morning. Love—Nigel."

She had been expecting such a message; she had known that it must come; yet when Hassan brought it into the garden, where she was sitting at the moment, she felt as if she had been struck. Hassan waited calmly beside her till, with an almost violent gesture, she showed him there was no answer. When he had gone she sat for a moment with the telegram on her knees; then she cried out for Ibrahim. He heard her voice, and came, with his sauntering gait, moving slowly among the rose-trees.

"I've a telegram from Cairo," she said.

She took up the paper and showed it to him.

"My lord Arminigel—he is comin' back?"

"Yes."

"That is very good noos, very nice noos indeed," said Ibrahim, with an air of sleepy satisfaction.

"He starts to-night, and will be here with the express to-morrow morning."

"This is a most bootiful business!" said Ibrahim, blandly. "My lord he has been away so long he will be glad to see us again."

She looked at him, but he did not look at her. Turning a flower in his white teeth, he was gazing towards the river, with an unruffled composure which she felt almost as a rebuke. But why should it matter to him? Baroudi had paid him. Nigel paid him. He had no reason to be upset.

"When he comes," she said, "he will take me away to the Fayyûm."

"Yes. The Fayyūm is very nice place, very good place indeed. There is everythin' there; there is jackal, pidgin, duck, lots and lots of sugar-cane; there is water, there is palm-trees; there is everythin' what any one him want."

"Ah!" she said.

She got up, with a nervously violent movement.

"What's the good of all that to you?" she said. "You're not going with us to the Fayyūm, I suppose."

He said nothing.

"Are you?" she exclaimed.

"Suttinly."

"You are coming. How do you know? Has Mr. Armine told you?"

"My lord, he tell me nothin', but I comin' with you, and Hamza him comin' too."

"Hamza is coming?"

"Suttinly."

She was conscious of a sensation of relief that was yet mingled with a faint feeling of dread.

"Why—why should Hamza come with us?" she asked.

"To be your donkey-boy. Hamza he very good donkey-boy."

"I don't know—I am not sure whether I shall want Hamza in the Fayyūm."

Ibrahim looked at her with a smiling face.

"In the Fayyūm you will never find good donkey-boy, my lady, but you will do always what you like. If you not like to take Hamza, Hamza very sad, very cryin' indeed, but Hamza he stay here. You do always what you think."

When he had finished speaking, she knew that Hamza

would accompany them; she knew that Baroudi had ordered that Hamza was to come.

"We will see later on," she said, as if she had a will in this matter.

She looked at her watch.

"It's time to start."

"The felucca him ready," remarked Ibrahim. "This night the *Loulia* sailin'; this night the *Loulia* he go to Armant."

Mrs. Armine frowned. Armant—Esneh—Kom Ombos —and then Aswàn! The arbitrariness of her nature was going to be scourged with scorpions by fate, it seemed. How was she to endure that scourging? But—there was to-day. When was she going to learn really to live for the day? What a fool she was! Still frowning, and without saying another word, she went upstairs quickly to dress.

It was past midnight when she returned to the villa. There was no moon; wind was blowing fiercely, lashing the Nile into waves that were edged with foam, and whirling grains of sand stripped away from the desert over the prairies and gardens of Luxor. The stars were blotted out, and the night was cold and intensely dark. She held on tightly to Ibrahim's arm as she struggled up the bank from the river, and almost felt her way to the house, from which only two lights gleamed faintly. The French windows of the drawing-room were locked, and they went round the house to the front door. As Ibrahim put up his hand to ring the bell, a sudden fear came to Mrs. Armine. Suppose Nigel had started earlier from Cairo than he had intended? Suppose he had returned and was then in the house? She caught Ibrahim's hand. He said something which was carried away and lost to her in the wind. She dropped his hand; he rang, and in a moment the door was opened by Hassan.

"Ask him if—if anything has happened, if there is any message, anything for me!" she said to Ibrahim directly she was in the house.

Ibrahim spoke to Hassan in Arabic.

"My lady, he says there is nothin'."

"Very well. I'll go to bed. Good night, Ibrahim."

And she went upstairs.

When she was in her bedroom she shut the door and sat down just as she was, with a veil over her face, the collar of her dust-coat turned up, her shining hair dishevelled by the angry hands of the gale. A lamp was burning on the dressing-table, upon which, very oddly arranged, stood a number of silver things, brushes, bottles, boxes, which were usually in the dressing-room. They were set out in a sort of elaborate and very fantastic pattern, which recalled to her sharply a fact. She had no longer a maid. She had got rid of Marie, who had left Luxor on the previous day, neither tearful nor, apparently, angry, but looking sharp, greedy, and half-admiringly inquisitive to the very last. Mrs. Armine had come to her two days before holding an open letter from Nigel, and had announced to her his decision that a lady's maid in the Fayyūm would be an impossibility, and that Marie would have to be left behind, for the time, at Luxor. And then had followed a little scene admirably played by the two women; Mrs. Armine deploring the apparent necessity of their separation, but without undue feeling or any exaggeration; Marie regretting "monsieur's" determination to carry " une dame si délicate, si fine " into "un monde si terrible, si sauvage," but at the same time indicating, with a sly intention and the most admirably submissive *nuances*, the impossibility of her keeping house in the villa alone with a group of Nubians. Both women had really enjoyed themselves, as talent must when exercising itself with perfect adroitness. Mrs. Armine had regretted Marie's decision, while at the same time applauding her maidenly *délicatesse,* and had presently, by chance, discovered that several charming purchases from Paris were no good to her, that two or three remarkably attractive gowns made her look "like nothing at all," and that, as she was going to the Fayyūm, she "couldn't be bothered with" some hats that were, as Marie had often said, *"plus chic que le diable!*" Then a wonderful "character" had been written out, signed, and had changed hands, with an exceedingly generous cheque. Certain carelessly delivered promises had been made which Marie knew would be kept. She had given a permanent address in France, and the curtain had slowly fallen. Ah, the pity of it that there had been no audience! But talent, like genius, should be its own consolation and reward.

So now Hassan arranged Mrs. Armine's "things." She was thankful that Marie had gone, yet she felt utterly lost without a maid. Never, since she was a young girl, had she been accustomed to do anything for herself that a good maid could do for her. And there was not a woman-servant in the house. She was tired, she was terribly strung up; her nerves were all on edge; her heart was aflame with a jealousy which, she knew too well, was destined to be fanned and not to be assuaged in the days that lay before her. And she felt profoundly depressed. It was awful to come home in such a condition in the dead of the night, and to be deprived of all one's comforts. When she saw those silver things all laid out wrongly, the brushes pointing this way and that, the combs fixed in them with the teeth upwards, the bottles of perfume laid on their sides instead of standing erect, the powder-boxes upside down, she felt ready to cry her eyes out. And no one to take away her hat, to loosen and brush her hair, to get her out of her gown, to unlace her shoes! And Nigel at nine o'clock to-morrow!

The wind roared outside. One of the hanging wooden shutters that protected the windows had got loose, and was now, at short intervals, striking against the wall with a violent sound that suggested to her a malefactor trying to break in. She knew what caused the reiterated noise; she knew she could probably stop it by opening the window for a moment and putting out her hand. And yet she felt afraid to do this, afraid to put out her hand into the windy darkness, lest it should be grasped by another hand. She was full of nervous fears.

As she sat there, she could scarcely believe she was in

Egypt. The roaring of the wind suggested some bleak and Northern clime. The shutter crashed against the wall. At last she could bear the noise no longer, and she got up, went out on to the landing, and called out: "Ibrahim!"

There was no answer. The lights were out. She felt afraid of the yawning darkness.

"Ibrahim! Ibrahim!" she cried.

She heard the sough of drapery, and a soft and striding step. Somebody was coming quickly. She drew back into her room, and Ibrahim appeared.

"My lady, what you want?"

She pointed to the window.

"The shutter—it's got loose. Can you fasten it? It's making such an awful noise. I shan't be able to sleep all night."

He opened the window. The wind rushed in. The lamp flared up and went out.

For two or three minutes Mrs. Armine heard nothing but the noise of the wind, which seemed to have taken entire possession of the chamber, and she felt as if she were its prey and the prey of the darkness. Something that was like hysteria seized upon her, a desperate terror of fate and the unknown. In the wind and in the darkness she had a grievous sensation of helplessness and of doom, of being lost for ever to happiness and light. And when the wind was shut out, when a match grated, a little glow leaped up, and Ibrahim, looking strangely tall and vast in the black woollen abâyeh which he had put on as a protection against the cold, was partially revealed, she sprang towards him with a feeling of unutterable relief.

"Oh, Ibrahim, what an awful night! I'm afraid of it!" she said.

Deftly he lit the lamp; then he turned to her and stared.

"My lady, you are all white, like the lotus what Rameses him carry."

She had laid her hand on his arm. Now she let it drop, sat down on the sofa, unpinned her hat and veil, and threw them down on the floor.

"It's the storm. I hate the sound of wind at night."

"The ginnee him ride in the wind," said Ibrahim, very seriously.

"The ginnee! What is that?"

"Bad spirit. Him come to do harm. Him bin in the room to-night."

They looked at each other in silence. Then Mrs. Armine said:

"Is the shutter quite safe now?"

"Suttinly."

"Then good night, Ibrahim."

"Good night, my lady."

He went over to the door.

"Suttinly the ginnee him bin in the room to-night," he said, solemnly.

She tried to smile at this absurdity, but her lips refused to obey her will.

"Who should he come for?" she asked.

"I dunno. P'raps he come to meet my Lord Arminigel. It is bad night to-night. Mohammed him die to-night. Him die on the night from Sunday Monday."

He drooped morosely and went out, softly closing the door behind him.

As soon as he had gone Mrs. Armine undressed, leaving her clothes scattered pell-mell all over the room, and got into her bed. She kept the lamp burning. She was afraid of the dark, and she knew she would not sleep. Although she laughed at Egyptian superstition, as she glanced about the room she was half unconsciously looking for the shadowy form of a ginnee. All night the wind roared, and all night she lay awake, wondering, fearing, planning, imagining, in terror of the future, yet calling upon her adroitness, her strong fund of resolution, to shape it as she willed.

And she would have helpers—Baroudi, Ibrahim, Hamza.

When at dawn the wind died down, and at last slumber, like a soft wave, came stealing over her, the last thing she saw with her imagination was Hamza, straight, enigmatic, grave, holding an upright wand in his hand.

Or was it the ginnee, who had come in out of the night to meet "my lord Arminigel"?

* * * * * *

What was that? Was it the ginnee moving, speaking? Was it——? There had surely been a movement in the room, a sound. She opened her eyes, and saw sunshine and some one by the bed.

"Ruby!"

She blinked, stared, lying perfectly still.

"Ruby!"

She felt a hand on one of her hands. The touch finally recalled her from sleep, and she knew the morning and Nigel. He stood beside the bed in loose travelling clothes, dusty, with short, untidy hair, and a radiant brown face, looking down on her, holding her hand.

"Did I frighten you? I didn't mean to. But I thought you must be awake by now."

There was no sound of reproach in his voice, but there was perhaps just a touch of disappointment. She sat up, leaning against the big pillow.

"And I meant to be at the station to meet you!" she said.

He sat down close to the bed, still keeping his hand on hers.

"You did?"

"Of course. It's this horrid habit I've got into of lying awake at night and sleeping in the morning. And there was such a storm last night."

"I know. The ginnee were abroad."

He spoke laughingly, but she said:

"How did you know that?"

"How? Why, in Egypt—but what do you mean?"

But she had recovered herself, was now fully awake, fully herself, entirely freed from the thrall of the night.

"How well you look!" she said.

"Work!" he replied. "Sun—life under the tent! It's glorious! How I want you to love it! But, I say, shan't we have some tea together? And then I'll jump into a bath. It's too cold for the Nile this morning. And I'm all full of dust. I'll ring for Marie."

He moved, but she caught his hand.

"Nigel!"

"Yes?"

"Don't ring for Marie."

"Why not?"

"It wouldn't be any use."

"What—is she ill?"

"She's gone."

"Gone!"

He looked at the confusion of the room, at the clothes strewn on the furniture and the floor.

"Now I understand all that," he said. "But what was the matter? Did she steal something, or—perhaps I ought to have had another woman in the house."

"No, no; it wasn't that. I sent her away quite amicably; because I thought she'd be in our way in the Fayyūm. What could we do with her in a tent?"

"You're going to manage without a maid?"

A radiant look of pleasure came into his face.

"You're a trump!" he said.

He bent down, put his hands gently on her shoulders, and gave her a long kiss.

"And this is how you're managing!" he added, lifting himself up, and speaking with a sort of tender humour as again he looked at the room. "I must learn to maid you."

And he went about rather clumsily getting the things together, picking them up by the wrong end, and laying them in a heap on the sofa.

"I'll do better another time," he said, when he had finished, rather ruefully surveying his handiwork. "And now I'll call Hassan and get tea, and while we're having it I'll tell you about our camp in the Fayyûm. To think of your giving up your maid!"

He kissed her again, with a lingering tenderness, and went out.

As soon as he was gone she got up. She had to search for a wrapper. She did not know where any of her things were. How maddening it was to be without a maid! More than once, now that Nigel was back and she could not go to Baroudi, she almost wished that she had kept Marie. Would it have been very unwise to keep her? She pulled out drawer after drawer. She was quite hot and tired before she had found what she wanted. What would life be like in a tent? She almost sickened at the thought of all that was before her. Ah! here was the wrapper at last. She tore it out from where it was lying with reckless violence, and put it on anyhow; then suddenly her real nature, the continuous part of her, asserted itself. She went to the mirror and adjusted it very carefully, very deftly. Then she twisted up her hair simply, and considered herself for a moment.

Had the new truth stamped itself yet upon her face, her body?

She saw before her a woman strongly, strikingly alive, thrilling with life. The eyes, released from sleep, were ardent, were full of the promises of passion; the lips were fresh, surely, and humid; the figure was alluring and splendid; the wonderful line of the neck had kept all its beauty. She had grown younger in Egypt, and she knew very well why. For her the new truth was clearly stamped, but not for Nigel. He would read it wrongly; he would take it for himself, as so many deceived men from the beginning of time have taken the truths of women, thinking "All this is for me." She looked long at herself, and she rejoiced in the vital change that had come over her, and, rejoicing, she came to the resolve of a vain woman. She must exert all her will to keep with her this Indian summer. She must school her nature, govern her passions, drill her mind to accept with serenity what was to come—dulness, delay, the long fatigues of playing a part, the ennui of tent life, of this *solitude à deux* in the Fayyūm. She must not permit this opulence of beauty to be tarnished by the ravages of jealousy; for jealousy often destroys the beauty of women, turns them into haggard witches. But she would not succumb; for, in her creed beauty was everything to a woman, and the woman who had lost her beauty had ceased to count, was scarcely any more to be numbered among the living. This sight and appreciation of herself suddenly seemed to arm her at all points. Her depression, which had peopled the night with horrors and the morning with apprehensions, departed from her. She was able to believe that the future held golden things, because she was able to believe in her own still immense attraction.

That day she contented Nigel, she fascinated him, she charmed him with her flow of animal spirits. He could deny her nothing. And when, laughingly, she begged him, as she had dispensed with a maid, to let her have her own special donkey-boy and donkey in the Fayyûm, he was ready to acquiesce.

"We'll take Mohammed, of course, if you wish," he said, heartily, "though there are lots of donkey-boys to be got where we are going."

"I've given up Mohammed," she said.

He looked surprised.

"Have you? What's he done?"

"Nothing specially. But I prefer Hamza."

"The praying donkey-boy!"

"Yes."

She paused; then, looking away from him, she said slowly:

"There's something strange to me and interesting about him. I think it comes, perhaps, from his intense belief in his religion, his intense devotion to the Moslem's faith. I—I can't help admiring that, and I should like to take Hamza with us. He's so different from all the others."

Then, with a changed and lighter tone, she added:

"Besides, his donkey is the best on the river. It comes from Syria, and is a perfect marvel. Give me Hamza, his donkey, and Ibrahim as my suite, and you shall never hear a complaint from me, I promise you."

"Of course you shall have them," he said. "I like the man to whom his beliefs mean something, even if they're not mine and could never be mine."

So the fate of Hamza and Ibrahim was very easily settled.

But when Nigel called Ibrahim, and told him that he had decided on taking him and Hamza to the Fayyūm, and that he was to tell Hamza at once, Ibrahim looked a little doubtful.

"All what my gentleman want I do," he said. "But Hamza do much business in Luxor; I dunno if him come to the Fayyūm."

He glanced deprecatingly at Mrs. Armine.

"I very glad to come, but about Hamza I dunno."

He spoke with such apparent sincerity that she was almost deceived, and thought that perhaps some difficulty had really arisen.

"Offer him his own terms," exclaimed Nigel, "and I'll bet he'll be glad to come."

"I go to see, my gentleman."

"You shall have him, Ruby, whatever his price," said Nigel.

Ibrahim, with great difficulty, he said, made a bargain with Hamza, and on the following day the Villa Androud was left in Hassan's charge, and the Armines went north by the evening express to Cairo, where they were to stay two days and nights, in order that Mrs. Armine might see the Pyramids and the Sphinx. Nigel had already taken rooms at the Mena House, with a terrace exactly opposite to the Great Pyramid, and giving on to the sand of the desert.

They breakfasted at Shepheard's, then hired a victoria to drive up Ismail's road under the meeting lebbek-trees. Nigel was in glorious spirits. It seemed to him that morning as if his life were culminating, as if he were destined to a joy of which he was scarcely worthy. An unworldly man, and never specially fond of society or anxious about its edicts and its opinions, he did not suffer, as many men might have done, under his knowledge of its surprised pity for him, or even contempt. But in his secret heart he was glad that he was cut out of the succession to his family's title and the estates. Had he succeeded to them, his position would at once have become more difficult, his situation with Ruby far more complicated. As things were, they two were free as the wind. His soul leaped up to their freedom.

"I feel like a nomad to-day!" he exclaimed. "By Jove, though! isn't the wind cold? It always blows in the winter over these flats. Wrap yourself well up, darling."

He put up his hand to draw the furs more closely round her. When with her now he so easily felt protective that he was perpetually doing little things for her, and he did them with a gentleness of touch that, coming from a man of his healthy strength and vigour, revealed the progress made by the inner man in absence.

"I must be your maid," he added.

"But you'll be working and shooting," she said, speaking out of the depths of her furs in a low voice.

Her face was shrouded in a veil which seemed to muffle her words, and he only just heard them.

"You come first. I am going to look after you before anything else," he said.

She pulled up her veil till her lips were free of it.

"But I want your work to come first," she said, speaking with more energy. "I hate the woman who marries a man because she admires his character, and who then seeks by every means to change it, to reduce him from a real man to—well, to a sort of male lady's maid. No, Nigel; stick to your work, and I'll manage all right."

She felt just then that she could not endure it if he were always intent on her in the Fayyûm. And yet she wished him to be her slave, and she always wished to be adored by men. But now there was something within her which might, perhaps, in the fulness of time even get the upper hand of her vanity.

"We'll see," he answered. "It'll be all right about the work, Ruby. You see the Pyramids well now."

She looked across the flats to those great tombs which draw the world to their feet.

"I wish it wasn't so horribly cold," she said.

And Baroudi was away in the gold of the south, and perhaps with the "Full Moon."

"It won't be half so bad when we get to Mena House. There's always a wind on this road in winter."

"And in the Fayyūm? Will it be cold there?"

"No, not like this. Only at nights it gets cold sometimes, and there's often a thick mist."

"A thick mist!"

"But we shall be warm and cosy in our tent, and we shall know nothing about it."

And the *Loulia* was floating up the Nile into the heart of the gold! Her heart sank. But then she remembered her resolution in the villa. And her vanity, and that which a moment ago had seemed to be fighting against it, clasped hands in resistant friendship.

The victoria rolled smoothly; the horses trotted fast in the brisk air; the line of the desert, pale and vague in the windy morning, grew more distinct, more full of summons; the orifice that was the end of the avenue gaped like a mouth that opens more widely. A line of donkeys appeared, with here and there a white camel with tasselled trappings, surrounded by groups of shouting Egyptians, who stared at the carriage with avaricious eyes. "Ah—ah!" shouted the coachman. The horses broke into a gallop, turned into a garden on the right, and drew up before the Mena House.

A minute later Mrs. Armine was standing on a terrace that ended in a sea of pale yellow sand. Nigel followed her, but only after some minutes.

"You seem to know everybody here," she said to him, in a slightly constrained voice, as he came to stand beside her.

"Well, there are several fellows from Cairo come here to spend Sunday."

"With their wives apparently."

"Yes, some of them. Of course last winter I got to know a good many people. It's much warmer here. We get all the sun, and there's much less wind. And isn't the Great Pyramid grand?"

He took her gently by the arm.

"The Sphinx is beyond. I want you to see that for the first time just before nightfall, Ruby."

"Whatever you like," she said.

Her voice still sounded constrained. On the veranda and in the hall of the hotel she had had to run the gauntlet, and now that she was married again, and had abandoned the defiant life which she had led for so many years, somehow she had become less careless of opinion, of the hostility of women, than she had formerly been. She wished to be accepted again. As Lady Harwich she could have forced people to accept her.

As she looked at the Great Pyramid, she was saying that to herself, and Nigel's words about the Sphinx fell upon inattentive ears. Although he did not know it, in bringing her to Mena House just at this moment he had taken a step that was unwise. But he was walking in the dark.

At lunch in the great Arabic hall officers from the garrisons of Cairo and Abbassieh, and their womenkind, were in great force. Acquaintances of Nigel's sat at little tables to the right and left of them. In other parts of the room were scattered various well-known English people, who stared at Mrs. Armine when they chose to imagine she did not see them. Not far off Lord and Lady Hayman and the Murchisons reappeared.

A more effective irritant to Mrs. Armine's temper and nerves at this moment than this collection of people afforded could scarcely have been devised by her most subtle enemy. But not by a glance or movement did she betray the fact. She had had time to recover herself, to regain perfect outward self-control. But within her a storm was raging. Into the chamber of her soul, borne upon the wings of the wind, were flocking the ginnees out of the dense darkness of night. And when the twilight came, throwing its pale mystery over the desert, and the wonders the desert kept, they had taken possession of her spirit.

The travellers who, during the day, had peopled the waste about the Pyramids had gone back to Cairo by tram and carriage, or were at tea in the hotel, when the Armines, mounted on donkeys, rode through the twilight towards the Sphinx. They approached it from behind. The wind had quite gone down, and though the evening was not warm, the sharpness of the morning had given place to a more gentle briskness that was in place among the sands. Far off, across the plains and the Nile, the lights of Cairo gleamed against the ridges of the Mokattam. Through the empty silence of this now deserted desert they rode in silence, till before them, above the grey waste of the sand, a protuberance arose.

"Do you see that, Ruby?" Nigel said, pulling at his donkey's rein.

"That thing like a gigantic mushroom? Yes. What is it?"

"The Sphinx."

"That!" she exclaimed.

"Yes, but only the back of its head. All the body is concealed. Wait till you've ridden round it and seen it from the front."

She said nothing, and they rode on till they came to the edge of the deep basin in which the sacred monster lies with the sand and its ceaseless fame about it, till they had skirted the basin's rim, and faced it full on the farther bank. There they dismounted, and Nigel ordered their donkey-boys to lead the beasts away till they were out of earshot. The dry sound of their tripping feet, over the stones and hard earth which edged the sand near by, soon died down into the twilight, and the Armines were left alone.

Although the light of day was rapidly failing, it had not entirely gone; day and night joined hands in a twilight mystery which seemed not only to fall from the sky, so soon to be peopled with stars, but also to rise from the pallor of the sands, and to float about the Sphinx. In the distance the Great Pyramid was black against the void.

Mrs. Armine at first stood perfectly still looking at the monster. Then she made Nigel a sign to spread her dust-cloak upon the ridge of the sand, and she sat down on it, and looked again. She did not speak. The pallor of the twilight began to grow dusky, as if into its yellow grey and grey white, from some invisible source a shadowy black was filtering. A cool air stirred, coming from far away where the sands stretch out towards the Gold Coast. It failed, then came again, with a slightly greater force, a more definite intention.

Nigel was standing, but presently, as Ruby did not move, he sat down beside her, and clasped his brown hands round his knees so tightly that they went white at the knuckles. He stole a glance at her, and thought that her face looked strangely fixed and stern, almost cruel in its repose, and he turned his eyes once more towards the Sphinx.

And then he forgot Ruby, he forgot Egypt, he forgot everything except that greatest creation which man has ever accomplished; that creation which by its inexorable calm and prodigious power rouses in some hearts terror and sets peace in some, stirs some natures to aspiration, and crushes others to the ground with an overwhelming sense of their impotence, their smallness, their fugitive existence, and their dark and mysterious fate.

Upon Mrs. Armine the effect of the Sphinx, whatever it might have been at a less critical moment in her life, at this moment was cruel. The storm had broken upon her and she faced the uttermost calm. She was the prey of conflicting forces, wild beasts of which herself was the cage. And she was confronted by the beast of the living rock which, in its almost ironic composure, its power purged of passion, did it deign to be aware of her she felt could only, with a strange stillness, mock her. She was a believer only in the little life, and here lay the conception of Eternity, struck out of the stone of the waste by man, to say to her with its motionless lips, "Thou fool!" And as she had within her resolution, will, and an unsleeping vanity, this power which confronted her not only dimly distressed, but angered her. She felt angry with Nigel. She forgot, or chose not to remember, that the Sphinx was the wonder of the world, and she said to herself that she knew very well why Nigel had brought her by night to see it. He had brought her to be chastened, he had brought her to be rebuked. In the heat of her nervous fancy it almost seemed to her for a moment as if he had divined something of the truth that was in her, truth that struck hard at him, and his hopes of happiness, and all his moral designs, and as if he had brought her to be punished by the Sphinx. In the grasp of the monster she writhed, and she hated herself for writhing. Once in her presence Baroudi had sneered at the Sphinx. Now she remembered his very words: "We Egyptians, we have other things to do than to go and stare at the Sphinx. We prefer to enjoy our lives while we can, and not to trouble about it." She remembered the shrug of his mighty shoulders that had accompanied the words. Almost she could see them and their disdainful movement before her. Yes, the Sphinx was fading away in the night, and Baroudi was there in front of her. His strong outline blotted out from her the outline of the Sphinx. The evening star came out, and the breeze arose again from its distant place in the sands, and whispered round the Sphinx.

She shivered, and got up.

"Let us go; I want to go," she said.

"Isn't it wonderful, Ruby?"

"Yes. Where are the Arabs?"

She could no longer quite conceal her secret agitation, but Nigel attributed it to a wrong cause, and respected it. The Sphinx always stirred powerfully the spiritual part of him, made him feel in every fibre of his being that man is created not for time, but for Eternity. He believed that it had produced a similar effect in Ruby. That this effect should distress her did not surprise him, but roused in his heart a great tenderness towards her, not unlike the tenderness of a parent who sees the tears of a child flow after a punishment the justice of which is realized. The Sphinx had made her understand intensely the hatefulness of certain things.

When he had helped her on to her donkey he kept his arm about her.

"Do you realize what it has been to me to see the Sphinx with you?" he whispered.

The night had fallen. In the darkness they went away across the desert.

And the Sphinx lay looking towards the East, where the lights of Cairo shone across the flats under the ridges of the Mokattam.

XXII

The Fayyūm is a great and superb oasis situated upon a plateau of the desert of Libya, wonderfully fertile, rich, and bland, with a splendid climate, and springs of sweet waters which, carefully directed into a network of channels, spreading like wrinkles over the face of the land, carry life and a smiling of joy through the crowding palms, the olive and fruit trees, the corn and the brakes of the sugar-cane. The Egyptians often call it "the country of the roses," and they say that everything grows there. The fellah thinks of it as of a Paradise where man can only be happy. Every Egyptian who has ever set the butt end of a gun against his shoulder sighs to be among its multitudinous game. The fisherman longs to let down his net into the depths of its sacred lake. The land-owner would rather have a few acres between Sennoures and Beni Suwêf than many in the other parts of Egypt. The man who is amorous yearns after the legendary beauty of its unveiled women, with their delicately tattooed chins, their huge eyes, and their slim and sinuous bodies. And scarcely is there upon the Nile a brown boy whose face will not gleam and grow expressive with desire at the sound of the words "El-Fayyūm."

It is a land of Goshen, a land flowing with milk and honey, a land of the heart's desire, this green tract of sweet and gracious fertility to which the Bahr-Yûsuf is kind.

But to Mrs. Armine it was from the very first a hateful land.

Their camp was pitched on a piece of brown waste ground, close to a runlet of water, near a palm-grove that shut out from them the native houses of the great village or country town of Sennoures. The land which Nigel's fellahin were reclaiming and had reclaimed—for much of it was already green with luxuriant crops—was farther away, where the oasis runs flush with the pale yellow, or honey-coloured, or sometimes spectral grey sands of the desert of Libya. But Nigel, when he first came to the Fayyūm, had first gone into camp among the palms of Sennoures, and there had heard the Egyptian Pan in the night; and he wanted to renew certain impressions, to feel them decked out, as it were, with novel graces now that he was no longer lonely; so he had ordered the camp to be pitched by the little stream that he knew, in order to savour fully the great change in his life.

The railway from Cairo goes to Sennoures, so they came by train, and arrived rather late in the afternoon. Three days later the Sacred Carpet was to depart from Cairo on its journey to Mecca, and at Madinat-al-Fayyūm, and at other stations along the route, there were throngs of natives assembled to bid farewell to the pilgrims who were departing to accompany it and to worship at the Holy Places. Small and cheap flags of red edged with a crude yellow fluttered over the doors or beneath the hanging shutters of many dwellings, and the mild and limpid atmosphere was full of the chanting of the songs of pilgrimage in high and nasal voices. Once at a roadside station there was for some unexplained reason a long delay, during which Mrs. Armine sat at the window and looked out upon the crowd, while Nigel got down to stretch his legs and see the people at closer quarters. Loud and almost angry hymns rose up not only from some of the starting pilgrims, but also from many envious ones who would never be "hâjjee." Presently, just before the carriage door, a strange little group was formed; a broad, sturdy man with a brutal, almost white-skinned face garnished with a bristling black beard but no moustache, who wore the green turban, an elderly man with staring, sightless eyes, carrying a long staff, and three heavily veiled women, in thin robes partially covered with black, loose-sleeved cloaks, whose eyelids were thickly adorned with kohl, whose hands were dyed a deep orange-colour with the henna, and who rattled and clinked as they moved and the barbaric ornaments of silver and gold which circled their arms and ankles shifted upon their small-boned limbs. The blind man was singing loudly. The women, staring vacantly, held the corners of their cloaks mechanically to their already covered faces. The man with the bristling beard talked violently with friends, and occasionally, interrupting himself abruptly, joined almost furiously in the blind man's hymn. On the platform lay a few bundles wrapped in gaudy cloths and handkerchiefs. From outside the station came the perpetual twittering of women.

As Mrs. Armine looked at these people Nigel came up.

"They are going to Mecca," he said. "You see those bundles? The poor things will be away for months, and that is all they are taking."

The blind man shouted his hymn. Fixing his small and vicious eyes upon Mrs. Armine, the man with the beard joined in. A horn sounded. Nigel got into the carriage, and the train moved slowly out of the station. Mrs. Armine stared at the man with the beard, who kept his eyes upon her, always roaring his hymn, until he was out of sight. His expression was actively wicked. Yet he was starting at great expense with infinite hardships before him, to visit and pray at the Holy Places. She remembered how Baroudi had stared at her while he sang.

"What strange people they are!" said Nigel.

"Yes, they are very strange."

"One can never really know them. There is an eternal barrier between us, the great stone wall of their faith. To-day all the world seems going on pilgrimage. We too, Ruby!"

Even at Sennoures, when they got down, the station was crowded, and the air was alive with hymns. Ibrahim met them, and Hamza was outside the fence with the donkey for Mrs. Armine. He was joining in the singing, and his long eyes held a flame. But when he saw Mrs. Armine, his voice ceased, and he looked at her in silence. As she greeted him, she felt an odd mingled sensation of fear and of relief. He was a link between her and Baroudi, yet he looked a fatal figure, and she could never rid herself of the idea that some harm, or threatening of great danger, would come to her through him.

As they left the station and rode towards the palm-trees, the noise of the hymns grew less, but even when they came in sight of the tents the voices of the pilgrims were still faintly audible, stealing among the wrinkled trunks, through the rich, rankly growing herbage, over the running waters, to make a faint music of religion about their nomad's home.

But after sunset the voices died away. The train had carried the pilgrims towards Cairo, and, trooping among the palm-trees, or along the alleys of Sennoures, the crowd dispersed to their homes.

And a silence fell over this opulent land, which already Mrs. Armine hated.

She hated it as a woman hates the place which in her life is substituted for the place where is the man who has grasped her and holds her fast, whatever the dividing distance between them.

That night, as she sat in the tent, she saw before her the orange garden that bordered the Nile, the wild geraniums making a hedge about the pavilion of bamboo, she heard the loud voice of the fellah by the shadûf. Was it raised in protest or warning? Did she care? Could she care? Could any voice stop her from following the voice that called her on? And what was it in Baroudi that made his summons to her so intense, so arbitrary? What was it in him that governed her so completely? Now that he was far away she could ask herself a question that she could not ask when she was near him.

He was splendid in physique, but so were other men whom she had known and ruled, not been ruled by. He was bold, perhaps indifferent at bottom, though sometimes, in certain moments, on the surface far from indifferent. Others had been like that, and she had not loved them. He was intensely passionate. (But Nigel was passionate, though he kept a strong hand upon the straining life of his nature.) He was very strange.

He was very strange. She understood and could not understand him. He was very strange, and full of secret violence in which religion and vice went hand in hand. And his religion was not canting, nor was his vice ashamed. The one was as bold and as determined as the other. She seemed to grasp him, and did not grasp him. Such a failure piques a woman, and out of feminine pique often rises feminine passion. He was intent upon her. Yet part of him escaped her. Did he love her? She did not know. She knew he drove her perpetually on towards greater desire of him. Yet even that driving action might not be deliberate on his part. He seemed too careless to plot, and yet she knew that he plotted. Was he now at Aswân with some dancing-girl of his own people? Not one word had she heard of him since the day which had preceded the night of the storm when the ginnee had come in the wind. Abruptly he had gone out of her life. At their last meeting he had said nothing about any further intercourse. Yet she knew that he meant to meet her again, that he meant—what? His deep silence did not tell her. She could only wonder and suspect, and govern herself to preserve the bloom of her beauty, and, looking at Ibrahim and Hamza, trust to his intriguing cleverness to "manage things somehow." Yet how could they be managed? She looked at the future and felt hopeless. What was to come? She knew that even if, driven by passion, she were ready to take some mad, decisive step, Baroudi would not permit her to take it. He had never told her so, but instinctively she knew it. If he meant anything, it was something quite different from that. He must mean something, he must mean much; or why was Hamza out here in the green depths of the Fayyûm?

Nigel had gone to Sennoures to order provisions, leaving her to rest after the journey from Cairo. She got up from the sofa in the sitting-room tent, which was comfortable in a very simple way but not at all luxurious, went to the opening, and looked out.

Night had fallen, the stars were out, and a small moon, round which was a luminous ring of vapour, lit up the sky, which was partially veiled by thin wreaths of cloud. The densely growing palms looked like dark wands tufted with enormous bunches of feathers. Among them she saw a light. It came from a tent pitched at some distance, and occupied by a middle-aged German lady who was travelling with a handsome young Arab. They had passed on the road close by the camp when the Armines were having tea, and Nigel had asked Ibrahim about them. Mrs. Armine remembered the look on his face when, having heard their history, he had said to her, "Those are the women who ruin the Europeans' prestige out here." She had answered, "*That* is a thing I could never understand!" and had begun to talk of other matters, but she had not forgotten his look. If—certain things—she might be afraid of Nigel.

Dogs barked in the distance. She heard a faint noise from the runlet of water in front of the camp. From the heavily-cumbered ground, smothered with growing things except just where the tents were pitched, rose a smell that seemed to her autumnal. Along the narrow road that led between the palms and the crops to the town, came two of their men leading in riding camels. A moment later a bitter snarling rose up, mingling with the barking of the dogs and the sound of the water. The camels were being picketed for the night's repose. The atmosphere was not actually cold, but there was no golden warmth in the air, and the wonderful and exquisitely clean dryness of Upper Egypt was replaced by a sort of rich humidity, now that the sun was gone. The vapour around the moon, the smell of the earth, the distant sound of the dogs and the near sound of the water, the feeling of dew which hung wetly about her, and the gleam of the light from that tent distant among the palm-trees, made Mrs. Armine feel almost unbearably depressed. She longed with all her soul to be back at Luxor. And it seemed to her incredible that any one could be happy here. Yet Nigel was perfectly happy and every Egyptian longed to be in the Fayyūm.

The sound of the name seemed to her desolate and sad. But Baroudi meant something. Even now she saw Hamza, straight as a reed, coming down the shadowy track from the town. She must make Nigel happy—and wait. She must make Nigel very happy, lest she should fall below Baroudi's estimate of her, lest she should prove herself less clever, less subtle, than she felt him to be.

Hamza's shadowy figure crossed a little bridge of palm-wood that spanned the runlet of water, turned and came over the waste ground noiselessly into the camp. He was walking with naked feet. He came to the men's tent, where, in a row, with their faces towards the tent door, the camels were lying, eating barley that had been spread out for them on bits of sacking. When he reached it he stood still. He was shrouded in a black abâyeh.

"Hamza!"

Mrs. Armine had called to him softly from the tent-door.

"Hamza!"

He flitted across the open space that divided the tents, and stood beside her.

She had never had any conversation with Hamza. She had never heard him say any English word yet but "yes." But to-night she had an uneasy longing to get upon terms with him. For he was Baroudi's emissary in the camp of the Fayyūm.

"Are you glad to be in my service, Hamza?" she said. "Are you glad to come with us to the Fayyūm?"

"Yes," he said.

She hesitated. There was always something in his

appearance, in his manner, which seemed to fend her off from him. She always felt as if with his mind and soul he was pushing her away. At last she said:

"Do you like me, Hamza?"

"Yes," he replied.

"You have been to Mecca, haven't you, with Mahmoud Baroudi?"

"Yes."

He muttered the word this time. His hands had been hanging at his sides, concealed in his loose sleeves, but now they were moved, and one went quickly up to his breast, and stayed there.

"What are you doing?" Mrs. Armine said, with a sudden sharpness; and, moved by an impulse she could not have explained, she seized the hand at his heart, and pulled it towards her. By the light of the young moon she saw that it was grasping tightly a sort of tassel made of cowries which hung round his neck by a string. He covered the shells with his fingers, and showed his teeth. She let his hand go.

"What is it?" she asked.

"Yes," he answered.

She turned and went into the tent, and he flitted away like a shadow.

That night, when Nigel came in from Sennoures, she said to him:

"What is the meaning of those tassels made of shells that Egyptians sometimes wear round their necks?"

"What sort of shells?" he asked.

"Cowries."

"Cowries—oh, they're supposed to be a charm against the evil eye and bad spirits. Where have you seen one?"

"On a donkey-boy up the Nile, at Luxor."

She changed the conversation.

They were sitting at dinner on either side of a folding table that rested on iron legs. Beneath their feet was a gaudy carpet, very thick and of a woolly texture, and so large that it completely concealed the hard earth within the circle of the canvas, which had a lining of deep red, covered with an elaborate pattern in black, white, yellow, blue, and green. The tent was lit up by an oil-lamp, round which several night moths revolved, occasionally striking against the globe of glass. The tent-door was open, and just outside stood Ibrahim, with his head and face wrapped up in a shawl with flowing fringes, to see that the native waiter did his duty properly. Through the opening came the faint sound of running water and the distant noise of the persistent barking of dogs. The opulent smell of the rich and humid land penetrated into the tent and mingled with the smell from the dishes.

Nigel's face was radiant. They had got right away from modern civilization into the wilds, and, manlike, he felt perfectly happy. He looked at Ruby, seeking a reflection of his joy, yet a little doubtful, too, realizing that this was an experiment for her, while to him it was an old story to which she was supplying the beautiful interest of love. She answered his look with one that set his mind at rest, which thrilled him, yet which only drew from him the prosaic remark:

"The cook isn't so bad, is he, Ruby?"

"Excellent," she said. "I don't know when I've had such a capital dinner. How can he do it all in a tent?"

She moved her chair.

"This table's a little bit low," she said. "But I've no business to be so tall. In camp one ought to be the regulation size."

"Have you been uncomfortable?" he exclaimed, anxiously.

"No, no—not really. It doesn't matter."

"I'll have it altered, made higher somehow, to-morrow. We must have everything right, as we're going to live in camp for some time."

She got up.

"I won't take coffee to-night," she said. "It would be too horrid to sleep badly in a tent."

"You'll see, you'll sleep splendidly out here. Every

one does in camp. One is always in the air, and one gets thoroughly done by the evening."

"Yes, but I shan't be working so hard as you do."

She went to the tent-door.

"How long shall we be in the Fayyūm?" she asked, carelessly. "How long were you in it last year?"

"Off and on for nearly six months."

She said nothing. He struck a match and lit a cigar.

"But of course now it's different," he said. "If you like it, we can stay on, and if you don't we can go back presently to the villa."

"And your work?"

"I ought to be here, so I hope you will like it, Ruby."

He joined her at the tent-door.

"But this winter I mean to live for you, and to try to make you happy. We'll just see how you like being here. Do you think you will like it? Do you feel, as I do, the joy of being in such perfect freedom?"

He put his arm inside hers.

"It's a tremendous change for you, but is it a happy change?" he asked.

"It's wonderful here," she answered; "but it's so strange that I shall have to get accustomed to it."

As she spoke, she was longing, till her soul seemed to ache, to take the early morning train to Cairo. Accustomed for years to have all her caprices obeyed, all her whims indulged by men, she did not know how she was going to endure this situation, which a passionate love alone could have made tolerable. And the man by her side had that passionate love which made the dreary Fayyûm his Heaven. She could almost have struck him because he was so happy.

"There's one thing I must say I should love to do before we go away from Egypt," she said, slowly.

She seemed to be led or even forced to say it.

"What's that?"

"I should love to go up the Nile on a dahabeeyah."

"Then you shall. When we leave here and pass through

Cairo, I'll pick out a boat, and we'll send it up to Luxor, go on board there, and then sail for Assouan. But you mustn't think we shall get a *Loulia*."

He laughed.

"Millionaires like Baroudi don't hire out their boats," he added. "And if they did, I couldn't pay their price while Etchingham's so badly let."

Her forehead was wrinkled by a frown. She hated to hear a man who loved her speak of his poverty. It had become a habit of her mind to think that no man had a right to love her unless he could give her exactly what she wanted.

"Shall we go out, Ruby?"

"Very well."

They stepped out on to the waste ground. His hand was still on her arm, and he led her down to the stream. The young moon was already setting. The starry sky was flecked here and there with gossamer veils of cloud. A heavy dew was falling upon the dense growths of the oasis, and in the distance of the palm-grove, where gleamed the lamp from the tent of the German lady and the young Arab, a faint and pearly mist was rising. Nigel drew in his breath, then let it out. It went in vapour from his lips.

"We've left the dryness of Upper Egypt," he said. "This is the country of fertility, the country where things grow. The dews at night are splendid. But wait a moment. I'll get you a cloak. I'm your maid, remember."

He fetched a cloak and wrapped it round her.

"I suppose the *Loulia* is far up the river," he said. "Perhaps at Assouan. I wonder if we shall see Baroudi some day again. I think he's a good sort of fellow; but after all, one can never get really quite in touch with an Eastern. I used to think one could. I used to swear it, but——"

He shook his head and puffed at his cigar. Quite unconsciously he had taken the husband's tone. There was something in the very timbre of his voice which seemed to assume Ruby's agreement. She longed to startle him, to say she was far more in touch with an Eastern than she could ever be with him, but she thought of the dahabeeyah, the Nile, the getting away from here.

"To tell the truth," she said, "I have always felt that. There is an impassable barrier between East and West."

She looked at the distant light among the palm-trees. Then, with contempt, she added:

"Those who try to overleap it must be mad, or worse."

Nigel's face grew stern.

"Yes," he said. "I loathe condemnation. But there are some things which really are unforgivable."

He swung out his arm towards the light.

"And that is one of them. I hate to see that light so near us. It is the only blot on perfection."

"Don't look at it," she murmured.

His unusual expression of vigorous, sane disgust, and almost of indignation, partly fascinated and partly alarmed her.

"Don't think of it. It has nothing to do with us. Hark! What's that?"

A clear note, like the note of a little flute, sounded from the farther side of the stream, was reiterated many times. Nigel's face relaxed. The sternness vanished from it, and was replaced by an ardent expression that made it look almost like the face of a romantic boy.

"It's—it's the Egyptian Pan by the water," he whispered.

His arm stole round her waist.

"Come a little nearer—gently. That's it! Now listen!"

The little, clear, frail sound was repeated again and again.

The young moon went down behind the palm-trees. Its departure, making the night more dark, made the distant light in the grove seem more clear, more definite, more brilliant.

It drew the eyes, it held the eyes of Bella Donna as the Egyptian Pan piped on.

XXIII

MRS. ARMINE summoned all her courage, all her patience, all her force of will, and began resolutely, as she mentally put it, to earn her departure from the land which she hated more bitterly day by day. The situation she was in, so different from any that she had previously known, roused within her a sort of nervous desperation, and this desperation armed her and made her dangerous. And because she was dangerous, she seemed often innocently happy, and sometimes ardently happy; she seemed to have cast away from her any lingering remnants of the manner of a great courtesan which had formerly clung about her. Nigel would have denied that there had been such remnants; nevertheless, he felt and rejoiced in the change that came. He said to himself that he was justified of his loving experiment. He had restored to Ruby her self-respect, her peace of mind and body, and in doing so he had won for himself a joy that he had not known till now.

In that joy his nature expanded, his energies leaped up, his mind kindled, his heart glowed and burned. He felt himself twice the man that he had formerly been. He flung himself into his work with almost a giant's strength, into his pleasure, riding, shooting, fishing, with the enthusiasm of a boy for the first time freed from tutelage.

Mrs. Armine was rewarded for her effort of cunning by the happiness of her husband, and by his gratitude and devotion to her. For she was clever enough to put him into the place the world thought she ought to occupy, into the humble seat of the grateful. She succeeded very soon in infecting his mind with the idea that it was good of her to have married him, that she had given up not a little in doing so. She never made a complaint, but very often she indicated, as if by accident, that for the sake of the upward progress she was enduring a certain amount of definite hardship cheerfully. There was scarcely a day, for instance, when she did not contrive to recall to his mind the fact that, for his sake, she was doing without a maid for the first time in her life. Yet she never said, "I wish I had kept Marie." Her method was, "How thankful I am we decided to get rid of Marie, Nigel! She would have been wretched here. The life would have killed her, though I manage to stand it so splendidly. But servants never will put up with a little discomfort. And it's so good of you not to mind my looking anyhow, and always wearing the same old rag." Such things were said with a resolutely cheerful voice which announced a moral effort.

As they sat at dinner, she would say, perhaps: "Isn't it extraordinary, Nigel, how soon one gets not to care what one is eating, so long as one can satisfy one's hunger? I remember the time when, for a woman, I was almost an epicure, and now I can swallow Mohammed's dinners with positive relish. Do give me another help of that extraordinary muddle he calls a stew."

And in bed that night, or over a last solitary pipe outside the tent, Nigel would be thinking, "By Jove, Ruby is a trump to put up with Mohammed's messes after the food she's always been accustomed to!" Whereas, before, he had been congratulating himself on having engaged at a high rate the greatest treasure of a camp cook that could be found in the whole of Egypt.

Perpetually, in a hundred ways, she brought to his memory the extravagant luxury in which for so many years she had lived. Yet she never seemed to be regretting, but always to be congratulating herself on the fact, that she had abandoned it for a different, more Spartan way of life. Often, in fact generally, she talked as if they were poor people, as if she had married a quite poor man.

"I can't let you be reckless," she would say, when perhaps he suggested something that would put them to extra expense. "It isn't as if we were rich. I love spending money, but I should hate to run you into debt."

And if Nigel began to explain that he could perfectly well afford whatever it was, she would gently, and gaily too, ignore or sweep away his remarks with a "You forget how different your position is now that your brother's got an heir." Once, however, he persisted, and made a sort of statement of his affairs to her, his object being to prove to her that they had "plenty to go on with." The result was scarcely what he had anticipated. For a moment she seemed to be struck dumb with a strong surprise. Then, apparently recovering herself, she said decisively, "If that is all we've got, I am perfectly right to be parsimonious. And besides, it's an excellent thing for me to have to think about money. I've always been accustomed to spend far too much. I've lived much too extravagantly, too brilliantly, all my life. A change to simplicity and occasional self-denial will do me all the good in the world, whether I like it at first or not."

And she smothered a sigh, and smiled at him with a sort of gentle determination. But she never overacted her part, she never underlined anything. Directly she saw that she had gained her end, had "got home," she passed on to a different topic. Never did she persistently play the martyr. She knew how soon a man secretly gets sick of the martyr-wife. But, in one way or another, she kept Nigel simmering in appreciation of her.

And in contenting his soul she did not forget to content him in other ways; she never allowed him to lose sight of the fact that she was still a beautiful and voluptuous woman, and that she belonged wholly to him. And so gradually she woke up in him the peculiar and terrible need of her that a certain type of woman can wake in a certain type of man. She taught him to be grateful to her for a double joy: the moral joy of the high-minded man who has, or who thinks he has, through a woman in some degree fulfilled his ideal of conduct, and the physical joy of the completely natural and vigorous man who legitimately links with his moral satisfaction a satisfaction wholly different. To both spirit and body she held the torch, and each was warmed by the glow, and made cheerful and glad by the light.

Nigel had cared for her in England, had loved her in

the Villa Androud; but that care, that love, were as nothing to the feeling for her that sprang up in him in the midst of the springing green things that made a Paradise of the Fayyūm. He was a man who got very near to Nature, whose heart beat very near to Nature's generous heart, and often, when he stood shoulder-high in a silver-green sea of sugar-cane, or looked up to the tufted palms that made a murmuring over his head, or listened to the rustle of corn in the sunshine, or to the swish of the heavily-podded doura in the light wind that came in from the desert, he would compare his growing love for Ruby to the growing of Nature's children in this beneficent clime. And the luxuriant richness of the green world round about him seemed to have its counterpart within him.

But there was the desert, too, always near to remind him of the arid wastes of the world—of the arid wastes that needed reclaiming in humanity, in himself.

And in his great joy he never lost one of his most beautiful natural graces, the grace of an unostentatious humility.

The racial reticence of the Englishman about the things he cares for most kept him from telling his wife of what was happening in his mind and heart, despite his apparent frankness, which often seemed that of a boy; and some of it she was too devoid of all spirituality, all moral enthusiasm, to divine. But she summed him up pretty accurately, knew as a rule pretty thoroughly "where she was with him"; and though she sometimes wondered how things could be as they were in him, or in any one, still she knew that so they were.

She acted her part well, though day by day, in the acting of it, her nervous desperation increased; but when, now and then, her self-control was for a moment shaken, she succeeded in leading Nigel to attribute any momentary sharpness, cynicism, or even bitterness, to some failure in himself which had awakened the doubts of the woman long trampled on. Subtly she recalled to him the night after the scene in the garden of the Villa Androud; she reminded him—without words—of the words she had spoken then. He seemed to hear her saying: "After this morning you will have to prove your belief in me to me, thoroughly prove it, or else I shall not believe it. It will take a little time to make me feel quite safe with you, as one can only feel when the little bit of sincerity in one is believed in and trusted." And he remembered the resolve he had taken on that night of crisis, to restore this woman's confidence in goodness by having a firm faith in the goodness existing in her. And he condemned himself and braced himself for new efforts. Those efforts were not difficult for him to make now that he had Ruby all to himself, now that he saw her utterly divorced from her old life and companions, now that he held her in the breast of Nature, now that he knew —as how could he not know?—that she was living virtuously, sanely, simply, and, as he thought, splendidly and happily, despite the lingering backward glances she sometimes cast at the old luxury foregone. It is very difficult for the human being who finds perfect happiness in a life to realize that such a life to another may be a torment.

And Ruby made few mistakes. When she was with her husband, her now unpainted face was serene. She worked bravely to earn her release from a life that was unsuited to her whole temperament, and that was utterly odious to her.

But had not Hamza and Ibrahim been in the camp with her, she often said to herself that she could not have endured this period. That they were there meant that she was not forgotten, that while she was being patient, in a distant place, somewhere upon the great river, in the golden climate of Upper Egypt, some one else was being patient too.

Surely it meant, it must mean, that!

But she was haunted by a jealousy that, instead of being diminished by time and absence, increased with each passing day, even waking up in her a vital force of imagination she had not suspected she possessed. She knew men as a race *au fond*—knew their fickleness, swift forgetfulness, readiness to be content with the second best, so different from the far greater Epicureanism of women; knew their uneasy appetites, their lack of self-restraint; and, adding to this sum of knowledge her personal knowledge of Baroudi as a young, strong, and untrammelled man of the East, she was confronted with visions which tortured her cruelly. There were times when her mind ran riot, throwing him among all the sensual pleasures which he loved. And then she was more than heart-sick; she was actually body-sick. She felt ill; she felt that she ached with jealousy, as another may ache with some physical disease. She had a longing to perform some frantic physical act.

And then she remembered her beauty, and that, at all costs, she must preserve it as long as possible, and she secretly cursed the unbridled nature within her. But the climate of the Fayyūm was very kind to her, and this life in the open, in the unvitiated air that blew through the palms from the virgin deserts of Libya, gave to her health such as she had never known till now, despite her mental torture. And that body-sickness which came from her jealousy was like a fit which seized her and passed away.

Egypt brought back her youth, or, at the least, prolonged and increased steadily the shining and warmth of her Indian summer. And with that shining and warmth the desire to live fully, to use her present powers in the way that would bring her happiness, grew perpetually in strength and ardour. She longed for the man who suited her, and for the *luxe* that he could give her. With her genuine physical passion for Baroudi there woke the ugly greed that was an essential part of her nature, the greed of the true materialist who cares nothing for a simplicity that has not cost the eyes out of somebody's head. She was a woman who loved to know that some one was ruining himself for her. She took an almost physical pleasure in the spending of money. And often her mind echoed the words of Hassan, when he looked across the Nile to the tapering mast of the *Loulia* and murmured, "Mahmoud Baroudi is rich! Mahmoud Baroudi is rich!" And she yearned to go, not only to Baroudi, but to his gold, and she remembered her fancy when she sat by the Nile, that the gleaming gold on the water was showered towards her by him to comfort her in her solitude.

At last a crisis came.

After staying for a short time at Sennoures, the camp had been moved from the village to the outskirts of the oasis, so that Nigel might be close to his land. Here the rich fertility, the green abundance of growing things, trailed away into the aridity of the desert, and at night, from the door of the tent, Mrs. Armine could look out upon the pale and vague desolation of the illimitable sands stretching away into the illimitable darkness. Just at first the vision fascinated her, and she lent an ear to the call of the East, but very soon she was distressed by the sight of the still and unpeopled country, which suggested to her the nameless solitudes into which many women are driven out when the time of their triumph is over. She did not speak of this to Nigel, but, pretending that the wind at night from the desert chilled her even between the canvas walls of the tent, she had the tent turned round with its orifice towards the oasis. And she strove to ignore the desert.

Nevertheless, despite what was indeed almost a horror of its spaces, she now found that she felt more strongly their fascination, which seemed calling her, but to danger or sorrow rather than to any pleasure or permanent satisfaction. She often felt an uneasy desire to be more intimate with the thing which she feared, and which woke up in her a prophetic dread of the future when the Indian summer would have faded for ever. And when one day Nigel suggested that he should take two or three days' holiday, and that they should remove the camp into the wilds at the north-eastern end of the sacred lake of Kurûn, where Ibrahim and Hamza said he could get some first-rate duck-shooting, and Ruby could come to close quarters with the reality of the Libyan desert, she assented almost eagerly. Any movement, any change, was welcome to her; and— she had to be more intimate with the thing which she feared.

So one morning the riding camels kneeled down, the tents collapsed, were rolled up and sent forward, and they started to go still farther into the wilds.

They made a détour in the oasis to give their Bedouins time to pitch their camp in the sands, and Ibrahim an hour or two to prepare everything for their arrival. It was already afternoon when they were on the track that leads to the lake, leaving the groves of palms behind them and the low houses of the fellahîn, moving slowly towards the sand-hills that appeared far off, where huddled the patched and discoloured tents of the gipsies and the almost naked fishermen who are the only dwellers in this strange and blanched desolation, where the sands and the salty waters meet in a wilderness of tamarisk bushes.

It was a grey and windless day, and the sky looked much lower than it usually does in Egypt. The atmosphere was sad. Clouds of wild pigeons flew up to right and left of them, circling over the now diminishing crops and the little runlets of water that soon would die away where sterility's empire began. In low, yet penetrating, voices the camel men sang the songs of the sands, as they ran on, treading softly with naked feet. Hamza, who accompanied the little caravan with his donkey in case Mrs. Armine grew tired of her camel, holding his hieratic wand, kept always softly and unweariedly behind them.

And thus, always accompanied by the hum and the twittering of a melancholy music, they went on towards the lake.

Upon Nigel's beast were slung his guns. He was eagerly looking forward to his holiday. He had been toiling really hard with his fellahîn, often almost up to his knees in mud and water, driving the sand-plough, working the small and primitive engines, digging, planting, even following the hand-plough drawn by a camel yoked to a donkey. He was in grand condition, hard as nails, burnt by the sun, joyful with the almost careless joy that is born of a health made perfect by labour. The desolation before them to him seemed a land of promise, for he was entering it with Ruby, and in it there were thousands of wild duck, and jackals that slunk out by night among the stunted tamarisk bushes.

"We seem to be going to the end of the world," she said.

She was swaying gently to and fro with the movement of her camel, which had just turned to the right, after following for an immense time a straight track that was cut through the crops, and that never deviated to right or left. Now sand appeared. On their left, and parallel to them, crept a sluggish stream of water between uneven banks of sand. And the track was up and down, and here and there showed humps, and deep ruts, and sometimes holes. The crops began to be sparser; no more houses or huts were visible; but far away in the white and wintry distance, looking almost like discolourations upon a sheet, were scattered low brown and black tents, which seemed to be crouching on the desolate ground.

"Does any one live out here beyond us?" she added. "Are those things really tents?"

"Yes, Ruby."

"It seems incredible that any human beings should deliberately choose to live here."

"You haven't ever felt the call of the wild?" he asked.

She looked at him, and said, quickly:

"Oh, yes. But it's different for us. We come here to get a new experience, to have a thorough change, and we can get away whenever we like. But just imagine choosing to live here permanently!"

"I'd rather live here than in almost any town."

He was silent for a moment, and his face lost its joyous expression and became almost eagerly anxious. Then he said:

"Ruby, do you hate all this?"

"Hate it! No, it's a novelty; it's strange; it excites me, interests me."

"You are sure?"

He had suddenly thought of her sitting-room in the Savoy Into what a violently different life he had conveyed her!—into a life that he loved, and that was well fitted for a man to live. He loved such a life, but perhaps he had been, was being selfish. He tried to read her face, and was suddenly full of doubts and fears.

"I like roughing it, of course," he added. "But, I say, you mustn't give in to what I like if it doesn't suit you. We men are infernally selfish."

She saw her opportunity.

"Don't you know yet that women find most of their happiness in pleasing the men they love?" she said.

"But I want to please you."

"So you shall presently."

"How?"

"By taking me up the Nile."

She had sown in his mind the belief that she was living for him unselfishly. He resolved to pay her with a sterling coin of unselfishness. Never mind the work! In this first year he must think always first of her, must dedicate himself to her. And in making her life to flower was he not reclaiming the desert?

"I will take you up the Nile," he said. "Always be frank with me, Ruby. If—if things that suit me don't suit you, tell me so straight out. I think the one thing that binds two people together with hoops of steel is absolute sincerity. Even if it hurts, it's a saviour."

"Yes, but I am absolutely sincere when I say that I love to live in your life."

She could afford to say that now, and despite the increasing desolation around them her heart leaped at a prospect of release, for she knew how his mind was working, and she heard the murmur of Nile water round the prow of a dahabeeyah.

That night they camped in an amazing desolation.

The great lake of Kurûn, which looks like an inland sea, and which is salt almost as the sea, is embraced at its northern end by another sea of sand. The vast slopes of the desert of Libya reach down to its waveless waters. The desolation of the desert is linked with the desolation of this unmurmuring sea, the deep silence of the wastes with the deep silence of the waters.

Never before had Mrs. Armine known such a desolation, never had she imagined such a silence as that which lay around their camp, which brooded over this desert, which brooded over the greenish grey waters of this vast lake which was like a sea.

She spoke, and her voice seemed to be taken at once as its prey by the silence. Even her thought seemed to be seized by it, and to be conveyed away from her like a living thing whose destiny it was to be slain. She felt paltry, helpless, unmeaning, in the midst of this arid breast of Nature, which was pale as the leper is pale. She felt chilled, even almost sexless, as if all her powers, all her passions and her desires, had been grasped by the silence, as if they were soon to be taken for ever from her. Never before had anything that was neither human nor connected in any way with humanity's efforts and wishes made such a terrific impression upon her.

She hid this impression from Nigel.

The long camel-ride had slightly fatigued her, despite the great strength of body which she had been given by Egypt. She busied herself in the usual way of a woman arrived from a journey, changed her gown, bathed in a collapsible bath made of India rubber, put eau de Cologne on her forehead, arranged her hair before a mirror pinned to the sloping canvas. But all the time that she did these things she was listening to the enormous silence, was feeling it like a weight, was shrinking, or trying to shrink away from its outstretched, determined arms. From without came sometimes sounds of voices that presented themselves to her ears as shadows, skeletons, spectres, present themselves to the eyes. Was that really Ibrahim? Was that Nigel speaking, laughing? And that long stream of words, did it flow from Hamza's throat? Or were those shadows outside, with voices of shadows, trying to hold intercourse with shadows? Presently tea was ready, and she came out into the waste.

They were at a considerable distance from the lake, looking down on it from the slight elevation of a gigantic slope of sand, which rose gradually behind them till in the distance it seemed to touch the stooping grey of the low horizon. Everywhere white and yellowish white melted into grey and greenish grey. The only vegetation was a great maze of tamarisk bushes, which stretched from the flat sand-plain on their left to the verge of the lake, and far out into the water, making a refuge and a shelter for the thousands upon thousands of wild duck that peopled the watery waste. Now, unafraid, they were floating in the open, casting great clouds of velvety black upon the still surface of the lake, which, owing to some atmospheric effect, looked as if it sloped upward like the sands till it met the stooping sky. Very far off, almost visionary, like blacknesses held partly by the water, and partly by the vapours that muffled the sky, were two or three of the clumsy boats of the wild, almost savage natives who live on the fish of the lake. Almost imperceptibly they moved about their eerie business.

"Just look at the duck, Ruby!" said Nigel, as she came out. "What a place for sport!"

For once their usual rôles were reversed; he was practical, while she was imaginative, or at least strongly affected by her imagination. He had been looking to his guns, making arrangements with a huge and nearly black dweller of the tents to show him the best sport possible for a fixed sum of money.

"But it's the devil to get within range of them," he added. "I shall have to do as the natives do, I expect."

"What's that?" she asked, with an effort.

"Strip, and wade in up to my neck, carrying my gun over my head, and then keep perfectly still till some of them come within range."

He laughed with joyous anticipation.

"I've told Ibrahim he must have a roaring big fire for me when I get back."

"Are you going to-day?"

"Yes, I think I'll have just an hour. D'you feel up to

riding the donkey to the water's edge, and coming out on the lake with me?"

She hesitated. In this waste and in this silence she felt almost incapable of a decision. Then she said:

"No, I think I've had enough for to-day. You must bring me back a duck for dinner."

"I swear I will."

He gripped her hands when he went. He was full of the irrepressible joy of the sportsman starting out for his pleasure.

"What will you do till I come back?"

"Rest. Perhaps I shall read, and I'll talk to Ibrahim. He always amuses me."

"Good. I'm going to ride the donkey and take Hamza."

Just as he was mounting, he turned round, and said:

"Ruby, I'm having my time now. You shall have yours. You shall have the best dahabeeyah to be got on the Nile, the *Loulia,* if Baroudi will hire it out to us."

"Oh, the *Loulia* would cost us too much," she said, "even if it could be hired."

"We'll get a good one, anyhow, and you shall see every temple—go up to Halfa, if you want to. And now pray for duck with all your might."

He rode away down the sand slope towards the lake, and presently, with Hamza and the native guide, was but a moving speck in the pallid distance.

Mrs. Armine watched them from a folding chair, which she made Ibrahim carry out into the sand some hundreds of yards from the camp.

"Leave me here for a little while, Ibrahim," she said.

He obeyed her, and strolled quietly away, then presently squatted down to keep guard.

At first Mrs. Armine scarcely thought at all. She stared at the sand slopes, at the sand plains, at the sand banks, at the wilderness of tamarisk, at the grey waters spotted with duck, at the little moving black things that, like insects, crept towards them. And she felt like—what? Like a nothing. For what seemed a very long time she felt like that. And then, gradually, very gradually, her self began to wake, began to release itself from the spell of place, and to struggle forward, as it were, out of the shattering grip of the silence. And she burned with indignation in the chill air of the desert.

Why had she let herself be brought, even to spend only three or four days, to such a place as this? Had she ever had even a momentary desire to see more solitary places than the place from which they had come? Where was Baroudi at this moment? What was he feeling, doing, thinking? She fastened her mind fiercely upon the thought of him, and she saw herself in exile. Always, until now, she had felt the conviction that Baroudi had some plan in connection with her, and that quiescence on her part was necessary to its ultimate fulfilment. She had felt that she was in the web of his plan, that she had to wait, that something devised by him would presently happen—she did not know what—and that their intercourse would be resumed.

Now, influenced by the desolation towards utter doubt and almost frantic depression, as she came back to her full life, which had surely been for a while in suspense, she asked herself whether she had not been grossly mistaken. Baroudi had never told her anything about the future, had never given her any hint as to what his meaning was. Was that because he had had no meaning? Had she been the victim of her own desires? Had Baroudi had enough of her and done with her? Something, that was compounded of something else as well as of vanity, seemed still to be telling her that it was not so. But to-day, in this terrible greyness, this melancholy, this chilly pallor, she could not trust it. She turned.

"Ibrahim! Ibrahim!" she cried out.

He rose from the sands and sauntered towards her. He came and stood silently beside her.

"Ibrahim," she began.

She looked at him, and was silent. Then she called on her resolute self, on the self that had been hardened, coarsened, by the life which she had led.

"Ibrahim, do you know where Baroudi is—what he has been doing all this time?" she asked.

"What he has bin doin' I dunno, my lady. Baroudi he doos very many things."

"I want to know what he has been doing. I must, I will know."

The spell of place, the spell of the great and frigid silence, was suddenly and completely broken. Mrs. Armine stood up in the sand. She was losing her self-control. She looked at the dreary prospect before her, growing sadder as evening drew on; she thought of Nigel perfectly happy, she even saw him down there a black speck in the immensity, creeping onward towards his pleasure, and a fury that was vindictive possessed her. It seemed to her absolutely monstrous that such a woman as she was should be in such a place, in such a situation, waiting in the sand alone, deserted, with nothing to do, no one to speak to, no prospect of pleasure, no prospect of anything. A loud voice within her seemed suddenly to cry, to shriek, "I won't stand this. I won't stand it."

"I'm sick of the Fayyūm," she said fiercely, "utterly sick of it. I want to go back to the Nile. Do you know where Baroudi is? Is he on the Nile? I hate, I loathe this place."

"My lady," said Ibrahim, very gently, "there is good jackal-shootin' here."

"Jackal-shooting, duck-shooting—so you think of nothing but your master's pleasure!" she said, indignantly. "Do you suppose I'm going to sit still here in the sand for days, and do nothing, and see nobody, while—while——"

She stopped. She could not go on. The fierceness of her anger almost choked her. If Nigel had been beside her at that moment, she would have been capable of showing even to him something of her truth. Ibrahim's voice again broke gently in upon her passion.

"My lady, for jackal-shootin' you have to go out at night. You have to go down there when it is dark, and stay there for a long while, till the jackal him come. You tie a goat; the jackal him smell the goat and presently him comin'."

She stared at him almost blankly. What had all this rhodomontade to do with her? Ibrahim met her eyes.

"All this very interestin' for my Lord Arminigel," said Ibrahim, softly.

Mrs. Armine said nothing, but she went on staring at Ibrahim.

"P'r'aps my gentleman go out to-night. If he go, you take a little walk with Ibrahim."

He turned, and pointed behind her, to the distance where the rising sand-hill seemed to touch the stooping sky.

"You take a little walk up there."

Still she said nothing. She asked nothing. She had no need to ask. All the desolation about her seemed suddenly to blossom like the rose. Instead of the end of the world, this place seemed to be the core, the warm heart of the world.

When at last she spoke, she said quietly:

"Your master will go jackal-shooting to-night."

Ibrahim nodded his head.

"I dessay," he pensively replied.

The soft crack of a duck-gun came to their ears from far off among the tamarisk bushes beside the green-grey waters.

"I dessay my Lord Arminigel him goin' after the jackal to-night."

XXIV

THE dinner in camp that night was quite a joyous festival. Nigel brought back two duck, Ibrahim made a fine fire of brushwood to warm the eager sportsman, and Ruby was in amazing spirits. She played to perfection the part of ardent housewife. She came and went in the sand, presiding over everything. She even penetrated into the cook's tent with Ibrahim to give Mohammed some hints as to the preparation of the duck.

"This is your holiday," she said to Nigel. "I want it to be a happy one. You must make the most of it, and go out shooting all the time. They say there's any amount of jackals down there in the tamarisk bushes. Are you going to have a shot at them to-night?"

Nigel stretched out his legs, with a long sigh of satisfaction.

"I don't know, Ruby. I should like to, but it's so jolly and cosy here."

He looked towards the fire, then back at her.

"I'm not sure that I'll go out again," he said.

"I dare say you're tired."

"No, that's not it. The truth is that I'm tremendously happy in camp with you. And I love to think of the desolation all round us, and that there isn't a soul about, except a few gipsies down there, and a few wild, half-naked fishermen. We've brought our own oasis with us into the Libyan Desert. And I think to-night I'll be a wise man and stick to the oasis."

She smiled at him.

"Then do!"

In the midst of her smile she yawned.

"I shall go to bed directly," she said.

She seemed to suppress another yawn.

"You mean to go to bed early?" he asked.

"Almost directly. Do you mind? I'm dog tired with the long camel ride, and I shall sleep like twenty tops."

She put her hand on his shoulder. Her whole face was looking sleepy.

"You old wretch," she said. "What do you mean by looking so horribly wide awake?"

He put his hand over hers, and laughed.

"I seem to be made of iron in this glorious country. I'm not a bit sleepy."

She stifled another yawn.

"Then I'll"—she put up her hand to her mouth—"I'll sit up a little to keep you company."

"Indeed, you shan't. You shall go straight to bed,

and when you're safely tucked up I think perhaps I will just go down and have a look for the jackals. If you're going to sleep, I might as well——"

He drew down her face to his and gave her a long kiss.

"I'll put you to bed first, and when you're quite safe and warm and cosy, I'll make a start."

She returned his kiss.

"No, I'll see you off."

"But why?"

"Because I love to see you starting off in the night to the thing that gives you pleasure. That's my pleasure. Not always, because I'm too selfish. On the Nile you'll have to attend to me, to do everything I want. But just for these few days I'm going to be like an Eastern woman, at the beck of my lord and master. So I must see you start, and then—oh, how I shall sleep!"

He got up.

"P'r'aps I'll be out till morning. I wonder if Hamdi's got a goat."

He went away for his gun. In a very few minutes he left the camp, gaily calling to her, "Sleep well, Ruby! You look like a sorceress standing there all lit up by the fire. The flames are flickering over you. Good night—good night!"

His steps died away in the sands, his voice died away in the darkness.

She waited, standing perfectly still by the fire, for a long time. Her soul seemed running, rushing over the sands towards the ridge that met the sky, but her will kept her body standing beside the flames, until at last the sportsmen were surely far enough away.

"Ibrahim!"

"My lady?"

"How are we going?"

She was whispering to him beside the fire.

"Does it matter the camel-men knowing? Are they to know? Am I to ride or walk?"

"You leave everythin' to Ibrahim. You go in your tent, and presently I come."

She went at once into the tent, and sat down on a folding chair. A little round iron table stood before it. She leaned her arms on the table and laid her face against the back of her hand. Her cheek was burning. She sprang up, went to her dressing-case, unlocked it, drew out the *boîte de beauté* which Baroudi had given her in the orange-garden, and quickly made her face up, standing before the glass that was pinned to the canvas. Then she put on a short fur coat. The wind would be cold in the sands. She wondered how far they had to go.

And if Nigel should unexpectedly return, as nearly all husbands did on such occasions?

She could not bother about that. She felt too desperate to care; she felt in the grasp of fate. If the fate was to be untoward, so much the worse for her—and for Nigel. She meant to go beyond that ridge of the sand. That was all she knew. Quickly she buttoned the fur coat and put on a hat and gloves.

"Now we goin' to start."

Ibrahim put his muffled head in at the door of the tent.

"Walking?" she asked.

"We goin' to start walkin'."

When she came out, she found that the brushwood fire had been pulled to pieces.

"Down there they not see nothin'," said Ibrahim, pointing towards the darkness before them.

"And the men? Does it matter about the men?" she asked perfunctorily. She did not feel that she really cared.

"All the men sleepin', except Hamza. Him watchin'."

The tents of the men were at some distance. She looked, and saw no movement, no figures except the faint and grotesque silhouettes of the hobbled camels.

"I say that I follow my Lord Arminigel."

They started into the desert. As they left the camp, Mrs. Armine saw Hamza behind her tent, patrolling with a matchlock over his shoulder.

The night was dark and starless; the breeze, though slight and wavering over the sands, was penetrating and cold. The feet of Mrs. Armine sank down at each step into the deep and yielding sands as she went on into the blackness of the immeasurable desert. And as she gazed before her at the hollow blackness and felt the immensity of the unpeopled spaces, it seemed to her that Ibrahim was leading her into some crazy adventure, that they were going only towards the winds, the desolate sands, and the darkness that might be felt. He did not speak to her, nor she to him, till she heard, apparently near them the angry snarl of a camel. Then she stopped.

"Did you hear that? There's some one near us," she said.

"My lady come on! That is a very good dromedary for us."

"Ah!" she said.

She hastened forward again. In two or three seconds the camel snarled furiously again.

"The Bedouin he make him do that to tell us where he is," said Ibrahim.

He cried out some words in Arabic. A violent guttural voice replied out of the darkness. In a moment, under the lee of a sand dune, they came upon two muffled figures holding two camels, which were lying down. Upon one there was a sort of palanquin, in which Mrs. Armine took her seat, with a Bedouin sitting in front. A stick was plied. The beast protested, filling the hollow of the night with a complaint that at last became almost leonine; then suddenly rose up, was silent, and started off at a striding trot.

Mrs. Armine could not measure either the time that elapsed or the space that was covered during that journey. She was filled with a sense of excitement and adventure that she had never experienced before, and that made her feel oddly young. The dark desert, swept by the chilling breeze, became to her suddenly a place of strong hopes and of desires leaping towards fulfilment. She was warmed through and through by expectation, as she had not been warmed by the great camp fire that had been kindled to greet Nigel. And when at last in the distance there shone out a light, like an earth-bound star, to her all the desert seemed glowing with an almost exultant radiance.

But the light was surely far away, for though the dromedary swung on over the desert, it did not seem to her to grow clearer or brighter, but like a distant eye it regarded her with an almost cruel steadiness, as if it calmly read her soul.

And she thought of Baroudi's eyes, and looking again at the yellow light, she felt as if he were watching her calmly from some fastness of the sands to which she could not draw near.

In the desert it is difficult to measure distances. Just as Mrs. Armine was thinking that she could never gain that light, it broadened, broke up into forms, the forms of leaping flames blown this way and that by the stealthy wind of the waste, became abruptly a fire revealing vague silhouettes of camels, of crouching men, of tents, of guard dogs, of hobbled horses. She was in the midst of a camp pitched far out in a lonely place of the sands within sight of no oasis.

The dromedary knelt. She was on her feet with Ibrahim standing beside her.

For a moment she felt dazed. She stood still, consciously pressing her feet down against the sand which glowed in the light from the flames. She saw eyes—the marvellous, birdlike eyes of Bedouins—steadily regarding her beneath the darkness of peaked hoods. She heard the crackle of flames in the windy silence, a soft grating sound that came from the jaws of feeding camels. Dogs snuffed about her ankles.

"My lady, you comin' with me!"

Mechanically she followed Ibrahim away from the fire, across a strip of sand to a large tent that stood apart. As she drew near to it her heart began to beat violently and irregularly, and she felt almost like a girl. For years she had not felt so young as she felt to-night. In this dark desert, among these men of Africa, all her worldly knowledge, all her experience of men in civilized countries seemed of no use to her. It was as if she shed it, cast it as a snake casts its skin, and stood there in a new ignorance that was akin to the wondering ignorance of youth. The canvas flap that was the door of the tent was fastened down. Ibrahim went up to it and called out something. For a moment there was no answer. During that moment Mrs. Armine had time to notice a second smaller tent standing, with Baroudi's, apart from all the others. And she fancied, but was not certain, that as for an instant the breeze died down, she heard within it a thin sound like the plucked strings of some instrument of music. Then the canvas of the big tent was lifted, light shone out from within, and she saw the strong outline of a man. He looked into the night, drew back, and she entered quickly and stood before Baroudi. Then the canvas fell down behind her, shutting out the night and the desert.

Baroudi was dressed in Arab costume. His head was covered with a white turban spangled with gold, his face was framed in snowy white, and his great neck was hidden by drapery. He wore a kuftán of striped and flowered silk with long sleeves, fastened round his waist with lengths of muslin. Over this was a robe of scarlet cloth. His legs were bare of socks, and on his feet were native slippers of scarlet morocco leather. In his left hand he held an immensely long pipe with an ivory mouthpiece.

Mrs. Armine looked from him to his tent, to the thick, bright-coloured silks which entirely concealed the canvas walls, to the magnificent carpets which blotted out the desert sands, to the great hanging lamp of silver, which was fastened by a silver chain to the peaked roof, to the masses of silk cushions of various hues that were strewn about the floor. Once again her nostrils drew in the faint but heavy perfume which she always associated with Baroudi, and now with the whole of the East, and with all Eastern things.

That racing dromedary had surely carried her through the night from one world to another. Suddenly she felt tired; she felt that she longed to lie down upon those great silk cushions, between those coloured walls of silk that shut out the windy darkness and the sad spaces of the sands, and to stay there for a long time. The courtesan's lazy, luxurious instinct drowsed within her soul, and her whole body responded to this perfumed warmth, to this atmosphere of riches created by the man before her in the core of desolation.

She sighed, and looked at his eyes.

"And how is Mr. Armeen?" he said, with the faintly ironic inflection which she had noticed in their first interview alone. "Has he gone out after the jackal?"

What his intention was she did not know, but he could not have said anything to her at that moment that would have struck more rudely upon her sensuous pleasure in the change one step had brought her. His words instantly put before her the necessity for going presently, very soon, back to the camp and Nigel, and they woke up in her the secret woman, the woman who still retained the instincts of a lady. This lady realized, almost as Eve realized her nakedness, the humiliation of that rush through the night from one camp to another, the humiliation that lay in the fact that it was she who sought the man, that he had her brought to him, did not trouble to come to her. She reddened beneath the paint on her face, turned swiftly round, bent down, and tried to undo the canvas flap of the tent. Her intention was to go out, to call Ibrahim, to leave the camp at once. But her hands trembled and she could not undo the canvas. Still bending, she struggled with it. She heard no movement behind her. Was Baroudi calmly waiting for her to go? Some one must have pegged the flap down after she had come in. She would have to kneel down on the carpet to get at the fastenings. It seemed to her, in her nervous anger and excitement, that to kneel in that tent would be a physical sign of humiliation; nevertheless, after an instant of hesitation, she sank to the ground and pushed her hands forcibly under the canvas, feeling almost frantically for the ropes. She grasped something, a rope, a peg—she did not know what—and pulled and tore at it with all her force.

Just then the night wind, which blew waywardly over the sands, now rising in a gust that was almost fierce, now dying away into a calm that was almost complete, failed suddenly, and she heard a frail sound which, by its very frailty, engaged all her attention. It was a reiteration of the sound which she thought she had heard as she waited outside the tent, and this time she was no longer in doubt. It was the cry of an instrument of music, a stringed instrument of some kind, plucked by demure fingers. The cry was repeated. A whimsical Eastern melody, very delicate and pathetic, crept to her from without.

It suggested to her—women.

Her hands became inert, and her fingers dropped from the tent-pegs. She thought of the other tent, of the smaller tent she had seen, standing apart near Baroudi's. Who was living in that tent?

The melody went on, running a wayward course. It might almost be a bird's song softly trilled in some desolate place of the sands, but——

It died away into the night, and the night wind rose again.

Mrs. Armine got up from her knees. Her hands were trembling no longer. She no longer wished to go.

"Arrange some of those cushions for me, Baroudi," she said. "I am tired after my ride."

He had not moved from where he had been standing when she came in, but she noticed that his long pipe had dropped from his hand and was lying on the carpet.

"Where shall I put them?" he asked, gravely.

She pointed to the side of the tent which was nearest to the smaller tent.

"Against the silk, two or three cushions. Then I can lean back. That will do."

She unbuttoned her fur jacket.

"Help me!" she said.

He drew it gently off. She sat down, and pulled off her gloves. She arranged the cushions with care behind her back. Her manner was that of a woman who meant to stay where she was for a long time. She was listening intently to hear the music again, but her face did not show that she was making any effort. Her self was restored to her, and her self was a woman who in a certain world, a world where women crudely, and sometimes quite openly, battle with other women for men, had for a long time resolutely, successfully, even cruelly, held her own.

Baroudi watched her with serious eyes. He picked up his pipe and let himself down on his haunches close to where she was leaning against her cushions. The night wind blew more strongly. There was no sound from the other tent. When Mrs. Armine knew that the wind must drown that strange, frail music, even if the hidden player still carelessly made it, she said, with a sort of brutality:

"And if my husband comes back to camp before my return there?"

"He will not."

"We can't know."

"The dromedary will take you there in fifteen minutes."

"He may be there now. If he is there?"

"Do you wish him to be there?"

He had penetrated her thought, gone down to her desire. That sound of music, that little cry of some desert lute plucked by demure fingers, perhaps stained with the henna, the colour of joy, had rendered her reckless. At that moment she longed for a crisis. And yet, at his question, something within her recoiled. Could she be afraid of Nigel? Could she cower before his goodness when it realized her evil? Marriage had surely subtly changed her, giving back to her desires, prejudices, even pruderies of feeling that she had thought she had got rid of for ever long ago. Some spectral instincts of the "straight" woman still feebly strove, it seemed, to lift their bowed heads within her.

"Things can't go on like this," she said. "I don't know what I wish. But I am not going to allow myself to be treated as you think you can treat me. Do you know that in Europe men have ruined themselves for me—ruined themselves?"

"You liked that!" he intercepted, with a smile of understanding. "You liked that very much. But I should never do that."

He shook his head.

"I would give you many things, but I am not one of those what the Englishman calls 'dam fools.'"

The practical side of his character, thus suddenly displayed, was like a cool hand laid upon her. It was like a medicine to her fever. It seemed for a moment to dominate a raging disease—the disease of her desire for him—which created, to be its perpetual companion, a furious jealousy involving her whole body, her whole spirit.

"Because you don't care for me," she said, after a moment of hesitation, and again running, almost in despite of herself, to meet her humiliation. "Every man who cares for a woman can be a fool for her, even an Eastern man."

"Why do I come here," he said, "two days through the desert from the Sphinx?"

"It amuses you to pursue an Englishwoman. You are cruel, and it amuses you."

Her cruelty to Nigel understood Baroudi's cruelty to her quite clearly at that moment, and she came very near to a knowledge of the law of compensation.

His eyes narrowed.

"Would you rather I did not pursue you?"

She was silent.

"Would you rather be left quietly to your life with Mr. Armeen?"

"Oh, I'm sick of my life with him!" she cried out, desperately. "It would be better if he were in camp tonight when I got back there; it would be much better!"

"And if he were in camp—would you tell him?"

Contempt crawled in his voice.

"You are not like one of our women," he said. "They know how to do what they want even behind the shutters of their husbands' houses. They are clever women when they walk in the ways of love."

He had made her feel like a child. He had struck hard upon her pride of a successful demi-mondaine.

"Of course I shouldn't tell him!" she said. "But perhaps it would be better if I did. For I'm tired of my life."

Again the horrible melancholy which so often comes to women of her type and age, and of which she was so almost angrily afraid, flowed over her. She must live as she wished to live in these few remaining years. She must break out of prison quickly, or, when she did break out, there would be no freedom that she could enjoy. She had so little time to lose. She could tell nothing to Baroudi of all this, but perhaps she could make him feel the force of her desire in such a way that an equal force of answering desire would wake in him. Perhaps she had never really exerted herself enough to put forth, when with him, all the powers of her fascination, long tempered and tried in the blazing furnaces of life.

The gusty wind died down across the sands, and again she heard the frail sound of the desert lute. It wavered into her ears, like something supple, yielding, insinuating.

There was a woman in that tent.

And she, Bella Donna, must go back to camp almost directly, and leave Baroudi with that woman! She was being chastised with scorpions to-night.

"Why did you come to this place?" she said.

"To be with you for an hour."

The irony, the gravity, that seemed almost cold in its calm, died out of his eyes, and was replaced by a shining that changed his whole aspect.

There was the divine madness in him too, then. Or was it only the madness that is not divine? She did not ask or care to know.

The night wind rose again, drowning the little notes of the desert lute.

* * * * *

That night, without being aware of it, Mrs. Armine crossed a Rubicon. She crossed it when she came out of the big tent into the sands to go back to the camp by the lake. While she had been with Baroudi the sky had partially cleared. Above the tents and the blazing fire some stars shone out benignly. A stillness and a pellucid clearness that were full of remote romance were making the vast desert their sacred possession. The aspect of the camp had changed. It was no longer a lurid and mysterious assemblage of men, animals, and tents, half revealed in the light of blown flames, half concealed by the black mantle of night, but a tranquil and restful picture of comfort and of repose, full of the quiet detail of feeding beasts, and men smoking, sleeping, or huddling together to tell the everlasting stories and play the games of draughts that the Arabs love so well.

But blackness and gusty storm were within her, and made the vision of this desert place, governed by the huge calm of the immersing night in this deep hour of rest, almost stupefying by its contrast with herself.

Baroudi had gone out first to speak with Ibrahim. She saw him, made unusually large and imposing by the ample robes he wore, the innumerable folds of muslin round his head, stride slowly across the sand and mingle with his attendants, who all rose up as he joined them. For a moment she stood quite still just beyond the shadow of the tent.

The exquisitely cool air touched her, to make her know that she was on fire. The exquisite clearness fell around her, to make her realize the misty confusion of her soul. She trembled as she stood there. Not only her body, but her whole nature was quivering.

And then she heard again the player upon the lute, and she saw a faint ray of light upon the sand by the tent she had not entered. She buttoned her fur jacket, twisted her gloves in her hands, and looked towards the ray. There was a hard throbbing in her temples, and just beneath her shoulders there came a sudden shock of cold, that was like the cold of menthol. She looked again at the camp fire; then she stole over the sand, set her feet on the ray, and waited.

For the first time she realized that she was afraid of Baroudi, that she would shrink from offending him almost as a dog shrinks from offending its master. But would it anger him if she saw the lute-player? He had not taken the trouble to silence that music. He treated women *de haut en bas*. That was part of his fascination for them—at any rate, for her. What would he care if she knew he had a woman with him in the camp, if she saw the woman?

And even if he were angry? She thought of his anger, and knew that at this moment she would risk it—she would risk anything—to see the woman in that tent. Thinking with great rapidity in her nervous excitement and bitter jealousy, become tenfold more bitter now that the moment had arrived for her departure, she imagined what the woman must be: probably some exquisite, fair Circassian, young, very young, fifteen or sixteen years old, or perhaps a maiden from the Fayyūm, the region of lovely dark maidens with broad brows, oval faces, and long and melting black eyes. Her fancy drew and painted marvellous girls in the night. Then, as a louder note, almost like a sigh, came from the tent, she moved forward, lifted the canvas, and looked in.

The interior was unlike the interior of Baroudi's tent. Here nothing was beautiful, though nearly everything was gaudy. The canvas was covered with coarse striped stuff, bright red and yellow, with alternate red and yellow rosettes all round the edge near the sand, which was strewn with bits of carpet on which enormous flowers seemed to be writhing in a wilderness of crude green and yellow leaves. Fastened to the walls, in tarnished frames, were many little pictures—oleographs of the most blatant type, chalk drawings of personages such as might people an ugly dream; men in uniforms with red noses and bulbous cheeks; dogs, cats, and sand-lizards, and coloured plates cut out of picture papers. Mingled with these were several objects that Mrs. Armine guessed to be charms, a mus-haf, or copy of the Koran, enclosed in a silver case which hung from a string of yellow silk; one or two small scrolls and bits of paper covered with Arab writing; two tooth-sticks in a wooden tube, open at one end; a child's shoe tied with string, to which were attached bits of coral and withered flowers; several tassels of shells mingled with bright blue and white beads; a glass bottle of blessed storax; and a quantity of Fatma hands, some very large and made of silver gilt, set with stones and lumps of a red material that looked like sealing-wax, others of silver and brass, small and practically worthless. There was also the foot of some small animal set in a battered silver holder. On a deal table stood a smoking oil lamp of mean design and cheap material. Underneath it was a large wooden chest or coffer, studded with huge brass nails, clamped with brass, and painted a brilliant green. Near it, touching the canvas wall, was a mattress covered with gaudy rugs that served as a bed.

In the tent there were two people. Although the thin sound of the music had suggested a woman to Mrs. Armine, the player was not a woman, but a tall and large young man, dressed in a bright yellow jacket cut like a "Zouave," wide drawers of white linen, yellow slippers, and the tarbush. Round his waist there was a girdle, made of a long and narrow red and yellow shawl with fringes and tassels. He was squatting cross-legged on the hideous carpet, holding in his large, pale hands, artificially marked with blue spots and tinted at the nails with the henna, a strange little instrument of sand-tortoise, goat-skin, wood, and catgut, with four strings from which he was drawing the plaintive and wavering tune. He wore a moustache and a small, blue-black beard. His eyes were half shut, his head drooped to one side, his mouth was partly open, and the expression upon his face was one of weak and sickly contentment. Now and then he sang a few notes in a withdrawn and unnatural voice, slightly shook his large and flaccid body, and allowed his head to tremble almost as if he were seized with palsy. Despite his breadth, his large limbs, and his beard, there was about his whole person an indescribable effeminacy, which seemed heightened, rather than diminished, by his bulk and his virile contours. A little way from him on the mattress a girl was sitting straight up, like an idol, with her legs and feet tucked away and completely concealed by her draperies.

Mrs. Armine looked from the man to her with the almost ferocious eagerness of the bitterly jealous woman. For she guessed at once that the man was no lover of this girl, but merely an attendant, perhaps a eunuch, who ministered to her pleasure. This was Baroudi's woman, who would stay here in the tent beside him, while she, the fettered, European woman, would ride back in the night to Kurûn. Yet could this be Baroudi's woman, this painted, jewelled, bedizened creature, almost macawlike in her bright-coloured finery, who remained quite still upon her rugs—like the macaw upon its perch—indifferent, somnolent surely, or perhaps steadily, enigmatically watchful, with a cigarette between her painted lips, above the chin, on which was tattooed a pattern resembling a little, indigo-coloured beard or "imperial"? Could he be attracted by this face, which, though it seemed young under its thick vesture of paint and collyrium, would surely not be thought pretty by any man who was familiar with the beauties of Europe and America, this face with its heavy features, its sultry, sullen eyes, its plump cheeks, and sensual lips?

Yes, he could. As she looked, with the horrible intuition of a feverishly strung up and excited woman Mrs. Armine felt the fascination such a creature held to tug at a man like Baroudi. Here was surely no mind, but only a body containing the will, inherited from how many Ghawázee ancestors, to be the plaything of man; a well-made body, yes, even beautifully made, with no heaviness such as showed in the face, a body that could move lightly, take supple attitudes, dance, posture, bend, or sit up straight, as now, with the perfect rigidity of an idol; a body that could wear rightly cascades of wonderfully tinted draperies, and spangled, vaporous tissues, and barbaric jewels, that do not shine brightly as if reflecting the modern, restless spirit, but that are somnolent and heavy and deep, like the eyes of the Eastern women of pleasure.

The player upon the desert lute had not seen that some one stood in the tent door. With half-shut eyes he continued playing and singing, lost in a sickly ecstasy. The woman on the gaudy rug sat quite still and stared at Mrs. Armine. She showed no surprise, no anger, no curiosity. Her expression did not change. Her motionless, painted mouth was set like a mouth carved in some hard material. Only her bosom stirred with a regular movement beneath her coloured tissues, her jewels and strings of coins.

Mrs. Armine stepped into the tent and dropped the flap behind her. She did not know what she was going to do, but she was filled with a bitter curiosity that she could not resist, with an intense desire to force her way into this woman's life, a life so strangely different from her own, yet linked with it by Baroudi. She hated this woman, yet with her hatred was mingled a subtle admiration, a desire to touch this painted toy that gave him pleasure, a longing to prove its attraction, to plumb the depth of its fascination, to learn from it a lesson in the strange lore of the East. She came close up to the woman and stood beside her.

Instantly one of the painted hands went up to her jacket, and gently, very delicately, touched its fur. Then the other hand followed, and the jacket was felt with wondering fingers, was stroked softly, first downwards, then upwards, while the dark and heavy eyes solemnly noted the thin shine of the shifting skin. The curiosity of Mrs. Armine was met by another but childlike curiosity, and suddenly, out of the cloud of mystery broke a ray of light that was naïve.

This naïveté confused Mrs. Armine. For a moment it seemed to be pushing away her anger, to be drawing the sting from her curiosity. But then the childishness of this strange rival stirred up in her a more acrid bitterness than she had known till now. And the wondering touch became intolerable to her. Why should such a creature be perfectly happy, while she with her knowledge, her experience, her tempered and perfected powers, lived in a turmoil of misery? She looked down into the Ghawázee's eyes, and suddenly the painted hands dropped from the fur, and she was confronted by a woman who was no longer naïve, who understood her, and whom she could understand.

The voice of the lute-player died away, the thin cry of the strings failed. He had seen. He rose to his feet, and said something in a language Mrs. Armine could not understand. The girl replied in a voice that sounded ironic, and suddenly began to laugh. At the same moment Baroudi came into the tent. The girl called out to him, pointed at Mrs. Armine, and went on laughing. He smiled at her, and answered.

"What are you saying to her?" said Mrs. Armine, fiercely. "How dare you speak to her about me? How dare you discuss me with her?"

"P'f! She is a child. She knows nothing. The camel is ready."

The girl spoke to him again with great rapidity, and an air of half-impudent familiarity that sickened Mrs. Armine. Something seemed to have roused within her a sense of boisterous humour. She gesticulated with her painted hands, and rocked on her mattress with an abandon almost negroid. Holding his lute in one pale hand, and stroking his blue-black beard with the other, her huge and flaccid attendant looked calmly on without smiling.

Mrs. Armine turned and went quickly out of the tent. Baroudi spoke again to the girl, joined in her merriment, then followed Mrs. Armine. She turned upon him and took hold of his cloak with both her hands, and her hands were trembling violently.

"How dared you bring me here?" she said. "How dared you?"

"I wanted you. You know it."

"That's not true."

"It is true."

"It is not true. How could you want me when you had that dancing-girl with you?"

He shrugged his shoulders, almost like one of the Frenchmen whom he had met ever since he was a child.

"You do not understand the men of the East, or you forget that I am an Oriental," he said.

A sudden idea struck her.

"Perhaps you are married, too?" she exclaimed.

"Of course I am married!"

His eyes narrowed, and his face began to look hard and repellent.

"It is not in our habits to discuss these things," he said.

She felt afraid of his anger.

"I didn't mean——"

She dropped her hands from his cloak.

"But haven't I a right?" she began.

She stopped. What was the use of making any claim upon such a man? What was the use of wasting upon him any feeling either of desire or of anger? What was the use? And yet she could not go without some understanding. She could not ride back into the camp by the lake and settle down to virtue, to domesticity with Nigel. Her whole nature cried out for this man imperiously. His strangeness lured her. His splendid physique appealed to her with a power she could not resist. He dominated her by his indifference as well as by his passion. He fascinated her by his wealth, and by his almost Jewish faculty of acquiring. His irony whipped her, his contempt of morality answered to her contempt. His complete knowledge of what she was warmed, soothed, reposed her.

But the thought of his infidelity to her as soon as she was away from him roused in her a sort of madness.

"How am I to see you again?" she said.

And all that she felt for him went naked in her voice.

"How am I to see you again?"

He stood and looked at her.

"And what is to happen to me if he has found out that I have been away from the camp?"

"Hamza will make an explanation."

"And if he doesn't believe the explanation?"

"You will make one. You will never tell him the truth."

It was a cold command laid like a yoke upon her.

"He can never know I have been here. To-night, directly you are gone, I strike my tents and go back to Cairo. I do not choose to have any bad affairs with the English so long as the English rule in Egypt. I am well looked upon by the English, and so it must continue. Otherwise my affairs might suffer. And that I will not have. Do you understand?"

She looked at him, and said nothing.

"We have to do what we want in the world without losing anything by it. Thus it has always been with me in my life."

She thought of all she had lost long ago by doing the thing she desired, and again she felt herself inferior to him.

"And this, too, we shall do without losing anything by it," he said.

"This? What?"

"Go back to Kurûn. Tell me. Will you not presently need to have a dahabeeyah?"

"And if we do?"

"You shall have the *Loulia.*"

"You mean to come with us?"

"Are you a child? I shall let it to your husband at a price that will suit his purse, so that you may be housed as you ought to be. I shall let it with my crew, my servants, my cook. Then you must take your husband away with you quietly up the Nile."

Again Mrs. Armine was conscious of a shock of cold.

"Quietly up the Nile?" she repeated.

"Yes."

"What is the use of that?"

"Perhaps he will like the Nile so much that he will not come back."

He looked into her eyes. She heard the snarl of a camel.

"Your camel is ready," he said.

They walked towards the fire where Ibrahim was awaiting them. Before Mrs. Armine had settled herself in the palanquin Baroudi moved away without another word, and as the camel rose, complaining in the night, she saw him lift the canvas of the Ghawázee's tent and disappear within it.

When she reached the camp by the lake, Nigel had not returned. She undressed quickly, got into bed, and lay there shivering, though heavy blankets covered her.

Just at dawn Nigel came back.

Then she shut her eyes and pretended to sleep.

Always she was shivering.

XXV

"Ruby," Nigel said, as he stood with her on the deck of the *Loulia* and looked up at the Arabic letters of gold inscribed above the doorway through which they were going to pass, "what is the exact meaning of those words? Baroudi told us that day at Luxor, but I've forgotten. It was some lesson of fate, something from the Koran. D'you remember?"

She turned up her veil over the brim of her burnt-straw hat. "Let me see!" she said.

She seemed to make an effort of memory, and lines came on her generally smooth forehead.

"I fancy it was 'The fate of every man have we bound about his neck,' or something very like that."

"Yes, that was it. We discussed it, and I said I wasn't a fatalist."

"Did you? Come along. Let's explore."

"Our floating home—yes."

He took hold of her arm.

"If my fate is bound about my neck, it's a happy fate," he said—"a fate I can wear as a jewel instead of bearing as a burden."

They went down the steps together, and vanished through the doorway into the shadows beyond.

The *Loulia* was moored at Keneh, not far from the temple of Denderah. She had been sent up the river from

Assiout, where Baroudi had left her when he had finished his business affairs and was ready to start for Cairo. It was Nigel's wish that he and his wife should join her there.

"Denderah was the first temple you and I saw together," he said. "Let's see it more at our leisure. And let us ask Aphrodite to bless our voyage."

"Hathor! What, are you turning pagan?" she said.

He laughed as he looked into her blue eyes.

"Scarcely; but she was the Egyptian Goddess of Beauty, and I don't think she could deny her blessing to you."

Then she was looking radiant!

That cold which had made her shudder in the night by the sacred lake had been left in the desolation of Libya. Surely, it could never come to her here in the golden warmth of Upper Egypt. She said to herself that she would not shudder again now that she had escaped from that blanched end of the world where desperation had seized her.

The day of departure for the Nile journey had come, and Nigel and she set foot upon the *Loulia* for the first time as proprietors.

They passed the doors of the servants' cabins, and came into their own quarters. Ibrahim followed softly behind with a smiling face, and Hamza, standing still in the sunshine beneath the golden letters, looked after them imperturbably.

Baroudi's "den" had been swept and garnished. Flowers and small branches of mimosa decorated it, as if this day were festal. The writing-table, which had been loaded with papers, was now neat and almost bare. But all, or nearly all, Baroudi's books were still in their places. The marvellous prayer rugs strewed the floor. Ibrahim had set sticks of incense burning in silver holders. Upon the dining-room table, beyond the screen of mashrebeeyah work, still stood the tawdry Japanese vase. And the absurd cuckoo clock uttered its foolish sound to greet them.

"The eastern house!" said Nigel. "You little thought you would ever be mistress of it, did you, Ruby? How wonderful these prayer rugs are! But we must get rid of that vase."

"Why?" she said hastily, almost sharply.

He looked at her in surprise.

"You don't mean to say you like it? Besides, it doesn't belong to the room. It's a false note."

"Of course. But it appeals to my sense of humour—like that ridiculous cuckoo clock. Don't let's change anything. The incongruities are too delicious."

"You are a regular baby!" he said. "All right. Shall we make Baroudi's 'den' your boudoir?"

She nodded, smiling.

"And you shall use it whenever you like. And now for the bedrooms!"

"More incongruities," he said. "But never mind. They looked delightfully clean and cosy."

"Clean and cosy!" she repeated, with a sort of light irony in her beautiful voice. "Is that all?"

"Well, I mean——"

"I know. Come along."

They opened the doors and looked into each gay and luxurious little room. And as Mrs. Armine went from one to another, she was aware of the soft and warm sensation that steals over a woman returning to the atmosphere which thoroughly suits her, and from which she has long been exiled. Here she could be in her element, for here money had been lavishly spent to create something unique. She felt certain that no dahabeeyah on the Nile was so perfect as the *Loulia*. Every traveller upon the river would be obliged to envy her. For a moment she secretly revelled in that thought; then she remembered something; her face clouded, her lips tightened, and she strove to chase from her mind that desire to be envied by other women.

Nigel and she must avoid the crowds that gather on the Nile in the spring. They must tie up in the unfrequented places. Had she not reiterated to him her wish to "get away from people," to see only the native life on the river? Those "other women" must wait to be envious, and she, too, must wait. She stifled an impatient sigh, and opened another door. After one swift glance within, she said:

"I will have this cabin, Nigel."

"All right, darling. Anything you like. But let's have a look."

For a moment she did not move.

"Don't be selfish, Ruby!"

She felt fingers touching her waist at the back, gripping her with a sort of tender strongness; and she closed her eyes, and tried to force herself to believe they were Baroudi's fingers of iron.

"Or I shall pick you up and lift you out of the way."

When Nigel spoke again, she opened her eyes. It was no use. She was not to have that illusion. She set her teeth and put her hands behind her, feeling for his fingers. Their hands met, clasped. She fell back, and let him look in.

"Why, this must be Baroudi's cabin!" he said.

"I dare say. But what I want it for is the size. Don't you see, it's double the size of the others," she said, carelessly.

"So it is. But they are ever so much gayer. This is quite Oriental, and the bed's awfully low."

He bent down and felt it.

"It's a good one, though. Trust Baroudi for that. Well, dear, take it; I'll turn in next door. We can easily talk through the partition"—he paused, then added in a lower voice—"when we are not together. Now there's the other sitting-room to see and then shall we be off to Denderah with Hamza, while Ibrahim sees to the arrangement of everything?"

"Yes. Or—shall we leave the other room till we come back, till it's getting twilight? I don't think I want to see quite everything just at once."

"You're becoming a regular child, saving up your pleasure. Then we'll start for Denderah now."

"Yes."

She drew her veil over her face rather quickly, and walked down the passage, through the arch in the screen, and out to the brilliant sunshine that flooded the sailors' deck. For though the Nubians had spread an awning over their heads, they had not let down canvas as yet to meet the white and gold of the bulwarks forward. And there was a strong sparkle of light about them. In the midst of that sparkle Hamza stood, a little away from the crew, who were tall, stalwart, black men, evidently picked men, for not one was mean or ugly, not one lacked an eye or was pitted with smallpox.

As Mrs. Armine came up the three steps from the cabins, walking rather hurriedly, as if in haste to get to the sunshine, Hamza sent her a steady look that was like a quiet but determined rebuke. His eyes seemed to say to her, "Why do you rush out of the shadows like this?" And she felt as if they were adding, "You who must learn to love the shadows." His look affected her nerves, even affected her limbs. At the top of the steps she stood still, then looked round, with a slight gesture as if she would return.

"What is it, Ruby?" asked Nigel. "Have you forgotten anything?"

"No, no. Is it this side? Or must we have the felucca? I forget."

"It's this side. The *Loulia* is tied up here on purpose. The donkeys, Hamza!"

He spoke kindly, but in the authoritative voice of the young Englishman addressing a native. Without changing his expression, Hamza went softly and swiftly over the gangway to the shore, climbed the steep brown bank, and was gone—a flash of white through the gold.

"He's a useful fellow, that!" said Nigel. "And now, Ruby, to seek the blessing of the Egyptian Aphrodite. It will be easily won, for Aphrodite could never turn her face from you."

As their tripping donkeys drew near to that lonely temple, where a sad Hathor gazes in loneliness upon the courts that are no longer thronged with worshippers, Mrs. Armine fell into silence. The disagreeable impression she had received here on her first visit was returning. But on her first visit she had been tired, worn with travel. Now she was strong, in remarkable health. She would not be the victim of her nerves. Nevertheless, as the donkeys covered the rough ground, as she saw the pale façade of the temple confronting her in the pale sands, backed by the almost purple sky, she remembered the carven face of the goddess, and a fear that was superstitious stirred in her heart. Why had Nigel suggested that they should seek the blessing of this tragic Aphrodite? No blessing, surely, could emanate from this dark dwelling in the sands, from this goddess long outraged by desertion.

They dismounted, and went into the temple. No one was there except the chocolate-coloured guardian, who greeted them with a smile of welcome that showed his broken teeth.

"May your day be happy!" he said to them in Arabic.

"He ought to say, 'May all your days on the Nile be happy,' Ruby," said Nigel.

"He only wants the day on which we pay him to be happy. On any other day we might die like dogs, and he wouldn't care."

She stood still in the first court, and looked up at the face of Hathor, which seemed to regard the distant spaces with an eternal sorrow.

"I think you count too much on happiness, Nigel," she added. She felt almost impelled by the face to say it. "I believe it's a mistake to count upon things," she added.

"You think it's a mistake to look forward, as I am doing, to our Nile journey?"

"Perhaps."

She walked on slowly into the lofty dimness of the temple.

"One never knows what is going to happen," she added. And there was almost a grimness in her voice.

"And it all passes away so fast, whatever it is," he

said. "But that is no reason why we should not take our happiness and enjoy it to the utmost. Why do you try to damp my enthusiasm to-day?"

"I don't try. But it is dangerous to be too sure of happiness beforehand."

She was speaking superstitiously, and she was really speaking to herself. At first she had been thinking of, speaking to, him as if for his own good, moved by a sort of dim pity that surely belonged rather to the girl she had been than to the woman she actually was. Now the darkness of this lonely temple and the knowledge that it was Aphrodite's—she thought always of Hathor as Aphrodite—preyed again upon her spirit as when she first came to it. She felt the dreadful brevity of a woman's, of any woman's triumph over the world of men. She felt the ghastly shortness of the life of physical beauty. She seemed to hear the sound of the movement of Time rushing away, to see the darkness of the End closing about her, as now the dimness of this desolate shrine of beauty and love grew deeper round her.

Far up, near the forbidding gloom of the mighty roof, there rose a fiercely petulant sound, a chorus of angry cries. Large shadows with beating wings came and went rapidly through the forest of heavy columns. The monstrous bats of Hathor were disturbed in their brooding reveries. A heavy smell, like the odour of a long-decaying past, lifted itself, as if with a slow, determined effort, to Mrs. Armine's nostrils. And ever the light of day failed slowly as she and Nigel went onward, drawn in despite of themselves by the power of the darkness, and by the mysterious perfumes that swept up from the breast of death.

At last they came into the sanctuary, the "Holy of Holies" of Denderah, where once were treasured images of the gods of Egypt, where only the King or his high priest might venture to come, at the fête of the New Year. They stood in its darkness, this woman who was longing to return to the unbridled life of her sensual and disordered past, and this man who, quite without vanity, believed that he had been permitted to redeem her from it.

The guardian of the temple, who had followed them softly, now lit a ribbon of magnesium, and there sprang into a vague and momentary life reliefs of the King performing ceremonies and accomplishing sacrifices. Then the darkness closed again. And the fragmentary and short vision seemed to Mrs. Armine like the vision of her little life as a beautiful woman, and the coming of the darkness to blot it out like the coming of the darkness of death to cover her for ever with its impenetrable mantle.

What she had told Meyer Isaacson in his consulting-room was true. When she thought sincerely, she believed in no future life. She could not conceive of a spirit life. Nor could she conceive of the skeletons of the dead in some strange resurrection being reclothed with the flesh which she adored, being inhabited again by the vitality which makes skeleton and flesh living man or woman. This life was all to her. And when the light in which it existed and was perceived died away and was consumed, she believed that the vision could never reappear.

Now, in this once so sacred place, she seemed for a moment to plunge into the depths of herself, to penetrate into the inmost recesses of her nature. In London, before Nigel came into her life, had she not been like Hathor in her temple, hearing the sound of the departing feet of those who had been her worshippers? And with Nigel had come a wild hope of worldly eminence, of great riches, of a triumph over enemies. And that hope had faded abruptly. Yet through her association with Nigel she had come to another hope. And this hope must be fulfilled, before the inevitable darkness that would fall about her beauty. Nigel would never be the means to the end she had originally had in view. Yet his destiny was to serve her. He had his destiny, and she hers. And hers was not a great worldly position, or any ultimate respectability. She could not have the first, and so she would not have the second. Perhaps she was born for other things—born to be a votary of Venus, but not to content any man as his lawful wife. The very word "lawful" sent a chill through her blood now. She was meant for lawlessness, it seemed. Then she would fulfil her destiny, without pity, without fear, but not without discretion. And her destiny was to emerge from the trap in which she was confined. So she believed.

Yet would she emerge? In the darkness of Hathor's sanctuary, haunted by the face of the goddess and by the sad thoughts of deserted womanhood which it suggested to her self-centred mind, she resolved that she would emerge, that nothing should stop her, that she would crush down any weakening sentiments and thoughts if they came to heart or mind. Egypt, in which one desire had been rendered useless and finally killed in her, had given to her another, had brought to her a last chance—she seemed to know it was that—of happiness, of ugly yet intense joy. In Egypt she had blossomed, fading woman though she had been. She had renewed her powers of physical fascination. Then she must emerge from the trap and go to fulfil her destiny. She would do so. Silently, and as if making the vow to the Egyptian Aphrodite in the darkness of her temple, she swore to do so. Nigel had brought her there—had he not?—that Hathor might bless her voyage. Moved by a fierce impulse, and casting away pity, doubt, fear, everything but flamelike desire, she called upon Hathor to bless her voyage—not their voyage, but only hers. She called upon the goddess of beauty, the pagan goddess of the love that was not spiritual.

And she almost felt as if she was answered.

Yet only the enormous bats cried fiercely to her from far up in the dimness. She only heard their voices and the beating of their wings.

"Let's go, Ruby. I don't know why, but to-day I hate this place."

She started at the sound of his voice close to her. But she controlled herself immediately, and replied, quietly:

"Yes, let us go. We are only disturbing the bats."

As they went out, she looked up to the column from which Hathor gazed as if seeking for her worshippers, and she whispered adieu to the goddess.

As soon as they were on board of the *Loulia* Nigel gave

the order to cast off. He seemed unusually restless, and in a hurry to be *en route*. With eagerness he spoke to the impassive Reis, whose handsome head was swathed in a shawl, and who listened imperturbably. He went about on the sailors' deck watching the preparations, seeing the ropes hauled in, the huge poles brought out to fend them from off the bank, the gigantic sail unfurled to catch the evening breeze, which was blowing from the north, and which would take them up against the strong set of the current. And when the water curled and eddied about the *Loulia's* prow, and the shores seemed slipping away and falling back into the primrose light of the north, and into the great dahabeeyah there came that mysterious feeling of life which thrills through the moving vessel, he flung up his arms, and uttered an exclamation that was like a mingled sigh and half-suppressed shout. Then he laughed at himself, and turned to look for Ruby.

She was alone on the upper deck, standing among some big palms in pots, with her hands on the rail, and gazing towards him. She had taken off her hat and veil, and the breeze stirred, and the gold of the departing sun lit up the strands of her curiously pale yet shining hair. He sprang up the companion to stand beside her.

"We're off!" he said.

"How glad you seem! You called me a child. But you're like a mad boy—mad to be moving. One would think you had——No, that wouldn't be like a boy."

"What do you mean?"

"I was going to say one would think you had an enemy in Keneh and were escaping from him."

"Him! Her, you should say."

"Her?"

"Hathor. That temple of Denderah seemed haunted to-day."

He pulled off his hat to let the breeze get at his hair, too.

"When we were standing in the sanctuary I seemed to be smelling death and corruption. Ugh!"

His face changed at the memory.

"And the cries of those bats! They sounded like menacing spirits. I was a fool to go to such a place to ask a blessing on our voyage. My attempt at paganism was punished, and no wonder, Ruby. For I don't think I'm really a bit of a pagan; I don't think I see much joy in the pagan life, that is so much cracked up by some people. I don't see how the short life and the merry one can ever be really merry at all. How can a man be merry with a darkness always in front of him?"

"What darkness?"

"Death—without immortality."

She said nothing for a moment. Then she asked him:

"Do you look upon death merely as a door into another life?"

"I believe it is. Don't you?"

"Yes. Then you don't dread death?"

"Don't I—now? It would be leaving so much now. And besides, I love this life; I revel in it. Who wouldn't, with health like mine? Feel that arm!"

She did not move. He took her hand and pressed her fingers against his muscles.

"It's like iron," she said, taking away her hand. "But muscle and health are not exactly the same thing, are they?"

"No; of course not. But did you ever see a man look more perfectly well than I do?"

As he stood beside her, radiant now, upright, with the breeze ruffling his short, fair hair, his enthusiastic blue eyes shining with happiness, he did look like a young god of health and years younger than his age.

"Oh, you look all right," she said; "just like lots of other men who go in for sport and keep themselves fit."

He laughed.

"You won't pay me the compliment I want. Look at those barges loaded with pottery! All those thousands of little vases—*koulal*, as the natives call them—are made in Keneh. I've seen the men doing it—boys too—the wet clay spinning round the brown finger that makes the orifice. How good it is to see the life of the river! There's always something new, always something interesting, humanity at work in the sunshine and the open air. Who wouldn't be a fellah rather than a toiler in any English town? Here are the shadûfs! All the way up the Nile we shall see them, and we shall hear the old shadûf songs, that sound as if they came down from the days when they cut the Sphinx out of the living rock, and we shall hear the drowsy song of the water-wheels, as the sleepy oxen go round and round in the sunshine; and we shall see the women coming in lines from the inland villages with the water-jars poised on their heads. If only we were back in the days when there were no steamers and the Nile must have been like a perpetual dream! But never mind. At least we refused Baroudi's steam-tug. So we shall just go up with the wind, or be poled up when there is none, if we aren't tied up under the bank. That's the only way to travel on the Nile, but of course Baroudi uses it, as one uses the railway, to go to business."

He stopped, as if his mind had taken a turn towards some other line of thought; then he said:

"Isn't it odd that you and I should be established in Baroudi's boat, when we've never seen him again since the day we had tea on it? I almost thought——"

"What?"

"I almost thought perhaps he'd run up by train to give us a sort of send-off."

"Why should he?"

"Of course it wasn't necessary. Still, it would have been an act of pretty politeness to you."

"Oh, I think the less pretty politeness European women have from these Orientals the better!" she said, almost with a sneer.

"You're thinking of that horrible German woman in the Fayyūm. But Baroudi's very well looked on by the English in Egypt. I found that out in Cairo, when I left you to go to the Fayyūm. He's quite a *persona grata* for an Egyptian. Everybody seems ready to do him a good turn. That's partly why he's been so successful in all he's undertaken."

"I dare say he's not bad in his way, but as long as we've got his lovely boat I can do quite well without him," she said, smiling. "Where are we going to tie up to-night, and when?"

"When it gets dark. The Reis knows where. Isn't it glorious to be quite free and independent? We can stop wherever we like, in the lonely places, where there'll be no tourists to bother us."

"Yes," she said, echoing his enthusiasm, while she looked at him with smiling eyes. "Let's avoid the tourists and stop in the lonely places. Well, I'm going down now."

"Why? What are you going to do? The sun will soon be setting. We ought to see the first afterglow from the *Loulia* together."

"Call me, then, when it comes. But I'm going to take a lesson in coffee-making as they do it out here. It will amuse me to make our coffee after lunch. Besides, it will be something to do. And I want to take an interest in everything, in all the trifles of this odd new life."

He put his arm around her shoulder.

"Splendid!" he said.

His hand tightened upon her.

"But you must come for the afterglow."

"Call me, and I'll come."

As she went down the companion, he leaned over the rail and asked her:

"Who's going to give you your lesson in coffee-making?"

"Hamza," she answered.

And she disappeared.

XXVI

"ALL the way up the Nile we shall hear the old shadûf songs," Nigel had said, when the *Loulia* set sail from Keneh.

As Mrs. Armine went down to meet Hamza, she was aware of the loud voices of the shadûf men. They came from both banks of the Nile—powerfully from the eastern, faintly from the western bank soon to be drowned in the showers of gold from the sinking sun. Yet she could hear that even those distant voices were calling loudly, that in their faintness there was violence. And she thought of the fellah's voice that cried to her in the orange-garden, and how for a moment she had thought of flight before she had found herself in a prison of prayer. Now she was in another prison. But even then the inexorable hands had closed upon her, and the final cry of the fellah had thrilled with a savage triumph. She had remembered "Aïda" that day. She remembered it again now. Then, in her youth, she had believed that the passion which had wrecked her was the passion of her life, a madness of the senses, a delirium of the body which could never be repeated in later years for another object. How little she had known herself or life! How little she had known the cruel forces of mature age. That passion of her girlhood seemed to her like an anæmic shadow of the wolfish truth that was alive in her now. In those days the power to feel, the power to crave, to shudder with jealousy, to go almost mad in the face of a menacing imagination, was not full-grown. Now it was full-grown, and it was a giant. Yet in those days she had allowed the shadow to ruin her. In these she meant to be more wary. But now she was tortured by a nature that she feared.

The die was cast. She had no more thought of escape or of resistance. The supreme selfishness of the materialist, which is like no other selfishness, was fully alive within her. Believing not at all in any future for her soul, she desired present joy for her clamorous body as no one not a materialist could ever desire. If she failed in having what she longed for now, while she still retained the glow of her Indian summer, she believed she would have nothing more at all, that all would be finally over for her, that the black gulf would gape for her and that she would vanish into it for ever. She was a desperate woman, beneath her mask of smiling calm, when the *Loulia* set sail and glided into the path of the golden evening.

Nevertheless, directly she had descended the shallow steps, and come into the luxurious cabin that was to be her boudoir, she was conscious of a feeling of relief that was almost joy. The comfort, the perfect arrangements of the *Loulia* gave her courage. She was able to look forward. The soul of her purred with a sensual satisfaction. She went on down the passage to the room of the fountain and of the gilded ball. But to-day the fountain was not playing, and the little ball floated upon the water in the marble basin like a thing that had lost its life. She felt a slight shock of disappointment. Then she remembered that they were moving. Probably the fountain only played when the dahabeeyah was at rest. The grotesque monster, like a dragon with a dog's head, which she had seen on her first visit, looked down on her from its bracket. And she felt as if it welcomed her. The mashrebeeyeh lattices were closed over the windows, but the sliding doors that gave on to the balcony were pushed back, and let in the light of evening, and a sound of water, and of voices along the Nile. She sat down on the divan, and almost immediately Hamza came in.

"You are going to show me how to make Turkish coffee, Hamza?" she said, in her lazy and careless voice.

"Yes," he replied.

"Where shall we do it?"

He pointed towards the raised balcony in the stern.

"Out there!" she said.

She seemed disappointed, but she got up slowly and followed him out. The awning was spread so that the upper deck was not visible. When she saw that, the cloud passed away from her face, and as she sat down to receive her lesson, there was a bright and hard eagerness and attention in her eyes and about her lips.

Hamza had already brought a brazier with iron legs, which was protected from the wind by a screen of canvas. On the polished wood close to it there were a shining saucepan containing water, a brass bowl of freshly roasted and pounded coffee, two small open coffee-pots with handles that stuck straight out, two coffee-cups, a tiny bowl of powdered sugar, and some paper parcels which held sticks of mastic, ambergris, and seed of cardamom. As soon as Mrs. Armine was seated by the brazier Hamza, whose face looked as if he were quite alone, with slow and almost dainty delicacy and precision proceeded with his task. Squatting down upon his haunches, with his thin brown legs well under his reed-like body, he poured the water from the saucepan into one of the copper pots, set the pot on the brazier, and seemed to sink into a reverie, with his enigmatic eyes, that took all and gave nothing, fixed on the burning coals. Mrs. Armine was motionless, watching him, but he never looked at her. There was something animal in his abstraction. Presently there came from the pot a murmur. Instantly Hamza stretched out his hand, took the pot from the brazier and the bowl of coffee from the ground, let some of the coffee slip into the water, stirred it with a silver spoon which he produced from a carefully folded square of linen, and set the pot once more on the brazier. Then he unfolded the paper which held the ambergris, put a carat weight of it into the second pot and set that, too, on the brazier. The coffee began to simmer. He lit a stick of mastic, fumigated with its smoke the two little coffee-cups, took the coffee-pot, and gently poured the fragrant coffee into the pot containing the melted ambergris, let it simmer for a moment there, poured it out into the coffee-cups, creaming and now sending forth with its own warm perfume the enticing perfume of ambergris, added a dash of the cardamom seed, and then, at last, looked towards Mrs. Armine.

"It's ready? Then—then shall I put the sugar in?" she said.

"Yes," said Hamza, looking steadily at her.

She stretched out her hand, but not to the sugar bowl. Just as she did so a voice from over their heads called out:

"Ruby! Ruby!"

"Come down here!" she called, in answer.

"But I want you to come up and see the sunset and the afterglow with me."

"Come down here first," she called.

"Right!"

The coffee-making was finished. Hamza got up from his haunches, lifted up the brazier, and went softly away, carrying it with a nonchalant ease almost as if it were a cardboard counterfeit weighing nothing.

In a moment Nigel came into the dim room of the fountain.

"Where are you? Oh, there! We mustn't miss our first sunset."

"Coffee!" she said, smiling.

He came out on to the balcony, and she gave him one of the little cups.

"Did you make it yourself?"

"No. But I will to-morrow. Hamza has been showing me how to."

He took the cup.

"It smells delicious, as enticing as perfumes from Paradise. I think you must have made it."

"Drink it, and believe so—you absurd person!" she said, gently.

He sipped, and she did likewise.

"It's perfect, simply perfect. But what has been put into it to give it this peculiar, delicious flavour, Ruby?"

"Ah, that's my secret."

She sipped from her little cup.

"It is extraordinarily good," she said.

She pointed to the small paper packets, which Hamza had not yet carried off.

"The preparation is almost like some sacred rite," she said. "We put in a little something from this packet, and a little something from that. And we smoke the cups with one of those burning sticks of mastic. And then, at the very end, when the coffee is frothing and creaming, we dust it with sugar. This is the result."

"Simply perfect."

He put his cup down empty.

"Look at that light!" he said, pointing over the rail to the yellow water which they were leaving behind them. "Have you finished?"

"Quite."

"Then let's go on deck—coffee-maker."

They were quite alone. He put his arm around her as she stood up.

"Everything you give me seems to me different from other things," he said—"different, and so much better."

"Your imagination is kind to me—too kind. You are foolish about me."

"Am I?"

He looked into her eyes, and his kind and enthusiastic eyes became almost piercing for an instant.

"And you, Ruby?"

"I?"

"Could you ever be foolish about me?"

For a moment his joy seemed to be clouded by a faint and creeping doubt, as if he were mentally comparing her condition of heart with his, and as if the comparison were beginning—only just beginning—dimly to distress him. She knew just how he was feeling, and she leaned against him, making her body feel weak.

"I don't want to," she said.

"Why not?"

Already the cloud was evaporating.

"I don't want to suffer. I want to be happy now in the short time I have left for happiness."

"Why do you say 'the short time'?"

"I'm not young any more. And I've suffered enough in my life."

"But through me! How could you suffer? Don't you trust me completely even yet?"

"It isn't that. But—it's dangerous for a woman to be foolish about any man. It's a folly to care too much."

She spoke with a sincerity there was no mistaking, for she was thinking about Baroudi.

"Only sometimes. Only when one cares for the weak, or the insincere. We—needn't count the cost, and hesitate."

She let him close her lips, which were opening for a reply, and while he kissed her she listened to the voices of the shadûf men ever calling on the banks of the river.

When they were on the upper deck those voices seemed to her louder. That evening it was a sunset of sheer gold. The cloudless sky—so it seemed—would brook no other colour; the hills would receive no gift that was not a gift of gold. A pageant of gold that was almost barbaric was offered to Mrs. Armine. Out of the gold the voices cried from banks that were turning black. Always, in Egypt, the gold turns the barques on the Nile, its banks, the palm-trees that sometimes crown them, the houses of the native villages, black. And so it was that evening, but Nigel only saw and thought of the gold.

"At last we are sailing into the gold," he said. "This makes me think of a picture that I love."

"What picture?"

"A picture by Watts, called 'Progress.' In it there is a wonderful glow. I remember I spoke of it to Meyer Isaacson on the evening when I introduced him to you."

She had been leaning over the rail on the starboard side of the boat. Now she lifted her arms, stood straight up, then sat down in a beehive chair, and leaned back against the basket-work, which creaked as if protesting.

"To Meyer Isaacson!" she said. "What did you say about it?"

He turned, set his back against the rail, and looked at her in her hooded shelter.

"We spoke of progress. The picture's an allegory, of

course, an allegory of the spiritual progress of the world, and of each one of us. I remember telling Isaacson how firmly I believed in the triumph of good in the world and the individual."

"And what did he say?"

"Isaacson? I don't know that he quite took my view."

"He's a tiny bit of a suspicious man, I think."

"Perhaps he wants more solid proof—proof you could point to and say, 'Look there! I rely on that!' than I should."

"He's ever so much more *terre à terre* than you are."

"Oh, Ruby, I don't know that!"

"Yes, he is. He's a delightfully clever and a very interesting man, but, though he mayn't think it he's *terre à terre*. He sees with extraordinary clearness, but only a very little way, and he would never believe anything important existed beyond the range of his vision. You are not like that!"

"He's a thousand times cleverer than I am."

"Yes, he's so clever that he's distrustful. Now, for instance, he'd never believe in a woman like me."

"Oh——" he began, in a tone of energetic protest.

"No, he wouldn't," she interrupted, quietly. "To the end of time he would judge me by the past. He would label me 'woman to beware of' and my most innocent actions, my most impulsive attempts to show forth my true and better self he would entirely misinterpret, brilliant man though he is. Nigel, believe me, we women know!"

"But, then, surely you must dislike Isaacson very much!"

"On the contrary, I like him."

"I can't understand that."

"I don't require of him any of the splendid things that —well, that I do require of you, because I could never care for him. If he were to play me false, even if he were to hate me a thousand times more than he does, it wouldn't upset me, because I could never care for him."

"You think Isaacson hates you!" he exclaimed.

He had forgotten the gold of the sunset, the liquid gold of the river. He saw only her, thought only of what she was saying, thinking.

"Nigel, tell me the truth. Do you think he likes me?"

He looked down.

"He doesn't know you. If he did——"

"If he did, it would make not a bit of difference."

"I think it would; all the difference."

She smilingly shook her head.

"I should always wear my label, 'woman to beware of.' But what does it matter? I'm not married to him. If I were, ah, then I should be the most miserable woman on earth—now!"

He sat down close to her in another beehive chair.

"Ruby, why did you say 'now' like that?"

"Oh," she spoke in a tone of lightness that sounded assumed, "because now I've lived in an atmosphere not of mistrust. And it's spoilt me completely."

He felt within him a glow strong and golden as the glow of the sunset. At last she had forgotten their painful scene in the garden. He had fought for and had won her soul's forgetfulness.

"I'm glad," he said, with the Englishman's almost blunt simplicity—"I'm glad. I wish Isaacson knew."

She felt as if she frowned, but not a wrinkle came on her forehead.

"I didn't tell you," he added, "but I wrote to Isaacson the other day."

"Did you?"

Her hands met in her lap, and her fingers clasped.

"Yes, I sent him quite a good letter. I told him we were going up the Nile in Baroudi's boat, and how splendid you were looking, and how immensely happy we were. I told him we were going to cut all the travellers, and just live for our two selves in the quiet places where there are no steamers and no other dahabeeyahs. And I told him how magnificently well I was."

"Oh, treating him as the great Doctor, I suppose!"

She unclasped her hands, and took hold of the rudimentary arms of her chair.

"No. But I felt expansive—riotously well—when I was writing, and I just stuck it down with all the rest."

"And the rest?"

She leaned forward a little, as if she wanted to see the sunset better, but soon she looked at him.

"Oh, I let him understand just how it is between you and me. And I told him about the dahabeeyah, what a marvel it is, and about Baroudi, and how Ibrahim put Baroudi up to the idea of letting it to us."

"I see."

"How these chairs creak!" he said. "Yours is making a regular row."

She got up.

"You aren't going down again?"

"No. Let us walk about."

"All right."

He joined her and they began slowly to pace up and down, while the gold grew fainter in the sky, fainter upon the river. She kept silence, and perhaps communicated her wish for silence to him, for he did not speak until the sunset had faded away, and the world of water, green flats, desert, and arid hills grew pale in the pause before the afterglow. Then at last he said:

"What is it, Ruby? What are you thinking about so seriously?"

"I don't know."

She looked at him, and seemed to take a resolve.

"Yes, I do."

"Have I said something that has vexed you? Are you vexed at my writing to Isaacson to tell him about our happiness?"

"Not vexed, no. But somehow it seems to take off the edge of it a little. But men don't understand such things, so it's no use talking of it."

"But I want to understand everything. You see, Isaacson is my friend. Isn't it natural that I should let him know of my happiness?"

"Oh, yes, I suppose so. Never mind. What does it matter?"

"You dislike my having written to him?"

"I'm a fool, Nigel—that's the truth. I'm afraid of everything and everybody."

"Afraid! You're surely not afraid of Isaacson?"

"I tell you I'm afraid of everybody."

She stopped by the rail, and looked towards the west.

"To me happiness seems such a brittle thing that any one might break it. And men—forgive me!—men generally have such clumsy hands."

He leaned on the rail beside her, turning himself towards her.

"You don't mean to say that you think Isaacson could ever break our happiness, even if he wished to?"

"Why not?"

"Don't you understand me at all?"

There was in his voice a tremor of deep feeling.

"Do you think," he went on, "that a man who is worth anything at all would allow even his dearest friend to come between him and the woman whom he loved and who was his? Do you think that I would allow any one, woman or man, to come between me and you?"

"Are you sure you wouldn't?"

"What a tragedy it must be to be so distrustful of love as you are!" he said, almost with violence.

"You haven't lived my life."

She, too, spoke almost with violence, and there was violence in her eyes.

"You haven't lived for years in the midst of condemnation. Your friend, Doctor Isaacson, secretly condemns me. I know it. And so I'm afraid of him. I don't pretend to have any real reason—any reason that would commend itself to a man. Women don't need such reasons for their fears."

"And yet you say that you like Isaacson!"

"So I do, in a way. At least, I thought I did, till you told me you'd written to him to tell him about us and our life on the Nile."

He could not help smiling.

"Oh!" he said, moving nearer to her. "I shall never understand women. What a reason for dislike of a man hundreds of miles away from us!"

"Hundreds of miles—yes! And if your letter brought him to us! Suppose he took it into his head to run out and see for himself if what you wrote was true?"

"Ruby! How wild you are in your suppositions!"

"They're not so wild as you think. Doctor Isaacson is just the man to do such a thing."

"Well, even if he did——?"

"Do you want him to?" she interrupted.

He hesitated.

"You do want him to."

She said it bitterly.

"And I thought I was enough!" she exclaimed.

"It isn't that, Ruby—it isn't that at all. But I confess that I should like Isaacson to see for himself how happy we are together."

"Did you say that in your letter?"

"No, not a word of it. But I did think it when I was writing. Wasn't it a natural thought? Isaacson was almost my confidant—not quite, for nobody was quite— about my feelings and intentions towards you before our marriage."

"And if he could have prevented the marriage, he would have prevented it."

"And because of that, if it's true, you wouldn't like him to see us happy together?"

"I don't want him here. I don't want any one. I feel as if he might try to separate us, even now."

"He might try till the Day of Judgment without succeeding. But you are not quite fair to him."

"And he would never be fair to me. There's the afterglow coming at last."

They watched it in silence giving magic to the western hills and to the cloudless sky in the west. It was suggestive of peace and of remoteness, suggestive of things clarified, purged, made very wonderfully pure, but not coldly pure. When it died away into the breast of the softly advancing night, Nigel felt as if it had purged him of all confusion of thought and feeling, as if it had set him quite straight with himself.

"That makes me feel as if I understood everything just for a moment," he said. "Ruby, don't let us get into any difficulties, make any difficulties for ourselves out here. We are having such a chance for peace, aren't we? We should be worse than mad if we didn't take it, I think. But we will take it. I understand that your life has made you suspicious of people. I believe I understand your fears a little, too. But they are groundless as far as I am concerned. Nobody on earth could ever come between you and me. Only one person could ever break our union."

"Who?"

"Yourself. Hark! the sailors are singing. I expect we are going to tie up."

That night, as Mrs. Armine lay awake in the cabin which was Baroudi's, and which, in contrast to all the other bedrooms on the *Loulia,* was sombre in its colouring and distinctively Oriental, she thought of the conversation of the afternoon, and realized that she must keep a tighter hold over her nerves, put a stronger guard upon her temper. Without really intending to, she had let herself run loose, she had lost part of her self-control. Not all, for as usual when she told some truth, she had made it serve her very much as a lie might have served her. But by speaking as she had about Meyer Isaacson she had made herself fully realize something—that she was afraid of him, or that in the future she might become afraid of him. Why had Nigel written just now? Why had he drawn Isaacson's attention to them and their lives just now? It was almost as if—and then she pulled herself up sharply. She was not going to be a superstitious fool. It was, of course, perfectly natural for Nigel to write to his friend. Nevertheless, she wished ardently that Isaacson was not his friend, that those keen doctor's eyes, which seemed to sum up the bodily and mental states of woman or man with one bright and steady glance, had never looked upon her.

And most of all she wished that they might never look upon her again.

XXVII

In the house in Cleveland Square, on a morning in late January, Meyer Isaacson read Nigel's letter.

"Villa Androud,
"Luxor, Upper Egypt, Jan. 21st.
"Dear Isaacson,

"Here at last is a letter, the first I've sat down to write to you since the note telling you of my marriage. I had your kind letter in answer, and showed it to Ruby, who was as pleased with it as I was. She liked you from the first, and I think has always wished to know you better since you went to cheer her up in her London solitude. Some day I suppose she will have the chance, but now we are on the eve of cutting ourselves off from every one and giving ourselves up to the Nile. You are surprised, perhaps? You thought I should be hard at it in the Fayyūm, looking after my brown fellows? Well, I'm as keen as ever on the work there, and if you could have seen me not many days ago, nearly up to my knees in mud, and as oily and black as a stoker, you'd know it. My wife was in the Fayyūm with me, and has been roughing it like a regular Spartan. She packed off her French maid so as to be quite free, and has been living under the tent, riding camels, feeding anyhow, and, in short, getting a real taste of the nomad's life in the wilds. She cottoned to it like anything, although no doubt she missed her comforts now and then. But she never complained, she's looking simply splendid—years younger than she did when you saw her in London—and won't hear of having another maid, though now she might quite well get one. For I felt I oughtn't to keep her too long in the wilds just at first, although she was quite willing to stay, and didn't want to take me away from my work. I knew she was naturally anxious to see something of the wonders of Egypt, and the end of it was that we decided to take a dahabeeyah trip on the Nile, and are on the eve of starting. You should see our boat, the *Loulia!* she's a perfect beauty, and, apart from a few absurd details which I haven't the time to describe, would delight you. The bedrooms are Paris, but the sitting-rooms are like rooms in an Eastern house. You'll say Paris and the East don't go together. Granted! But it's very jolly to be romantic by day and soused in modern comfort at night. Now isn't it? Especially after the Fayyūm. And we've actually got a fountain on board, to say nothing of prayer rugs by the dozen which beat any I've seen in the bazaars of Cairo. For we haven't hired from Cook, but from an Egyptian millionaire of Alexandria called Mahmoud Baroudi, whom we met coming out, and who happened to want a tenant for his boat just in the nick of time. It isn't my money he needs, though I'm paying him what I should pay Cook for a first-rate boat, but he doesn't like leaving his crew and servants with nothing to do. He says they get into mischief. He was looking out for a rich American—like nearly every one out here—when he happened to hear from one of our fellows, a first-rate chap called Ibrahim, that we wanted a good boat, and so the bargain was made. Our plans are pretty vague. We want to get right away from trippers, and just be together in all the delicious out-of-the-way places on the river; see the temples and tombs quietly, enter into the life of the natives—in fact, steep ourselves to the lips in Nile water. I can't tell you how we are both looking forward to it. Isaacson, we're happy! Out here in this climate, this air, this clearness—like radiant sincerity it is, I often think— it's difficult not to be happy; but I think we're happier even than most people out here—at any rate I'm sure I am—I'll dare to say than any one else out here. And I'll say it with audacity and without superstitious fears of the future. The sun's streaming in over me as I write; I hear the voices of the watermen singing; I see my wife in the garden walking to the river bank, and I've got this trip before me. And—just remembered it!—I'm superbly well. Never in my life have I been in such splendid health. They say a perfectly healthy man should be unconscious of his body. Well, when I get up in the morning, all I know is that I say to myself, 'You're in grand condition, old chap!' And I think that consciousness means more than any unconsciousness. Don't you? I've no use for all your knowledge, your skill, out here—no use at all. Are there really people being ill in London? Are your consulting-rooms crowded? I can't believe it, any more than I can believe in the darkness of London days. What a selfish brute I am! You're hating me, aren't you? But it's so good to be happy. When I'm happy, I always feel that I'm fulfilling the law. If you want to fulfil the law better, come to Egypt. But you ought to bring *the* woman with you into the sunshine. I can't say any more; I needn't say any more. Now, you understand that it's all right. Do you remember our walk home from the concert that night, and how I said, 'I want to get into the light, the real light'? Well, I'm in it, and how I wish that you and every one else could be in it too! Forgive my egoism. Write to me at this address when you have time. Come to the Nile when next you take a holiday, and, with many messages from us both,

"Believe us

"Your friends,

"N. A. and R. A.

"I sign for her. She's still in the garden, where I'm just going."

A letter of success. A letter subtly breathing out from every line the message, "You were wrong." A letter of triumph, devoid of the cruelty that triumph often holds. A letter, surely, for a true friend to rejoice in?

Meyer Isaacson held it for a long while in his hands, forgetful of the tea that was standing at his elbow.

The day was dark and grim, a still, not very cold, but hopeless day of the dawning year. And he, was he not holding sunshine? The strange thing was that it did not warm him, that it seemed rather to add a shadow to London's dimness.

Mrs. Armine without a maid! He scarcely knew why, but that very small event, the dismissal of a maid, seemed almost to bristle up at him out of his friend's letter. He knew smart women well, and he knew that the average smart woman would rather do without the hope of Heaven than do without her maid. Mrs. Armine must have changed indeed since she was Mrs. Chepstow. Could she have changed so much? Do people of mature age change radically when an enthusiastic influence is brought to bear upon them?

All day long Isaacson was pondering that question.

Nigel was knocking at a door. Had it opened to him? Would it ever open? He thought it would. Probably he thought it had.

He and his wife were going away to be together "in all the delicious out-of-the-way places on the Nile," and they were "happier than most people"—even than most people in the region of gold.

And yet two sons had been born to Lord Harwich, and Nigel had been cut out of the succession!

When he had read that news, Isaacson had wondered what effect it would have in the *ménage* on the Nile—how the greedy woman would bear it.

Apparently she had borne it well. Nigel did not even mention it.

And the departure of that maid! Mrs. Armine without a maid! Again that night as Isaacson sat alone reading Nigel's letter that apparently unimportant fact seemed to bristle up from the paper and confront him. What was the meaning of that strange renunciation? What had prompted it? "She packed off her French maid so as to be quite free." Free for what?

The doctor lit a cigar, and leaned back in a deep armchair. And he began to study that cheery letter almost as a detective studies the plan of a house in which a crime has been committed. When his cigar was smoked out, he laid the letter aside, but he still refrained for a while from going to bed. His mind was far away on the Nile. Never had he seen the Nile. Should he go to see it, soon, this year, this spring? He remembered a morning's ride, when the air of London was languorous, had seemed for a moment almost exotic. That air had made him wish to go away, far away, to the land where he would be really at home, where he would be in "his own place." And then he had imagined a distant country where all romances unwind their shining coils. And he had longed for events, tragic, tremendous, horrible, even, if only they were unusual. He had longed for an incentive which would call his secret powers into supreme activity.

Should he go to the Nile very soon—this spring?

He looked again at the letter. He read again those apparently insignificant words:

"She packed off her French maid, so as to be quite free."

XXVIII

The next day was Sunday. Meyer Isaacson had no patients and no engagements. He had deliberately kept the day free, in order that he might study, and answer a quantity of letters. He was paying the penalty of his great success, and was one of the hardest worked men in London. At the beginning of the New Year he had even broken through his hitherto inflexible rule, and now he frequently saw patients up till half-past seven o'clock. He dined out much less than in former days, and was seldom seen at concerts and the play. Success, like a monster, had gripped him, was banishing pleasure from his life. He worked harder and harder, gained ever more and more money, rose perpetually nearer to the top of his ambition. Not long ago royalty had called him in for the first time, and been pleased to approve both of him personally and of his professional services. The future, no doubt, held a title for him. All the ultra-fashionable world thronged to consult him. Even since the Armines' departure he had gone up several rungs of the ladder. His strong desire to "arrive"—and arrival in his mind meant far more than it does in the minds of most men—and his acute pleasure in adding perpetually to his fortune, drove him incessantly onward. In his few free hours he was slowly and laboriously writing a work on poisons, the work for which he had been preparing in Italy during his last holiday. On this Sunday he meant to devote some hours to it. But first he would "get through" his letters.

After a hasty breakfast, he shut himself up in his study. London seemed strangely quiet. Even here within four walls, and without looking at the outside world, one felt that it was Sunday; one felt also that almost everybody was out of town. A pall of grey brooded over the city. Isaacson turned on the electric light, stood for a moment in front of the fire, then went over to his writing-table. The letters he intended to answer were arranged in a pile on the right hand side of his blotting-pad. Many of them—most of them—were from people who desired to consult him, or from patients about their cases. These letters meant money. Numbers of them he could answer with a printed card to which he would only have to add a date and a name. Monotonous work, but swiftly done, a filling up of many of the hours of his life which were near at hand.

He sat down, took a packet of his printed engagement forms, and a pen, put them before him, then opened one of the letters:

"4, MANTON STREET, MAYFAIR, Jan. 2.
"DEAR DOCTOR ISAACSON:
"My health," etc., etc.

He opened another:

"200, PARK LANE, Jan. ——
"DEAR DOCTOR ISAACSON:
"I don't know what is the matter with me, but——" etc., etc.

He took up a third:

"1x, BERKELEY SQUARE, Jan. ——
"DEAR DOCTOR ISAACSON:
"That strange feeling in my head has returned, and I should like to see you about it," etc., etc.

Usually he answered such letters with energy, and certainly without any disgust. They were the letters he wanted. He could scarcely have too many of them. But to-day a weariness overtook him; almost more than a weariness, a sort of sick irritation against the life that he had chosen and that he was making a marvellous success of. Illness, always illness! Pale faces, disordered nerves, dyspepsia, melancholia, anæmia, all the troop of ills that afflict humanity, marching for ever into his room! What company for a man to keep! What company! Suddenly he pushed away the printed forms, put down his pen, and got up.

He knew quite well what was troubling him. It was the letter he had had from the Nile. At first it had disturbed him in one way. Now it was disturbing him in another. It was a call to him from a land which he knew he must love, a call to him from his own place. For his ancestors had been Jews of the East, and some of them had been settled in Cairo. It was a call from the shining land. He remembered how one night, when Nigel and he were talking about Egypt, Nigel had said: "You ought to go there. You'd be in your right place there."

If he did go there! If he went soon, very soon—this spring!

But how could he take a holiday in the spring, just when everybody was coming to town? Then he told himself that he was saying nonsense to himself. People went abroad in the spring, to India, Sicily, the Riviera, the Nile. Ah, he was back again on the Nile! But so many people did not go abroad. It would be madness for a fashionable doctor to be away just when the season was coming on. Well, but he might run out for a very short time—for a couple of weeks, something like that. Two nights from London to Naples; two nights at sea in one of the new, swift boats, the *Heliopolis*, perhaps; a few hours in the train, and he would be at Cairo. Five nights' travelling would bring him to the first cataract. And he would be in the real light.

He stared at the electric bulbs that gleamed on either side of the mantelpiece. Then he glanced towards the windows, oblongs of dingy grey looking upon fog and daylight darkness.

That would be good, to be in the real light!

Nigel's letter lay somewhere under the letters from patients. The Doctor went back to his table, searched for it, and found it. Then he came back to the fire, and studied the letter carefully again.

"Do you remember our walk home from the concert that night, and how I said, 'I want to get into the light, the real light'? Well, I'm in it, and how I wish that you and every one else could be in it too! . . . Come to the Nile when next you take a holiday."

It was almost an invitation to go; not quite an invitation, but almost. Isaacson seemed to divine that the man who wrote wished his friend to come out and see his happiness, but that he did not quite dare to ask him to come out; seemed to divine a hostile influence that kept the pen in check.

"I wonder if she knows of this letter?"

That question came into Isaacson's mind. The last words of the letter almost implied that she knew. Nigel had meant to tell her of it, had doubtless told her of it on the day when he wrote it. If Isaacson went to the Nile, there was one person on the river who would not welcome him. He knew that well. And Nigel, of course, did not really want him. Happy people do not really want friends outside to come into the magic circle and share their happiness. They may say they do, out of good-will. Even for a moment, moved by an enthusiastic impulse, they may think that they do. But true happiness is exquisitely exclusive in its desires.

"Armine would like me just to see it's all right, and then, when I've seen, he would like to kick me out."

That was how Isaacson summed up eventually Nigel's exact feeling towards him at this moment. It was hardly worth while undertaking the journey from England to gratify such a desire of the happy egoist. Better put the idea away. It was impracticable, and——

"Besides, it's quite out of the question!"

The Doctor returned to his table, and began resolutely to write answers to his letters, and to fix appointments. He went on writing until every letter was answered—every letter but Nigel Armine's.

And then again the strong desire came upon him to answer it in person, one morning to appear on the riverbank where the—what was the name?—the *Loulia* was tied up, to walk on deck, and say, "I congratulate you on your happiness."

How amazed his friend would be! And his enemy—what would her face be like?

Isaacson always thought of Mrs. Armine as his enemy. She had come into his life as a spy. He felt as if from the first moment when she had seen him she had hated him. She had got the better of him, and she knew it. Possibly now, because of that knowledge, she would like him better. She had won out. Or had she, now that Lord Harwich had an heir?

As he sat there with Nigel's letter before him, a keen, an almost intense curiosity was alive in Meyer Isaacson. It was not vulgar, but the natural curiosity of the psychologist about strange human things. Since the Armines had left London and he had known of their marriage, Isaacson had thought of them often, but a little vaguely, as of people who had quite gone out of his life for a time. He had to concentrate on his own affairs. But now, with this letter, despite the great distance between the Armines and himself, they seemed to be quite near him. All his recollection of his connection with them started up in his mind, vivid and almost fierce. Especially he remembered the clever woman, the turn of her beautiful head, the look in the eyes contradicting the lovely line of the profile, the irony of her smile, the attractive intonations of her lazy voice. He remembered his two visits to her, how she had secretly defied him. He recalled exactly her appearance when he had bade her good-bye for the last time, eight days before she had been married to Nigel. She had stood by the hearth, in a rose-coloured gown, with smoke-wreaths curling round her. And she had looked quite lovely in her secret triumph. But as he went out, he had noticed the tiny wrinkles near her eyes, the slight hardness about her cheek-bones, the cynical droop at the corners of her mouth.

And he had remembered these things when he learnt of the marriage, and he had foreseen disaster.

He smoothed out Nigel's letter, and he took up his pen to answer it. Since he could not answer it in person, he must despatch the substitute. But now the dreary quiet of the London Sunday distressed him as if it were noise. He found himself listening to it with a sort of anxiety; he felt as if he must struggle against it before he could write sincerely to Nigel. There was something paralyzing in this dark and foggy peace.

Why was he heaping up money, grasping at fame, dedicating himself to imprisonment within the limits of this house, within this sunless town? Why was he starving his love of beauty, his natural love of adventure, his quick feeling for romance? Or was it quick any longer? Things not encouraged die sometimes. Certainly, he was starving deliberately much of himself.

Again came the desire to let, for once, a strong impulse have its way, to forget, for once, that he was a man under strict discipline—the discipline of his own cruel will—or to remember and mutiny. For a moment his thoughts were almost like a schoolboy's. The fun of it! The fun of rapid packing, of saying to Henry (unboundedly amazed), "Call me a four-wheeler!" of the drive to Charing Cross, of the registering of the luggage, of the rapid flight through the wintry landscape till the grey sea beat up almost against the line, of the——

And presently Naples! A blue sea, the mountains of Crete, the iron ridges of Zante, and at last a laughing harbour, boats with bellying lateen sails manned by dark men in turbans, white houses, flat roofs, palm-trees!

It would be good! It would be splendid!

If he answered Nigel's letter, he would not yield to his impulse. And if he did not answer it——?

After long hesitation, he put the letter aside, he got out of a drawer his pile of manuscript paper, and he set himself to work. And presently he forgot that it was Sunday in London; he forgot everything except what he was doing. But in the evening, when he was dining alone, the longing to be off returned, and though he said to himself that he would not yield to it, he did not answer Nigel's letter. Absurdly, he felt that by not answering it he left the door open to this possible pleasure.

He never answered that letter. Day after day went by. He worked with unflagging energy. He seemed as attentive to, as deeply interested in, his patients as usual. But all the time that he sat in his consulting-room, that he listened to accounts of symptoms, that he gave advice and wrote out prescriptions, he was secretly playing with the idea that perhaps this spring he would take a holiday in Egypt. He had an ardent, though generally carefully controlled imagination. Just now he gave it the reins. In the darkest days he saw himself in sunlight. When he looked at the bare trees in the parks, they changed in a moment to opulent palms. He heard a soft wind stirring their mighty leaves. It spoke to him of the desert. Never before had he gained such definite pleasure from his imagination. Had he become a child again? It almost seemed so. If his patients only knew the present truths of the man whom they begged to lead them to health! If they only knew his wanderings while they were unfolding their tales of wonder and woe! But his face told nothing. It did not cry to them, "I am in Egypt!" And so they were never perturbed.

February slipped away.

If he really meant to go to the Nile, he must not delay his departure. Did he mean to go? So long now had he played with the delightful imagination of a voyage to the sun that he began to say to himself that he had had his pleasure and must rest satisfied. He even told himself the commonplace lie that the thought of a thing is more satisfactory than the thing itself could ever be, and that to him the real Egypt would prove a disappointment after the imagined Egypt of his winter dreams. And he decided that he would not go, that he had never intended to go.

On the day when he took this decision, he got a letter from a patient whom he had sent to winter on the Nile. She wrote from Luxor many details of her condition, which he read slowly and with care. Towards the end of the letter, perhaps made frolicsome by confession, she broke into gossip, related several little scandals of various hotels, and concluded with this paragraph:

"Quite an excitement has been caused here by the arrival of a marvellous dahabeeyah called the *Loulia*. She is the most lovely boat on the Nile, I am told, and every one is longing to go over her. But there is no chance for any of us. In the first place the *Loulia* is tied up at the western bank, on the Theban side of the river, and, in the second place, she belongs for the season to the Nigel Armines. And, as of course you remember, Mrs. Nigel Armine was Mrs. Chepstow, and *utterly impossible*. Now she is married again she may think she will be received, but she never will be. Of course, if she could have had the luck one day to become Lady Harwich, it might have become possible. A great position like that naturally makes people think differently. And, after all, the woman is married now. But no use talking about it! The twins have effectually knocked that possibility on the head. They say she nearly went mad with fury when she heard the news. It seems he had never given her a hint before the wedding. Wise man! He evidently knew his Mrs. Chepstow. Nevertheless, to give the devil her due, I hear she seems quite wrapped up in her husband. I saw him for a minute the other day, when I was crossing to go to the tombs of the Kings. He was looking awfully ill, I thought, such an extraordinary colour! I didn't see her, but they say she looks younger than ever, and much more beautiful than when she was in London. Marriage evidently suits her, though it doesn't seem to suit him," etc., etc.

This letter arrived by an evening post, and Isaacson read it after his day's work was done. When he had finished it, he took out from a drawer Nigel's letter to him, which he had kept, and compared the two. It was not necessary to do this, for Nigel's words were in his memory. Isaacson could not have said exactly why he did it. The sight of the two letters side by side made a strongly disagreeable impression upon him, and perhaps, in comparing them thus, he had almost unconsciously been seeking such an impression.

"Never in my life have I been in such splendid health."

"He was looking awfully ill—such an extraordinary colour!"

What had happened between the writing of the first letter and the writing of the last? What had produced this change?

After a few minutes, Isaacson put both the letters away and softly shut the drawer of the writing-table. He had dined. The night was his. He had his nargeeleh brought, and told Henry that he was not to be disturbed.

Not since that night of autumn when Nigel had said of Mrs. Chepstow, "She talks of coming to Egypt for the winter," had Isaacson taken the long and snake-like pipe-stem into his hand. Only when his mind was specially alive, almost excitedly alive, and when he wished to push that vitality to its limit, did he instinctively turn to the nargeeleh. Then his fingers and his lips needed it. His eyes needed it, too. Some breath of the East ran through him, stirring inherited instincts, inherited needs, to life. Now he turned out all the electric lights, he sat down in the dim glow from the fire, and he took once again, eagerly, between his thin fingers the snake-like stem of the nargeeleh. The water bubbled in the cocoanut. He filled his lungs with the delicious tumbák, he let it out in clouds through his nostrils.

London slept, and he sat there still. In his shining eyes the intense life of his mind was revealed. But there was no one to mark it, no one with him to love or to fear it.

At last, in the very deep of the night, he got up from his chair. He sat down at his writing-table. And he worked till the morning came, writing letters to patients whose names he looked out in his book of appointments, and whose addresses he turned up in the Red Book, or found in letters which he had kept by him, going through accounts, studying his bank-book, writing to his banker and his stockbroker, to hospitals with which he was connected, to societies for which he sometimes delivered addresses; doing a multitude of things which might surely —might they not?—have waited till day. And when at length there was a movement in the house which told of the servants awakening, he pushed the bell with a long finger.

Presently Henry came, trying to hide a look of amazement.

"Directly Cook's office in Piccadilly opens I shall want this letter taken there. The messenger must wait for an answer."

He held out a letter.

"Yes, sir."

"All these are for the post."

"Yes, sir."

"You might order Arthur to get ready my bath."

"Yes, sir."

The doctor stood up.

"I shall see patients to-day. To-morrow, or the next day, at latest, I shall leave London. I'm going to Egypt for a few weeks."

There was a pause. Then Henry uttered his formula.

"Yes, sir," he murmured.

He turned and went slowly out.

His sloping shoulders looked as if the Heavens had fallen—on them.

XXIX

Isaacson refused to get into the omnibus at the station in Cairo, and drove to Shepheard's Hotel in a victoria, drawn by a pair of lean grey horses with long manes and tails. The coachman was an Arab much pitted with smallpox, who wore the tarbush with European clothes. It was about three o'clock in the afternoon, and the streets of the enticing and confusing city were crowded. Isaacson sat up very straight and looked about him with eager eyes. He felt keenly excited. This was his very first taste of Eastern life. Never before had he set foot in his "own place." Already, despite the zest shed through him by novelty, he had an odd, happy feeling of being at home.

He saw here and there houses with white façades, before which palm-trees were waving. And in those houses he knew he could be very much at ease. The courtyards, the steps, the tiles, a fountain, small rugs, a divan, a carved dark door, a great screen of wood hiding an inner apartment—could he not see within? He had never entered that house there on the left, and yet he knew it. And this throng of Eastern men, with dark, keen, shining eyes, with heavy, slumbrous eyes, with eyes glittering with the yellow fires of greed; this throng, yellow-skinned, brown-skinned, black-skinned, with thin, expressive hands, with henna-tinted nails, with narrow, cunning wrists; this throng that talked volubly, that gesticulated, that gazed, observing without self-consciousness, summing up without pity, whose eyes took all and gave nothing—if he stepped out of the carriage, if he forsook the borrowed comforts and the borrowed delights of Europe, if he hid himself in this throng, would he not find himself for the first time?

He was sorry when the carriage drew up before the great terrace of the hotel. But he had not lost touch with the pageant. He realized that, almost with a sensation of exultation, when he came down from his room between four and five o'clock, and took a seat by the railing.

"Tea, sir?"

He nodded to the German waiter. Somewhere a band was playing melodies of Europe. That night he would seek in the native quarter the whining and syncopated tunes of the East.

The tea was brought, and an Arab approached with papers: the "*Sphinx,*" a French paper published in Cairo, and London papers, the "*Times,*" the "*Morning Post.*" Isaacson bought two or three, vaguely. It was but rarely he felt vague, but now, as he sipped his tea, his excitement was linked with something else, that seemed misty and nebulous, yet not free from a sort of enchantment. By the railing, before and beneath him, a world of many of his dreams—his nargeelèh dreams—flowed by. The abruptness of his decision to come—that made half the enchantment of his coming, made a wonder of his arrival. The boy in him was alive to-day, but with the boy there stood the dreamer.

The terrace, of course, was crowded. People of many nations sat behind and on each side of Meyer Isaacson, walked up and down the broad flight of steps that connected the terrace with the pavement, stared, gesticulated, gossiped. There was a clatter of china. Girls in long veils munched cakes, and, more delicately, ate ices tinted pink, pale green, and almond colour. Elderly ladies sat low in basket chairs, almost dehumanized by sight-seeing. Antiquarians argued and protested, shaking their forefingers, browned by the sun that shines in the desert. American business men, on holiday, smoked large cigars, and invited friends from New York, Boston, Washington to dinner. European boys, smartly dressed, full of life and gaiety, went eagerly up and down excitedly retailing experiences. And perpetually carrriages drove up, set down, and departed, while a lean, beautifully clad Arab with grey hair noted hours, prices, numbers, in a mysterious book.

But Meyer Isaacson all the time was watching the Easterns who passed and repassed in the noisy street. He had not even glanced keenly once at the crowd of travellers to see if there were any whom he knew, patients, friends, enemies. His usual sharp consciousness of those about him was for once completely in abeyance.

Presently, however, his attention was transferred from the street to the terrace, carried thither, so it seemed to him, by a man who moved from the one to the other. There passed in front of him slowly one of the most perfectly built mail phaetons he had ever seen. It was very high and large, but looked elegantly light, and it was drawn by a pair of superb Russian horses, jet-black, full of fiery spirit, matched to a hair, and with such grand action that it was an æsthetic pleasure to look upon them moving.

Sitting alone in the front of the phaeton was the man who, almost immediately, was to draw Isaacson's attention to the terrace. He was Mahmoud Baroudi. He was dressed in a light grey suit, and wore the tarbush. Behind him sat a very smart little English groom, dressed in livery, with a shining top-hat, breeches, and top-boots. The phaeton was black with scarlet wheels. The silver on the harness glittered with polish; the chains which fastened the horses to the scarlet pole gleamed brilliantly in the sunshine. But it was Baroudi, his extraordinary physique, his striking, nonchalant face, and his first-rate driving, which attracted all eyes, which held Isaacson's eyes. He pulled up his horses in front of the steps. The groom was down in a moment. Baroudi gave him the reins, got out, and walked up to the terrace. He stood for a moment, looking calmly round; then brought his right hand to his tarbush as he saw a party of French friends, which he immediately joined. They welcomed him with obvious delight. Two of them, perfectly dressed Parisian women, made room for him between them. As he sat down, smiling, Isaacson noticed his slanting eyebrows and his magnificent throat, which looked as strong as the throat of a bull.

"My dear Isaacson! Is it possible? I should almost as soon have expected to meet the Sphinx in Cleveland Square!"

A tall man, not much over thirty, with light, imaginative, yet penetrating eyes, stood before him, and with a "May I?" sat down beside him, after cordially grasping his hand.

"Starnworth, you're one of the few men—I might say almost the only man—I'm glad to meet at this moment. Where have you just come from, or where are you just going? I can't believe you are going to stay in Cairo."

"No. I've been in Syria, just arrived from Damascus. I've been with a caravan—yes, I'll have some tea. I'm going to start to-morrow or next day from Mena House for another little desert trip."

"Little! How many days?"

"Oh, I don't know," said the newcomer, negligently. "Three weeks out and three weeks back, I believe—something like that—to visit an oasis where there are some extraordinary ruins. But why are you here? What induced you to leave your innumerable patients?"

After a very slight hesitation Isaacson answered:

"A whim."

"The deuce! Can doctors who are the rage permit themselves to be governed by whims?"

This man, Basil Starnworth, was an English nomad who for years had steeped himself in the golden East, who spoke Arabic and innumerable Eastern dialects, who was more at home with Bedouins than with his own brothers, and who was a mine of knowledge about the natives of Syria, of Egypt, and the whole of Northern Africa—about their passions, their customs, their superstitions, and all their ways of life. Isaacson had cured him of a malarial fever contracted on one of his journeys. That night they dined together, and after dinner Starnworth took Isaacson to see some of the native quarters of the town.

It was towards eleven o'clock when Isaacson found himself sitting in a small, rude café that was hidden in the very bowels of Cairo. Through winding alleys they had reached it—alleys full of painted ladies, alleys gleaming with the lights shed from solitary candles set within entries tinted mauve, and blue, and scarlet, or placed half-way up narrow flights of whitewashed stairs. And in these winding alleys, mingled with human cries, and laughter, and murmured invitations, and barterings, and refusals, there had been music that seemed to wind on and on in ribands of sound—music that was hoarse and shrill and weary, that was piercing, yet at the same time furtive—music that was provocative, and yet that was often sad, with a strange sadness of the desert and of desire among the sands. Even now, in the maze around this café, there was another maze of sound, the tripping notes of Eastern dance tunes, the wail of the African hautboy, the twitter of little flutes that set the pace for the pale Circassians, the dull murmur of daraboukkehs.

An old Arab who was "hâjjee" brought them coffee, straight from the glowing embers. Starnworth took from his pocket a little box of tobacco and cigarette-papers, and deftly rolled two cigarettes. There were but few people in the café, and they were Easterns—two Egyptians, a negro, and three soldiers from the Soudan, black, thin almost as snakes, with skins so dry that they looked like the skins of some reptiles of the sands. And these Easterns were almost motionless, and seemed to be sunk in dreams

"Why did you bring me here?" asked Isaacson.

"It bores you?"

"No. But I want to know why you chose this café out of all the cafés of Cairo."

"It's a very old and, among Easterns, very famous resort of smokers of hashish. You notice the blackened walls, the want of light. The hashish smoker does not desire any luxury or brightness. He wants his dream, and he gets it here. You would scarcely suppose it, but there are rich Egyptians of the upper classes, men who are seen at official receptions, who go to the great balls at the smart hotels, and who slink in here secretly night after night, mingle with the lowest riff-raff, to have their dream beneath this blackened roof. There is one coming in now."

As he spoke, Mahmoud Baroudi appeared in the doorway. He was dressed in native costume—very poorly dressed; wore a dingy turban, and a long gibbeh of discoloured cloth. With the usual salaam, muttered in his throat, he went into the farthest and darkest corner of the café and squatted down on the floor. The old Arab carried to him in a moment a gozeh, a pipe resembling a nargeeleh, but without the snake-like handle. Baroudi took it for a moment, inhaled the smoke of the hashish, and poured it out from his mouth and nostrils.

"He looks like a poor Egyptian," said Isaacson, almost in a whisper.

"He is a millionaire. By the way, didn't you see him this afternoon?"

"Where?"

"At Shepheard's. He drove up just before I saw you, in a phaeton."

"The man with the Russian horses! Surely, it's impossible!"

"This afternoon he was the cosmopolitan millionaire. To-night he sinks down into his native East."

"Who is he?"

"Mahmoud Baroudi."

"Mahmoud Baroudi!" repeated Isaacson, slowly and softly.

An old man who had crept in began to sing in a high and quavering voice a song of the smokers of hashish, accompanying himself upon an instrument of tortoise and goat-skin. A youth in skirts began to posture and dance an unfinished dance of the dreamer who has been led by hashish into a world that is sweet and vague.

"I'll tell you about him later," whispered Starnworth.

That night they sat up in the hotel till the third time of the Moslem's prayer was near at hand. Starnworth, pleased to have an auditor who was much more than merely sympathetic, who understood his Eastern lore as if with a mind of the East, poured forth his curious knowledge. And Isaacson gripped it as only the Jew can grip. He listened and listened, saying little, until Starnworth began to speak of the strange immutability that is apparent in Islam, and of how the East must ever, despite the most powerful outside influences, remain utterly the East.

"Or so it seems up to now," he said.

He illustrated and emphasized his contention by a number of striking examples. He spoke of Arabs, of Egyptians he had known intimately, whom he had seen subjected to every kind of European influence, whom he had even seen apparently "Europeanized," as he put it, but who, when the moment came, had shown themselves "native" to the core.

"And it is even so when there is mingled blood," he said. "For instance, that man you saw to-night smoking hashish, wrapped up in that dirty old gibbeh, had a Greek mother, and may have—no doubt has—some aptitudes, some characteristics that are Greek, but they are dominated, almost swallowed up by the East that is in him."

"Do you know him?"

"I have never spoken to him, but I have heard a great deal about him—from Egyptians, mind you, as well as Europeans. With the English, and foreigners generally, he is an immense success. He is a very clever man, and has excellent qualities, I believe. But he is of the East. He is capable of giving one—who does not know very much—the most profound surprises. To ordinary eyes he shows nothing, nothing of what he is. He seems calm, dominating, practical, even cold and businesslike, full always of the most complete self-possession, calculating, but generous, and kind, charming, polished, suave and indifferent, with a sort of tremendously masculine indifference. I have often seen him in society. Even to me he has given that type of impression."

"And what is the real man?"

"Red-hot under the crust, a tremendous hater and a simply tremendous lover. But he hates with his soul and he loves with his body—they say. They say he's the slave of his soul in hatred, the slave of his body in love. He's committed crimes for women, if I ever get truth from my native friends. And I believe I am one of the few Europeans who can get a good deal of truth from the natives."

"Crimes, you say?"

"Yes," returned Starnworth, with his odd, negligent manner, which suggested a man who would undertake a desert journey full of tremendous hardships clad in a dressing-gown and slippers.

"But not for his own women, not for the beauties of the East. Baroudi is one of the many Egyptians who go mad over the women of Europe and of the New World, who go mad over their fairness of skin, their delicate colouring and shining hair. There was a dancer at the opera house here one season—a Dane she was, all fairness, the Northern sunbeam type——"

"I know."

"He spent thousands upon her. Gave her a yacht, took her off in it to the Greek islands and Naples. Presently she wanted to marry."

"Him?"

"A merchant of Copenhagen, a very rich man. Baroudi was charming about it. The merchant came out to Cairo during the dancer's second season at the opera. Baroudi entertained him, became his friend, talked business, impressed the Dane immensely with his practical qualities, put him up to some splendid 'specs.' Result—the Dane was ruined, and went back to Copenhagen minus his fortune and—naturally—minus his lady-love."

"And what became of her?"

"I forget. Don't think I ever knew. She vanished from the opera house. But the best of it is that the Dane to this day swears by Baroudi, and thinks it was his own folly that did for him. There are much worse things than that, though. Baroudi's a man who would stick at absolutely nothing once he got the madness for a woman into his body. For instance——"

He told stories of Baroudi, stories which the Europeans of Egypt knew nothing of, but which some Egyptians knew and smiled at; one or two of them sounded very ugly to European ears.

"He's a Turco-Egyptian, you know," Starnworth said, presently, "and has the cunning that comes from the Bosphorus grafted on to the cunning that flourishes beneath the indifference of the Sphinx. We should call him a rank bad lot"—the dressing-gown and slippers manner was very much in evidence just here—"but the Turco-Egyptian has a different code from ours. I must say I admire the man. He's got so much grit in him. Worker, lover, hater—there's grit and go in each. Whichever bobs up, bobs up to win right out. But it's the madness for women that really rules the fellow's life, according to Egyptians who are near him and who know him well. And that's so with far more men of Eastern blood than you would suppose, unless you'd lived among them and knew them as I do. Arabs will literally run crazy for a fair face. So will Egyptians. And once they are dominated, they are dominated to an extent an Englishman would scarcely be able to understand. I knew an Arab of the Sahara who broke down the palm-wood door of an auberge at El-Kelf and cut the throat of the Frenchwoman who kept it, cut it while she was screaming her soul out—and only to get the few francs in the till to send to a girl in Paris he'd met at the great Exhibition. And the old Frenchwoman had befriended that man for over sixteen years, had almost brought him up from a boy, had written his letters for him to the tourists and sportsmen whose guide he was. Mahmoud Baroudi would do as much for a woman, once he'd got the madness for her into his body, but he'd do it in a more brainy way."

Starnworth talked on and on. The time of the third prayer was at hand when at last he said good-night. Turning at the door, just as he was going out, he looked at Isaacson with his light and imaginative eyes.

"A different code from ours, you see!" he murmured.

He went out and gently shut the door.

Although it was so late and Isaacson had that day arrived from a journey, he felt strongly alive, and as if no power to sleep were in him. Of course, he must go to bed, nevertheless. Slowly he began to undress, slowly and reluctantly.

And he was in Cairo, actually in Cairo! All around him in the night was Cairo, with its houses full of Egyptians sleeping, with its harîms, with its mosques! Not far away was the Sphinx looking east in the sand!

He pottered about his room. He did things very slowly. Eastern life, as it had flowed from the lips of Starnworth, went before his imagination like a great and strange procession. And in this procession Mahmoud Baroudi drove Russian horses, and walked, almost like a mendicant, in a discoloured gibbeh. And then the procession stopped, and Isaacson saw the dingy café in the entrails of Cairo, and Mahmoud Baroudi crouched upon the floor drawing the smoke of the hashish into his nostrils.

At last Isaacson was in pajamas and ready for bed. But still his mind was terribly wide awake. The papers he had bought in the afternoon were lying upon his table. Should he read a little to compose his mind? He took up a paper—the *Morning Post*—opened it, and glanced casually over the middle page.

"Sudden death of the Earl of Harwich."

So Nigel's brother was gone, and, but for the twin boys so recently arrived, Mrs. Armine would at this moment be Countess of Harwich!

Isaacson read the paragraph quickly; then he put the paper down and opened his window. He wanted to think in the air. As he leaned out to the silent city, faintly, as if from very far off, he heard a cry that thrilled through his blood and set his pulses beating.

From a minaret a mueddin was calling the faithful to prayer, at "fegr," when the sun pushes the first ray of steel-coloured light, like the blade of a distant lance, into the breast of the East.

"Al-là-hu-akbar! Al-là-hu-ak-bar!"

XXX

ISAACSON had come out to Egypt with no settled plan. The only thing he knew was that he meant to see Nigel Armine. He had not cabled or written to let Nigel know he was coming, and now that he was in Cairo he did not attempt to communicate with the *Loulia*. He would go up the Nile. He would find the marvellous boat. And one day he would stand upon a brown bank above her, he would see his friend on the deck, would hail him, would cross the gangway and walk on board. Nigel would be amazed.

And Mrs. Armine?

Many times on shipboard Isaacson had wondered what look he would surprise in the eyes of Bella Donna when he held out his hand to her. Those eyes had already defied him. They had laughed at him ironically. Once they had almost seemed to menace him. What greeting would they give him in Egypt?

That the death of Lord Harwich would recall Nigel to England he scarcely supposed. The death had been sudden. It would be impossible for Nigel to arrive for the funeral. And Isaacson knew what had been the Harwich view of the connection with Mrs. Chepstow, what Lady Harwich had thought and said of it. Zoe Harwich was very outspoken. It was improbable that Nigel's trip on the Nile would be brought to an end by his brother's death. Still, it was not impossible. Isaacson realized that, and on the following day, meeting a London acquaintance in the hotel, a man who knew everything about everybody, he spoke of the death casually, and wondered whether Armine would be leaving the Nile for England.

"Not he! Too seedy!" was the reply.

Isaacson remembered the letter he had had in London from his patient at Luxor.

"What's the matter?" he asked.

"Sunstroke, they say. He went out at midday without a hat—just the sort of thing Armine would do—went out diggin' for antiquities, and got a touch of the sun. I don't think it's serious. But there's no doubt he's damned seedy."

"D'you know where the boat is—the *Loulia?*"

"Somewhere between Luxor and Assouan, I believe. Armine and his wife are perfect turtle-doves, you know, always keep to themselves and get right away from the crowd. One never sees 'em, except by chance. She's playin' the model wife. Wonder how long it'll last!"

In his laugh there was a sound of cynical incredulity. When he had strolled away, Isaacson went round to Cook's office, and took a sleeping compartment in the express train that started for Luxor that evening. He would see the further wonders of Cairo, the Pyramids, the Sphinx, Sakkara—later, when he came down the Nile, if he had time; if not, he would not see them at all. He had not travelled from England to see sights. That was the truth. He knew it now, despite the longing that Cairo, the real Cairo of the strange, dimly-lit and brightly-tinted interiors, of the shrill and weary music, of the painted girls and the hashish smokers, and of that voice which cried aloud in the mystic hour the acclamation of the Creator—had waked in his Eastern nature to sink into the life which his ancestors knew—the life of the Eastern Jews. He knew what his real purpose had been.

Yet he left Cairo with regret. Starnworth had asked him to come on that six weeks' desert journey. He longed to do that, too. With this cessation of work, this abrupt and complete change of life, had come an almost wild desire for liberty, for adventure. This persistent worker woke to the great, stretching life outside—outside of his consulting-room, of the grey sea that ringed the powerful Island, outside of Europe, a little weary, a little over-civilized. And a voice that seemed to come from the centre of his soul clamoured for wild empires, for freedoms unutterable. It was as if the walls of his consulting-room fell with a noise of the walls of Jericho. And he looked out upon what he needed, what he had always needed, subconsciously. But he could not take it yet.

In the train he slept but little. Early in the morning he was up and dressed. From his window he saw the sunrise, and, for the first time was moved by the hard wonder of barren hills in an Eastern land. Those hills on the left bank of the river, glowing with delicate colours, hills with dimples that looked like dimples in iron, with outlines that were cruel and yet romantic, stirred his imagination and made him again regret his life. Why had he never been here before? Why had he grown to middle age encompassed by restrictions? A man like Starnworth had a truer conception of life than he. Even now, at this moment, he was not running quite free. And then he thought of the *Loulia*. Was he not really a man in pursuit? Suppose he gave up this pursuit. No one constrained him to it. He was here with plenty of money, entirely independent. If he chose to hire a caravan, to start away for the Gold Coast, there was no one to say him nay. He could go, if he would, forgetting that in the world there were men who were sick, forgetting everything except that he was in liberty and in a land where he was at home.

And then he asked himself whether he would have the power to forget that in the world there were men who were sick. And he remembered the words in a letter and other spoken words of an acquaintance in an hotel—and he was not sure.

The Armines, when they arrived at Luxor, had walked to their villa. When Isaacson arrived he refused all frantic offers of conveyance, and set out to walk to his hotel. It was the height of the tourist season, and Luxor was a centre for travellers. They swarmed, even at this early hour, in the little town. When Isaacson reached the bank of the Nile he saw a floating wharf with a big steamer moored against it, on which Cook's tourists were promenading, breakfasting, leaning over the rail, calling to and bargaining with smiling brown people on the shore. Beyond were a smaller mail steamer and a long line of dahabeeyahs flying the Union Jack, the Stars and Stripes, flags of France, Spain, and other countries. Donkeys cantered by, bearing agitated or exultant sight-seers, and pursued by shouting donkey-boys. Against the western shore, flat and sandy, and melting into the green of crops which, in their turn, melted into the sterility that holds the ruins of Thebes, lay more dahabeeyahs, the high, tapering masts of which cut sharply the crude, unclouded blue of a sky which announced a radiant day. Already, at a little after nine, the heat was very great. Isaacson revelled in it. But he longed to take a seven-thonged whip and drive out the happy travellers. He longed to be alone with the brown children of the Nile.

On the terrace of the Winter Palace Hotel he saw at once people whom he knew. Within the bay of sand formed by its crescent stood or strolled throngs of dragomans, and as he approached, one of them, who looked compact of cunning and guile, detached himself from a group, came up to him, saluted, and said:

"Good-morning, sir. You want a dahabeeyah? I get

you a very good dahabeeyah. You go on board to-day—not stay at the hotel. One night you sleep. When morning-time come, we go away from all these noisy peoples, we go 'mong the Egyptian peoples. Heeyah"—he threw out a brown hand with fingers curling backward—"heeyah peoples very vulgar, make much noise. You not at all happy heeyah, my nice gentleman!"

The rascal had read his thought.

"What's your name?"

"Hassan ben Achmed."

"I'll see you later."

Isaacson went up the steps and into the great hotel.

When he had had a bath and made his toilet, he came out into the sun. For a moment he stood upon the terrace rejoicing, soul and body, in the radiance. Then he looked down, and saw the long white teeth of Hassan displayed in a smile of temptation and understanding. Beyond those teeth was the river, to which Hassan was inviting him in silence. He looked at the tapering masts, and—he hesitated. Hassan showed more teeth.

At this moment the lady patient who had written to Isaacson from the Nile and mentioned Nigel came up with exclamations of wonder and delight, to engage all his attention. For nearly an hour he strolled from end to end of the crescent and talked with her. When at last she slowly vanished in the direction of the temple of Luxor, accompanied by a villainous-looking dragoman who was "the most intelligent, simple-minded old dear" in Upper Egypt, Isaacson, with decision, descended the steps and stood on the sand by Hassan.

"Where's that dahabeeyah you spoke about?" he said. "I'll go and have a look at her."

That evening, just before sunset he went on board the *Fatma* as proprietor.

He had been bargaining steadily for some hours, and felt weary, though triumphant, as he stood upon the upper deck, with Hassan in attendance, while the crew poled off from the bank into the golden river. Despite the earnest solicitations of the lady patient and various acquaintances staying in Luxor, he had given the order to remove to the western bank of the Nile. There he could be at peace.

Friends of his cried out adieux from the road in front of the shops and the great hotel. Unknown donkey-boys saluted. Tourists stood at gaze. He answered and looked back. But already a new feeling was stealing over him; already he was forgetting the turmoil of Luxor. The Reis stood on the raised platform in the stern, still as a figure of bronze, with the gigantic helm in his hand. The huge sail hung limp from the mast. Then there came a puff of wind. Slowly the shore receded. Slowly the *Fatma* crept over the wrinkled gold of the river towards the unwrinkled gold of the west. And Isaacson stood there, alone among his Egyptians, and saw his first sunset on the Nile. Over the gold from Thebes came boats going to the place he had left. And the boatmen sang the deep and drowsy chant that set the time for the oars. Mrs. Armine had often heard it. Now Isaacson heard it, and he thought of the beating pulse in a certain symphony to which he had listened with Nigel, and of the beating pulse of life; and he thought, too, of the destinies of men that often seem so fatal. And he sank down in the magical wonder of this old and golden world.

"Don't tie up near any other dahabeeyah."

"No, gentlemans," said Hassan.

Again the crew got out their poles. Two men stripped, went overboard with a rope, and, running along the shore, towed the *Fatma* up stream against the tide till she came to a lonely place where two men were vehemently working a shadûf. There they tied up for the night.

The gold was fading. Less brilliant, but deeper now, was the dream of river and shore, of the groves of palms and the mountains. Here and there, far off, a window, touched by a dying ray of light, glittered out of the softened dusk. Isaacson leaned over the rail. This evening, after his long months of perpetual work in a house in London, deprived of all real light, he felt like a man taken by the hand and led into Heaven. Behind him the naked fellahîn, unmindful of his presence, cried aloud in the fading gold.

For a long while he stood there without moving. His eyes were attracted, were held, by a white house across the water. It stood alone, and the river flowed in a delicate curve before it by a low tangle of trees or bushes. The windows of this house gleamed fiercely as restless jewels. At last he lifted himself up from the rail.

"Who lives in that house?" he asked of Hassan.

"An English lord, sah. My Lord Arminigel."

"What house is it? What's the name?"

"The Villa Androud, my kind gentlemans."

"The Villa Androud!"

So that was where Armine had gone for his honeymoon with Bella Donna! The windows glittered like the jewels many men had given to her.

Night fell. The song of the fellahîn failed. The stars came out. Just where the *Loulia* had lain the *Fatma* lay. And under the stars, on deck, Isaacson dined alone. Tomorrow at dawn he would start on his voyage up river. He would follow where the *Loulia* had gone. When dinner was finished, he sent Hassan away, and strolled about on the deck smoking his cigar. Through the tender darkness of the exquisite night the lights of Luxor shone, and from somewhere below them came a faint but barbaric sound of native music.

To-morrow he would follow where the *Loulia* had gone.

The lady patient that morning had been very communicative. One of her chief joys in life was gossip. Her joy in gossip was second only to her joy in poor health. And she had told her beloved doctor "all the news." The news of the Armine *ménage* was that Nigel Armine had got sunstroke in Thebes and been "too ill for words," and that the *Loulia*, after a short stay near Luxor, had gone on up the Nile, and was now supposed to be not far from the temple of Edfou. Not a soul had been able to explore the marvellous boat. Only a young American doctor, very susceptible indeed to female charm, had been permitted to set foot on her decks. He had diagnosed "sunstroke," had prescribed for Nigel Armine, and had come away "positively raving" about Mrs. Armine—"silly fellow." Isaacson would have liked a word with him, but he had gone to Assouan.

On the lower deck the boatmen began to sing.

Isaacson paced to and fro. The gentle and monotonous exercise, now accompanied by monotonous though ungentle music, seemed to assist the movement of his thought. When he left the garrulous lady patient, he might have gone to the post-office and telegraphed to the *Loulia*. It was possible to telegraph to Edfou. Since he intended to leave Luxor and sail up the Nile, surely the natural thing to do was to let his friend know of his coming. Why had he not done the natural thing? Some instinct had advised him against the completely straightforward action. If Nigel had been alone on the *Loulia* the telegram would have been sent. That Isaacson knew. But Nigel was not alone. A spy was with him, she who had come to spy out the land when she had come to Cleveland Square. Perhaps it was very absurd, but the remembrance of Bella Donna prevented Isaacson now from announcing his presence on the Nile. He was resolved to come to her as she had once come to him. She had appeared in Cleveland Square carrying her secret reason with her. He would appear in the shadow of the temple of Horus. And his secret reason? Perhaps he had none. He was a man who was often led by instinct.

And he trusted very much in his instinctive mistrust of Bella Donna.

The *Fatma* was no marvellous boat like the *Loulia*. She was small, poorly furnished, devoid of luxury, and not even very comfortable! That night Isaacson lay on a mattress so thin that he felt the board beneath it. The water gurgled close to him against the vessel's side. It seemed to have several voices, which were holding secret converse together in the great stillness of the night. For long he lay awake in the darkness. How different this darkness seemed from that other darkness of London! He thought of the great temples so near him, of the tombs of the Kings, of all those wonders to see which men travelled from the ends of the earth. And he was sailing at dawn, he who had seen nothing! It seemed a mad thing to do. His friends had been openly amazed when he had been forced to tell them of his immediate departure. And he wanted, he longed, to see the wonders that were so near him in the night; Karnak with its pylons, its halls, its statues; the Colossi sitting side by side in their plain, with the springing crops about their feet; the fallen King in the Ramesseum, and that sad King who gazes for ever into the void beneath the mountain.

He longed to see these things, and many others that were near him in the night.

But he longed still more to look for a moment into the eyes of a woman, to take the hand and gaze at the face of a man. And he was glad when, at dawn, he heard the movement of naked feet and the murmur of voices above his head, when, presently, the dahabeeyah shivered and swayed, and the Nile water spoke in a new and more ardent way as it held her in its embrace.

He was glad, for he knew he was going towards Edfou.

XXXI

Upon a hard and habitual worker an unexpected holiday sometimes has a weakening rather than a strengthening effect, in the first days of it. Later may come from it vitality and a renewal of energy. Just at first there steals over the worker a curious lassitude. Parts of him seem to lie down and sleep. Other parts of him are dreaming.

So it was now with Meyer Isaacson.

He got up from his Spartan bed feeling alert and animated. He went up on deck full of curiosity and expectation. But as the day wore on, the long day of golden sunshine, the dream of the Nile took him slowly, quietly, to its breast. Strange were the empty hours to this man whose hours were generally so full. And the solitude was strange. For he sent Hassan away, and sat alone on the upper deck—alone save for the Reis, who, like a statue, stood behind him holding the mighty helm.

The *Fatma* travelled slowly, crept upon the greenish-brown water almost with the deliberation of some monstrous water-insect. For she journeyed against the tide, and as yet there was little wind, though what there was blew from the north. The crew had to work hard in the burning sun-rays, going naked upon the bank and straining at the tow-rope. Isaacson sat in a folding chair and watched their toil. For years he had not known the sensation of watching in absolute idleness the strenuous exertion of others. Those exertions emphasized his inertia, in which presently the mind began to take part with the body. The Nile is exquisitely monotonous. He was coming under its spell. Far off and near, from the western and eastern banks of the river, he heard almost perpetually the creaking song of the sakeeyas, the water-wheels turned by oxen. They made the leit motiv of this wonderful, idle life. Antique and drowsy, with a plaintive drowsiness, was their continual music, which very gradually takes possession of the lonely voyager's soul. The shadûf men, in their long lines leading the eyes towards the south, sang to the almost brazen sky. And heat reigned over all.

Was this pursuit? Where was the *Loulia*? To what secret place had she crept against the repelling tide? It began to seem to Isaacson that he scarcely cared to know. He was forgetting his reason for coming to Egypt. He was forgetting his friend, his enemy; he was forgetting everything. The heat increased. The puffs of wind died down. Towards noon the Reis tied up, that the sweating crew might rest.

A table was laid on deck, and Isaacson lunched under an awning. When he had finished and the Egyptian waiter had cleared away, Hassan came to stand beside his master and entertain him with conversation.

"Are there many orange plantations on the Nile?" asked Isaacson, presently, looking towards the bank, which was broken just here and showed a vista of trees.

Hassan spoke of Mahmoud Baroudi. Once again Isaacson heard of him, and now of his almost legendary wealth. Then came a flood of gossip in pigeon-English. Hamza was presently mentioned, and Isaacson learnt of Hamza's pilgrimage to Mecca with Mahmoud Baroudi, and of his present service with "my Lord Arminigel" upon the *Loulia*. Isaacson did not say that he knew "my Lord." He kept his counsel, and he listened, till at last Hassan's volubility seemed exhausted. The crew were sleeping now. There was no prospect of immediate departure, and, to create a diversion, Hassan suggested a walk through the orange gardens to the house they guarded closely.

Lazily Isaacson agreed. He and the guide crossed the gangway, and soon disappeared into the Villa of the Night of Gold.

When the heat grew less, as the day was declining, once more the *Fatma* crept slowly on her way. She drew ever towards the south with the deliberation of a water-insect which yet had a purpose that kept it on its journey.

She rounded a bend of the Nile. She disappeared.

And all along the Nile the sakeeyahs lifted up their old and melancholy song. And the lines of bending and calling brown men led the eyes towards the south.

XXXII

On a morning at ten o'clock the *Fatma* arrived opposite to Edfou, and Hassan came to tell his master. The *Loulia* had not been sighted. Now and then on the gleaming river dahabeeyahs had passed, floating almost broadside and carried quickly by the tide. Now and then a steamer had churned the Nile water into foam, and vanished, leaving streaks of white in its wake. And the dream had returned, the dream that was cradled in gold, and that was musical with voices of brown men and sakeeyas, and that was shaded sometimes by palm-trees and watched sometimes by stars. But no dahabeeyah had been overtaken. The *Fatma* travelled slowly, often in an almost breathless calm. And Isaacson, if he had ever wished, no longer wished her to hasten. Upon his sensitive and strongly responsive temperament the Nile had laid a spell. Never before had he been so intimately affected by an environment. Egypt laid upon him hypnotic hands. Without resistance he endured their gentle pressure; without resistance he yielded himself to the will that flowed mysteriously from them upon his spirit. And the will whispered to him to relax his mind, as in London each day for a fixed period he relaxed his muscles—whispered to him to be energetic, determined, acquisitive no more, but to be very passive and to dream.

He did not land to visit Esneh. He would have nothing to do with El-Kab. Hassan was surprised, inclined to be argumentative, but bowed to the will of the dreamer. Nevertheless, when at last Edfou was reached, he made one more effort to rouse the spirit of the sight-seer in his strangely inert protector; and this time, almost to his surprise, Isaacson responded. He had an intense love of purity and of form in art, and even in his dream he felt that he could not miss the temple of Horus at Edfou. But he forbade Hassan to accompany him on his visit. He was determined to go alone, regardless of the etiquette of the Nile. He took his sun-umbrella, slipped his guide-book into his pocket, and slowly, almost reluctantly, left the *Fatma*. At the top of the bank a donkey was waiting. Before he mounted it he stood for a moment to look about him. His eyes travelled up-stream, and at a long distance off, rising into the radiant atmosphere and relieved against the piercing blue, he saw the tapering mast of a dahabeeyah. No sail was set on it. The dahabeeyah was either becalmed or tied up. He wondered if it were the *Loulia,* and something of his usual alertness returned to him. For a moment he thought of calling up the snarling and indignant Hassan, whose piercing eyes might perhaps discern the dahabeeyah's identity even from this distance. Or he might go back to his boat, and tell the men to get out their poles again and work her up the river till he could see for himself. Then, in the golden warmth, the dream settled down once more about him and upon him. Why hurry? Why be disturbed? The alertness seemed to fade, to dissolve in his mind. He turned his eyes away from the distant mast, he got upon the donkey, and was taken gently to the temple.

No tourists were there. He sent the donkey-boy away, saying he would walk back to the river. He knew the consciousness that some one was waiting for him to go would take the edge off his pleasure. And he realized at once that he was on the threshold of one of the most intense pleasures of his life. Allured by a gift of money, the native guardian consented to desert him instead of dogging his steps. For the first time he stood in an Egyptian temple.

He remained for some time in the outer court, where the golden sunshine fell, attracted by the sacred darkness that seemed silently to be calling him, but pausing to savour his pleasure. Before him was a vista of empty golden hours. What need had he to hurry? Slowly he approached the hypostyle hall. All about him in the sunshine swarms of birds flew. Their vivacious chirping fell upon ears that were almost deaf. For already the great silence of the darkness beyond was flowing out to Isaacson, was encompassing him about. He reached the threshold and looked back. Through the high and narrow doorway between the towers he caught a glimpse of the native village, and his eyes rested for a moment upon the cupolas of a mosque. Behind him was a place of prayer. Before him was another place, which surely held in its arms of stone all the mystical aspirations, all the unuttered longings, all the starry desires and humble but passionate worship of the men who had passed away from this land of the sun, leaving part of their truth behind them to move through the ages of the souls of men.

He turned at last, and slowly, almost with precaution, he moved from the sunlight into the darkness.

And darkness led to deeper darkness. Never before in any building had Isaacson felt the call to advance so strongly as he felt it now. And yet he lingered. He was forced to linger by the perfect beauty of form which met him in this temple. Never before had any creation of man so absolutely satisfied all the secret demands of his brain and of his soul. He was inundated with a peace that praised, with a calm that loved and adored. This temple built for adoration created within him the need to adore. The perfection of its form was like a perfect prayer offered spontaneously to Him who created in man the power to create.

But though he lingered, and though he was strangely at peace, the darkness called him onward, as the desert calls the nomad who is travelling in it alone.

He was drawn by the innermost darkness of the sanctuary, the core of this house divine of the Hidden One. And he went on between the columns, and up the delicate stone approaches; and though he was always drawing near to a deeper darkness, and natural man is repelled by darkness rather than enticed by it, he felt as if he were approaching something very beautiful, something even divine, something for which, all unconsciously, he had long been waiting and softly hoping. For the spell of the dead architect was upon him, and the Holy of Holies lay beyond—that chamber with narrow walls and blue roof, which contains an altar and shrine of granite, where once no doubt stood the statue of Horus, the God of the Sun.

Isaacson expected to find in this sanctuary the representation of the Being to whom this noble house had been raised. It seemed to him that in this last mystery of beauty and darkness the God Himself must dwell. And he came into it softly, with calm but watchful eyes.

By the shrine, just before it, there stood a white figure. As Isaacson entered it moved, as if disturbed or even startled. A dress rustled.

Isaacson drew back. A chill ran through his nerves. He had been so deep in contemplation, his mind had been drawn away so far from the modern world, that this apparition of a woman, doubtless like himself a tourist, gave him one of the most unpleasant shocks he had ever endured. And in a moment he felt as if his sudden appearance had given an equally disagreeable shock to the woman. Looking in the darkness unnaturally tall, she stood quite still for an instant after her first abrupt movement, then, with an air of decision that was forcible, she came towards him.

Her gait seemed oddly familiar to Isaacson. Directly she stirred he was once more in complete command of his brain. The chill died away from his nerves. The normal man in him started up, alert, composed, enquiring.

The woman came up to him where he stood at the entrance to the sanctuary. Her eyes looked keenly into his eyes, as she was about to pass him. Then she did not pass him. She did not draw back. She just stood where she was and looked at him, looked at him as if she saw what her mind told her, told her loudly, fiercely, she could not be seeing, was not seeing. After an instant of this contemplation she shut her eyes.

"Mrs. Armine!" said Meyer Isaacson.

When he spoke, Mrs. Armine opened her eyes.

"Mrs. Armine!" he repeated.

He took off his hat and held out his hand.

"Then it was the *Loulia* I saw!" he said.

She gave him her hand and drew it away.

"You are in Egypt!" she said.

Although in the darkness her walk had been familiar to him, had prepared him for the coming up to him of Bella Donna, her voice now seemed utterly unfamiliar. It was ugly and grating. He remembered that in London he had thought her voice one of her greatest charms, one of her most perfectly tempered weapons. Had he been mistaken? Had he never heard it aright? Or had he not heard it aright now?

"What are you doing in Egypt?" she said.

Her voice was ugly, almost hideous. But now he realized that its timbre was completely changed by some emotion which had for the moment entire possession of her.

"What are you doing in Egypt?" she repeated.

Isaacson cleared his throat. Afterwards he knew that he had done this because of the horrible hoarseness of Mrs. Armine's voice.

"I was feeling overworked, run down. I thought I would take a holiday."

She was silent for a minute. Then she said:

"Did you let my husband know you were coming? Does he know you are in Egypt?"

In saying this her voice became more ugly, less like hers, as if the emotion that governed her just then made a crescendo, became more vital and more complex.

"No. I left England unexpectedly. A sudden impulse!"

He was speaking almost apologetically, without meaning to do so. He realized this, and pulled himself up sharply.

"I told no one of my plans. I thought I would give Nigel a surprise."

He said it coolly, with quite a different manner.

"Nigel!" she said.

Isaacson was aware when she spoke that he had called his friend by his Christian name for the first time.

"I thought I would give you and your husband a surprise. I hope you forgive me?"

After what seemed to him an immensely long time she answered:

"What is there to forgive? Everybody comes to the Nile. One is never astonished to see any one turn up."

Her voice this time was no longer ugly. It began to have some of the warm and the lazy charm that he had found in it when he met her in London. But the charm sounded deliberate, as if it was thrust into the voice by a strong effort of her will.

"I use the word 'see,'" she added. "But really here one can't see any one or anything properly. Let us go out."

And she passed out of the sanctuary into the dim but less dark hall that lay beyond. Isaacson followed her.

In the slightly stronger light he looked at her swiftly. Already she was putting up her hands to a big white veil, which she had pushed up over her large white hat. Before it fell, obscuring, though not concealing her, he had seen that her face was not made up and that it was deadly pale. But that pallor might be natural. Always in London he had seen her made up, and always made up white. Possibly her face, when unpowdered, unpainted, was white, too.

In the hall she stood still once more.

"You are an extraordinary person, Doctor Isaacson," she said. "Do you know it? I don't think any one else would come out suddenly like this to a place where he had a friend, without letting the friend know. Really, if it were not you, one might think it quite oddly surreptitious."

She finished with a little laugh.

"I think Nigel will be very much surprised," she added.

"I hope you don't mean unpleasantly surprised? As I told you, I intended——"

"Oh, yes, I know all that," she interrupted. "But surely, it seems—well, almost a little bit unfriendly to be on the Nile and never to let him know. And I suppose—how long have you been in Egypt?"

"Oh, a very short time. You must not think I've delayed. On the contrary——"

"If you had delayed, it would have been quite reasonable. You have never seen Egypt before, have you?"

"Never."

"How long were you at Luxor?"

"One night, on the boat opposite to Luxor."

"Then what did you see?"

"Nothing at all."

She put up one hand and pulled gently at her veil.

"I thought I would do all the sight-seeing as I came down the river."

"Most people do it coming up. And I find you in a temple."

"It is the first I have entered. I couldn't pass Edfou."

"Why?"

"Perhaps because I felt that I should meet you in it."

He spoke now with the lightness of an agreeable man of the world paying a compliment to a pretty woman.

"My good angel perhaps guided me into the Holy of Holies because you were—shall I say dreaming in it?"

She moved and walked on.

"Were you long in Cairo?" she said.

"One night."

She stopped again.

"What an extraordinary rush!" she said.

"Yes, I've come along quickly."

"I suppose you've only a very limited time to do it all in? You're only taking a week or two?"

She turned her head towards him, and it seemed to him that her eyes were glittering with a strange excitement, a strange eagerness under her veil.

"I don't know," said Isaacson, carelessly. "I may stay on if I like it. The fact is, Mrs. Armine, that having at last taken the plunge and deserted my patients, I'm enjoying myself amazingly. You've no idea how——"

"Your patients," she interrupted him again, "what will they do? Why, surely your whole practice will go to pieces!"

"It's very kind of you to trouble about that."

"Oh, I'm not troubling; I'm only wondering. I don't know you very well, but I confess I thought I had summed you up."

"Yes, and——?"

"And I thought you were a man of intense ambition, and a man who would rise to the very top of the tree."

"And now?"

"Well, this is hardly the way to do it. I'm—I'm quite sorry."

She said it very naturally. If his appearance had startled her very much—and that it had startled her almost terribly he felt certain—she was now recovering her equanimity. Her self-possession was returning.

"Women are very absurd," she continued. "They

always admire the man who gets on, who forces his way to the front of the crowd."

Walking onward slowly side by side they came into the great outer court. Isaacson had forgotten the wonderful temple. This woman had the power to grasp the whole of his attention, to fix it upon herself.

"Shall we sit down for a minute?" she said. "I'm quite tired with walking about."

She sauntered to a big block of stone on which a shadow fell, sat down carelessly, and put up a white and green sun-umbrella. For the first time since they had met Isaacson, remembering the death of Lord Harwich, wondered at her costume.

"Ah," she said, "you've heard, of course!"

He was startled by her sudden comprehension of his thought.

"Heard! what, Mrs. Armine?"

"About my brother-in-law's sudden death."

"I saw it in the paper."

"Well, I don't happen to have any thin mourning with me."

Her voice had changed again. When she said that it was as hard as a stone.

Isaacson sat down near her. His block of stone was in the sunshine.

"Besides what does it matter here? And I never even knew Harwich, except by sight."

Isaacson said nothing, and after a pause she added:

"So I can't be very sorry. But Nigel's been very much upset by it."

"Has he?"

"Terribly. I dare say you know how sensitive he is?"

"Yes."

"He couldn't go back for the funeral. It was too far. He wouldn't have been in time."

"That was why he didn't go?"

Again he saw the eyes looking keenly at him from under the veil.

"It would have been absolutely no use. Lady Harwich cabled to say so."

"I see."

"She has always been against Nigel since he married me. You know what women are!"

He nodded.

"But the whole thing has upset Nigel dreadfully. That's why we are up here. He wanted to get away, out of reach of everybody, and just to be alone with me. He hasn't even come out with me this morning. He preferred to stay on the boat. He won't see a soul for two or three weeks, poor fellow! It's quite knocked him up, coming so suddenly."

"I'm sorry."

She turned her head towards him. She was holding the sun-umbrella very low down.

"How long were you at Luxor?" she asked, carelessly. "I forget. And weren't you in a hotel? Did you go straight on board your boat?"

"I went to the Winter Palace for a few hours."

"Did you? And hated the crowd, I suppose?"

"I didn't exactly love it."

"You can imagine poor Nigel's horror of it under the circumstances. And then, you know, he hasn't been very well lately. Nothing of any importance—nothing in your line—but he got a touch of the sun. And that, combined with this death, has made him shrink from everybody. I shall try to persuade him, though, to see you later on, in two or three weeks perhaps, when you're dropping down the Nile. You'll stay at the First Cataract, of course?"

"Probably."

"That'll be it, then. As you come down. You can easily find us. Our boat is called the *Loulia*."

"And so your husband's had a touch of the sun?"

"Yes; digging at Luxor. Of course, I got in a doctor at once, a charming man—Doctor Baring Hartley. Very clever—a specialist from Boston. He has the case in charge."

"Oh, you've got him on board?"

"No. Nigel wouldn't have any one. But he has the case in charge, and has gone up to Assouan to meet us there. Shall you run up to Khartoum?"

"I may."

"All these things are done so easily now."

"Yes."

"The railway has made everything so simple."

"Yes."

"I'd give worlds to go to Khartoum. People say it's much more interesting than anything up to the First Cataract."

"Then why not go there?"

"Perhaps we may. But not just yet. Nigel isn't in the mood for anything of that kind. Besides, wouldn't it look almost indecent? Travelling for pleasure, sight-seeing, so soon afterwards? It's a little dull for me, of course, but I think Nigel's quite right to lie low and see no one just for two or three weeks."

"May I light a cigar?"

"Of course."

Rather slowly Meyer Isaacson drew out his cigar-case, extracted a large cigar, struck a match, and lit it. His preoccupation with what he was doing, which seemed perfectly natural, saved him from the necessity of talking for a minute. When the cigar drew thoroughly, he spoke again.

"You don't think"—he spoke slowly, almost lazily, as if he were too content to care much either way about anything under heaven or earth—"you don't think your husband would wish to see me, as we are so very near? We've known each other pretty well. And just now you seemed to fancy he might almost be vexed at my coming out to Egypt without letting him know."

"That's just it," she said, with an answering laziness and indifference. "If he had been expecting you, possibly it mightn't hurt him in the least to see you. But Doctor Baring Hartley specially enjoined on me to keep him quite quiet—at any rate till we got to Assouan. Any shock, even one of pleasure, must be avoided."

"Really? I'm afraid from that that he must really be pretty bad."

"Oh, no, he isn't. He looks worse than he is. It's given him a bad colour, rather, and he gets easily tired. But he was ever so much worse a week ago. He's picking up now every day."

"That's good."

"He would go out digging at Thebes in the very heat of the day. I begged him not to, but Nigel is a little bit wilful. The result is I've had to nurse him."

"It's spoilt your trip, I'm afraid."

"Oh, as long as I get him well quickly, that doesn't matter."

"It will seem quite odd to pass by him without giving him a call," said Isaacson, retaining his casual manner and lazy, indifferent demeanour. "For I suppose I shall pass. You're not going up immediately?"

"We may. I don't know at all. If he wishes to go, we shall go. I shall do just what he wants."

"If you start off, then I shall be in your wake."

"Yes."

She moved her umbrella slightly to and fro.

"I do wish you could pay Nigel a visit," she said. Then, in a very frank and almost cordial voice, she added, "Look here, Doctor Isaacson, let's make a bargain. I'll go back to the dahabeeyah and see how he is, how he's feeling—sound him, in fact. If I think it's all right, I'll send you a note to come on board. If he's very down, or disinclined for company—even yours—I'll ask you to give up the idea and just to put off your visit for a few days, and come to see us at Assouan. After all, Nigel may wish to see you, and it might even do him good. I'm perhaps overanxious to obey doctor's orders, inclined to be too careful. Shall we leave it like that?"

"Thank you very much."

She got up, and so did he.

"Of course," she said, "if I do have to say no after all —I don't think I shall—but if I do, I know you'll understand, and pass us without disturbing my husband. As a doctor, you won't misunderstand me."

"Certainly not."

She pulled at her veil again.

"Well, then——" She held out her hand.

"Oh, but I'll go with you to your donkey," he said. "I suppose you came on a donkey? Or was it in a boat?"

"No; I rode."

"Then let me look for your donkey-boy."

"He went to see friends in the village, but no doubt he's come back. I'll find him easily."

But he insisted on accompanying her. They came out of the first court, through the narrow and lofty portal upon which traces of the exquisite blue-green, the "love colour," still linger. This colour makes an effect that is akin to the effect that would be made by a thin but intense cry of joy rising up in a sombre temple. Isaacson looked up at it. He thought it suggested woman as she ought to be in the life of a man—something exquisite, delicate, ethereal, touchingly fascinating, protected and held by strength. He was still thinking of the love colour, and of his companion when Hamza stood before them, still, calm, changeless as a bronze in the brilliant light of the morning. One of his thin and delicate hands was laid on the red bridle of a magnificent donkey. He looked upon them with his wonderfully expressive Eastern eyes, which yet kept all his secrets.

"What a marvellous type!" Isaacson said, in French, to Mrs. Armine.

"Hamza—yes."

"His name is Hamza?"

She nodded.

"He comes from Luxor. Good-bye again. And I'll send you the note some time this morning, or in the early afternoon."

With a quick easy movement, like that of a young woman, she was in the saddle, helped by the hand of Hamza.

Isaacson heard her sigh as she rode away.

XXXIII

Isaacson walked back alone into the temple. But the spell of the Nile was broken. He had been rudely awaked from his dream, and so thoroughly awaked that his dream was already as if it had never been. He was once more the man he normally was in London—a man intensely, Jewishly alert, a man with a doctor's mind. In every great physician there is hidden a great detective. It was a detective who now walked alone in the temple of Edfou, who penetrated presently once more to the sombre sanctuary, and who stayed there for a long time, standing before the granite shrine of the God, listening mentally in the absolute silence to the sound of an ugly voice.

When the heat of noon approached, Isaacson went back to the *Fatma*. He did not know at all how long a time had passed since Mrs. Armine had left him, and when he came on board, he enquired of Hassan whether any message had come for him, any note from the dahabeeyah that lay over there to the south of them, drowned in the quivering gold.

"No, my nice gentlemans," was the reply, accompanied by a glance of intense curiosity.

Questions immediately followed.

"That boat is the *Loulia*," said Isaacson, impatiently, pointing up river.

"Of course, I know that, my gentlemans."

Hassan's voice sounded full of an almost contemptuous pity.

"Well, I know the people on board of her. They—one of them is a friend of mine. That'll do. You can go to the lower deck."

Isaacson began to pace up and down. He pushed back the deck chairs to the rail in order to have more room for movement. Although the heat was becoming intense, and despite the marvellous dryness of the atmosphere, perspiration broke out on his forehead and cheeks, he could not cease from walking. Once he thought with amazement of his long and almost complete inertia since he had left Luxor. How could he have remained sunk in a chair for hours and hours, staring at the moving water and at the monotonous banks of the Nile? Close to the *Fatma* two shadûf men were singing and bending, singing and bending. And had the shadûf songs lulled him? Had they pushed him towards his dream? Now, as he listened to the brown men singing, he heard nothing but violence in their voices. And in their rhythmical movements only violence was expressed to him. When lunch came, he ate it hastily, without noticing what he was eating. Soon after he had finished, coffee was brought, not by the waiter, but by Hassan, who could no longer suppress another demonstration of curiosity.

"No message him comin', my nice gentlemans."

He stood gazing at his master.

"No?" said Isaacson, with a forced carelessness.

"All the men bin sleepin', the Reis him ready to start. We stop by the *Loulia*, and we take the message ourselfs."

"No. I'm not going to start at present. It's too hot."

Hassan showed his long teeth, which looked like the teeth of an animal: Isaacson knew a protest was coming.

"I'll give the order when I'm ready to start. Go below to my cabin—in the chair by the bed there's a field-glass"—he imitated the action of lifting up to the eyes, and looking through, a glass—"just bring it up to me, will you?"

Hassan vanished, and returned with the glass.

"That'll do."

Hassan waited.

"You can go now."

Slowly Hassan went. Not only his face but his whole body looked the prey of an almost venomous sulkiness. Isaacson picked up the glass, put it to his eyes, and stared up river. He saw faintly a blurred vision. Hassan had altered the focus. The sudden gust of irritation which shook Isaacson revealed him to himself. As his fingers quickly readjusted the glass to suit his eyesight, he stood astonished at the impetuosity of his mind. But in a moment the astonishment was gone. He was but a gazer, entirely concentrated in watchfulness, sunk as it were in searching.

The glass was a very powerful one, and of course Isaacson knew it; nevertheless, he was surprised by the apparent nearness of the *Loulia* as he looked. He could appreciate the beauty of her lines, distinguish her colour, the milky white picked out with gold. He could see two flags flying, one at her mast-head, one in the stern of her; the awning that concealed the upper deck. Yes, he could see all that.

He slightly lowered the glass. Now he was looking straight at the balcony that bayed out from the chamber of the faskeeyeh. There was an awning above it, but the sides were not closed in. As he looked, he saw a figure, like a doll, moving upon the balcony close to the rail. Was it Mrs. Armine? Was it his friend, the man who was sick? He gazed with such intensity that he felt as if he were making a severe physical effort. His eyes began to ache. His eyelids tickled. He rubbed his eyes, blinked, put up the glasses, and looked again.

This time he saw a small boat detach itself from the side of the *Loulia*, creep upon the river almost imperceptibly. The doll was still moving by the rail. Then, as the boat dropped down the river, coming towards Isaacson, it ceased to move.

Isaacson laid down the glass. As he did so, he saw the crafty eyes of Hassan watching him from the lower deck. He longed to give Hassan a knock-down blow, but he pretended not to have seen him.

He sat down on a deck-chair, out of range of Hassan's eyes, and waited for the coming of the messenger of Bella Donna.

Although his detective's mind had told him what the message must be, something within him, some other part of him, strove to contradict the foreknowledge of the detective, to protest that till the message was actually in his hands he could know nothing about it. This protesting something was that part of a man which is driven into activity by his secret and strong desire, a desire which his instinct for the naked truth of things may declare to be vain, but which, nevertheless, will not consent to lie idle.

He secretly longed for the message to be what he secretly knew it would not be.

At last he heard the plash of oars quite near to the *Fatma* and deep voices of men chanting, almost muttering, a monotonous song that set the time for the oars. And although it rose up to him out of a golden world, it was like a chant of doom.

He did not move, he did not look over the side. The chant died away, the plash of the oars was hushed. There was a slight impact. Then guttural voices spoke together.

A minute later Hassan came up the companion, carrying a letter in his curling dark fingers.

"The message him comin', him heeyah!"

Isaacson took the letter.

"You needn't stay."

Hassan did not move.

"I waitin' for——"

"Go away!"

Isaacson had never before spoken so roughly, so almost ferociously to a dependant. When Hassan had gone, ferociously Isaacson opened the letter. It was not very long, and his eyes seized every word of it almost at a glance—seized every word and conveyed to his brain the knowledge, undesired by him, that the detective had been right.

"Loulia, Nile, Wednesday.

"Dear Doctor,

"I find it is better not. When I came on board again I found Nigel reading over one of the notices of Harwich's death. I had begged him to put them away, and not to brood over the inevitable. (We only got the papers giving an account of Harwich yesterday.) But being so seedy, poor boy, I suppose he naturally turns to things that deepen depression. I ought not to have left him. But he insisted on my taking a ride and visiting the temple, which I had never been in before. I persuaded him to put away the papers, and am devoting myself to cheering him up. We play cards together, and I make music, and I read aloud to him. The great thing is—now that he has taken a decided turn for the better—not to excite him in any way. Now you, dear doctor—you mustn't mind my saying it—are rather exciting. You have so much mentality yourself that you stir up one's mind. I have always noticed that. Fond as he is of you, just at this moment I fear you would exhaust Nigel. He gets hot and excited *so* easily since the sunstroke. So *please pass us by without a call*, and do be kind and wait for us at Assouan. In a very few days we shall be able to receive you, and then, when he is a little stronger, you can be of the greatest help to Nigel. Not as a doctor—you see we have one, and mustn't leave him; *medical etiquette*, you know!—but as a friend. It is so delightful to feel you will be at Assouan. If you are the least anxious about your friend, when you get to Assouan ask for Doctor Baring Hartley, if you like, Cataract Hotel. He will set your mind at rest, as he has set mine. It is only a question of keeping very quiet and getting up strength.

"Sincerely yours,

"Ruby Armine.

"P. S. Don't let your men make too much noise when passing us. Nigel sleeps at odd times. Perhaps wiser to pole up along the opposite bank."

Yes, the detective had been right—of course.

Isaacson read the letter again, and this time slowly. The handwriting was large, clear, and determined, but here and there it seemed to waver, a word turned down. He fancied he detected signs of——

He read the postscript four times. If the handwriting had ever wavered, it had recovered itself in the postscript. As he gazed at it, he felt as if he were looking at a proclamation.

He heard a sound, almost as if a soft-footed animal were padding towards him.

"My gentlemans, the Noobian peoples waitin' for what you say to the nice lady."

BELLA DONNA

Isaacson got up and looked over the rail.

Below lay a white felucca containing two sailors, splendidly handsome black men, who were squatting on their haunches and smoking cigarettes. In the stern of the boat, behind a comfortable seat with a back, was Hamza, praying. As Isaacson looked down, the sailors saluted. But Hamza did not see him. Hamza bowed down his forehead to the wood, raised himself up, holding his hands to his legs, and prostrated himself again. For a moment Isaacson watched him, absorbed.

"Hamza very good donkey-boy, always prayin'."

It was Hassan's eternal voice. Isaacson jerked himself up from the rail.

"Ask if the lady expected an answer," he said. "They don't speak English, I suppose?"

"No, my gentlemans.'

He spoke in Arabic. A sailor replied. Hamza always prayed.

"The lady him say p'raps you writin' somethin'."

"Very well."

Isaacson sat down, took a pen and paper. But what should be his answer? He read Mrs. Armine's letter again. She was Nigel's wife, mistress of Nigel's dahabeeyah. It was impossible, therefore, for him to insist on going on board, not merely without an invitation, but having been requested not to come. And yet, had she told Nigel his friend was in Egypt? Apparently not. She did not say she had or she had not. But the detective felt certain she had held her peace. Well, the sailors were waiting, and even that bronze Hamza could not pray for ever.

Isaacson dipped the pen in the ink, and wrote.

"That's for the lady," he said, giving the note to Hassan.

As Hassan went down the stairs, holding up his djelabieh, Isaacson got up and looked once more over the rail. His eyes met the eyes of Hamza. But Hamza did not salute him. Isaacson was not even certain that Hamza saw him. The sailors threw away the ends of their cigarettes.

They bent to the oars. The boat shot out into the gold. And once more Isaacson heard the murmuring chant that suggested doom. It diminished, it dwindled, it died utterly away. And always he leant upon the rail, and he watched the creeping felucca, and he wished that he were in it, going to see his friend.

What was he going to do?

Again he began to pace the deck. It was not very far to Assouan—Gebel Silsile, Kom Ombos, then Assouan. It was some hundred and ten kilometres. The steamers did it in thirteen hours. But the *Fatma*, going always against the stream, would take a much longer time. At Assouan he could seek out this man, Baring Hartley.

But she had suggested that!

How entirely he distrusted this woman!

Mrs. Armine and he were linked by their dislike. He had known they might be when he met her in London. To-day he knew that they were. It seemed to him that he read her with an ease and a certainty that were not natural. And he knew that with equal ease and certainty she read him. Their dislike was as a sheet of flawless glass through which each looked upon the other.

He picked up the field-glass again, and held it to his eyes.

The felucca was close to the *Loulia* now. And the doll upon the balcony was once more moving by the rail.

He was certain this doll was Mrs. Armine, and that she was restless for his answer.

The tiny boat joined the dahabeeyah, seemed to become one with it. The doll moved and disappeared. Isaacson put down the glass.

In his note to Mrs. Armine, the note she was reading at that moment, he had politely accepted her decision, and written that he would look out for them at Assouan. He had written nothing about Doctor Hartley, nothing in answer to her postscript. His note had been shorter than hers, rather careless and perfunctory. He had intended, when he was writing it, to convey to her the impression that the whole matter was a trifle and that he took it lightly. But he, too, had put his postscript. And this was it:

"P. S. I look forward to a real acquaintance with you at Assouan."

And now, if he gave the word to the Reis to untie, to pole off, to get out the huge oars, and to cross to the western bank of the river! Soon they would be level with the *Loulia*. A little later the *Loulia* would lie behind them. A little later still, and she would be out of their sight.

"God knows when they'll be at Assouan!"

Isaacson found himself saying that. And he felt as if, as soon as the *Fatma* rounded the bend of the Nile and crept out of sight on her slow way southwards, the *Loulia* would untie and drop down towards the north. He felt it? He knew it as if he had seen it happen.

"Hassan!"

When Hassan answered, Isaacson bade him tell the Reis that he and his men could rest all the afternoon.

"I'm going to Edfou again. I shall probably spend some hours in the temple."

"Him very fine temple."

"Yes. I shall go alone and on foot."

A few minutes later he set out. He gained the temple, and stayed in it a long time. When he returned to the *Fatma*, the afternoon was waning. In the ethereal distance the *Loulia* still lay motionless.

"We goin' now?" asked Hassan.

Isaacson shook his head.

"We goin' to-night?"

"I'll tell you when I want to go. You needn't keep asking me questions."

The dragoman was getting terribly on Isaacson's nerves. For a moment Isaacson thought of dismissing him there and then, paying him handsomely and sending him ashore now, on the instant. The impulse was strong, but he resisted it. The fellow might possibly be useful. Isaacson looked at him meditatively and searchingly.

"What can I doin' for my gentlemans?"

"Nothing, except hold your tongue."

Hassan retired indignantly.

While he had looked at Hassan, Isaacson had considered a proposition and rejected it. He had thought of sending the dragoman with a note to the *Loulia*. It would be simple enough to invent an excuse for the note. Hassan might see Nigel—would see Nigel, if a hint were given him to do so. But he would no doubt also see Mrs. Armine; and—if Isaacson's instinct were not utterly astray in a wilderness of absurdity and error—she would make more use of Hassan than he ever could. The dragoman's face bore the sign-manual of treachery stamped upon it. And Mrs. Armine would be more clever in using treachery than Isaacson. He appreciated her talent at its full value.

While he had been in the temple of Edfou he had come to a conclusion with himself. Entirely alone in the semi-darkness of the most perfect building, and the most perfectly calm building, that he had ever entered, he had known his own calm and what his instinct told him in it. Had he not spent those hours in Edfou, possibly he might have denied the insistent voice of his instinct. Now he would heed that voice, certain that it was no unreasonable ear that was listening.

He saw the tapering mast of the *Loulia* against the thin, magical gold of the sky at sunset. He saw it against the even more magical primrose, pale green, soft red, of the after-glow. He saw it black as ink in the livid spasm of light that the falling night struck away from the river, the land, the sky. And then he saw it no more.

His sailors began to sing a song of the Nile, sitting in a circle around a bowl that had been passed from hand to hand. He dined quickly.

Hassan came to ask if he might go ashore. He had friends in the native village, and wished to see them. Isaacson told him to go. A minute later, with a swish of skirts, the tall figure vanished over the gangway and up the bank.

The sailors went on singing, throwing back their heads,

swaying them, rocking gently to and fro and from side to side. They were happy and intent.

Isaacson let five minutes go by; then he followed Hassan's example. He crossed the gangway, climbed the bank, and stood still on the flat ground which dominated the river.

The night was warm, almost lusciously warm, and very still. The sky was absolutely clear, but there was no moon, and the river, the flats, the two ranges of mountains that keep the Nile, were possessed by a gentle darkness. As Isaacson stood there, he saw the lights on the *Fatma* gleaming, he heard the sad and tempestuous singing of his men, and the barking of dogs on hidden houses keeping guard against imagined intruders. When he looked at the lights of the *Fatma*, he realized how the boat stood to him for home. He felt almost desolate in leaving her to adventure forth in the night.

But he turned southwards and looked up-river. Far away—so it seemed, now the night was come—isolated in the darkness, was a pattern of lights. And high above them, apparently hung in air, there was a blue jewel. Isaacson knew it for a lamp fixed against the mast of the *Loulia*. He put his hand down to his hip-pocket. Yes, his revolver was safely there. He lit a cigar, then, moved by an after-thought, threw it away. Its tip hissed as it struck the river. He looked at that blue jewel, at the diaper of yellow below it, and he set out upon his nocturnal journey.

At first he walked very slowly and cautiously. But soon his eyes, which were exceptionally strong-sighted, became accustomed to the gloom, and he could see his way without difficulty. Now and then he looked back, rather as a man going into a tunnel on foot may look back to the orifice which shows the light of day. He looked back to his home. And each time it seemed to have receded from him. And at last he felt he was homeless. Then he looked back no more, but always forward to the pattern of light that marked where the *Loulia* lay. And then—why was that?— he felt more homeless still. Perhaps he was possessed by the consciousness of moving towards an enemy. Men feel very differently in darkness and in light. And in darkness their thought of an individual sometimes assumes strange contours. Now Isaacson's imagination awoke, and led his mind down paths that were dim and eerie. The blue jewel that hung in air seemed like the cruel eye of a beautiful woman that was watching him as he walked. He felt as if Bella Donna had mounted upon a tower to spy out his progress in the night. With this fancy he played a sort of horrible game, until deep in his mind a conviction grew that Mrs. Armine had actually somehow divined his approach. How? Women have the strangest intuitions. They know things that—to speak by the card—they cannot know.

Surely Bella Donna was upon her tower.

He stopped at the edge of a field of doura. What was the use of going further?

He looked to the north, then turned and looked to the south, comparing the two distances that lay between him and his own boat, between him and the *Loulia*. His mind had said, "If I'm nearer to the *Fatma* I'll go back; if I'm nearer to the *Loulia* I'll go on." His eyes, keenly judging the distances, told him he was nearer to the *Loulia* than to his own boat. The die was cast. He went on.

Surely Bella Donna knew it, spied it from her tower.

Now he heard he knew not where, violent voices of fellahîn, of many fellahîn talking, as it seemed, furiously in the darkness. The noise suggested a crowd roused by some strong emotion. It sounded quite near, but not close. Isaacson stood still, listened, tried to locate it, but could not. The voices rose in the night, kept perpetually at a high, fierce pitch, like voices of men in a frenzy. Then abruptly they failed, as if the night, wearied with their importunity, had fallen upon the speakers and choked them. And the silence, broken only by the faint rustle of the doura, was startling, was almost dreadful.

Isaacson walked more quickly, fixing his eyes on those lights to the south. As he drew near to them, he was conscious of a sort of cold excitement, cold because at its core lay apprehension. When he was very near to them and could distinguish the solidity of the darkness out of which they were shining, he walked slowly, and then presently stood still. And as he stood still the Nubian sailors on the *Loulia* began to sing the song about Allah which Mrs. Armine had heard from the garden of the Villa Androud on her first evening in Upper Egypt.

First a solo voice, vehement, strange to Western ears, immensely expressive, like the voice of a mueddin summoning the faithful to prayer, cried aloud, "Al-lah! Al-lah! Al-lah!" And this voice was accompanied by a deep and monotonous murmur, and by the ground bass of the daraboukkeh. Then the chorus of male voices joined in.

As Isaacson stood a little way off on the lonely bank of the Nile in this deserted place—for the *Loulia* was tied up far from any village, in a desolate reach of the river—he thought that he had never heard till now any music at the same time so pitiless and so sad, so cruel, and yet, at moments, so full of a rough and artless yearning. It seemed heavy with the burthen of fate, of that from which a man cannot escape, though he strive with all his powers and cry out of the very depths of his heart.

Like a great and sombre cloud the East settled down upon Isaacson as he heard that song of the dark people. And as he stood in the cloud something within him responded to these voices, responded to the souls that were behind them.

Once, one morning in London, besieged by the commonplace, he had longed for events, tragic, tremendous, horrible even, if only they were unusual, if only they were such as would lift him into sharp activity. Had that longing resulted in—now?

He put out one lean, dark hand, and pulled at the heavily podded head of a doura plant. And the voices sang on, and on, and on.

Suddenly, with a sharp and cruel abruptness, they ceased.

"Al——" and silence! The name of the dark man's God was executed upon their lips.

Isaacson let go the podded head of the doura. He waited. Then, as the deep silence continued, he went on till the outline of the big boat was distinct before his eyes, till he saw that the blue light was a lamp fixed against an immense mast that bent over and tapered to a delicate point. He saw that, and yet he still seemed to see Bella Donna upon her tower; Bella Donna, the eternal spy, whose beautiful eyes had sought his secrets between the walls of his consulting-room.

Very cautiously he went now. He looked warily about him. But he saw no more upon the bank. It was not high here. Without a long descent he would be able to see into the chambers of the *Loulia,* unless their shutters were closed against the night. It was strange to think that he was close to Nigel, and that Nigel believed him to be in Cleveland Square, unless Mrs. Armine had been frank. Now he saw something moving upon the bank, furtively creeping towards the lights, as if irresistibly attracted, and yet always afraid. It was a wretched pariah dog, starving, and with its yellow eyes fixed upon the thing that contained food; a dog such as that which crept near to Mrs. Armine as she sat in the garden of the villa, while Nigel, above her, watched the stars. As Isaacson came near to it, it shivered and moved away, but not far. Then it sat down and shook. Its ribs were like the ribs of a wrecked vessel.

Isaacson was close to the *Loulia* now. He could see the balcony in the stern where the doll had moved by the rail. It was lit by one electric burner, and was not closed in with canvas, though there was a canvas roof above it. Beyond it, through two large apertures, Isaacson could see more light that gleamed in a room. He stood still again. Upon the balcony he saw a long outline, the outline of a deck-chair with a figure stretched out in it. As he saw this the silence was again broken by music. From the lighted room came the chilly and modern sound of a piano.

Then Bella Donna had come down from her tower! Or had she never been there?

Isaacson looked at the long outline, and listened. His

mind was full of that other music, the cry of Mohammedanism in the African night. This music of Europe seemed out of place, like a nothing masquerading beneath the stars. But in a moment he listened more closely; he moved a step nearer. He was searching in his memory, was asking himself what that music expressed, what it meant to him. No longer was it banal. There was a sound in it, even played upon a piano, even heard in this night and this desolate place between two deserts, of the elemental.

Bella Donna was playing that part of "The Dream of Gerontius" where the soul of man is dismissed to its Maker.

"Proficiscere, anima Christiana, de hoc mundo!" (Go forth upon thy journey, Christian soul! Go from this world!)

She was playing that, and the stretched figure in the long chair was listening to it.

At that moment Isaacson felt glad that he had come to Egypt—glad in a new way.

"Go forth . . . go from this world!"

Almost he heard the deep and irreparable voice of the priest, and in the music there was disintegration. In it the atoms parted. The temple crumbled to let the inmate come forth.

Presently the music ceased. The murmur of a voice was audible. Then one of the oblongs of light beyond the balcony was broken up by a darkness. And the darkness came out, and bent above the stretched figure in the chair. An instant later the electric burner that gave light to the balcony was extinguished. Nigel and his wife were together in the dimness, with the lighted room beyond them.

When the light was turned out, the pariah dog got up stealthily and crept much nearer to the *Loulia*. Its secret movement, observed by Isaacson, made an unpleasant impression upon him. He drew a parallel between it and himself, and felt himself to be a pariah, because of what he was doing. But something within him that was much stronger than his sense of discretion, and of "the right thing" for a decently bred man to do, had taken him to this place in the night, kept him there, even prompted him to imitate the starving dog, and to move nearer to those two who believed themselves isolated in the dimness.

He was determined to hear the voice of the stretched figure in the long chair.

The light that issued from the room of the faskeeyeh faintly illuminated part of the balcony. Isaacson heard the murmuring voice of Mrs. Armine again. Then one of the oblongs was again obscured, and the room was abruptly plunged in darkness. As Mrs. Armine returned, Isaacson stole down the shelving bank and took up a position close to the last window of this room. The crew and the servants were all forward on the lower deck, which was shut in closely by canvas. On the upper deck of the boat there was no one. If Mrs. Armine had lingered after putting out the light, she would perhaps have seen the figure of a man. But she did not linger. Isaacson had felt that she would not linger. And he was out of range of the vision of any one on the balcony, although now so close to it that it was almost as if he stood upon it. The Nile flowed near his feet with a sucking murmur that was very faint in the night. There was no other sound to interfere between him and the two voices.

A dress rustled. He thought of the sanctuary in the temple of Edfou. Then a faint and strangely toneless voice, that he did not recognize, said:

"That's ever so much better. I do hate that strong light."

"But who is that in the chair, then?" Isaacson asked himself, astonished. "Have they got some one on board with them?"

"Electric light tries a great many people."

Isaacson knew the voice which said that. It was Mrs. Armine's voice, gentle, melodious, and seductive. And he thought of the hoarse and hideous sound which that morning he had heard in the temple.

"Do sit down by me," said the first voice.

Could it really be Nigel's? This time there was in it a sound that was faintly familiar to Isaacson—a sound to which he listened almost as a man may regard a shadow and say to himself, "Is that shadow cast by my friend?"

A dress rustled. And the tiny noise was followed by the creak of a basket chair.

"Don't you think you're a little better to-night?" said Mrs. Armine.

The other sighed.

"No."

"Doctor Baring Hartley said you would recover rapidly."

"Ruby, he doesn't understand my case. He can't understand it."

"But he seemed so certain. And he's got a great reputation in America."

"But he doesn't understand. To-night I feel—when you were playing 'Gerontius' I felt that—that I must soon go. 'Proficiscere, anima Christiana, de hoc mundo'—I felt as if somewhere that was being said to me."

"Nigel!"

"It's strange that I, who've always loved the sun, should be knocked over by the sun, isn't it? Strange that what one loves should destroy one!"

"But—but that's not true, Nigel. You are getting better, although you don't think so."

"Ruby"—the voice was almost stern, and now it was more like the voice that Isaacson knew—"Ruby, I'm getting worse. To-day I feel that I'm going to die."

"Let me telegraph for Doctor Hartley. At dawn to-morrow I shall send the boat to Edfou——"

"If only Isaacson were here!"

There was a silence. Then Mrs. Armine said:

"What could Doctor Isaacson do more than has been done?"

"He's a wonderful man. He sees what others don't see. I feel that he might find out what's the matter."

"Find out! But, Nigel, we know it's the sun. You yourself——"

"Yes, yes!"

"To-morrow I'll wire for Doctor Hartley to come down at once from Assouan."

"It's this awful insomnia that's doing for me. All my life I've slept so well—till now. And the rheumatic pains: how can the sun—Ruby, sometimes I think it's nothing to do with the sun."

"But, then, what can it be? You know you would expose yourself, though I begged and implored——"

"But the heat's nothing new to me. For months in the Fayyûm I worked in the full glare of the sun. And it never hurt me."

"Nigel, it was the sun. One may do a thing ninety-nine times, and the hundredth time one pays for it."

A chair creaked.

"Do you want to turn, Nigel? Wait, I'll help you."

"Isn't it awful to lose all one's strength like this?"

"It'll come back. Wait! You're slipping. Let me put my arm behind you."

"Yes, give me your hand, dearest!"

After a pause he said:

"Poor Ruby! What a time for you! You never guessed you'd married a miserable crock, did you?"

"I haven't. Any one may get a sunstroke. In two or three weeks you'll be laughing at all this. Directly it passes you'll forget it."

"But I have a feeling sometimes that—it's a feeling—of death."

"When? When?"

"Last night, in the night. I felt like a man just simply going out."

"I never ought to have let Doctor Hartley go. But you said you wanted to be alone with me, didn't you, Nigel?"

"Yes. I felt somehow that Hartley could be of no use—that no ordinary man could do anything. I felt as if it were Fate, and as if you and I must fight it together. I felt as if—perhaps—our love——"

The voice died away.

Isaacson clenched his hands, and moved a step backward. The shivering pariah dog slunk away, fearing a blow.

"What was that?" Nigel said.

"Did you hear something?"

"Yes—a step."

"Oh, it's one of the men, no doubt. Shall I play to you a little more?"

"Can you without putting on the light? I'm afraid of the light now and—and how I used to love it!"

"I'll manage."

"But you'll have to take away your hand! Wait a minute. Oh, Ruby, it's terrible! To-night I feel like a man on the edge of an abyss, and as if, without a hand, I must fall—I——"

Isaacson heard a dry, horrid sound, that was checked almost at once.

"I never—never thought I should come to this, Ruby."

"Never mind, dearest. Any one——"

"Yes—yes—I know. But I hate—it isn't like a man to—— Go and play to me again."

"I won't play 'Gerontius.' It makes you think sad things, dreadful things."

"No, play it again. It was on your piano that day I called—in London. I shall always associate it with you."

The dress rustled. She was getting up.

Isaacson hesitated no longer. He went instantly up the bank. When he had reached the top he stood still for a moment. His breath came quickly. Below, the piano sounded. Bella Donna had not seen him, had not, without seeing him, divined his presence. He might go while she played, and she would never know he had been there eavesdropping in the night. No one would ever know. And to-morrow, with the sun, he could come back openly, defying her request. He could come back boldly and ask for his friend.

"Proficiscere, anima Christiana, de hoc mundo!"

He would come back and see the face that went with that changed voice, that voice which he had hardly recognized.

"Go forth upon thy journey, Christian soul! Go from this world!"

He moved to go away to those far-off lights which showed where the *Fatma* lay, by Edfou.

"Go forth . . . go from this world!"

Was it the voice of a priest? Or was it the irreparable voice of a woman?

Suddenly Isaacson breathed quietly. He unclenched his hands. A wave—it was like that—a wave of strong self-possession seemed to inundate him. Now, in the darkness on the bank, a great doctor stood. And this doctor had nothing to do with the far-off lights by Edfou. His mission lay elsewhere.

"Go forth—go forth from this world!"

He walked along the bank, down the bank to the gangway which connected the deck of the *Loulia* forward with the shore. He pushed aside the dropped canvas, and he stepped upon the deck. A number of dark eyes gravely regarded him. Then Hamza detached himself from the hooded crowd and came up to where Isaacson was standing.

"Give that card to your master, and ask if I can see him."

"Yes!" said Hamza.

He went away with the card. There was a pause.

Then abruptly, the sound of the piano ceased.

XXXIV

AFTER the cessation of the music there was a pause, which seemed to Isaacson almost interminably prolonged. In it he felt no excitement. In a man of his type excitement is the child of uncertainty. Now all uncertainty as to what he meant to do had left him. Calm, decided, master of himself as when he sat in his consulting-room to receive the suffering world, he waited quietly for the return of his messenger. The many dark eyes stared solemnly at him, and he looked back at them, and he knew that his eyes told them no more than theirs told him.

When Hamza went with the card, he had shut behind him the door at the foot of the stairs, which divided the rooms on the *Loulia* from the deck. Presently as no one came, Isaacson looked at this door. He saw above it the Arabic inscription which Baroudi had translated for Mrs. Armine and he wondered what it meant. His eyes were almost fascinated by it and he felt it must be significant, that the man he had seen crouching beneath the black roof of the hashish café had set it there to be the motto of his wonderful boat. But he knew no Arabic, and there was no one to translate the golden characters. For Ibrahim that night was unwell, and was sleeping smothered in his haik.

The white door opened gently, and Hamza reappeared. He made a gesture which invited Isaacson to come to him. Isaacson felt that he consciously braced himself, as a strong man braces himself for a conflict. Then he went over the deck, down the shallow steps, and was led by Hamza into the first saloon of the *Loulia*, that room which Baroudi had called his "den," and which Mrs. Armine had taken as her boudoir. It was lit up. The door on the far side, beyond the dining-room, was shut. And Mrs. Armine was standing by the writing-table, holding Isaacson's card in her hand.

As soon as Isaacson had crossed the threshold, Hamza went out and shut the door gently.

Mrs. Armine was dressed in black, and on her cheeks were two patches of vivid red, of red that was artificial and not well put on. Isaacson believed that she had rushed from the piano to make up her face when she had learnt of his coming. She looked towards him with hard interrogation, at the same time lifting her hand.

"Hush, please!" she said, in a low voice. "He doesn't know you are here. He's asleep."

Her eyes went over his face with a horrible swiftness, and she added, "I was playing. I have been playing him to sleep."

As if remembering, she held out her hand to Isaacson. He went over to her softly and took it. As he did so, she made what seemed an involuntary and almost violent movement to draw it away, checked herself, and left her hand in his, setting her lips together. He noticed that in one of her eyelids a pulse was beating. He held her hand with a gentle, an almost caressing decision, while he said, imitating her withdrawn way of speaking:

"I'm afraid my coming at this hour has surprised you very much. Do forgive me, but——"

"What about my note?" she asked.

"May I sit down? What marvellous rugs! What an extraordinary boat this is!"

"Oh, sit—the divan! Yes, the rugs are fine—of course."

Hastily, and moving without her usual grace, she went to the nearest divan. He followed her. She sat down, but did not lean back. She had dropped his card on the floor.

"You read my note! Well, then——?"

It seemed to Isaacson that within his companion there was at this moment a violent mental struggle going on as to what course she should take, now, immediately; as if something within her was clamouring for defiance, something else was pleading for diplomacy. He felt that he was close to an almost red-hot violence, and wondered intensely whether it was going to have its way. He wondered, but he did not care. For he knew that nothing his companion did could change his inward decision. And even in a moment that was like a black thing lit up by tragic fires he enjoyed his alert mentality, as an athlete enjoys his power to give a tremendous blow even if he has just seen a sight that has waked in him horror.

"Well, then?" she repeated, always speaking in a very low voice, though not in a whisper.

A cuckoo clock sounded. She sprang up.

"That wretched——!"

She went over to the clock, tore the little door in the front out, inserted her fingers in the opening. There was a dry sound of tearing and splintering. She came back with minute drops of blood on her fingers.

"It drives Nigel mad!" she said. "It ought to have been stopped long ago. You got my note, and I your answer."

"And of course you think that I ought not to have come to-night."

She looked at him and sat down again. And by the way of her sitting down he knew that she had come to a decision as to conduct.

"I suppose you felt uneasy, and thought you would like to enquire a little more of me. Was that it?"

"I did feel a little uneasy, I confess."

"How did you come to-night?"

"I walked."

"Walked? Alone?"

"Quite alone."

"All that way! I'll send you back in the felucca."

"Oh, that will be all right."

"No, no, you shall have the felucca."

She touched an electric bell. Hamza came.

"The felucca, Hamza."

"Yes."

He went.

"They'll get it ready."

She moved some cushions. Isaacson noticed a yellowish tinge about her temples, just beyond the corners of her eyes above the cheek-bones. Most of her face was not made up, though there were one or two dabs of powder as well as the rouge.

"They'll get it ready in a moment," she repeated.

She turned towards him, smiling suddenly.

"And so you felt uneasy, and thought you'd hear a little more, and came at night so as not to startle or disturb him. That was good of you. The fact is, I didn't tell him I had met you to-day. I intended to, but when I got here I gave up the idea."

"Why was that?"

"He'd been reading all the notices about Harwich, and they'd utterly upset him."

Suddenly she noticed the tiny drops of blood on her fingers.

"Oh!" she said.

She put her hand up to the front of her gown, drew out a handkerchief, and pressed her fingers with it.

"How stupid of me!"

Hamza appeared.

"Ah, the felucca is ready!" said Mrs. Armine.

Isaacson leaned back quietly, and made himself comfortable on the broad divan.

"In a minute, Hamza!" she said.

Hamza went away.

"That's a marvellous fellow you've got," said Isaacson.

Although he spoke almost under his breath, he managed to introduce into his voice the quiet sound of a man of the world very much at his ease, and with a pleasant half-hour before him. "I saw him praying this afternoon."

"Praying?"

"Yes, when he brought your note."

A look of horror crept over her face, and was gone in an instant.

"Oh, all these people pray."

She sat more forward on the divan, almost like one about to get up. Isaacson crossed one leg over the other.

"What you told me this morning did make me uneasy about your husband," he said, leaving the Mohammedan world abruptly.

"Then I must have spoken very carelessly," she said, quickly.

"All the time they were talking, she made perpetual slight movements, and was never perfectly still.

"Then you are not at all uneasy about his condition?"

"I—I didn't say that. Naturally, a wife is a little anxious if her husband has been ill. But he is so much better than he was that it would be foolish of me to be upset."

"I confess this morning you roused my professional anxiety."

"I really don't see why."

"Well, you know, we doctors become very alert about signs and symptoms. And you let drop one or two words which made me fear that possibly your husband might be worse than you supposed."

Doctor Baring Hartley is in charge of the case."

"Well, but he isn't here!"

"He's coming here to-morrow."

"I understood he was waiting for you at Assouan. You'll forgive me for venturing to intrude into this affair, but as an old friend of your husband——"

"Doctor Hartley is at Assouan, but he will come down to-morrow to see his patient. You don't seem to realize that Assouan is close by, just round the corner."

"I know it is only a hundred and ten kilometres away."

"In a steam launch or by train that's absolutely nothing. He'll be here to-morrow."

"Then your husband feels worse?"

"Not at all."

"But if you've sent for Doctor Hartley?"

"I've only done that because instead of going up at

once to Assouan, as we had intended, we've decided to remain here for the present. Nigel enjoys the quiet, and I dare say it's better for him. You forget he's just lost his only brother."

"You mean that I am wanting in delicacy in thrusting myself into your mutual grief?"

He spoke very simply, very quietly, but there was a note in his voice of inflexible determination.

"I don't wish to say that," she answered.

And her voice was harder than his.

"But I'm afraid you think it. I'll be frank with you, Mrs. Armine. Here is my friend, ill, isolated from medical help——"

"For the moment only."

"Isolated for the moment from medical help in a very lonely place——"

"My dear doctor!" She raised her narrow eyebrows. "To hear you talk, one would think we were at the end of the world instead of in the very midst of civilization and people."

"And here, by chance"—he saw her mouth set itself in a grimness which made her look suddenly middle-aged—"by chance, am I, an old acquaintance, a good friend, and, if I may say so of myself, a well-known medical man. Is it not natural if I come to see how the sick man is?"

"Oh, quite; and I've told you how he is."

"Isn't it natural if I ask to see the sick man himself?"

Her mouth went suddenly awry. She pressed her hand on a cushion. "No, I don't think it is when his wife asked you not to come to see him, because it would upset him, and because he had specially told her that for two or three weeks he wished to see nobody."

"Are you quite sure your husband wouldn't wish to see me?"

"He doesn't wish to see anybody for a few days."

"Are you quite sure that if he knew I was here he wouldn't wish to see me?"

"How on earth can one be quite sure of what other

people would think, or want, if this, or that, or the other?"

"Then why not find out?"

"Find out?"

"By asking. I certainly am not the man to force myself upon a friend against his will. But I should be very much obliged to you if you would tell your husband I'm here, and ask him whether he wouldn't like to see me."

"You really wish me to wake an invalid up in the dead of night, just as he's been got off to sleep, in order to receive a visitor! Well, then, I flatly refuse."

"Oh, if he is really asleep!"

"I told you that just before you arrived I had been playing the piano to him and that he had fallen asleep. I don't think you are very considerate this evening, Doctor Isaacson."

She got up.

"A doctor, I think, ought to know better."

The little pulse in her eyelid was beating furiously.

He stood up, too.

"A doctor," he said, very quietly, "I think does know better than one who is not a doctor how to treat a sick man. What you said to me in the temple this morning, and what I heard when I was in Cairo and at Luxor before I came up the river, has alarmed me about my friend, and I must request to be allowed to see him."

"At Cairo and Luxor! What did you hear at Cairo and Luxor?"

"At Cairo I heard from a man that your husband was too ill to travel, and therefore certainly could not under any circumstances have gone to England when he heard of his brother's death. At Luxor from a woman I heard very much the same story."

"Of course, and probably with plenty of embroidery and exaggeration."

"Perhaps. But sunstroke can be a very serious thing."

"I never heard you were a specialist in sunstroke."

"And is Doctor Baring Hartley, who is watching this case from Assouan?"

They looked at each other for a minute in silence. Then she said:

"Perhaps I've been a little unjust to-night. I've had a good deal of trouble lately, and it's upset my nerves. I know you care for Nigel, and I'm grateful to you for your friendly anxiety. But perhaps you don't realize that you've expressed that anxiety in a way that—well, that has seemed to reflect upon me, upon my conduct, and any woman, any wife, would resent that, and resent it keenly."

"I'm sorry," he said, coldly. "In what way have I reflected upon you?"

"Your words, your whole manner—they seem to show doubt of my care of and anxiety about Nigel. I resent that."

"I'm sorry," he said again, and again with almost icy coldness.

Her lips trembled.

"Perhaps, being a man, you don't realize how it hurts a woman who has been through a nervous strain when some one pushes in from outside and makes nothing of all she has been doing, tacitly belittles all her care and devotion and self-sacrifice, and tries, or seems to wish to try, to thrust himself into her proper place."

"Oh, Mrs. Armine, you are exaggerating. I wish nothing of that kind. All I wish is to be allowed to use such medical talent as God has given me in the service of your husband and my friend."

Her lips ceased from trembling. "I cannot insult Doctor Baring Hartley by consenting to bring is another doctor behind his back," she said. And now her voice was as cold, as hard, as decisive as his own. "I am astonished that you should be so utterly indifferent to the etiquette of your own profession," she added.

"I will make that all right with Doctor Hartley when I get to Assouan."

"There will be no need for that."

"Do you mean that you are going to refuse absolutely to allow me to see your husband?"

"I do. In any case, you could not see him to-night, as he is asleep——"

She stopped. Through the silent boat there went the sharp, tingling noise of an electric bell.

"As he is asleep." She spoke more quickly and unevenly. "And to-morrow Doctor Hartley will be here, and I shall go by what he says. If he wishes a consultation——"

Again the bell sounded. She frowned. Hamza appeared at the door leading from the deck. He closed the door behind him, crossed the cabin without noise, opened the farther door, and vanished, shutting it with a swift gentleness that seemed almost unnatural.

"Then it will be a different matter, and I shall be very glad indeed to have your opinion. I know its value"—she looked towards the door by which Hamza had gone out—"but I must treat Doctor Hartley with proper consideration. And now I must say good night."

Her voice still hurried. Quickly she held out her hand.

"The felucca will take you home. And to-morrow, as soon as Doctor Hartley has been here and I have had a talk with him and heard what he thinks, I'll let you know all about it. It's very good of you to bother."

But Isaacson did not take the outstretched hand.

"Your husband is awake," he said, abruptly.

Her hand dropped.

"I think, I'm sure, that if he knew I was here he would be very glad to see me. I know you'll tell him, and let him decide for himself."

"But I'm sure he is asleep. I left him asleep."

"That bell——"

She smiled.

"Oh, that wasn't Nigel! That was my French maid. She's very glorified here. She makes Hamza attend upon her, hand and foot."

As she spoke, Isaacson remembered the words in Nigel's letter: "She packed off her French maid so as to be quite free."

"Oh, your maid!" he said.

And his voice was colder, firmer.

"Yes."

"But surely it may have been your husband who rang?"

"No, I don't think so. I'm quite sure not. Once Nigel gets off to sleep he doesn't wake easily."

"But I thought he suffered from insomnia!"

Directly he had said the words, Isaacson realized that he had made a false step. But it was too late to retrieve it. She was upon him instantly.

"Why?" she said, sharply. "Why should you think that?"

"You——"

"I never said so! I never said a word of it!"

She remembered the steps Nigel had said he heard when they were together upon the balcony, and beneath the rouge on her face her cheeks went grey.

"I never said a word of it!" she reiterated, with her eyes fastened upon him.

"You spoke of having 'got him off to sleep'—of having 'played him to sleep.' I naturally gathered that he had been sleeping badly, and that sleep was very important to him. And then the clock!"

He pointed to the broken toy from Switzerland.

But the greyness persisted in her face. He knew that his attempted explanation was useless. He knew that she had realized his overhearing of her conversation with Nigel. Well, that fact, perhaps, cleared some ground. But he would not show that he knew.

"Your vexation about the clock proved that the patient was sleeping badly and was sensitive to the least noise."

She opened her lips twice as if to speak, and shut them without saying anything; then, as if with a fierce effort, and speaking with a voice that was hoarse and ugly as the voice he had heard in the temple, she said:

"It's very late, and I'm really tired out. I can't talk any more. I've told you that Nigel is asleep and that I decline to wake him for you or for any one. The doctor who understands his case, and whom he himself has chosen to be in charge of it, is coming early to-morrow. The felucca is there"—she put out her hand towards the nearest door—"and will take you down the river. I must ask you to go. I'm tired."

She dropped her hand.

"This boat is my house, Doctor Isaacson, and I must seriously ask you to leave it."

"And I must insist, as a doctor, on seeing your husband."

All pretence was dropped between them. It was a fight.

"This is great impertinence," she said. "I refuse. I've told you my reason."

"I shall stop here till I see your husband," said Isaacson.

And he sat down again very quietly and deliberately on the divan.

"And if you like, I'll tell you my reason," he said.

But she did not ask him what it was. Through the sheet of glass he looked at her, and it was as if he saw a pursued hare suddenly double.

"It's too utterly absurd all this argument about nothing," she said, suddenly smiling, and in her beautiful voice. "Evidently you have been the victim of some ridiculous stories in Cairo or Luxor. Some kind people have been talking, as kind people talked in London. And you've swallowed it all, as you swallowed it all in London. I suppose they said Nigel was dying and that I was neglecting him, or some rubbish of that sort. And so you, as a medical Don Quixote, put your lance in rest and rush to the rescue. But you don't know Nigel if you think he'd thank you for doing it."

In the last sentence her voice, though still preserving its almost lazy beauty, became faintly sinister.

"Nigel knows me as the world does not," she continued, quietly. "And the one who treats me wrongly, without the respect due to me as his wife, will find he has lost Nigel as a friend."

Isaacson felt like a man whose enemy has abruptly unmasked a battery, and who faces the muzzles of formidable guns.

"You don't know Nigel."

She said it softly, almost reflectively, and with a little droop of the head she emphasized it.

"You had better do what I ask you to do, Doctor Isaacson. If you wish to do Nigel good, you had better not try to force yourself in against my will in the dead of the night, when I'm tired out and have begged you to go. You had better let me ask Doctor Hartley for a consultation to-morrow, and tell Nigel, and call you in. That's the best plan—if you want to be nice to Nigel."

She sat down again on the divan, at a short distance from him, and close to the door by which Hamza had gone out.

"Nigel and I have talked this all over," she said, with a quiet sweetness.

"Talked this over?" Isaacson said.

With his usual quickness of mind he had realized the exact strength of the strategic position she had so suddenly and unexpectedly taken up. For the moment he wished to gain time. His former complete decision as to what he meant to do was slightly weakened by her presentation of Nigel, the believer. From his knowledge of his friend, he appreciated her judgment of Nigel at its full value. What she had just said was true, and the truth bristled like a bayonet-point in the midst of the lies by which it was surrounded.

"Talked this over? How can that be?"

"Very easily. When two people love each other there is nothing they do not discuss—even their enemies."

"My dear Mrs. Armine, no melodrama, please!"

"Melodrama or not, Doctor Isaacson, I promise you it is a fact that my friends are Nigel's friends, and that my enemies would, at a very few words from me, find that in Nigel they had an enemy."

"If you are speaking of me, your husband would never be my enemy."

"Do you know why he never told you we were going to be married?"

"It was no business of mine."

"His instinct informed him that you mistrusted me. Since then a good deal of time has passed. A man who loves his wife, and has proved her devotion to him, does not care about those who mistrust and condemn her. Their mistrust and condemnation reflect upon him, and not only on his love, but on his pride. I advise you, when you come to Nigel as a doctor, to come as my friend, otherwise I don't think you'll have an opportunity of doing him much good."

The cleverness of Isaacson, that cleverness which came from the Jewish blood within him, linked hands with the defiant adroitness of this woman even to-night and in the climax of suspicion. Why, with her powers, had she made such a tragic mess of her life? Why, with her powers, had she never been able to run straight along the way that leads to happiness? Useless questions! Their answer must be sought for far down in the secret depths of character. And now?

"If you come to Nigel when I call you in it will be all right, not otherwise, believe me."

She sat back on the divan. The greyness had gone out of her face. She looked now at her ease. Isaacson remembered how this woman had got the better of him in London, how she had looked as she stood in her room at the Savoy, when he saw her for the last time before she married his friend. She had been dressed in rose colour that day. Now she was in black—for Harwich. It seemed that for evening wear she had brought some "thin mourning." Did he mean her to get the better of him again?

"But you will not call me in," he said bluntly.

"Why not? As a doctor I rather believe in you."

"Nevertheless, you will not call me in."

"If Doctor Hartley desires a consultation, I promise you that I will. I hope you won't make your fee too heavy. You must remember we are almost poor people now."

It was very seldom that Isaacson changed colour, but at these words his dark face slowly reddened.

"If you suppose that—that I want to make money——" he began.

"It's always nice, if one takes a holiday, to be able to pay one's expenses. But I know you won't run Nigel in for too much."

Isaacson got up. His instinct was to go, to get away at once from this woman. For a moment he forgot the voice he had heard in the night; he forgot the words it had said. His egoism and his pride spoke, and told him to get away.

She read him. She got up, too, came away from her place near the door, and said, with a smile:

"You are going?"

He looked at her. He saw in her eyes the look he had seen in them when he had bade her good-bye at the Savoy after his useless embassy.

"You are going?"

"Yes," he said. "I am! Going to see your husband!"

And before she could speak or move, he was at the door through which Hamza had passed; he had opened it and disappeared, shutting it softly behind him.

XXXV

WITH such abrupt and adroit decisiveness had Meyer Isaacson acted, so swift and cunning had been his physical carrying out of his sudden resolve—a resolve, perhaps, determined by her frigid malice—that for a moment Mrs. Armine lost all command of her powers—even, so it seemed, all command of her thoughts and desires. When the door shut and she was alone, she stood where she was and at first did not move a finger. She felt dull, unexcited, almost sleepy, and as one who is dropping off to sleep sometimes aimlessly reiterates some thought, apparently unconnected with any other thought, unlinked with any habit of the mind, she found herself, in imagination, with dull eyes, seeing the Arabic characters above the doorway of the *Loulia*, dully and silently repeating the words Baroudi had chosen as the motto of the boat in which this thing—Isaacson's departure to Nigel—had happened:

"The fate of every man have we bound about his neck."

So it was. So it must be. With an odd and almost grotesque physical response to the meaning which at this moment she but vaguely apprehended, she let her body go. She shrank a little, drawing her shoulders forward, like one on whom a burden that is heavy is imposed. About her neck had been bound this fate. But the movement, slight though it was, recalled the woman who had defied and had bled the world—had defied the world of women, and had bled the world of men. And, like a living thing, there sprang up in her mind the thought:

"I'm the only woman on board this boat."

And she squared her shoulders. The numbness passed, or she flung it angrily from her. And she had the door open and was through the doorway in an instant, and crying out in the long corridor that led to the room of the faskeeyeh:

"Nigel! Nigel! What do you think of my surprise?"

There were energy and beauty in the cry, and she came into the room with a sort of soft rush that was intensely feminine. The men were there. Nigel was sitting up, but leaning against cushions on the divan close to the upright piano, on which stood the score of "Gerontius." Isaacson was standing before him, bending, and holding both his hands strongly, in an attitude that looked almost violent. Behind him, in the Eastern house of Baroudi the spray of the little fountain aspired, and the tiny gilded ball rose and fell with an airy and frivolous movement.

Mrs. Armine was not reasoning as she came in to these two. She was acting purely on the prompting of an instinct long proved by life. There was within her no mental debate. She did not know how long she had stood alone. She did not ask herself whether Meyer Isaacson had had time to say anything, or, if he had had time, what it was likely that he had said. She just came in with this soft rush, went to her husband, sat down touching him, put her hand on his shoulder, with the fingers upon his neck, and said:

"What do you think of my surprise? I dared it! Was I wrong? Has it done you any harm, Nigel?"

As she spoke she looked at the face of Isaacson and she knew that he had not spoken. A natural flush came to join the flush of rouge on her cheeks.

"Nigel, you've got to forgive me!" she said.

"Forgive you!"

The weak voice spoke with a stronger note than it had found on the balcony. Isaacson let go his friend's hands. He moved. The almost emotional protectiveness that had seemed mutely to exclaim, "I'll save you! Here's a hand— here are two strong hands—to save you from the abyss!" died out of his attitude. He stood up straight. But he kept his eyes fastened on his friend. Never in his consulting-room had he looked at any patient as he now looked at Nigel Armine, with such fiercely searching eyes. His face said to the leaning man before him: "Give up your secrets. I mean to know them all."

"Forgive you!" Nigel repeated.

Feebly he put out one hand and touched his wife. He was looking almost dazed.

"And to-night, when I—when I said, 'If only Isaacson were here!' did you know then?"

"That he was coming? Yes, I knew. And I nearly had to tell you—so nearly! But, you see, a woman can keep a secret."

"How did you know?"

He looked at Isaacson. But Isaacson let her answer. It was enough for him that he was with his friend. He did not care about anything else. And all this time he was at doctor's work.

"We met this morning in the temple of Edfou, and I told Doctor Isaacson about your sunstroke, and asked him to come up to-night and see you."

She lied with the quiet aplomb which Isaacson remembered almost enjoying in the Savoy Restaurant one night, when they were grouped about a supper-table. Quietly then she had handed him out the lies which he knew to be lies. She had made him presents of them, and as he had received her presents then, he received them now, but a little more indifferently. For he was deeply attentive to Nigel.

That colour, that dropped wrist, the cruel emaciation, the tremulous hands, the pathetic eyes that seemed crying for help—what did they indicate? And there were other symptoms, even stronger, in Nigel that already had almost assailed the doctor, as if clamouring for his notice and striving to tell a story.

"But why are you here, in Egypt?" asked Nigel. "You didn't come out because——?"

"No, no," said Isaacson.

"But then"—a smile that was rather like tears came into the sick man's face—"but then perhaps you came to —to see our happiness! You remember my letter, Ruby?"

"Yes," she said.

His hand still lay on hers.

"Well, since then it's been a bad time for me. But that happiness has never failed me—never."

"And it never shall," she said.

As she spoke she looked up again at Isaacson, and he read a cool menace in her eyes. Those eyes repeated what her voice had told him on the other side of that door. They said: "My enemy can never find a friend in my husband." But now that Isaacson saw these two people together, he realized the truth of their relations as words could never have made him realize them.

There was a little silence, broken only by the tiny whisper of the faskeeyeh. Then Mrs. Armine said gently:

"Now, Nigel, you've had your surprise, and you ought to sleep. Doctor Isaacson's coming back to-morrow to have a consultation with Doctor Hartley at four o'clock."

She spoke as if the whole matter were already arranged.

"Sleep! You know I can't sleep. I never can sleep now."

"Is the insomnia very bad?" asked Isaacson, quietly.

"I never can sleep scarcely. The nights are so awful."

"Yes, Nigel, dearest. But to-night I think you will sleep."

"Why to-night?"

"Because of this happy surprise I arranged for you. But I shall be sorry I arranged it if you get excited. Do you know how late it is? It is past eleven. You must let Doctor Isaacson go to the felucca. Our bargain was that to-night he should not attempt to hear all about you or enter into the case. It would not be fair to Doctor Hartley."

"Damn Doctor Hartley!" murmured the sick man, almost peevishly.

"I know. But we must behave nicely to him. Be good now, and go to bed. I have told Doctor Isaacson a lot, and I know you'll sleep now you can feel he's near you."

"I don't want anything more to do with Hartley. He knows nothing. I won't have him to-morrow."

He spoke crossly.

"Nigel!"

She put her hand upon his.

"Forgive me, dearest! Oh, what a brute I am!"

Tears came into his eyes.

"I martyrize her, I know I do," he said to Isaacson; "but I don't believe it's my fault. I do feel so awfully ill!"

His head drooped. Isaacson felt his pulse. Nigel gazed down at the divan, staring with eyes that had become filmy. Mrs. Armine looked at Isaacson, and he, with a doctor's memory that was combined with the memory of a man who had formerly been conquered, compared this poor pulse that fluttered beneath his sensitive fingers with another pulse which once he had felt beating strongly—a pulse which had made him understand the defiance of a life.

"You had better get to bed," he said to Nigel, letting his

wrist go, and watching it sharply as it dropped to the cushions. "I shall give you something to make you sleep."

Mrs. Armine opened her lips, but this time he sent her a look which caused her to shut them.

"I don't know whether you are in the habit of taking anything—whether you are given anything at night. If so, to-night it is to be discontinued. You are to touch nothing except what I am going to give you. Directly you are in bed I'll come."

"But——" Nigel began, "we haven't——"

"Had any talk. I know. There'll be plenty of time for that. But Mrs. Armine is quite right. It is late, and you must go at once to bed."

Nigel made a movement to get up. Mrs. Armine quickly and efficiently helped him, put her arm around him, supported his arm, led him away into the narrow corridor from which the bedrooms opened. They disappeared through a little doorway on the left.

Then Isaacson sat down and waited, looking at the leaping spray and at the gilded trifle that was its captive. Presently his eyes travelled away from that, and examined the room and everything in it. That man whom he had seen driving the Russian horses, and squatting on the floor of the hashish café, might well be at home here. And he himself—could not he be at home here, with these marvellous prayer-rugs and embroideries, into which was surely woven something of the deep and eternal enigma of the East? But his friend and—that woman?

Actively, now, he hated Mrs. Armine. He was a man who could hate well. But he was not going to allow his hatred to run away with him. Once, in a silent contest between them, he had been worsted by her. In this second contest he now declined to be worsted. One fall was enough for this man who was not accustomed to be overthrown. If his temper and his pride were his enemies, he must hold them in bondage. She had struck at both audaciously that night. But the blow, instead of driving him away, had sent him straight to the sick man. That stroke of hers had miscarried. But Isaacson recognized her power as an opponent.

A consultation to-morrow at four with this young doctor! So that was ordained, was it, by Bella Donna?

His energy of mind soon made him weary of sitting, and he got up and went towards the balcony which so lately he had been watching from the bank of the Nile. As he stepped out upon it he saw a white figure by the rail, and he remembered that Hamza had been with Nigel, and had disappeared at his approach. He had not given Hamza a thought. The sick man had claimed all of him. But now, in this pause, he had time to think of Hamza.

As he came out upon the balcony the Egyptian turned round to look at him.

Hamza was dressed in white, with a white turban. His arms hung at his sides. His thin hands, the fingers opened, made two dark patches against his loose and graceful robe. His dark face, seen in the night, and by the light which came from the room of the faskeeyeh, was like an Eastern dream. In his eyes lay a still fanaticism. Those eyes drew something in Isaacson. He felt oddly at home with them, without understanding what they meant. And he thought of the hashish-smoker, and he thought of the garden of oranges, surrounding the little secret house, to which the hashish-smoker sometimes came. These Easterns dwell apart—yes, despite the coming of the English, the so-called "awakening" of the East—in a strange and romantic world, an enticing world. Had Bella Donna undergone its charm? Unconsciously his eyes were asking this question of this Eastern who had been to Mecca, who prayed—how many times a day!—and was her personal attendant. But the eyes gave him no answer. He came a little nearer to Hamza, stood by the rail, and offered him a cigarette. Hamza accepted it, with a soft salute, and hid it somewhere in his robe. They remained together in silence. Isaacson was wondering if Hamza spoke any English. He looked full of secrets, that were still and calm within him as standing water in a sequestered pool, sheltered by trees in a windless place. Starnworth, perhaps, would have understood him—Starnworth who understood at least some of the secrets of the East. And Isaacson recalled Starnworth's talk in the night, and his parting words as he went away—"A different code from ours!"

And the secret of the dahabeeyah, of the beautiful *Loulia*—was it locked in that breast of the East?

In the silence Isaacson's mind sought converse with Hamza's, strove to come into contact with Hamza's mind. But it seemed to him that his mind was softly repelled. Hamza would not recognize the East that was in Isaacson, or perhaps he felt the Jew. When the voice of Mrs. Armine was heard from the threshold of the lighted chamber these two had not spoken a word. But Isaacson had learnt that in any investigation of the past, in any effort to make straight certain crooked paths, in any search after human motives, he would get no help from this mind that was full of refusal, from this soul that was full of prayer.

"Doctor Isaacson!"

A dress rustled.

"You are out here—with Hamza?"

She stood in one of the doorways.

"Will you please come and give my husband the sleeping draught?"

"Certainly."

When they were in the room by the fountain she said:

"Of course, you know, this is all wrong. We're not doing the right thing by Doctor Hartley at all. But I don't like to thwart Nigel. Convalescents are always wilful."

"Convalescents!" he said.

"Yes, convalescents."

"You think your husband is convalescent?"

"Of course he is. You didn't see him in the first days after his sunstroke."

"That's true."

"Please give him the draught, or whatever it is, and then we really must try and get some rest."

As she said the last words he noticed in her voice the

sound of a woman who had nearly come to the end of her powers of resistance.

"It won't take a moment," he said. "Where is he?"

"I'll show you."

She went in front of him to a cabin, in which, on a smart bed, Nigel lay supported by pillows. One candle was burning on a bracket of white wood, giving a faint light. Mrs. Armine stood by the head of the bed looking down upon the thin, almost lead-coloured face that was turned towards her.

"Now Doctor Isaacson is going to make you sleep."

"Thank God. The rheumatism's awfully bad to-night."

"Rheumatism?" said Isaacson.

Already he had poured some water into a glass, and dropped something into it. He held the glass towards Nigel, not coming quite near to him. To take the glass, it was necessary for the sick man to stretch out his arm. Nigel made a movement to do this; but his arm dropped, and he said, almost crossly:

"Do put it nearer."

Then Isaacson put it to his mouth.

"Rheumatism?" he repeated, when Nigel had swallowed the draught.

"Yes. I have it awfully badly, like creatures gnawing me almost."

He sighed, and lay lower in the bed.

"I can't understand it. Rheumatism in this perfect climate!" he murmured.

Mrs. Armine made an ostentatious movement as if to go away and leave them together.

"No, don't go, Ruby," Nigel said.

He felt for her hand.

"I want you—you two to be friends," he said. "Real friends. Isaacson, you don't know what she's been in— in all this bad time. You don't know."

His feeble voice broke.

"I'll be here to-morrow," said Isaacson, after a pause.

"Yes, come. You must put me—right."

Mrs. Armine could not accompany Isaacson to the felucca or say a word to him alone, for Nigel kept, almost clung to, her hand.

"I must stay with him till he sleeps," she almost whispered as Isaacson was going.

She was bending slightly over the bed. Some people might have thought that she looked like the sick man's guardian angel, but Isaacson felt an intense reluctance to leave the dahabeeyah that night.

He looked at Mrs. Armine for a moment, saw that she fully received his look, and went away, leaving her still in that beautifully protective attitude.

He came out on deck. The felucca was waiting. He got into it, and was rowed out into the river by two sailors. As they rowed they began to sing. The lights of the *Loulia* slipped by, yellow light after yellow light. From above the blue light looked down like a watchful eye. The darkness of the water, like streaming ebony, took the felucca and the fateful voices. And the tide gave its help to the oarsmen. The lights began to dwindle when Isaacson said to the men:

"Hush!"

He held up his hand. The Nubians lay on their oars, surprised. The singing died in their throats.

Across the water there came a faint but shrill sound of laughter. Some one was laughing, laughing, laughing, in the night.

The Nubians stared at each other, the man who was stroke turning his head towards his companion.

Faint cries followed the laughter, and then—was it not the sound of a woman, somewhere sobbing dreadfully?

Isaacson listened till it died away.

Then, with a stern, tense face, he nodded to the Nubians.

They bent again to the oars, and the felucca dropped down the Nile.

XXXVI

WHEN she had sent her note to the *Fatma*, Mrs. Armine had secretly telegraphed to Doctor Hartley, begging him to come to the *Loulia* as quickly as possible. She had implied to Isaacson that he would arrive about four the next day. Perhaps she had forgotten, or had not known how the trains ran from Assouan.

However that was, Doctor Hartley arrived many hours before the time mentioned by Mrs. Armine for a consultation, and was in full possession of the case and in command of the patient while Isaacson was still on the *Fatma*.

Isaacson had not slept all night. That dream of the Nile into which he had softly sunk was gone, was as if it never had been. His instinct was to start for the *Loulia* at daybreak. But for once he denied this instinct. Cool reason spoke in the dawn saying, "Festina lente." He listened. He held himself in check. After his sleepless night, in which thought had been feverish, he would spend some quiet, lonely hours. There was, he believed, no special reason, after the glance he had sent to Mrs. Armine just before he went out of Nigel's cabin, why he should hurry in the first hour of the new day to the sick man he meant to cure. Let the sleeping draught do its work, and let the clear morning hours correct any fever in his own mind.

And so he rested on deck, while the sun climbed the pellucid sky, and he watched the men at the shadûf. The sunlight struck the falling water and made it an instant's marvel. And the marvel recurred, for the toil never ceased. The naked bodies bent and straightened. The muscles stood out, then seemed to flow away, like the flowing water, cn the arms under the bronze-coloured skin. And from lungs surely made of brass came forth the fierce songs that have been thrown back from the Nile's brown banks perhaps since the Sphinx first set his unworldly eyes towards eternity.

But though Isaacson deliberately paused to get himself very thoroughly and calmly in hand, paused to fight with possible prejudice and drive it out of him, he did not delay till the hour fixed by Mrs. Armine. Soon after one o'clock in the full heat of the day, he set out in the tiny tub which was the only felucca on board of the *Fatma*, and he took Hassan with him. Definitely why he took Hassan, he perhaps could not have stated. He just thought he would take him, and did.

Very swiftly he had returned with the tide in the night. Now, in the eye of day, he must go up river against it. The men toiled hard, lifting themselves from their seats with each stroke of the oars and bracing their legs for the strain. But the boat's progress was slow, and Isaacson sometimes felt as if some human strength were striving persistently to repel him. He had the sensation of a determined resistance which must be battled with ruthlessly. And now and then his own body was tense as he watched his men at their work. But at last they drew near to the *Loulia*, and his keen, far-seeing eyes searched the balcony for figures. He saw none. The balcony was untenanted. Now it seemed to him as if in the fierce heat, upon the unshaded water, the great boat was asleep, as if there was no life in her anywhere; and this sensation of the absence of life increased upon him as they came nearer and nearer. All round the upper deck, except perhaps on the land side of the boat, which he could not see, canvas was let down. Shutters were drawn over the windows of the cabins. The doors of the room of the fountain were open, but the room was full of shadow, which, from his little boat, the eyes of Isaacson could not penetrate. As they came alongside no voice greeted them. He began to regret having come in the hour of the siesta. They glided along past green shutter after green shutter till they were level with the forward deck. And there, in an attitude of smiling attention, stood the tall figure of Ibrahim.

Isaacson felt almost startled to find his approach known, to receive a graceful greeting.

He stepped on board followed closely by Hassan. The deck was strewn with scantily clad men, profoundly sleeping. Isaacson addressed himself in a low voice to Ibrahim.

"You understand English?"

"Yes, my gentleman. You come to meet the good doctor who him curin' my Lord Arminigel. He bin here very long time."

"He's here already?"

Ibrahim smiled reassuringly.

"Very long time, my gentleman. Him comin' here to live with us till my lord him well."

And Ibrahim turned, gathered together his gold-coloured skirts, and mounted the stairs to the upper deck. Isaacson hesitated for a moment, then followed him slowly. In that brief moment of hesitation the words had gone through Isaacson's mind: "I ought to have been here sooner."

As he mounted and his eyes rose over the level of the top step of the companion, he was aware of a slight young man, very smartly dressed in white ducks, a loose silk shirt, a low, soft collar and pale, rose-coloured tie, a perfectly cut grey jacket with a small blue line in it, rose-coloured socks, and white buckskin boots, who was lying almost at full length in a wide deck-chair against cushions, with a panama hat tilted so far down over his eyes that its brim rested delicately upon his well-cut, rather impertinent short nose. From his lips curled gently pale smoke from a cigarette.

As Isaacson stepped upon the Oriental rugs which covered the deck, this young man gently pushed up his hat, looked, let his legs quietly down, and getting on his feet, said:

"Doctor Isaacson?"

"Yes," said Isaacson coming up to him.

The young man held out his hand with a nonchalant gesture.

"Glad to meet you. I'm Doctor Baring Hartley, in charge of this sunstroke case aboard here. Came down to-day from Assouan to see how my patient was getting on. Will you have a cigarette?"

"Thanks."

Doctor Isaacson accepted one.

"Fine air at Assouan! This your first visit to the Nile?"

The young man spoke with scarcely a trace of American accent. With his hat set back, he was revealed as brown-faced, slightly freckled, with very thick, dark hair, that was parted in the middle and waved naturally, though it looked as if it had been crimped; a small moustache, rather bristling, because it had been allowed only recently to grow on a lip that had often been shaved; a round, rather sensual chin; and large round eyes, in colour a yellow-brown. In these eyes the character of the man was very clearly displayed. They were handsome, and not insensitive; but they showed egoism, combined with sensuality. He looked very young, but was just over thirty.

"Yes, it's my first visit."

"Won't you sit down?"

He spoke with the ease of a host, and sank into his deck chair, laying his hat down upon his knees and stretching out his legs, from which he pulled up the white ducks a little way. Isaacson sat down on a smaller chair, leaned forward, and said, in a very practical, businesslike voice:

"No doubt Mr. or Mrs. Armine—or both of them, perhaps, has explained how I have come into this affair? I'm an old friend of your patient."

"So I gathered," said Doctor Hartley, in a voice that was remarkably dry.

"I knew him long before he was married, very long before he was ever a sick man, and being out here, and hearing about this sudden and severe illness, of course I called to see how he was."

"Very natural."

"Probably you know my name as a London consulting physician."

"Decidedly. Your success, of course, is great, Doctor

Isaacson. Indeed, I wonder you are able to take a holiday. I wonder the ladies will let you go."

He smiled, and touched his moustache affectionately.

"Why the ladies, especially?"

"I understood your practice lay chiefly among the neurotic smart women of London."

"No."

Isaacson's voice echoed the dryness of Doctor Hartley's.

"I'm sorry."

"May I ask why?"

"On the other side of the water we find them—shall I say the best type of patients?"

"Ah!"

Isaacson remembered the sentence of Mrs. Armine which had sent him straight to the sick man. He seemed to detect her cruel prompting in the half-evasive yet sufficiently clear words just spoken.

"Now about Mr. Armine," he said, brushing the topic of himself away. "I am sure——"

But Doctor Hartley interrupted with quiet firmness. One quality he seemed to have in the fullest abundance. He seemed to be largely self-possessed.

"It always clears the ground to be frank, I find," he said, smoothing out some creases in his ducks. "I don't require a consultation, Doctor Isaacson. I don't consider it a case that needs a consultation at present. Directly I do, I shall be glad to call you in."

Isaacson looked down at the rug beneath his chair.

"You consider Mr. Armine going on satisfactorily?" he asked, looking up.

"It's a severe case of sunstroke. It will take time and care. I have decided to stay aboard for a few days to devote myself entirely to it."

"Very good of you."

"I have no doubt whatever of very soon pulling my patient round."

"You don't see any complications in the case?"

"Complications?"

The tone was distinctly, almost alertly, hostile. But Isaacson reiterated coolly:

"Yes, complications. You are quite satisfied this is a case of sunstroke?"

"Quite."

The word came with a hard stroke, that was like the stroke of finality.

"Well, I'm not."

Doctor Hartley stared.

"I know you have come over with a view to a consultation," he said, stiffly. "But my patient has not demanded it, and as I think it entirely unnecessary, you will recognize that we need not pursue this conversation."

"You say the patient does not wish for my opinion on the case?" said Isaacson, allowing traces of surprise to escape him.

"I do. He is quite satisfied to leave it in my hands. He told me so this morning when I arrived."

"I am not reflecting for a moment on your capacity, Doctor Hartley. But, really, in complex cases, two opinions——"

"Who says the case is complex?"

"I do. I was extremely shocked at the appearance of Mr. Armine when I saw him last night. If you had ever known him in health, you would have been as shocked as I was. He was one of the most robust, the most brilliantly healthy, strong-looking men I have even seen."

As he spoke, Armine seemed to stand before Isaacson as he had been.

"The change in him, mind and body, is appalling," he concluded.

And there was in his voice an almost fearful sincerity.

Doctor Hartley fidgeted. He moved his hat, pulled down his ducks, dropped his cigarette on the rug, then rather hastily and awkwardly put it out with his foot. Sitting with his feet no longer cocked up but planted firmly on the rug, he said:

"Of course, an attack like this changes a man. What

else could you expect? Really! What else could you expect? I noticed all that! That's why I am going to stay. Upon my word"—as he spoke he seemed to work himself into vexation—"upon my word, Doctor Isaacson, to hear you, anyone would suppose I had been making light of my patient's condition."

Isaacson was confronted with fluffy indignation.

"You'll be accusing me of professional incompetence next, I dare say," continued Doctor Hartley. "I have not told you before, but I'll tell you now, that I consider it a breach of the etiquette that governs our profession, your interfering with my patient."

"How interfering?"

"I hear you gave him something last night—something to make him sleep."

"I did."

"Well, it's had a very bad effect upon him."

"Is he worse to-day?"

Isaacson, unknown to himself, said it with an almost fierce emphasis. Doctor Hartley drew his lips tightly together.

"This is not a consultation," he said coldly.

"I ask as a friend of the patient's, not as a doctor."

"His night was not good."

He shut his lips tightly again. His face and his whole smartly-dressed body expressed a rather weak but very lively hostility.

"He's asleep now," he added.

"Asleep now?"

"Yes. He'll sleep for several hours. *I* have put him to sleep."

Isaacson's body suddenly felt relaxed, as if all the muscles of it were loosened. For several hours his friend would sleep. For a moment he enjoyed a sense of fascinating relief. Then his consciousness of relief awoke him to another and fuller consciousness of why this relief had come to him, of that which had preceded it, and given it its intensity.

BELLA DONNA

He must take off the gloves.

"Look here, Doctor Hartley," he said. "I don't want to put you out. I am really not a vulgar, greedy doctor pushing myself into a case with which I have no concern, for some self-interested motive. I can assure you that I have more than enough to do with illness in London and should be thankful to escape from it here. I want a holiday."

"Take one, my dear Doctor Isaacson," remarked Doctor Hartley, imperturbably—"take one, and leave me to work."

"No. Professional etiquette or no professional etiquette, I can't take one while my friend is in such a condition of illness. I can't do that."

"I'm really afraid you'll have to, so far as this case is concerned. I'm an American, and I'm not going to be pushed away from a thing I've set my hand to—pushed away discourteously, and against the desires of those who have called me in. Never in the course of my professional experience has another physician butted in—yes, that's the expression for it: butted right in—without 'With,' or 'By your leave,' as you have. It's simply not to be borne. And I'm not the man to bear what's not to be borne. Really, if one didn't know you to be a doctor, one would almost take you for a Bowery detective. Straight, now, one would!"

"Where's Mrs. Armine?" said Isaacson abruptly. "Is she asleep too?"

"She is."

The languid impertinence of the voice goaded Isaacson. Scarcely ever, if ever, before had he felt such an almost physical longing for violence. But he did not lose his self-restraint, although he suffered bitterly in keeping it.

"Have you any idea how long she is going to sleep?"

"Some hours."

"What? Do you mean that you have put her to sleep, too?"

"I have ventured to do so. Her night had not been good."

Isaacson remembered the sounds that had come to him over the Nile.

"You have given her a sleeping draught?" he said.

"I have."

"But she was expecting me here. She was expecting me here for a consultation."

"I beg your pardon. You were good enough to say you meant to come. Mrs. Armine has been scrupulously delicate and courteous to me. That I know. You placed her in a very difficult position. She explained matters when I arrived."

She had "explained matters"! Isaacson felt rather as if he were fighting an enemy who had laid a mine to check or to destroy him, and had then retreated to a distance.

"Last night, Doctor Hartley," he said, very quietly and coldly, "Mr. Armine, in Mrs. Armine's presence, expressed a strong wish to put himself in my hands. I came here with not the least intention of being impolite, but since you have chosen to make things difficult for me I must speak out. Last night Mr. Armine said, 'I don't want anything more to do with Hartley. He knows nothing. I won't have him to-morrow.' Mrs. Armine was with us and heard these words."

A violent flush showed through the brown on the young man's face. His round eyes stared with an expression of crude amazement that was almost laughable.

"He—he said——" he began. Then abruptly, allowing an American drawl to appear in his voice, he said, "Pardon! But I don't believe it."

"It's quite true, nevertheless."

"I don't believe it. That's a fact. I've seen Mr. Armine, and he was most delighted to welcome me. He put himself entirely in my hands. He asked me to 'save' him."

Suddenly Isaacson felt a sickness at his heart.

"I must see him," he almost muttered.

"I won't have him disturbed," said Doctor Hartley, with now the transparently open enmity of a very conceited man who had been insulted. "As his physician I forbid you to disturb my patient."

BELLA DONNA

The two men looked at one another in silence.

"After what occurred last night, and what has occurred here to-day, I cannot go without seeing either Mr. or Mrs. Armine," Isaacson said at last.

Was Nigel's weakness of mind, the sad product of his illness of body, to fight against his friend, to battle against his one chance of recovery? That would complicate matters. That—Isaacson clearly recognized it—would place him at so grave a disadvantage that it might render his position impossible. What had been the scene last night after he had left the *Loulia?* How had it affected the sick man? Again he seemed to hear that dreadful laughter, the cries that had followed upon it!

"If I am not to see Mr. Armine as a doctor, then I must ask to see him as a friend."

"For a day or two I shall not be able to give permission for any one to see him, except Mrs. Armine and myself, and of course his servant, Hamza."

Isaacson sent a sudden, piercing look, a look that was like something sharp that could cut deep into the soul, to the man who faced him. Just for a moment a suspicion besieged him, a suspicion hateful and surely absurd, yet—for are not all things possible in the cruel tangle of life?—that might be grounded on truth. Before that glance the young doctor moved, with a start of uneasiness, despite his self-possession.

"What—what d'you mean?" he almost stammered. "What d'you mean?" He felt mechanically at his tie. "I don't understand you," he said. Then, recovering himself, as the strangely fierce expression died away from the eyes which had learnt what they wanted to know, he added:

"I certainly shall not give permission for you to see Mr. Armine. You would disturb and upset him very much. He needs the greatest quiet and repose. The brain is a fearfully sensitive organ."

Now, suddenly, Isaacson felt as if he was with an obstinate boy, and any anger he had felt against his companion evaporated. Indeed, he was conscious of a strong sensation of pity, mingled with irony. For a moment he had wronged the young doctor by a doubt, and for that moment he had a wish to make some amends. The man's unconsciousness of it did not concern him. It was to himself really that the amends were due.

"Doctor Hartley," he said almost cordially, "I think we don't quite understand one another. Perhaps that is my fault. I oughtn't to have repeated Mr. Armine's words. They were spoken and meant. But a sick man speaks out of his sickness. We doctors realize that and don't take too much account of what he says. You are here, I am sure, with no desire but to cure my poor friend. I am here with the same desire. Why should we quarrel?"

"I have no wish whatever to quarrel. But I will not submit to a man butting in from outside and trying to oust me from a case of which I have been formally given the control."

"I don't wish to oust you. I only wish to be allowed to co-operate with you. I only wish to hear your exact opinion of the case and to be allowed to form and give you mine. Come, Doctor Hartley, it isn't as if I were a pushing, unknown man. In London I'm offered far more work than I can touch. It will do your medical reputation no harm to call me in, in consultation. Without undue conceit, I hope I can say that. And if—if you have got hold of the idea that I'm on the Nile to make money, disabuse your mind of it. This is a case in which a little bit of my own personal happiness is wrapped up. I've—I've a strong regard for this sick man. That's the truth of it."

Doctor Hartley looked at him, looked away, and looked at him again.

"I don't doubt your friendship for Mr. Armine," he said, at last, laying a faint stress upon the penultimate word.

"Will you let me discuss the case amicably with you? No formal consultation! Just let me hear your views fully, and mention anything that occurs to me."

"Occurs? But you haven't examined the patient. You

haven't made any thorough examination, or entered into the circumstances of the case."

"No. But I've seen the patient."

"Only for a very few minutes, I understand. How can you have formed a definite opinion?"

"I did not say I had. But one or two things struck me."

Doctor Hartley stared with his handsome, round eyes.

"For instance, the patient's sallow colour, the patient's rheumatic pains, the patient's breath, and—did you happen to observe it? But no doubt you did!—the patient's dropped wrist."

The young doctor's face had become more serious. He looked much less conscious of himself at this moment.

"Dropped wrist!" he said.

"Yes."

'Of course! Muscular weakness brought on quite naturally by prolonged illness. The man has simply been knocked down by this touch of the sun. Travellers ought to be more careful than they are out here."

"I suppose you're aware that the patient has already lived and worked in Egypt for many months at a time. He has land in the Fayyūm, and has been cultivating it himself. He's no novice in Egypt, no untried tourist. He's soaked in the sun without hurt by the month together."

"As much as that?" said Hartley.

"Isn't it rather odd that so early in the year as February he should be stricken down by the spring sunshine?"

"It is queer—yes, it is queer," assented the other.

He crossed one leg over the other and looked abstracted.

"I suppose Mr. Armine himself thought the illness was brought about by the sun?" said Isaacson, after a minute.

"Well—oh, from the first it was an understood thing that he'd got a touch of the sun. There's no doubt whatever about that. He went out at noon, and actually dug at Thebes without covering his head. Sheer madness! People saw him doing it."

"And it all came on after that?"

"Yes, the serious symptoms. Of course he wasn't in very good health to start with."

"No?"

"He'd been having dyspepsia. Caught a chill one evening bathing in the Nile—somewhere off Kous, I believe it was. That rendered him more susceptible than usual."

"Naturally. So that he was already unwell before he did that foolish thing at Thebes?"

"He was seedy, but not really ill."

"What a long talk you're having!" said a voice.

Both men started, and into Doctor Baring Hartley's face there came a look of painful self-consciousness, as of one unexpectedly detected in an unpardonable action. He sprang up.

Mrs. Armine was standing near the top of the companion.

XXXVII

SHE came towards them.

"You've made friends without any introduction?"

She had on a hat and veil, and carried a fan in her hand.

"How can you be awake and up? But it's impossible, after the veronal I gave you. And such a night as you had! You mustn't——"

Doctor Hartley, still looking dreadfully guilty, was beside her. His solicitude was feverish.

"Really, I can't permit——" he almost stammered.

She looked at him.

"Your voices woke me!"

He was silent. He stood like a man who had been struck.

"How d'you do, Doctor Isaacson? Please forgive me for saying it, but, considering you are two doctors discussing the case of a patient sleeping immediately beneath you, you are not too careful to moderate your voices. Another minute and my husband would have been awake. He was moving and murmuring as it was. As for me—well, you just simply woke me right up, so I thought I would come and join you, and see whether I could keep you quiet."

Her face looked ghastly beneath the veil. Her voice, though she kept it very low, sounded bitter and harsh with irony, and there was something almost venomous in her manner.

"The question is," she added, standing midway between Hartley and Isaacson, "whether my unfortunate husband is to have a little rest or not. When we tied up here we really thought we should be at peace, but it seems we were mistaken. At any rate, I hope the consultation is nearly done, for my head is simply splitting."

Doctor Hartley was scarlet. He shot a vicious glance at Isaacson.

"There has been no consultation, Mrs. Armine," he said.

His eyes implored her forgiveness. His whole body looked pathetic, begging, almost like a chastised dog's.

"No consultation? Then what's the good of all this talky-talky? Have you waked me up by discussing the weather and the temples? That's really too bad of you!"

Her face worked for a second or two. It was easy to see that she was scarcely mistress of herself.

"I think I shall pack you both off to see Edfou," she continued, violently beginning to use her fan. "You can chatter away there and make friends to your hearts' content, and there'll be only the guardian to hear you. Then poor Nigel can have his sleep out whatever happens to me."

Suddenly she gaped, and put up her fan to her mouth.

"Ah!" she said.

The exclamation was like something between a sigh and a sob. Immediately after she had uttered it she cleared her throat.

"I told Doctor Isaacson his coming here to-day was absolutely useless," began Doctor Hartley. "I told him no consultation was required. I begged him to leave the case in my hands. Over and over again I——"

"Oh, you don't know Doctor Isaacson if you think that a courteous request will have any effect upon him. If he wants to be in a thing, he will be in it, and nothing in heaven or earth will stop him. You forget his nationality."

She yawned again, and moved her shoulders.

"You are wronging me grossly, and you know it!" Isaacson said, in a very low voice.

He had laid his hat down on a little straw table. Now he took it up. What was the good of staying? How could a decent man stay? And yet the struggle within him was bitter. If he could only have been certain of this man Hartley, perhaps there would have been no struggle. He might have gone with an almost quiet heart. Or if he had been certain of something else, absolutely certain, he might have remained and acted, completely careless in his defiance of the woman who hated him. But though his instinct was alive, telling him things, whispering, whispering all the time; even though his observation had on the previous night begun to back up his instinct, saying, "Yes, you must be right! You are right!" yet he actually knew nothing. He knew nothing except that this young man, between whose hands lay Nigel's life, was under the spell of Mrs. Armine.

He took up his hat and held it tightly, crushing the soft brim between his fingers. Doctor Hartley was looking at him with the undisguised enmity of the egoist tricked. He had had time to find out that Isaacson had begun subtly to induce him to do what he had refused to do. If Mrs. Armine had not appeared unexpectedly, Nigel Armine's case would have been, perhaps, pretty thoroughly discussed by the two doctors.

"Pushing trickster!"

His round eyes said that with all the vindictiveness of injured conceit.

"You are wronging me!" repeated Isaacson—"wronging me shamefully!"

Was he going? Yes, he supposed so. Yet he did not go.

"It's not a question of wronging any one," she said. "Facts are facts."

Her face was ravaged with physical misery. There was a battle going on between the sleeping draught she had taken and her will to be sleepless. She moved her shoulders again, with a sort of shudder, sideways.

"Nigel doesn't want you," she said.

"How can you say that? It's not true."

"It is true. Isn't it, Doctor Hartley? Didn't my husband——"

She yawned again, and put down her hand on the back of a chair to which she held tightly. "Didn't he ask you to remain on board and look after the case?"

"Certainly!" cried the young man, eagerly drinking in her returning favour. "Certainly!"

"Didn't he ask you to 'save him,' as he called it, poor, dear fellow?"

"That was the very word!"

"And last night?" said Isaacson, fixing his eyes upon her.

"Last night you startled him to death, rushing in upon him without warning or preparation. Wasn't it a cruel, dangerous thing to do in his condition, Doctor Hartley?"

"Most cruel! Unpardonably so! If anything had occurred you ought to have been held responsible, Doctor Isaacson."

"And then whatever it was you gave him, you forced it on him. And he had a perfectly terrible night in consequence."

"Not in consequence of what I gave him!" Isaacson said.

"It must have been."

"It was certainly not."

"He never had such a night before—never, till you interfered with him, and interrupted Doctor Hartley's treatment."

"Disgraceful!" exclaimed the young doctor. "I never

have heard of such conduct. If it were ever to be made public, your medical reputation would be ruined."

"And I shouldn't mind if it was, over that!" said Isaacson.

His fingers no longer crushed the brim of his hat, but held it gently.

"I shouldn't mind if it was. But I think if very great care is not taken with this case, it will not be my medical reputation that will be ruined over it."

As if mechanically Mrs. Armine pulled at the chair which she was holding. She drew it nearer her, and twisted it a little round.

"What do you mean?" said Doctor Hartley.

"Mr. Armine is a well-known man. Almost all the English travellers on the Nile, and most people of any importance in Cairo, know of his illness—have heard about his supposed sunstroke."

"Supposed!" interrupted the young doctor, indignantly. "Supposed!"

"All these people will know the name of the medical man in charge of the case—the medical man who declined a consultation."

"Will know?" said Hartley.

Under the attack of Isaacson's new manner his self-possession seemed slightly less assured.

"I shall be in Assouan and Cairo presently," said Isaacson.

Mrs. Armine yawned and pulled at the chair. Her face twitched under her veil. She looked almost terribly alive, as if indeed her mind were in a state of ferment. Yet there was in her aspect also a sort of half-submerged sluggishness. Despite her vindictive agitation, her purposeful venom, she seemed already partially bound by a cloud of sleep. That she had cast away her power to charm as useless was the greatest tribute that Isaacson had ever had paid to his seeing eyes.

"Really! What has that to do with me? Do you suppose I am attending this case surreptitiously?" said Hartley.

He forced a laugh.

"No; but I think it very possible that you may regret ever having had anything to do with it."

In spite of himself, the young doctor was impressed by this new manner of the older man. For a moment he was partially emancipated from Mrs. Armine. For a moment he was rather the rising, not yet risen, medical man than the fully risen young man in love with a fascinating woman. When he chose, Isaacson could hold almost anybody. That was part of the secret of his success as a doctor. He could make himself "believed in."

"Some mistakes ring through the world," Isaacson added quietly. "I should not care to be the doctor who made one of them."

Mrs. Armine, with a sharp movement, twisted the chair quite round, pulled at one side of her dress, and sat down.

"But surely——" Doctor Hartley began.

"This really is the most endless consultation over a case that ever was!" said Mrs. Armine.

She leaned her arms on the arms of the chair and let her hands hang down.

"Do, Doctor Hartley, make my husband over to Doctor Isaacson, if you have lost confidence in yourself. It will be much better. And then, perhaps, we shall have a little peace."

Doctor Hartley turned towards her as if pulled by a cord.

"Oh, but indeed I have not lost confidence. There is, as I have repeatedly said, nothing complicated——"

"You are really sure?" said Isaacson.

He fixed his dark eyes on the young man. Doctor Hartley's uneasiness was becoming evident.

"Certainly I am sure—for the present." The last words seemed to present themselves to him as a sort of life-buoy. He grasped them, clung to them. "For the present—yes. No doctor, of course, not the cleverest, can possibly say that no complications ever will arise in regard to a case. But for the present I am satisfied all is going quite as it should go."

But he turned up the tail of his last sentence. By his intonation it became a question, and showed clearly the state of his mind.

Isaacson had one great quality, the lack of which in many men leads them to distresses, sometimes to disasters. He knew when ice would bear, and directly it would bear, he was content to trust himself on it, but he did not stamp upon it unnecessarily, to prove it beyond its strength.

Suddenly he was ready to go, to leave this boat for a time. He had done as much as he could do for the moment, without making an actual scene. He had even perhaps done enough. That turned-up tail of a sentence nearly convinced him that he had done enough.

"That's well," he said.

His voice was inexpressive, but his face, turned full to the young doctor, told a powerful story of terribly serious doubt, the doubt of a big medical man directed towards a little one.

"That's well," he quietly repeated.

"Good-bye, Mrs. Armine," he said.

She was sunk in her chair. Her arms were still lying along its arms, with her hands hanging. As Isaacson spoke, from one of these hands her fan dropped down to the rug. She did not feel after it.

"Are you really going?" she said.

A faint smile twisted her mouth.

"Yes."

"Good-bye, then!"

He turned away from her slowly.

"Well, good-bye, Doctor Hartley," he said.

All this conversation, since the arrival on deck of Mrs. Armine, had been carried on with lowered voices. But now Isaacson spoke more softly, and his eyes for an instant went from Doctor Hartley to the tall figure sitting low in the chair, and back again to Hartley.

He did not hold out his hand. His voice was polite, but almost totally inexpressive.

Doctor Hartley looked quickly towards the chair too.

"Good-bye," he said, hesitatingly.

His youth was very apparent at this moment, pushing up into view through his indecision. Every scrap of Isaacson's anger against him had now entirely vanished.

"Good-bye!"

Mrs. Armine moved her head slightly, settling it against a large cushion. She sighed.

Isaacson walked slowly towards the companion. As the *Loulia* was a very large dahabeeyah, the upper deck was long. It was furnished like a drawing-room, with chairs, tables, and sofas. Isaacson threaded his way among these cautiously as if mindful of the sick man below. At length he reached the companion and began to descend. Just as he got to the bottom a whispering voice behind him said:

"Doctor Isaacson!"

He turned. Doctor Hartley was at the top of the steps.

"One minute! I'll come down!" he said, still whispering.

He turned back and glanced over his shoulder. Then, putting his two hands upon the two rails on either side of the steps, he was swiftly and rather boyishly down, and standing by Isaacson.

"I—we—I think we may as well have a word together before you go."

His self-possession was distinctly affected. Anxiety showed itself nakedly in his yellow-brown eyes, and there were wrinkles in his low forehead just below the crimpy hair.

"She's fallen asleep," he added, looking hard at Isaacson.

"Just as you like," Isaacson said indifferently.

"I think, after what has passed, it will be better."

Isaacson glanced round on the stretched-out Nubians, on Ibrahim and Hassan in a corner, standing respectfully but looking intensely inquisitive.

"We'd—we can go in here," said Doctor Hartley.

He led the way softly down the steps under the Arabic

inscription, and into the first saloon of the *Loulia*. As Isaacson came into it, instinctively he looked towards the shut door behind which—somewhere—Nigel was lying, asleep or not asleep.

"He'll sleep for some hours yet," said Doctor Hartley, seeing the glance. "Let's sit down here."

He sat down quickly on the nearest divan, and pulled his fingers restlessly.

"I didn't quite understand—that is—I don't know whether I quite gathered your meaning just now," he began, looking at Isaacson, then looking down between his feet.

"My meaning?"

"Yes, about this case."

"I thought you considered a consultation unnecessary."

"A formal consultation—yes. Still, you mustn't think I don't value a good medical opinion. And of course I know yours is a good one."

Isaacson said nothing. Not a muscle of his face stirred.

"The fact is—the fact is that, somehow, you have thoroughly put Mrs. Armine's back up. She thinks you altogether undervalue her devoted service."

"I shouldn't wish to do that."

"No, I knew! Still——"

He took out a handkerchief and touched his lips and his forehead with it.

"She has been really so wonderful!" he said—"waiting on him hand and foot, and giving herself no rest night or day."

"Well, but her maid? Wasn't she able to be of service?"

"Her maid? What maid?"

"Her French maid."

A smile of pity moved the corners of the young man's mouth.

"She hasn't got one. She sent her away long ago. Merely to please him. Oh, I assure you it isn't all milk and honey with Mr. Armine."

Isaacson motioned towards the inner part of the vessel.

"And she's not come back? The maid's never come back?"

"Of course not. You do so misunderstand her—Mrs. Armine."

Isaacson said nothing. He felt that a stroke of insincerity was wanted here, but something that seemed outside of his will forbade him to give it.

"That is what has caused all this," continued Hartley. "I shouldn't really have objected to a consultation so much, if it had come about naturally. But no medical man—you spoke very seriously of the case just now."

"I think very seriously of it."

"So do I, of course."

Doctor Hartley pursed his lips.

"Of course. I saw from the first it was no trifle."

Isaacson said nothing.

"I say, I saw that from the first."

"I'm not surprised."

There was a pause in which the elder doctor felt as if he saw the younger's uneasiness growing.

"You'll forgive me for saying it, Doctor Isaacson, but—but you don't understand women," said Hartley, at last. "You don't know how to take them."

"Perhaps not," Isaacson said, with an apparent simplicity that sounded like humility.

Doctor Hartley looked more at his ease. Some of his cool self-importance returned.

"No," he said. "Really! And I must say that—you'll forgive me?"

"Certainly."

"—that it has always seemed to me as if, in our walk of life, that was half the battle."

"Knowing how to take women?"

"Exactly."

"Perhaps you're right." He looked at the young man as if with admiration. "Yes, I dare say you are right."

Doctor Hartley brightened.

"I'm glad you think so. Now, a woman like Mrs. Armine——"

The mention of the name recalled him to anxiety. "One moment!" he almost whispered. He went lightly away and in a moment as lightly returned.

"It's all right! She'll sleep for some hours, probably. Now, a woman like Mrs. Armine, a beautiful, celebrated woman, wants a certain amount of humouring. And you don't humour her. See?"

"I expect you know."

Isaacson did not tell of that sheet of glass through which Mrs. Armine and he saw each other too plainly.

"She's a woman with any amount of heart, any amount. I've proved that." He paused, looked sentimental, and continued, "Proved it up to the hilt. But she's a little bit capricious. She wants to be taken the right way. I can do anything with her."

He touched his rose-coloured tie, and pulled up one of his rose-coloured socks.

"And the husband?" Isaacson asked, with a detached manner. "D'you find him difficult?"

"Between ourselves, very!"

"That's bad."

"He tries her very much, I'm afraid, though he pretends, of course, to be devoted to her. And she's simply an angel to him."

"Hard on her!"

"I sympathize with her very much. Of course, she's told me nothing. She's too loyal. But I can read between the lines. Tell me, though. Do you think him very bad?"

"Very."

Isaacson spoke without emotion, as if out of a solely medical mind.

"You don't—ah—you don't surely think him in any danger?"

Isaacson slightly shrugged his shoulders.

"But—h'm—but about the sunstroke! If it isn't sunstroke——?"

Hartley waited for an interruption. None came.

"If it isn't sunstroke entirely, the question is, what is it?"

BELLA DONNA

Isaacson looked at him in silence.

"Have you formed any definite opinion?" said Hartley, at last bringing himself to the point.

"I should have to watch the case, if only for a day or two before giving any definite opinion."

"Well, but—informally, what do you think about it? What did you mean upstairs about unless very great care was taken a—a—medical reputation might be—er—ruined over it. 'Ruined' is a very strong word, you know."

The egoist was evidently very much alarmed.

"And then you said that very possibly I might regret ever having had anything to do with it. That was another thing."

Isaacson looked down meditatively.

"I didn't, and I don't, understand what your meaning could have been."

"Doctor Hartley, I can't say very much. A doctor of any reputation who is at all known in the great world has to be guarded. This is not my case. If it were, things would be different. I may have formed an opinion or not. In any event, I cannot give it at present. But I am an older man than you. I have had great experience, and I should be sorry to see a rising young physician, with probably a big future before him, get into deep waters."

"Deep waters?"

Isaacson nodded gravely.

"Mrs. Armine may think this illness is owing to a sunstroke. But she may be wrong. It may be owing to something quite different. I believe it is."

"But what? What?"

"That has to be found out. You are here to find it out."

"I—I really believe a consultation——"

He hesitated.

"But there's her great dislike of you!" he concluded, naïvely.

Isaacson got up.

"If Mr. Armine gets rapidly worse——"

"Oh, but——"

"If he dies, and it's discovered afterwards that the cause of his illness had never been found out by his doctor, and that a consultation with a man—forgive me—as widely known as myself was refused, well, it wouldn't do you any good, I'm afraid."

"Good Heavens!" exclaimed the young man, getting up in a flurry. "But—but—look here, have you any idea what's the matter?"

"Unless there's a formal consultation, I must decline to say anything on that point."

Doctor Hartley dabbed his forehead with his handkerchief.

"I—I do wish you were on better terms with Mrs. Armine," he said. "I should be delighted to meet you in consultation. It would really be better, much better."

"I think it would. It often requires two brains working in accord to unravel a difficult case."

"Of course it does! Of course it does!"

"Well, I'm just down the river. And I may pole up little higher."

"Of course, if I demand another opinion——"

"Ah, that's your right."

"I shall exercise it."

"Women, even the best of women, don't always understand, as we do, the gravity of a situation."

"Just what I think!"

"And if—he should get worse——" said Isaacson, gravely, almost solemnly, and at this moment giving some rein to his real, desperately sincere feeling.

"Oh, but—do you think it's likely?"

Isaacson looked steadily at Hartley.

"I do—very likely."

"Whatever she wishes or says, I shall summon you at once. She will be thankful, perhaps, afterwards."

"Women admire the man who takes a strong line."

"They do!"

"And I think that you may be very thankful—afterwards."

"I'll tell you what, I'm going to call you in, in consultation, to-night. Directly the patient wakes and I've seen him, I shall insist on calling you in. I won't bear the whole responsibility alone. It isn't fair. And, as you say, she'll be glad afterwards and admire the strong line I— one takes."

They parted very differently from the way in which they had met.

Did the fate of Nigel depend upon whether the sensual or the ambitious part of the young American came out "top dog" in the worry that was impending? Isaacson called it to himself a worry, not a fight. The word seemed to suit best the nature in which the contest would take place.

Mrs. Armine's ravaged face would count for something in the struggle. Isaacson's cleverness was trusting a little to that, with a pitiless intuition that was almost feminine.

His eyes had pierced the veil, and had seen that the Indian summer had suddenly faded.

XXXVIII

RETURNED to the *Fatma*, Isaacson felt within him a sort of little collapse, that was like the crumbling of something small. For the moment he was below his usual standard of power. He was depressed, slightly overstrung. He was conscious of the acute inner restlessness that comes from the need to rest, of the painful wakefulness that is the child of a lack of proper sleep. As soon as he had arrived, he asked for tea.

"You can bring it," he said to Hassan.

When Hassan came up with the tea Isaacson gave him a cigarette, and, instead of getting rid of him, began to talk, or rather to set Hassan talking.

"What's the name of the tall boy who met us on the *Loulia?*"

"Ibrahim, my gentleman."

Ibrahim—the name that was mentioned in Nigel's letter as that of the Egyptian who had arranged for the hire by Nigel of the *Loulia*. Isaacson encouraged Hassan to talk about Ibrahim, while he kept still and sipped his tea and lemon.

It seemed that Ibrahim was a great friend of Hassan's; in fact, Hassan's greatest friend. He and Hassan were like brothers. Also, Hassan loved Ibrahim as he loved his father, and Ibrahim thought of Hassan with as much respect and admiration as he dedicated to his own mother.

Isaacson was impressed. His temples felt as if they were being pinched, as if somebody was trying gently to squeeze them together. Yet he was able to listen and to encourage, and to know why he was doing both.

Hassan flowed on with a native volubility, revealing his own and Ibrahim's affairs, and presently it appeared that at this moment Ibrahim was not at all pleased, not at all happy, on board the *Loulia*. Why was this? Isaacson asked. The reason was that he had been supplanted—he who had been efficient, devoted, inspired, and capable beyond what could be looked for from any other Egyptian, or indeed from any other sentient being. Hassan's hands became tragic and violent as he talked. He showed his teeth and seemed burning with fury. And who has done this monstrous thing? Isaacson dropped out the enquiry. Hamza—him who prayed. That was the answer. And it was through Ibrahim that Hamza had entered the service of my Lord Arminigel; it was Ibrahim's unexampled generosity and nobility that had brought Hamza to the chance of this treachery.

Then Ibrahim had been first in the service of the Armines?

Very soon Isaacson knew that Mohammed, "the best donkey-boy of Luxor," had been driven out to make room for Hamza, while "my Lord Arminigel" had been away in the Fayyūm, and that now Hamza had been permitted to take Ibrahim's place as the personal attendant on my lord.

"Hamza him wait on my lord, give him his drink, give

him his meat, give him his sick-food"—*i.e.*, medicine—"give him everythin'."

And meanwhile Ibrahim, though always well paid and well treated, had sunk out of importance, and was become, in the eyes of men, "like one dog what eat where him can and sleepin' nowheres."

Who had driven out Mohammed? Isaacson was interested to know that. He was informed, with the usual variations of the East, that Mrs. Armine had wanted Hamza. "She likin' him because him always prayin'." The last sentence seemed to throw doubt upon all that had gone before. But as Isaacson lay back, having dismissed Hassan, and strove to rest, he continually saw the beautiful Hamza before him, beautiful because wonderfully typical, shrouded and drenched in the spirit of the East, a still fanatic with fatal eyes.

And Hamza always gave Nigel his "sick-food."

When Isaacson had spoken to Mrs. Armine of Hamza praying, a strange look had gone over her face. It was like a look of horror. Isaacson remembered it very well. Why should she shrink in horror from Hamza's prayers?

Isaacson needed repose. But he could not rest yet. To sleep one must cease from thinking, and one must cease from waiting.

He considered Doctor Hartley.

He was accustomed in his consulting-room to read character, temperament, shrewdly, to probe for more than mere bodily symptoms. Would Doctor Hartley act out of his fear or out of his subjection to women? In leaving the *Loulia* Isaacson had really trusted him to act out of his fear. But suppose Isaacson had misjudged him! Suppose Mrs. Armine again used her influence, and Hartley succumbed and obeyed!

In that case, Isaacson resolved that he must act up to his intuition. If it were wrong, the consequences to himself would be very disagreeable—might almost be disastrous. If he were wrong, Mrs. Armine would certainly take care that he was thoroughly punished. There was in her an inflexible want of heart and of common humanity that made her really a dangerous woman, or a potentially dangerous woman. But he must take the risk. Although a man who went cautiously where his own interests were concerned, Isaacson was ready to take the risk. He had not taken it yet, for caution had been at his elbow, telling him to exhaust all possible means of obtaining what he wanted, and what he meant to have in a reasonable way and without any scandal. He had borne with a calculated misunderstanding, with cool impertinence, even with insult. But one thing he would not bear. He would not bear to be a second time worsted by Mrs. Armine. He would not bear to be driven away.

If Hartley was governed by fear, well and good. If not, Isaacson would stand a scene, provoke a scandal, even defy Nigel for his own sake. Would that be necessary?

Well, he would soon know. He would know that night. Hartley had promised to summon him in consultation that night.

"Meanwhile I simply must rest."

He spoke to himself as a doctor. And at last he went below, lay down in his cabin with the wooden shutters drawn over the windows, and closed his eyes. He had little hope of sleep. But sleep presently came. When he woke, he heard voices quite near him. They seemed to come from the water. He lay still and listened. They were natives' voices talking violently. He began to get up. As he put his feet to the floor, he heard a knock.

"Come in!" he called.

Hassan put in his head.

"The gentleman him here!"

"What gentleman? Not Doctor Hartley?"

"The sick gentleman."

Nigel! Was it possible? Isaacson sprang up and hurried on deck. There was a boat from the *Loulia* alongside, and on the upper deck was Doctor Hartley walking restlessly about. He heard Isaacson and turned sharply.

"You've come to fetch me?" said Isaacson.

BELLA DONNA

As he came up, he had noticed that already the sun had set. He had slept for a long time.

"There's been a—a most unpleasant—a most distressing scene!" Hartley said.

"Why, with whom?"

"With her—Mrs. Armine. What on earth have you done to set her against you? She—she—really, it amounts to absolute hatred. Have you ever done her any serious wrong?"

"Never!"

"I—I really think she must be hysterical. There's—there's the greatest change in her."

He paused. Then, very abruptly, he said:

"Have you any idea how old she is?"

"I only know that she isn't thirty-eight," said Isaacson.

"Isn't thirty-eight!"

"She is older than that. She once told me so—in an indirect way."

Hartley looked at him with sudden suspicion.

"Then you've—you and she have known each other very well?"

"Never!"

"Till now I imagined her about thirty, thirty-two perhaps, something like that."

"Till now?"

"Yes. She—to-day she looks suddenly almost like a—well—a middle-aged woman. I never saw such a change."

It seemed that the young man was seriously perturbed by the announced transformation.

"Sit down, won't you?" said Isaacson.

"No, thanks. I——"

He went to the rail. Isaacson followed him.

"Our talk quite decided me," Hartley said, "to call you in to-night. I felt it was necessary. I felt I owed it to myself as a—if I may say so—a rising medical man."

"I think you did."

"When she woke I told her so. But I'm sorry to say she didn't take my view. We had a long talk. It really was most trying, most disagreeable. But she was not herself. She knew it. She said it was my fault—that I ought not to have given her that veronal. Certainly she did look awful. D'you know"—he turned round to Isaacson, and there was in his face an expression almost of awe—"it was really like seeing a woman become suddenly old before one's very eyes. And—and I had thought she was quite—comparatively—young!"

"And the result of your conversation?"

"At first things were not so bad. I agreed—I thought it was only reasonable—to wait till Mr. Armine woke up and to see how he was then. He slept for some time longer, and we sat there waiting. She—I must say—she has charm."

Even in the midst of his anxiety, of his nervous tension, Isaacson could scarcely help smiling. He could almost see Bella Donna fighting the young man's dawning resolution with every weapon she had.

"Indeed she has!" he assented, without a touch of irony.

"Ah! Any man must feel it. At the same time, really she is a wreck now."

Isaacson's almost feminine intuition had evidently not betrayed him. That altered face had had a great deal to do with Doctor Hartley's definite resolve to have a consultation.

"Poor woman!" he added. "Upon my soul, I can't help pitying her. She knows it, too. But I expect they always do."

"Probably. But you've come then to take me to the *Loulia?*"

"I told her I really must insist."

"How did you find the patient when he woke?"

"Well, I must say I didn't like the look of him at all."

"No? Did he seem worse?"

"I really—I really hardly know. But I told her he was much worse."

"Why?"

"Why? Because I was determined not to go on with

the case alone, for fear something should happen. She denied it. She declared he was much better—stronger. He agreed with her, I must confess; said he felt more himself, and all that. But—but she seemed rather putting the words into his mouth, I fancied. I may have been wrong, but still—the fact is I'm positively upset by all that's happened."

He grasped the rail with both hands. Evidently he had only held his own against Bella Donna at the expense of his nervous system.

"When we left him, I told her I must get you in. She was furious, said she wouldn't have you, that you had always been against her, that you had nearly prevented her marriage with Mr. Armine, that you had maligned her all over London."

"Did she say any of this before her husband?"

"Not all that. No. We were in the first saloon. But I thought the men would have heard her. She really lost her head. She was distinctly hysterical. It was a most awkward position for me. But—but I was resolved to dominate her."

"And you did?"

"Well—I—I stuck to my point. I said I must and would have another opinion."

"Another?"

"Yours, of course. There's nobody else to be got at immediately. And after what you—what we both said and thought this afternoon, I won't wait till another doctor can be fetched from a distance."

"We'll start at once," said Isaacson, in a practical voice.

"Yes."

But the assent was very hesitating, and Hartley made no movement. Isaacson looked at him with sharply questioning eyes.

"I—I wish I was out of the case altogether," said the young man, weakly. "After this afternoon's row I seem to have lost all heart. I never have had such an unpleasant scene with any woman before. It makes the position extremely difficult. I don't know how she will receive us; I really don't. She never agreed to my proposition, and I left her looking dreadful."

"Mrs. Armine hates me. It's a pity. But I've got to think of the sick man. And so have you. Look here, Doctor Hartley, you and I have got over our little disagreement of this morning, and I hope we can be colleagues."

"I wish nothing better indeed," said the young man, earnestly.

"We'll go back to the *Loulia*. We'll see the patient. We'll have our consultation. And then if you still wish to get out of the case——"

"Really, I think I'd much rather. I've got friends waiting for me at Assouan."

"And I've got nobody waiting for me. Suppose the patient agrees, and you continue in the same mind, I'm willing to relieve you of all responsibility and take the whole thing into my own hands. And if at any time you come to London——"

"I may be coming this summer."

"Then I think I can be of use to you there. Shall we go?"

This time Doctor Hartley did move. A weight seemed lifted from his shoulders, and he went, almost with alacrity, towards the boat.

"After all, you are much my senior," he said, as they were getting in, "besides being an intimate friend of the patient. I don't think it would seem unnatural to any one."

"The most natural thing in the world!" said Isaacson, calmly. "Yes, Hassan, you can come with us. Come in the other boat. I may want you to do something for me later on."

The two doctors did not talk much as they were rowed towards the *Loulia*. Both were preoccupied. As they drew near to her, however, Doctor Hartley began to fidget. His bodily restlessness betrayed his mental uneasiness.

"I do hope she'll be reasonable," he said at length.

"I think she will."

"What makes you?"

"She's a decidedly clever woman."

"Clever—oh, yes, she is. She was very well known, wasn't she, once—in a certain way?"

"As a beauty—yes."

Isaacson's tone of voice was scarcely encouraging, and the other relapsed into silence and continued to fidget. But when they were close to the *Loulia*, almost under the blue light that shone at her mast-head, he said, in a low and secretive voice:

"I think you had better take the lead, as you are my senior. It will appear more natural."

"Very well. But I don't want to seem to——"

"No, no! Don't mind about me! I shall perfectly understand. I have chosen to call you in. That shows I am not satisfied with the way the case is going."

The felucca touched the side of the *Loulia*. Ibrahim appeared. He smiled when he saw them, smiled still more when he perceived beyond them the second boat with Hassan. Isaacson stepped on board first. Hartley followed him without much alacrity.

"I want to see Mrs. Armine," Isaacson said to Ibrahim. Ibrahim went towards the steps.

"Do you happen to know what that Arabic writing means?" Isaacson asked of Hartley, as they were about to pass under the motto of the *Loulia*.

"That—yes; I asked. It's from the Koran."

"Yes?"

"It means—the fate of every man have we bound about his neck."

"Ah! Rather fatalistic! Does it appeal to you?"

"I don't know. I haven't thought about it. I wonder how she'll receive us!"

"It will be all right," Isaacson said with cheerful confidence.

But he was wondering too.

The first saloon was empty. Ibrahim left them in it, and went through the doorway beyond to the after part of the vessel. Isaacson sat down on the divan, but Hartley moved about. His present anxiety was in proportion to his past admiration of Mrs. Armine. He had adored her enough once to be very much afraid of her now.

"I do—I must say I hope she won't make a scene," he said.

"Oh, no."

"Yes, but you didn't see her this afternoon."

"She was upset. Some people can't endure daytime sleep. She's had time now to recover."

But Hartley did not seem to be reassured. He kept looking furtively towards the door by which Ibrahim had vanished. In about five minutes it was opened again by Ibrahim. He stood aside, slightly bending and looking on the floor, and Mrs. Armine came in, dressed in a sort of elaborate tea-gown, grey in colour, with silver embroideries. She was carefully made up, but not made up pale. Her cheeks were delicately flushed with colour. Her lips were red. Her shining hair was arranged to show the beautiful shape of her head as clearly as possible and to leave her lovely neck quite bare. Everything that could be done to render her attractive had been very deftly done. Nevertheless, even Isaacson, who had seen the change in her that afternoon, and had been prepared for further change in her by Hartley, was surprised by the alteration a few hours had made in her appearance.

Middle-age, with its subtle indications of what old age will be, had laid its hands upon her, had suddenly and firmly grasped her. As before, since she had been in Egypt, she had appeared to most people very much younger than she really was, so now she appeared older, decisively older, than she actually was. When Isaacson had looked at her in his consulting-room he had thought her not young, nor old, nor definitely middle-aged. Now he realized exactly what she would be some day as a painted and powdered old woman, striving by means of clever corsets, a perfect wig, and an ingenious complexion to simulate that least artificial of all things, youth. The outlines of the face were sharper, cruder than before; the nose and chin looked more pointed, the cheek-bones much more salient. The mouth seemed to have suddenly "given in" to the thing it had hitherto successfully striven against. And the eyes burnt with a fire that called the attention to the dark night slowly but certainly coming to close about this woman, and to withdraw her beauty into its blackness.

Isaacson's thought was: "What must be the state of the mind which has thus suddenly triumphed over a hitherto triumphant body?" And he felt like a man who looks down into a gulf, and who sees nothing, but hears movements and murmurs of horror and despair.

Mrs. Armine came straight to Isaacson. Her eyes, fastened upon him, seemed to defy him to see the change in her. She smiled and said:

"So you've come again! It's very good of you. Nigel is awake now."

She looked towards Doctor Hartley.

"I hope Doctor Isaacson will be able to reassure you," she said. "You frightened me this afternoon. I don't think you quite realized what it is to a woman to have sprung upon her so abruptly such an alarming view of an invalid's condition."

"But I didn't at all mean——" began the young doctor in agitation.

"I don't know what you meant," she interrupted, "but you alarmed me dreadfully. Well, are you going to see my husband together?"

"Yes, we must do that," said Isaacson.

He was slightly surprised by her total lack of all further opposition to the consultation, although he had almost prophesied it to Hartley. Perhaps he had prophesied to reassure himself, for now he was conscious of a certain rather vague sense of doubt and of uneasiness, such as comes upon a man who, without actually suspecting an ambush, wonders whether, perhaps, he is near one.

"I dare say you would rather I was not present at your consultation?" said Mrs. Armine.

"It isn't usual for any one to be present except the doctors taking part in it," said Isaacson.

"The consultation comes after the visit to the patient," she said; "and of course I'll leave you alone for that. I should prefer to leave you alone while you are examining my husband, too, but I'm sorry to say he insists on my being there."

Isaacson was no longer in doubt about an ambush. She had prepared one while she had been left alone with the sick man. Hartley having unexpectedly escaped from the magic circle of her influence, she had devoted herself to making it invulnerable about her husband.

Nevertheless, he meant to break in at whatever cost.

"We don't want to oppose or irritate the patient, I'm sure," he said.

He looked towards Doctor Hartley.

"No, no, certainly not!" the young man assented, hastily.

"Very well, then!" said Mrs. Armine.

Her brows went down and her mouth contracted for an instant. Then she moistened her painted lips with the tip of her tongue and turned towards the door.

"I'll go first to tell him you are coming," she said.

She went out into the passage.

XXXIX

Isaacson glanced at Doctor Hartley before he followed her.

"I—doesn't she look strange? Did you ever see such an alteration?" almost whispered the young man.

Isaacson did not answer, but stepped into the passage.

Mrs. Armine was a little way down it, walking on rather quickly. Suddenly she looked round. Light shone upon her from above, and showed her tense and worn face, her features oddly sharpened and pointed, wrinkles clustering about the corners of her eyes. She seemed, under the low roof, unnaturally tall in her flowing grey robe, and this evening in her height there seemed to Isaacson to be something forbidding and almost dreadful. She held up one hand, as if warning the two men to pause for a moment. Then she went on, and disappeared through the doorway that faced them beyond the two rows of bedrooms.

"We are to wait, it seems," Isaacson said, stopping in the passage. "The patient is up then?"

"He wasn't when I left," murmured Hartley.

"Did you say whether he was to be kept in bed?"

"Oh, no. I don't know that there was any reason against his getting up, except his weakness. He has never taken to his bed."

"No?"

Mrs. Armine reappeared, and beckoned to them to come on. They obeyed her, and came into the farther saloon. As soon as Isaacson passed through the doorway, he saw Nigel sitting up on the divan, with cushions behind him, near the left-hand doorway which gave on to the balcony. He had a hat on, as if he had just been out there, and a newspaper on his knees. The saloon was not well lit. Only one electric burner covered with a shade was turned on. With the aid of the cushions he was sitting up very straight, as if he had just made a strong effort and succeeded in bracing up his body. Mrs. Armine stood close to him. His eyes were turned towards the two doctors, and as Isaacson came up to him, he said in a colourless voice, which yet held a faintly querulous sound:

"So you've come up again, Isaacson!"

"Yes."

"Very good of you. But I don't know why there should be all this fuss made about me. It's rather trying, you know. I believe it keeps me back."

Already Isaacson knew just what he had to face, what he had to contend with.

"I hate a fuss made about me," Nigel continued, "simply hate it. You must know that."

Isaacson, who had come up to him, extended his hand in greeting. But Nigel, whether he felt too weak too stretch out his hand, or for some other reason, did not appear to see it, and Isaacson at once dropped his hand, while he said:

"I don't think there is any reason to make a fuss. But, being so near, I just rowed up to see how you were getting on after your sleep."

"I didn't sleep at night," Nigel said quickly. "What you gave me did me no good at all."

"I'm sorry for that."

Nigel still sat up against the cushions, but his body now inclined slightly to the left side, where Mrs. Armine was standing, looking down on him with quiet solicitude.

"I had a very bad night—very bad."

"Then I'm afraid——"

"Doctor Hartley rowed down to fetch you here, I understood," Nigel interrupted.

There was suspicion in his voice.

"Yes," said Hartley, speaking for the first time, nervously. "I—I thought to myself, 'Two heads are better than one.'"

He forced a sort of laugh. Nigel twitched on the divan like a man supremely irritated, then looked from one doctor to the other with eyes that included them both in his irritation.

"Two heads—what for?" he said. "What d'you mean?"

He sighed heavily as he finished the question. Then, without waiting for an answer, he said to his wife:

"If only I could have a little peace!"

There was a frightful weariness in his voice, a sound that made Isaacson think of a cruelly treated child's voice. Mrs. Armine bent down and touched his hand as it lay on the newspaper which was still across his knees. She smiled at him.

"A little patience!" she murmured.

She raised her eyebrows.

"Yes, it's all very well, Ruby, but——" He looked again at Isaacson, with a distinct though not forcible hostility. "I know you want to doctor me, Isaacson," he said. "And she asked me to-night to see you. Last night it was different, but to-night I don't want doctoring. Frankly"—he sighed again heavily—"I only see any one to-night to please her. All I want is quiet. We came here for quiet. But we don't seem to get it."

He turned again to his wife.

"Even you are getting worn out. I can see that," he said.

Mrs. Armine's forehead sharply contracted. "Oh, I'm all right, Nigel," she said, quickly. She laughed. "I'm not going to let them begin doctoring me," she said.

"She's nursed me like a slave," Nigel continued, looking at the two men, and speaking as if for a defence. "There has never been such devotion. And I wish every one could know it." Tears suddenly started into his eyes. "But the best things and the best people in the world are not believed in, are never believed in," he murmured.

"Never mind, Nigel dear," she said, soothingly. "It's all right."

Isaacson, who with Hartley had been standing all this time because Mrs. Armine was standing, now sat down beside the sick man.

"I think true devotion will always find its reward," he said, quietly, steadily. "We only want to do you good, to get you quickly into your old splendid health."

"That's very good of you, of course. But you didn't do me good last night. It was the worst night I ever had."

Isaacson remembered the sound he had heard when the Nubians lay on their oars on the dark river.

"Let us try to do you good to-night. Won't you?" he said.

"All I want is rest. I've told her so. And I tell you so."

"Shall I stay on board to-night and see you to-morrow morning when you have had a night's rest?"

Nigel looked up at his wife.

"Aren't you quite near?" he asked Isaacson, in a moment.

"I'm not very far away, but——"

"Then I don't think we need bother you to stay. We've got Doctor Hartley."

"I—I'm afraid I shall have to leave you to-morrow," said the young man, who had several times looked, almost with a sort of horror, at Mrs. Armine's ravaged face. "You see I'm with people at Assouan. I really came out to Egypt in a sort of way in attendance upon Mrs. Craven Bagley, who is in delicate health. And though she's much stronger——"

"Yes, yes!" Nigel interrupted. "Of course, go—go! I want peace, I want rest."

He drooped towards his wife. Suddenly she sat down beside him, holding his hand.

"Would you rather not be examined to-night?" she asked him.

"Examined!" he said, in a startled voice.

"Well, dearest, these doctors——"

Nigel, with a great effort, sat up as before.

"I won't be bothered to-night," he said, with the weak anger of an utterly worn-out man. "I—I can't stand anything more. I—can't—stand——" His voice died away.

"We'd better go," whispered Hartley. "To-morrow morning."

He looked at Mrs. Armine, and moved towards the door. Isaacson got up.

"We will leave the patient to-night," he said to Mrs. Armine, in an expressionless voice.

"Yes?"

"But may I have a word with you, please, in the other room?"

Then he followed Hartley.

He caught him up in the passage.

"It's absolutely no use to-night," said Hartley. "Any examination would only make matters worse. He's not in a fit state mentally to go through it so late."

"I think it will be best to wait till to-morrow."

"And then, directly after the consultation is over, I must really get away. That is, if you are willing to——"

"You may leave everything in my hands."

"She hates me now!" the young man said, almost plaintively. "Did you ever see such a change?"

"I'm going to speak with her in the first saloon, so I'll leave you," said Isaacson.

Hartley had his hand on one of the cabin doors.

"Then I'll go in here. I sleep here."

"Good night," Isaacson said.

"Oh! you won't want me again?"

"Not to-night."

"Good night then."

He opened the cabin door and disappeared within, while Isaacson walked on to the first saloon.

He had to wait in it for nearly ten minutes before he heard Mrs. Armine coming. But he would not have minded much waiting an hour. He felt within him the determination of an iron will now completely assured. And strength can wait.

Mrs. Armine came in and shut the door gently behind her.

"I'm sorry to keep you waiting," she said. "I was taking my husband to his cabin. He's going to bed. Where is Doctor Hartley?"

"He's gone to his cabin."

Something in Isaacson's tone seemed suddenly to strike her, and she sent him a look of sharp enquiry.

"Will you sit down for a minute?" he said.

She sat down at once, still keeping her eyes fixed upon him. He sat down near her.

"Doctor Hartley is going away to-morrow morning," Isaacson said.

"He promised to stay several days with us to preside over my husband's convalescence."

"He's going away, and there's no question of convalescence."

"I don't understand you!"

"I'll make myself plain. Your husband is not a convalescent. Your husband is a very sick man."

"No wonder, when he's worried to death, when he's allowed no peace day or night, when he's given one thing on the top of another!"

"May I ask what you mean by that?"

"Didn't you come in last night, and force a sleeping draught upon him?"

"I certainly gave him something to make him sleep."

"And it didn't make him sleep."

"Because before it had had time to take effect he received a great shock," Isaacson said, quietly.

She moved.

"A great shock?"

She stared at him.

"At night, upon water, sound travels a very long way. Have you never noticed that?" he asked her.

Still she stared, and as he looked at her it seemed to him that the bony structure of her face became more salient.

"Last night," he said, as she did not speak, "I thought I heard something strange. I made my men stop rowing for a minute, and I listened. I am not surprised that the sleeping draught I gave your husband had no effect. Under the circumstances it probably even did him harm. But no doctor could have foreseen that."

She moved restlessly. Isaacson got up and stood before her.

"I'm going to speak plainly," he said. "Some time ago, in my consulting-room in London, you told me a good deal of the truth of yourself."

"You think——"

"I know. You told me then that your whole desire was to have a good time. How long are you going to put up with your present life?"

"Put up! You don't understand. Nigel has been very good to me, and I am very happy with him."

"If he's been good to you, don't you wish him to get well?"

"Of course I do. I've been waiting upon him hand and foot."

"And not even a maid to help you—although she did ring last night for Hamza, when we were here."

She looked down, and picked at the dim embroideries that covered the divan.

"I've nursed him till I've nearly made myself ill," she said, mechanically.

"I'm going to relieve you of that task."

She turned her face up towards him.

"No, you aren't!" she said. "I'm Nigel's wife, and that is my natural duty."

"Nevertheless, I'm going to relieve you of it."

The rock-like firmness of his tone evidently made upon her an immense impression.

"From to-night I take charge of this case."

Mrs. Armine stood up. She was taller than Isaacson, and now she stood looking down upon him.

"Nigel won't have you!" she said.

"He must."

"He won't—unless I wish it."

"You will never wish it."

"No."

"But you will pretend to wish it."

She continued to look down in silence. At last she breathed, "Why?"

"Because, if you don't, I shall not send for another doctor. I shall send for the police authorities."

She sank down again upon the divan. But her expression did not change. He believed that she succeeded in making her face a mere mask while she thought with a furious rapidity.

"You don't mean to say," she at length said, "that you think anything—that you suppose one of the servants—Ibrahim—Hamza——? I can't believe it! I could never believe it!"

"Do you wish me to cure your husband?"

"Of course I wish him to be cured."

"Then please go now and tell him that you have asked me to stay here for the night. I don't want him to see me to-night. I will see him as soon as he wakes to-morrow."

"But—he doesn't——"

"Just as you like! Either I stay here and take charge of this case, or I go back to the boat at Edfou and to-morrow I put myself into communication with the proper authorities."

She got up again slowly.

"Well, if you really believe you can pull Nigel round quickly!" she said.

She moved to the door.

"I'll see what he says!" she murmured.

Then she opened the door and went out.

That night Isaacson sent Hassan back to the *Fatma* to fetch some necessary luggage. For Mrs. Armine succeeded in persuading her husband to submit to a doctor's visit the next morning.

Isaacson had not been worsted. But as he went into one of the smart little cabins to get some sleep if possible, he felt terribly, almost unbearably, depressed.

For what was—what must be—the meaning of this victory?

XL

ISAACSON had asked himself at night the meaning of his victory. When the morning dawned, when once more he had to go to his work, the work which was his life, although sometimes he was inclined to decry it secretly in moments of fatigue, he asked no further questions. His business was plain before him, and it was business into which he could put his heart. Although he was not an insensitive man, he was a man of generous nature. He pushed away with an almost careless energy those small annoyances, those little injuries of life, which more petty people make much of and cannot easily forgive. The querulous man who was ready, out of his bodily weakness and his misdirected love, to make little of his friendship, even to thrust away his proffered help, he disregarded as man, regarded as so much nearly destroyed material which he had to repair, to bring back to its former flawlessness. He knew the real nature, the real soul of the man; he understood why they were warped, and he put himself aside, put his pride into his pocket, which he considered the proper place for it at that moment. But though he had gained his point by a daring half-avowal of what his intuition had whispered to him, he presently realized that if he were to win through with Nigel into the sunshine, he must act with determination; perhaps, too, with a cunning which the Eastern drops in his blood made not so unnatural to him as it might have been to most men as honest living as he was.

Mrs. Armine had been dominated for the moment. She had obeyed. She had done the thing she hated to do. But she was not the woman to run straight on any path that led away from her wishes; she now loathed as well as feared Meyer Isaacson, and she had a cruelly complete influence over her husband. And even any secret fear could not hold her animus against the man who understood her wholly in check. Like the mole, she must work in the dark. She could not help it.

What she had said of him to Nigel, between his first and his second visits to the *Loulia,* Isaacson did not know. Indeed, he scarcely cared to know. It was not difficult to divine how she had used her influence. Isaacson could almost hear her reciting the catalogue of his misdeeds against herself, could almost see her eyes as she murmured the insinuations which doubtless the sick man had believed —because in his condition he must believe almost anything she persistently told him.

Yet at a word from her he had agreed to accept all the ministrations of his friend, which at another word he had been willing to repel.

The fact was that secretly he was crying out for the powerful hand to save him from the abyss. And he believed in Isaacson as a doctor, however much he now resented Isaacson's mistrust, no longer to be doubted, of the woman his chivalry had lifted to a throne.

He received Isaacson with an odd mixture of thankfulness and reserve, put himself into the doctor's hands with almost a boy's confidence, but kept himself free, with a determination that in the circumstances was touching, however pitiful, from the stretched-out hands of the friend.

And Isaacson felt swiftly that though one contest was ended, and ended as he desired, another contest was at its beginning, a silent battle of influences about this good fellow, who, by his very virtue, had fallen so low.

But the doctor must come first. That coming might clear the ground for the friend. And so Isaacson, in the beginning, met Nigel's new reserve with another reserve, very unself-conscious apparently, very businesslike, practical, and, above all things, very calm.

Isaacson radiated calm.

He found his patient that first morning weary after another bad night, induced partly by the draught which had sent him to sleep in daylight, and this very conscious and physical misery, acting upon the mind, played into the Doctor's hands. He was able without difficulty to make a minute examination of the case. The patient, though so reserved at first in his manner, putting a barrier between himself and Isaacson, was almost pathetically talkative directly the conversation became definitely medical. But that conversation finished, he relapsed into his former almost stiff reserve, a reserve which seemed so strangely foreign to his real nature that Isaacson felt as if the man he knew and cared for had got up and left the room.

Mrs. Armine was waiting to hear the result of the interview. Doctor Hartley had taken his departure—fled, perhaps, is the word—at an early hour. In daylight her face looked even more ravaged than it had on the previous night. But her manner was coldly calm.

"What is the verdict?" she asked.

"I'm afraid I am not prepared to give a verdict. Your

husband is in a very weak, low state. If it had been allowed to continue indefinitely, the mischief might have become irreparable."

"But you can put him right?"

"Let's hope so."

She stood as if she were waiting for more definite information. But none came. After a silence Isaacson said:

"The first thing to be done is to get him away from here."

"Get him away! Where to?"

"You've still got your villa at Luxor, I believe?"

"Oh, yes."

"I suppose it is comfortable, well arranged?"

"Pretty well."

"And it's quiet and has a garden, I know."

"You've seen it?"

"Yes. My boat was tied up just opposite to it the night before I started up river."

"Oh!"

"Perhaps you'll be kind enough to give the order to the Reis to start for Luxor as soon as possible?"

"Very well," she said, indifferently.

Her whole look and manner now were curiously indolent and indifferent. Before she had been full of fiercely nervous life. To-day it seemed as if that life was withdrawn from her.

"I'll tell him now," she said.

And without any more questions she went away to the deck.

Soon afterwards there was a stir. Cries were heard from the sailors, and the *Loulia* began to move, floating northwards with the tide. When Nigel asked the reason, Isaacson said to him:

"This place is too isolated for an invalid. One can get at nothing here. You will be much more at your ease in your own home, and I can take better care of you there."

"We are going back to the villa?"

"Yes."

"I'm glad," Nigel said, slowly. "I never told her, but I was beginning to hate this boat; all this trouble has come upon me here. Sometimes—sometimes I have felt almost as if——"

He broke off.

"Yes?" Isaacson said, quietly.

"As if there were something that was fatal to me on board the *Loulia*."

"In the villa I shall get you back to your original health and strength."

The thin, lead-coloured face drooped forward, and the eyes that were full of a horrible malaise held for a moment the fires of hope.

"Do you really think I can ever get well?"

Isaacson did not reply for a moment. Then he said, "Will you make me a promise?"

"What is it?"

"Will you promise me to obey implicitly everything I order you to do?"

"Do you mean—as a doctor?"

"I do."

"I promise."

"Very well. If you carry out that promise, I think I can undertake to cure you. I think I can undertake that some day you will be once more the strong man who rejoices in his strength."

Tears came into Nigel's eyes.

"I wonder," he said. "I wonder."

"But remember," Isaacson said, almost with solemnity, "I shall expect from you implicit obedience to my medical orders. And the first of them is this: you are to swallow nothing which is not given to you by me with my own hand."

"Medicine, you mean?"

"I mean what I say—nothing; not a morsel of food, not a drop of liquid."

"Then my wife and Hamza——"

"Will you obey me?" Isaacson interrupted, almost sternly.

"Yes," Nigel said, in a weak voice.

"And now just lie quiet, and remember you are going towards your home, in which I intend to get you quite well."

And the *Loulia* floated down with the tide, slowly, and broadside to the great river, for there was no wind at all, and the weather was hot almost as a furnace. The *Fatma* untied, and followed her down. And the night came, and still they floated on broadside under the stars.

Nigel was now sleeping, and Meyer Isaacson was watching.

And in a cabin close by a woman was staring at her face in a little glass set in the lid of a gilded box, was staring, with desperation at her heart.

Hartley had said he believed she knew of the sudden collapse of her beauty. Believed! Before he had noticed it, she had perceived it, with a cold horror which, gathering strength, grew into a bitter despair. And with the despair came hatred, hatred of the man who by keeping her back from happiness had led her to this collapse. This man was Nigel. He thought he had saved her from her worst self. But really he had stirred this worst self from sleep. In London she had been almost a good woman, compared to the woman she was now. His bungling search after nobility of spirit had roused the devil within her. She longed to let him know what she really was. Often and often, while they two had been isolated together on the *Loulia*, she had been on the edge of telling him at least some fragments of the truth. Her nerves had nearly betrayed her when through the long and shining hours the dahabeeyah lay still on the glassy river, far away from the haunts of men, and she, sick with ennui, nearly mad because of the dulness of her life, had been forced to play at love with the man whose former strength and beauty diminished day by day.

Would it never end? Each day seemed to her an eternity, each hour almost a year. But she knew that she must be patient, though patience was no part of her character.

All through her life she had been an impatient and greedy woman, seizing on what she wanted and holding to it tenaciously. She had hidden her impatience with her charm, and so she had gained successes. But now, with so little time left to her for possible enjoyment, gnawed by desire and jealousy, she found her powers reluctant in their coming. Formerly she had exercised her influence almost without effort. Now she had to be stubborn in endeavour. And she knew, with the frightful certainty of the middle-aged woman, that the cruel exertions of her mind must soon tell upon her body.

Her terror, a terror which had never left her during these days and nights on the dahabeeyah, was that her beauty might fade before she was free to go to Baroudi. She knew now how strongly she had fascinated him, despite his seeming, almost cruel imperturbability. By her lowest powers, the powers that Nigel ignored and thought that he hated—though perhaps he too had been partially subject to them—she had grasped the sensual nature of the Egyptian. As Starnworth had told Isaacson, Baroudi had within him the madness for women. He had within him the madness for Bella Donna. But he knew how to wait for what he wanted. He was waiting now. The question that had presented itself to Mrs. Armine again and again during her exile with Nigel was this: "Will he wait too long?" She knew how fleeting is the Indian summer of women. And she knew, though she denied it to herself, that if she brought to Baroudi not an Indian summer as her gift, but a fading autumn, she would run the risk of being confronted by the blank cruelty that is so often the offspring of the Eastern conception of women.

Yet in her terror she had always been supported by a fierce energy of hope, until in the holy of holies of Horus she had come face to face with Isaacson.

And now!

Now she sat alone in her cabin, and she stared into the little mirror which Baroudi had given her in the garden of oranges.

And Isaacson watched over her husband.

"The fate of every man have we bound about his neck."

The Arabic letters of gold seemed to be pressing down upon her, to crush her body and spirit. She put down the box, and, almost savagely shut down the lid upon it.

And now that she no longer saw herself, she seemed to see Hamza praying, as he had prayed that day in the orange garden when she looked out of the window. Then she had felt that the hands of the East had grasped her, that they would never let her go, and something within her had recoiled, though something else had desired only that—to be grasped by Baroudi's hands.

The praying men had frightened her. Yet she believed in no God.

If there really was a God! If He looked upon her now!

She sprang up, and turned out the light.

* * * * * *

The next day the *Loulia* tied up under the garden of the Villa Androud, just beyond the stone promontory that diverted the strong current of the river. Nigel, too weak to walk up the bank to the house, was carefully carried by the Nubians. The surprised servants of the villa, who had had no notice of their master's arrival, hastened to throw back the shutters, to open the windows, letting in light and air. And Ibrahim once more began to look authoritative, for it seemed that Hamza's reign was over. From henceforth only Meyer Isaacson gave food and drink and "sick-food" to "my Lord Arminigel."

The change from dahabeeyah life to life on shore seemed at once to make a difference to the patient. When he was put carefully down in the white and yellow drawing-room, and, looking out through the French windows across the terrace, saw the roses blowing in the sandy garden, he heaved a sigh that was like a deep breathing of relief.

"I'm thankful to be out of the *Loulia*, Ruby," he said to his wife, who was standing beside the sofa on which he was resting.

"Are you, Nigel. Why?"

"I don't know. It seemed to oppress me. And you know that writing?"

"What writing?"

"Over the door as you went in."

"Oh, yes."

"I used to think of it in the night when I felt so awful, and it was like a weight coming down to crush me."

"That was fanciful of you," she said.

But she sent him a strange look of half-frightened suspicion.

He did not see it. He was looking out to the garden. From the Nile rose the voices of the sailors singing their song. He listened to it for a moment.

"What a strange time it's been since we first heard that song together, Ruby," he said.

"Yes."

"When we first heard it, I was so strong, so happy—strong to protect you, happy to have you to protect, and—and it's ended in your having to protect and take care of me."

She moved.

"Yes," she said again, in a dry voice.

"I—I think I'm glad we can't look into the future. One wants a lot of courage in life."

She said nothing.

"But I feel a little courage now. I never quite told you how it was with me on the *Loulia*. If I had stayed on her much longer, as we were, I should have died. I should have died very soon."

"No, no, Nigel."

"Yes, I should. But here"—he moved, stretched out his arms, sighed—"I feel that I shall get better, perhaps get well, even. How—how splendid if I do!"

"Well, I must go and look after things," she said.

"You're tired, aren't you?"

"No. Why should you think so?"

"Your voice sounds tired."

"It isn't that."

"What is it?"

"You know that for your sake I am enduring a companionship that is odious to me," she said, in a low voice.

At that moment, Meyer Isaacson came into the room.

"We must get the patient to bed as soon as possible," he said, in his quiet, practical, and strong voice.

"I'll go and see about the room," said Mrs. Armine.

She went away quickly.

When she got upstairs there were drops of blood on her lower lip.

XLI

NIGEL had come to hate the *Loulia*. They had no further need of her, and he begged his wife to telegraph to Baroudi in his name to take her away as soon as he liked.

"Ibrahim has his address, I know," he said.

The telegram was sent. In reply came one from Baroudi taking over the *Loulia*. The same day the Reis came up to the villa to receive backsheesh and to say farewell. He made no remark as to his own and his crew's immediate destiny, but soon after he had gone the *Loulia* untied, crossed the Nile, and was tied up again nearly opposite to the garden against the western bank. And in the evening the sailors could be heard in the distance "making the fantasia."

Mrs. Armine heard them as she walked alone in the garden close to the promontory, and she saw the blue light at the mast-head. The cabin windows were dark.

So this was the end of their voyage to the South!

She stood still near the wall of earth which divided the garden from the partially waste and partially cultivated ground which lay beyond it.

She had not thought that they would come back—three.

This was the end of their voyage. But what was to be the end?

Baroudi made no sign. He had never written to her one

word. She had never dared to write to him. He had not told her to write, and that meant he did not choose her to write. She was very much afraid of him, and her fear of him was part of the terrible fascination he held to govern her. She who had had so many slaves when she was young ended thus—in being herself a slave.

She sat down by the earth wall on the first stones of the promontory. The night was moonless; but in the clear nights of Egypt, even without the moon very near details can often be distinguished.

To the right of Mrs. Armine the brown earth bank shelved steeply to a shore that was like a sandy beach which an incoming tide had nearly covered. About it, in a sort of large basin of loose sand and earth, grew a quantity of bushes forming a not dense scrub. She had never been down to walk upon the sandy shore, though she had often descended to get into the felucca. But to-night, after sitting still for some time, she went down, and began to pace upon the sand close to the water's edge.

From here she could not see the house with its lighted windows, speaking to her of the life in which she was involved. She could see nothing except the darkness of the great river, the dark outline of the promontory, and of the top of the bank where the garden began, the dark and confused forms of the bushes tangled together. At her feet the silent water lay, like lake water almost, though farther out the current was strong.

"What am I going to do?" she kept on saying to herself, as she walked to and fro in this solitude. "What am I going to do?"

It was a strange thing, perhaps, that even at this moment Baroudi, the man at a distance, frightened her more than Isaacson, the man who was near. She did not know what either was going to do. She was the prey of a double uncertainty. Isaacson, she supposed, would bring her husband back to health, unless even now she found means to get rid of him. And Baroudi, what would he do? She looked across the river and saw the blue light. Why was the *Loulia* tied up there? Was Baroudi coming up to join her?

If he did come! She walked faster, quite unconscious that she had quickened her pace. If he did come she felt now that she could no longer be obedient. She would have to see him, have to force him to come out from his deep mystery of the Eastern mind and take notice of what she was feeling. His magnificent selfishness had dominated hers. But she was becoming desperate. The thought of her wrecked beauty haunted her always, though she was perpetually thrusting it away from her. She was resolved to think that there was very little change in her appearance, and that such change as there was would only be temporary. A little, only a little of what she wanted, and surely the Indian summer would return.

And then she thought of Meyer Isaacson up there in the house close to her, with his horribly acute eyes that proclaimed his horribly acute brain. That man could be pitiless, but not to Nigel. And could he ever be pitiless to her without being pitiless to Nigel?

She looked at the water, and now stood still.

If Baroudi were on board the *Loulia* to-night, she would get a boat and go to him—would not she?—and say she could not stand her life any longer, that she must be with him. She would let him treat her as he chose. Thinking of Nigel's kindness at this moment, she actually longed for cruelty from Baroudi.

But she must be with him.

If she could only be with Baroudi anywhere, anyhow, she would throw the memory of this hateful life with Nigel away for ever. She would never give Nigel another thought. There would be no time to waste over that.

"But what am I going to do? What am I going to do?"

That sentence came back to her mind. Flights of the imagination were useless. It was no use now to give the reins to imagination.

Baroudi must come up the river. He must be coming up, or the *Loulia* would surely not be tied up against the western shore. But perhaps she was there only for the night. Perhaps she would sail on the morrow.

Mrs. Armine felt that if the next morning the *Loulia* was gone she would be unable to remain in Luxor. She would have to take the train and go. Where? Anywhere! To Cairo. She could make some excuse; that she must get some clothes, mourning for Harwich. That would do. She would say she was going only for a couple of days. Nigel would let her go. And Meyer Isaacson?

What he wished and what he meant in regard to her Mrs. Armine did not know. And just at this moment she scarcely cared. The return to the villa and the departure of the *Loulia* seemed to have fanned the fire within her. While she was on the *Loulia,* in an enclosed place, rather like a beautiful prison, she had succeeded in concentrating herself to a certain extent on matters in hand. She had had frightful hours of ennui and almost of despair, but she had got through them somehow. And she had been in command.

Now Nigel had been taken forcibly out of her hands, and the beautiful prison was no more theirs. And this return to the home which had seen the opening of her life in Egypt strangely excited her. Once again the *Loulia* lay there where she had lain when Baroudi was on board of her; once again from the bank of the Nile Mrs. Armine heard the song of Allah in the distance, as on that night when she heard it first, and it was a serenade to her. But how much had happened between then and now!

Now in the house behind her there were two men—the man who did not know her and loved her, and the man who did know her and hated her.

But the man who knew her, and who had wanted her just as she was—he was not there.

She felt that she must see him again, quickly, that she must tell him all that had happened since she had set sail on the *Loulia.* And yet could she, dared she, leave Nigel alone with Meyer Isaacson?

She paced again on the sand, passing and repassing in front of the darkness of the bushes.

When Isaacson had stood before her in the temple of Edfou, she had had a moment of absolute terror—such a moment as can only come once in a life. A period of fear and of struggle, of agony even, had followed. Yet in that period there had been no moment quite so frightful. For she had confronted the known, not the utterly unexpected, and she had been fighting, and still she must fight.

But she must have a word from Baroudi, a look from Baroudi. Without these, she felt as if she might—as if she must do something stupid or desperate. She was coming to the end of her means, to the limit of her powers, perhaps.

The hardest blow she had had as yet had been Doctor Hartley's escape out of the circle of her influence. That escape had weakened her self-confidence, had been a catastrophe surely grimly prophetic of other catastrophes to come. It had even put into her mind a doubt that was surely absurd.

Suppose Nigel were to emancipate himself!

If he were gone, she would care nothing. She would not want Nigel to regret her. If she were gone, in a day he would be as one dead to her. He meant nothing to her except a weight that dragged upon her, keeping her from all that she was fitted for, from all that she desired. But while she remained with Nigel, her influence must be paramount. For Isaacson was at his elbow to take advantage of every opening. And she was sure Isaacson would give her no mercy, if once he got Nigel on his side.

What was she to do? What was she to do?

Secretly she cursed with her whole heart now the coldly practical, utterly self-interested side of Baroudi's nature. But she was afraid to defy it. She remembered his words:

"We have to do what we want in the world without losing anything by it."

And she saw him—how often!—going in at the tent-door through which streamed light, to join the painted odalisque.

She was reaching the limit of her endurance. She felt that strongly to-night.

On the day of their return to the villa Hamza had mysteriously left them, without a word.

Two or three times Nigel had asked for him. She had said at first that he had gone to see his family. Afterwards she had said that he stayed away because he was offended at not being allowed any more to wait upon his master: "Doctor Isaacson's orders, you know!" And Nigel had answered nothing. Where was Hamza? Mrs. Armine had asked Ibrahim. But Ibrahim, without a smile, had answered that he knew nothing of Hamza, and in Mrs. Armine's heart had been growing the hope that Hamza had gone to seek Baroudi, that perhaps he would presently return with a message from Baroudi.

And yet could any good, any happiness, ever come to her through the praying donkey-boy? Always she instinctively connected him with fatality, with evil followed by sorrow. The look in his eyes when they were turned upon her seemed like a quiet but steady menace. She had a secret conviction that he hated her, perhaps because she was what he would call a Christian. Strange if she were really hated for such a reason!

Once more she stood still by the edge of the river.

She heard the sailors still singing on the *Loulia*, the faint barking of dogs, perhaps from the village of Luxor. She looked up at the stars mechanically, and remembered how Nigel had gazed at them when she had wanted him to be wholly intent upon her. Then she looked again, for a long time, at the blue light which shone from the *Loulia's* masthead.

Behind her the bushes rustled. She turned sharply round. Ibrahim came towards her from the tangled darkness.

"What are you doing here?" she asked him. She spoke almost roughly. The noise had startled her.

"My lady, you better come in," said Ibrahim. "Very lonely heeyah. No peoples comin' heeyah!"

She moved towards the bank. He put his hand gently under her elbow to assist her. When they were at the top she said:

"Where's Hamza, Ibrahim?"

Ibrahim's boyish face looked grim.

"I dunno, my lady. I know nothin' at all about Hamza."

For the first time it occurred to Mrs. Armine that Ibrahim and Hamza were no longer good friends. She opened her lips to make some enquiry about their relation. But she shut them again without saying anything, and in silence they walked to the house.

On the following morning, when Mrs. Armine looked out of her window, the *Loulia* still lay opposite. She took glasses to see if there was any movement of the crew suggestive of impending departure. But all seemed quiet. The men were squatting on the lower deck in happy idleness.

Then Baroudi must presently be coming.

She decided to be patient a little longer, not to make that excuse to go to Cairo. With the morning she felt, she did not know why, more able to endure present conditions.

But as day followed day and Baroudi made no sign, and the *Loulia* lay always by the western shore with the shutters closed over the cabin windows, the intense irritation of her nerves returned, and grew with each succeeding hour.

Isaacson had not gone to stay at an hotel, but had, as a matter of course, taken up his abode at the villa, and he continued to live there. She was obliged to see him perpetually, obliged to behave to him with politeness, if not with suavity. His watch over Nigel was tireless. The rule he had made at the beginning of his stay was not relaxed. Nigel was not allowed to take anything from any hand but the Doctor's.

The relation between Doctor and patient was still a curious and even an awkward one. Although Nigel's trust in the Doctor was absolute, he had never returned to his former pleasant intimacy with his friend. At first Isaacson had secretly anticipated a gradual growth of personal confidence, had thought that as weakness declined, as a little strength began to bud out almost timidly in the poor, tormented body, Nigel would revert, perhaps unconsciously, to a happier or more friendly mood. But though the Doctor was offered the gratitude of the patient, the friend was never offered the cordiality of the friend.

Bella Donna's influence was stubborn. Between these two men the woman always stood, dividing them, even now when the one was ministering to the other, was bringing the other back to life, was giving up everything for the other.

For this prolonged stay in Egypt was likely to prove a serious thing to Isaacson. Not only was he losing much money by it now. Probably, almost certainly, he would lose money by it in the future. There were moments when he thought about this with a secret vexation. But they passed, and quickly. He had his reward in the growing strength of the sick man. Yet sometimes it was difficult to bear the almost stony reserve which took the colour out of his life in the Villa Androud. It would have been more difficult still if he too, like Bella Donna, had not had his work to do in the dark. Since they had arrived in Luxor he had been seeking for a motive. The moment came when at last he found it.

Prompted by him, Hassan played upon Ibrahim's indignation at having been supplanted for so long by Hamza, and drew from him the truth of Mrs. Armine's days while Nigel had been away in the Fayyūm.

Isaacson's treatment of Nigel's case had succeeded wonderfully. As the great heats began to descend upon Upper Egypt, the health of the invalid improved day by day. Mrs. Armine saw life returning into the eyes that had expressed a sick weariness of an existence suddenly overcast by the cloud of suffering. The limbs moved more easily as a greater vitality was shed through the body. The nights were no longer made a torment by the acute rheumatic pains. The parched mouth and throat craved no more perpetually for the cooling drinks that had not allayed their misery. Light could be borne without any grave discomfort, and the agonizing abdominal pains, which had made the victim writhe and almost desire death, had entirely subsided. From the face, too, the dreadful hue which had even struck those who had only seen Nigel casually had nearly departed. Though still very thin and pale, it did not look unnatural. It was now the face of a man who had recently suffered, and suffered much; it was not a face that suggested the grave.

Nigel would recover, was fast recovering. He would not be strong for a time, perhaps for a long time. But he was "out of the wood." One day he realized it, and told himself so, silently, with a sort of wonder mingled with a joy half solemn, half lively with the liveliness of the spirit that again felt the touch of youth.

The day that he realized it was the day that Isaacson found the motive he had in the dark been seeking.

And on that day, too, Mrs. Armine told herself that she could endure no longer. She must get away to Cairo, if only for two or three days. If Baroudi was not there, she must go to Alexandria and seek him. Baffled desire, enforced patience, the perpetual presence of Meyer Isaacson, with whom she was obliged to keep up a pretence of civility and even of gratitude, and the jealousy that grows like a rank weed in the soil of ignorance, rendered her at last almost reckless. She was sure if she remained longer in the villa she would betray herself by some sudden outburst. Isaacson had kept silence so long as to the cause of her husband's illness that she sometimes nearly deceived herself into thinking he did not know what it was. Perhaps she had been a fool to be so much afraid of him. She strove to think so, and nearly succeeded.

The *Loulia* lay always by the western shore of the Nile, but each night, when she looked from the garden, the cabin windows were dark. She had made enquiries of Ibrahim. But Ibrahim was no longer the smiling, boyish attendant who had been her slave. He performed his duties carefully, and was always elaborately polite, but he had an air of secrecy, of uneasiness, and almost of gloom, and when she mentioned Baroudi, he said:

"My lady, I know nothin'."

"Well, but on the *Loulia?*" she persisted. "The Reis—the crew——?"

"They knows nothin'. Nobody heeyah know nothin' at all."

Then she resolved to wait no longer, but to go and find out for herself. Perhaps it was the look of returning life in the eyes of her husband which finally decided her.

She came out on to the terrace where he was stretched in a long chair under an awning. A book lay on one of the arms of the chair, but he was not reading it. He was just lying there and looking out to the garden, and to the hills that edge the desert of Libya. Isaacson was not with him. He had gone away somewhere, perhaps for a stroll on the bank of the Nile.

Mrs. Armine sauntered up, with an indolent, careless air, and sat down near her husband.

"Dreaming?" she said, in her sweetest voice.

He shook his head.

"Waking!" he answered. "Waking up to life."

"You do look much stronger to-day."

"Stronger than yesterday?" he said, eagerly. "You think so? You notice it, Ruby?"

"Yes."

"That's strange. To-day I—I know that all is going to be right with me. To-day I know that presently—Ruby, think of it!—I shall be the man I once was."

"And I know it, too, Nigel—to-day—and that is why at last I feel I can ask you something."

"Anything—anything. I would do anything to please you after all this time of misery, and dulness for you!"

"It's a prosaic little request I have to make. I only want you to let me take the night train and run up to Cairo."

His face fell. He stretched out his hand to touch hers.

"Go away! Go to Cairo!" he said.

And his voice was reluctant.

"Yes, Nigel," she said, with gentle firmness. "I've

been looking over my wardrobe these last days, and I'm simply in rags."

"But your dresses——"

"It's not only my dresses—I really am in rags. Won't you let me go just for two days to get a few things I actually need? I'm not going to spend a lot of money."

"As if it was that!"

He pressed her hand, and his pressure showed his returning strength.

"It's being without you."

"For two days. And you'll have Doctor Isaacson. I want to go while he is still with us, so as not to leave you alone. And Nigel, while I'm gone, can't you manage to find out what we owe him? It must be an enormous sum."

Nigel suddenly looked preoccupied.

"I'd never thought of that," he said, slowly.

"No, because you've been ill. But I have often. And you must think of it now."

"Yes; he's saved my life. I can never really repay him."

"Oh, yes, you can. Doctors do these things for fixed sums, you know."

He shifted in his chair, and sent an uneasy glance to her.

"I wish—how I wish that you and Isaacson could be better friends!" he dropped out, at length.

"After all I've told you!" she exclaimed, almost with bitterness.

"I know, I know. But now that he's saved my life!"

"There are some things a woman can never forget, Nigel. I—of course, I am deeply grateful to Meyer Isaacson, the doctor. But Meyer Isaacson the man I never can be friends with. I must always tell you the truth, even if it hurts you."

"Yes, yes."

"While I'm in Cairo, find out what we owe him. For I suppose now you feel so much better he won't remain with us for ever."

"No, of course he must be wanting to go."

He spoke with hesitation. With the blameless selfishness of a sick man, he had taken a great deal for granted. She was making him feel that now. And he had to take it all in. How he depended on Isaacson! He looked at his wife. And how he depended on her, too! He was conscious again of his weakness, almost as a child might be. And these two human beings upon whom he was leaning were at enmity, not open but secret enmity. He did not know exactly how, or how much! But Ruby had told him often —things about Meyer Isaacson. And he knew that Isaacson had mistrusted her, and felt that he did so still.

"I may go, then?" she said.

He could not in reason forbid her. He thought of her long service.

"Of course, dearest, go. But surely you aren't going to-night?"

"If you'll let me. I shall only take a bag. And the sooner I go, the sooner I shall be back.'

"In two days?"

"In two days."

"And where will you stay?"

"At Shepheard's."

"I don't like your going alone. I wish you had a maid——"

"You've guessed it!" she said.

"What?"

He looked almost startled.

"I didn't like to tell you, but I will now. May I have a maid again?"

"That's what you want, to get a maid?"

She smiled, and looked almost shy.

"I've done splendidly without one. But still——"

From that moment he only pressed, begged her to go.

Isaacson returned to find it was all settled. When he was told, he only said, "I think it wonderful that Mrs. Armine has managed without a maid for so long."

Soon afterwards he went to his room, and was shut in

there for a considerable time. He said he had letters to write. Yet he sent no letters to the post that day.

Meanwhile Mrs. Armine, with the assistance of one of the Nubians, was packing a few things. Now that at last she was going to do something definite, she marvelled that she had been able to endure her life of waiting so long. This movement and planning in connection with a journey roused in her a secret excitement that was feverish.

"If only I were going away for ever!" she thought, as she went about her dressing-room. "If only I were never to see my husband and Isaacson again!"

And with that thought she paused and stood still.

Suppose it really were so! Suppose she found Baroudi, told him all that had happened, told him her misery, begged him to let her remain with him! He might be kind. He might for once yield to her wishes instead of imposing upon her his commands. There would be a great scandal; but what of that? She did not care any longer for public opinion. She only wanted now to escape from all that reminded her of Europe, of her former life, to sink into the bosom of the East and be lost in it for ever. The far future was nothing to her. All she thought about, all she cared for, was to escape at once and have the one thing she wanted, the thing for which the whole of her clamoured unceasingly. She was obsessed by the one idea, as only the woman of her temperament, arrived at her critical age, can be obsessed.

She might never come back. This might be her last day with Nigel.

In his room near to hers, Isaacson was sitting on his balcony, smoking the nargeeleh, and thinking that, too. He was not at all sure, but he was inclined to believe that this departure of Bella Donna was going to be a flight. Ought he to allow her to go? Instead of writing those letters, he was pondering, considering this. It was his duty, he supposed, not to allow her to go. If everything were to be known, people, the world would say that he ought to have acted already, that in any case he ought to act now. But he was not bothering about the world. He was thinking of his friend, how to do the best thing by him.

When he took his long fingers from the nargeeleh he had decided that he would let Bella Donna go.

And that evening, a little before sunset, she kissed her husband and bade him good-bye, wondering whether she would ever see him again. Then she held out her hand to Meyer Isaacson.

"Good-bye, Doctor! Take great care of him," she said, lightly.

Isaacson took her hand. Again now, at this critical moment, despite his afternoon's decision, he said to himself, not only "Ought I to let her go?" but "Shall I let her go?" And the influence of the latter question in his mind caused him unconsciously to grasp her hand arbitrarily, as if he meant to detain her. Instantly there came into her eyes the look he had seen in them when in the sanctuary of Edfou she had stood face to face with him—a look of startled terror.

"You promise only to stay two days, Ruby?"

Nigel's voice spoke.

"You promise?"

"I promise faithfully, Nigel," she said, with her eyes on Isaacson.

Isaacson dropped her hand. She sighed, and went out quickly.

XLII

THE departure of Mrs. Armine brought to Meyer Isaacson a sudden and immense feeling of relief. When he looked at his watch and knew that the train for Cairo had left the station of Luxor, when half an hour later Ibrahim came in to tell Nigel that "my lady" had gone off "very nice indeed," he was for a time almost joyous, as a man is joyous who has got rid of a heavy burden, or who is unexpectedly released from some cruel prison of circumstance. How much the enforced companionship with Mrs. Armine had oppressed him he understood fully now. And it was difficult for him to realize, more difficult still for him to sympathize with, Nigel's obvious regret at his wife's going, obvious longing for her to be back again by his side.

Isaacson's sympathy was not asked for by Nigel. Here the strong reserve existing between the two men naturally stepped in. Isaacson strove to dissimulate his joy, Nigel to dissimulate his feeling of sudden loneliness. But either Isaacson played his part the better, or his powers of observation were far more developed than Nigel's; for whereas he saw with almost painful clearness the state of his friend's mind on that first evening of their dual solitude, Nigel only partially guessed at his, or very faintly suspected it.

Their dinner together threatened at first to be dreary. For Mrs. Armine's going, instead of breaking down, had consolidated for the moment the reserve between them. But Isaacson's inner joyousness, however carefully concealed, made its influence felt, as joy will. Without quite knowing why, Nigel presently began to thaw. Isaacson turned the conversation, which had stumbled, had halted, to Nigel's condition of health, and then Nigel said, as he had already said to his wife:

"To-day I feel that I am waking up to life."

"Only to-day?" said the Doctor.

"Oh, I've been feeling better and better, but to-day it's as if a door that had been creaking on its hinges was flung wide open."

"I'm not surprised. These sudden leaps forward are often a feature of convalescence."

"They—they aren't followed by falling back, are they?" Nigel asked, with a sudden change to uneasiness.

"Sometimes, in fever cases especially. But in a case like yours we needn't anticipate anything of that kind."

The last words seemed to suggest to Nigel some train of thought, and after sitting in silence two or three minutes, looking grave and rather preoccupied, he said:

"By the way, what has been the matter with me,

exactly? What have I really had in the way of an illness? All this time I've been so occupied in being ill that I've never asked you."

The last words were said with an attempt at lightness.

"Have I?" he added.

"No, I don't think you have," said Isaacson, in a voice that suggested a nature at that moment certainly not inclined to be communicative.

"Has it been all sunstroke? But—but I'm sure it hasn't."

"No, I shouldn't put it down entirely to sunstroke. Hartley wasn't quite right there, I think."

"Well, then?"

Nigel had found a safe topic for conversation, or thought he had. It was sufficiently evident that he felt more at ease, and perhaps he was atoning for former indifference as to the cause of his misery by a real and keen interest about it now.

"You were unwell, you see, before you went out digging without a hat. Weren't you?"

"Yes, that bath in the Nile near Kous. It seemed all to begin somewhere about then. But d'you know, though I've never said so, even to you, I believe I really was not quite myself when I took that dip. I think it was because of that I got the chill."

"Very possibly."

"When I started, I was splendidly well. I mean when we went on board of the *Loulia*. It's as if it was something to do with that boat. I believe I began to go down the hill very soon after we started on her. But it was all so gradual that I scarcely noticed anything at first. My bath made things worse, and then the digging fairly finished me."

"Ah!"

The last course of the very light dinner was put on the table. Isaacson poured out some Vichy water and began to squeeze the juice of half a lemon into it. Nigel sat watching the process, which was very careful and deliberate.

"You don't tell me what exactly has been the matter," he said, at last.

"You've had such a complication of symptoms."

"That you mean it's impossible to give a name that covers them all?"

Isaacson squeezed the last drop almost tenderly into the tumbler, took up his napkin, and carefully dried his long, brown fingers.

" 'What's in a name?' " he quoted.

He looked across the table at Nigel, and questions seemed to be shining in his eyes.

"Do you mean that you don't want to tell me the name?" Nigel said.

It seemed that he was roused to persistence. Either curiosity or some other feeling was awakened within him.

"I don't say that. But you know we doctors often go cautiously—we don't care to commit ourselves."

"Hartley, yes. But that isn't true of you."

He paused.

"You are hedging," he said, bluntly.

Isaacson drank the Vichy and lemon. He put down the glass.

"You are hedging," Nigel repeated. "Why?"

"Isn't it enough for you to get well? What good will it do you to know what you have been suffering from?"

"Good! But isn't it natural that I should wish to know? Why should there be any mystery about it?"

He stopped. Then, leaning forward a little with one arm on the table, he said:

"Does my wife know what it is?"

"I've never told her," Isaacson answered.

"Well, but does she know?"

The voice that asked was almost suspicious. And the eyes that regarded Isaacson were now suspicious, too.

"How can I tell? She told me she supposed it to be a sunstroke."

"That was Hartley's nonsense. Hartley put that idea into her head. But since you came, of course she's realized there was more in it than that."

"I dare say."

Nigel waited, as if expecting something more. But Isaacson kept silence. Dinner was over. Nigel got up, and walking steadily, though not yet with the brisk lightness of complete strength and buoyancy, led the way to the drawing-room.

"Shall we sit out on the terrace?"

"If you like. But you must have a coat. I'll fetch it."

"Oh, don't you——"

But the doctor was gone. In a moment he returned with a coat and a light rug. He helped Nigel to put the coat on, took him by the arm, led him out to the chair, and, when he was in it, arranged the rug over his knees.

"You're awfully good to me, Isaacson," Nigel said, almost with softness, "awfully good to me. I am grateful."

"That's all right."

"We were speaking about it only to-day, Ruby and I. She was saying that we mustn't presume on your kindness, that we mustn't detain you out here now that I'm out of the wood."

"She wants to get rid of me! Then she must be coming back!" The thought darted through Isaacson's brain, upsetting a previously formed conviction which, to a certain extent, had guided his conduct during dinner.

"Oh, I'm in no hurry," he said, carelessly. "I want to get you quite strong."

"Yes, but your patients in London! You know I've been feeling so ill that I've been beastly selfish. I've thought only of myself. I've made a slave of my wife, and now I've been keeping you out of London all this time."

As he spoke, his voice grew warmer. His reserve seemed to be melting, the friend to be stirring in the patient. Although certainly he did not realize it, the absence of his wife had already made a difference in his feeling towards Isaacson. Her perpetual silent hostility was like an emanation that insensibly affected her husband. Now that was withdrawn to a distance, he reverted instinctively towards —not yet to—the old relation with his friend. He longed to get rid of all the difficulty between them, and this could only be done by making Isaacson understand Ruby more as he understood her. If he could only accomplish this before Ruby came back! Now this idea came to him, and sent warmth into his voice, warmth into his manner. Isaacson opened his lips to make some friendly protest, but Nigel continued:

"And d'you know who made me see my selfishness— realize how tremendously unselfish you've been in sticking to me all this time?"

Isaacson said nothing.

"My wife. She opened my eyes to it. But for her I mightn't have given a thought to all your loss, not only your material loss, but——"

Isaacson felt as if something poisonous had stung him.

"Please don't speak of anything of that kind!" he said.

"I know I can never compensate you for all you've done for us——"

"Oh, yes, you can!"

The Doctor's voice was almost sharp. Nigel was startled by it.

"We can? How?"

"You can!" Isaacson said, laying a heavy stress on the first word."

"How?"

"First, by never speaking to me of—of the usual 'compensation' patients make to doctors."

"But how can you expect me to accept all this devoted service and make no kind of return?"

"Perhaps you can make me a return—the only return I want."

"But what is it?"

"I—I won't tell you to-night."

"Then when will you tell me?"

Isaacson hesitated. His face was blazing with expression. He looked like a man powerfully stirred—almost like a man on the edge of some outburst.

"I won't tell you to-night," he repeated.

"But you must tell me."

"At the proper time. You asked me at dinner what had been the matter with you, what illness you had been suffering from. You observed that I didn't care to tell you then. Well, I'll tell you before you get rid of me."

"Get rid of you!"

"Yes, yes. Don't think I misunderstand what you've been trying to tell me to-night. You want to convey to me in a friendly manner that now I've accomplished my work it's time for me to be off."

Nigel was deeply hurt.

"Nothing of the sort!" he said. "It was only that my wife had made me understand what a terrible loss to you remaining out here at such a time must be."

"There is something I must make you understand, Armine, before I leave you. And when I've told you what it is, you can give me the only compensation I want, and I want it badly—badly!"

"And you won't tell me what it is now?"

"Not to-night—not in a hurry."

He got up.

"When are you expecting Mrs. Armine back?" he asked.

"In four nights. She wants a couple of full days in Cairo. Then there are the two night journeys."

"I'll tell you before she comes back."

Isaacson turned round, and strolled away into the darkness of the garden.

When he was alone there, he tacitly reproached himself for his vehemence of spirit, for the heat of his temper. Yet surely they were leading him in the right path. These words of Nigel had awakened him to the very simple fact that this association must come to an end, and almost immediately. He had been, he supposed now, drifting on from day to day, postponing any decision. Mrs. Armine was stronger than he. From her, through Nigel, had come to him this access of determination, drawn really from her decision. As he knew this, he was able secretly to admire for a moment this woman whom he actively hated. Her work in the dark would send him now to work in the light.

It was inevitable. While he had believed that very possibly her departure to Cairo was a flight from her husband, Isaacson had had a reason for his hesitation. If Bella Donna vanished, why torture Nigel further? Let him lose her, without knowing all that he had lost. But if she were really coming back, and if he, Isaacson, must go— and his departure in any case must shortly be inevitable— then, cost what it might, the truth must be told.

As he paced the garden, he was trying to brace himself to the most difficult, the most dreadful duty life had so far imposed upon him.

When he went back to the terrace, Nigel was no longer there. He had gone up to bed.

The next day passed without a word between the two men on the subject of the previous night. They talked on indifferent topics. But the cloud of mutual reserve once more enveloped them, and intercourse was uneasy.

Another day dawned.

Mrs. Armine had now been away for two nights, and, if she held to her announced plan, should leave Cairo on her return to Luxor on the evening of the following day. No letter had been received from her. The question in Isaacson's mind was, would she come back? If he spoke and she never returned, he would have stabbed his friend to the heart for no reason. But if she did return and he had not spoken?

He was the prey of doubt, of contending instincts. He did not know what to do. But deep down within him was there not a voice that, like the ground swell of the ocean, murmured ever one thing, unwearied, persistent?

Sometimes he was aware of this voice and strove not to hear it, or not to heed it, this voice in the depths of a man, telling him that in the speaking of truth there is strength, and that out of weakness no good ever came yet, nor ever will come till the end of all things.

But the telling of certain truths seems too cruel; and how can one be cruel to a man returning to life with almost hesitating steps?

Perhaps something would happen to decide the matter, something—some outside event. What it might be Isaacson could not say to himself. Indeed, it was almost childish to hope for anything. He knew that. And yet, unreasonably, he hoped.

And the event did happen, and on that day.

Late in the afternoon a telegram arrived for Nigel. Ibrahim brought it out to the terrace where the two men were together, and Nigel opened it with an eagerness he did not try to disguise.

"It's from her," he said. "She starts to-night, and will be here to-morrow morning early. She's in such a hurry to be back that she's only staying the one night in Cairo."

He looked across to Isaacson, who seemed startled.

"Is there anything the matter with you?" he asked.

"No. Why?"

"You don't look quite yourself."

"I feel perfectly well."

"Oh!"

Almost directly Isaacson made an excuse and got away. His decision was made. There was no more combat within him. But his heart was heavy, was sick, and he felt an acute and frightful nervousness, such as he could imagine being experienced by a man under sentence of death, who is not told on what day the sentence will be carried out. Apprehension fell over him like an icy rain in the sultry air.

He walked mechanically to the bank of the Nile.

To-day the water was like a sheet of glass, dimpled here and there by the wayward currents, and, because of some peculiar atmospheric effect, perhaps, the river looked narrower than usual, the farther bank less far off. Never before had Isaacson been so forcibly struck by the magical clearness of Egypt. Even in the midst of his misery, a misery which physically affected him, he stood still to marvel and to admire.

How near everything looked! How startlingly every detail of things stood out in this exquisite evening!

Presently his eyes went to the *Loulia*. She, too, looked strangely near, strangely distinct. He watched her, only because of that at first, but presently because he began to notice an unusual bustle on board. Men were moving rapidly about both on the lower and on the upper deck, were going here and there ceaselessly.

One man swarmed up the long and bending mast. Another clambered over the balcony-rail into the stern.

What did all this movement mean?

The master of the *Loulia* must surely be expected—the man Isaacson had seen driving the Russian horses, and, clothed almost in rags, squatting in the darkness of the hashish café in the entrails of Cairo.

And Bella Donna was hurrying back after only one night in Cairo!

Isaacson forgot the marvellous beauty of the declining day. In a few minutes he returned to the house. But immediately after dinner, leaving Nigel sitting on the terrace, he went again to the bank of the Nile.

The *Loulia* was illuminated from prow to stern. Light gleamed from every cabin window, and the crew had not only the daraboukkeh but the pipes on board, and were making the fantasia. Some of them, too, were dancing. Against a strong light on the lower deck, Isaacson saw black figures, sometimes relieved for a moment, moving with a wild grotesqueness, like crazy shadows.

He stood for several minutes listening, watching. He thought of a train travelling towards Luxor. Then he went quickly across the garden, and came to the terrace and Nigel.

The deep voice within him must be obeyed. He could resist it no longer.

"They're lively on the *Loulia* to-night," Nigel said, as he came up.

"Yes," Isaacson answered.

He stood while he lighted a cigar. Then he sat down near to his friend. The light from the drawing-room streamed out upon them from the open French window. The shrill sound of the pipes, the dull throbbing of the daraboukkeh, came to them from across the water.

"The whole vessel is lighted up," he added.

"Is she? Perhaps Baroudi has come up the river."

"Looks like it," said Isaacson.

He crossed, then uncrossed his legs. Never before had he felt himself to be a coward. He knew what he must do. He knew he would do it before Nigel and he went into the room behind them. Yet he could not force himself to begin. He thought, "When I've smoked out this cigar."

"You've never seen Baroudi," Nigel said. "He's one of the handsomest fellows I've ever clapped eyes on. As strong as a bull, I should think; enormously rich. A very good chap, too, I should say. But I don't fancy my wife liked him. He's hardly a woman's man."

"Why d'you think that?"

"I don't know. His manner, perhaps. And he doesn't seem to bother about them. But we only saw him about twice, except on the ship coming out. He dined here one night, and the next day we went over the *Loulia* with him, and we've never set eyes on him since. He went up river, and we went down, to the Fayyūm."

"But—but you went off alone to the Fayyûm, didn't you? At first, I mean?"

"Oh, yes. The morning after Baroudi had sailed for Armant."

"And Mrs. Armine was alone here for some time?"

"Yes. Just while I was getting things a little ship-shape for her. But we didn't have much luxury after all. However, she didn't mind that."

"Wasn't—don't you think it may have been rather dull for Mrs. Armine during that time?"

"Which time? D'you mean in the Fayyūm?"

"I mean, while you were away in the Fayyūm."

"I dare say it was. I expect it was. But why?"

"Well——"

Isaacson threw away his cigar.

"Not going to finish your cigar?" said Nigel.

He was evidently beginning to be surprised by his friend's words and manner.

"No," Isaacson said. "I don't want to smoke to-night; I want to talk. I must talk to you. You remember our conversation on the night of Mrs. Armine's departure?"

"About my illness?"

"Yes."

"Of course I do."

"I said then that I wouldn't accept the usual money compensation for anything I had been able to do for you."

"Yes, but——"

"And I told you you could compensate me in another way."

"What way?"

"That's what I'm going to try and tell you now. But—but it's not easy. I want you to understand—I want you to understand."

There was a moment of silence. Then Nigel said:

"But what? Understand what?"

"Armine, do you believe thoroughly in my friendship for you?"

"Yes."

"You believe, you know, it's a friendship that is quite disinterested?"

"I'm sure it is."

"And yet you have treated me all this time with almost as much reserve as if I had been a mere acquaintance."

Nigel looked uncomfortable.

"I didn't mean—I am deeply grateful to you," he said; "deeply grateful. You have saved my life."

"I have, indeed," Isaacson said, solemnly. "If I had not followed you up the river, you would certainly have died."

"Are you—you said you would tell me what was the matter with me."

"I'm going to."

"What was it?"

"The bath at Kous had nothing to do with it. As to sunstroke, you never had it. You began to feel unwell—didn't you?—soon after you started for your voyage?"

"Yes."

"Hasn't it ever struck you as very strange that you, a young man in magnificent health, living an outdoor life in one of the finest climates in the world, should be struck down by this mysterious illness?"

"Mysterious?"

"Well, wasn't it?"

"It was very odd. I always thought that, of course."

He leaned forward a little in his chair, fixing his eyes on Isaacson.

"What was my illness?"

"You've been suffering from lead-poisoning," said Isaacson, slowly, and with an effort.

"Lead?"—Nigel leaned farther forward, moving his hands along the arms of his reclining chair—"lead-poisoning?"

"Yes."

"I've been—you say I've been poisoned?"

"Poisoned from day to day, gradually poisoned through a considerable period of time."

"Poisoned!"

Nigel repeated the word heavily, almost dully. For a moment he seemed dazed.

"If I had not arrived in time, you would have been killed, undoubtedly."

"Killed! But—but who, in the name of God, should want to kill me?"

Isaacson was silent.

"I say, who should want to kill me?" reiterated Nigel.

And this time there was a sound of violence in his voice.

"There was somebody on board of the *Loulia* who must have wished for your death."

"But who—who? The Nubians? Ibrahim? Hamza?"

Isaacson did not answer. He could not answer at that moment.

"I treated them well, I paid them well, they had everything they could possibly want. They had an easy time. They all seemed fond of us. They were fond of us. I know they were."

"I don't say they were not."

"Then what d'you mean? There was nobody else on board with me."

"Yes, there was."

"There was? Then I never saw him! Do you mean to say there was some one hidden on board? What are you talking about, Isaacson?"

He was becoming greatly, almost angrily excited.

"Armine, the compensation I want is this. I don't want to clear out and leave you here in Egypt; I want to take you away with me."

"Take me away? Where to?"

"Anywhere—back to England."

"We are going to England as soon as I'm quite strong. But you haven't told me! You say I've been poisoned. I want to know by whom."

*   *   *   *   *   *

"But perhaps you don't know! Do you know?"

Isaacson got up. He felt as if he could not speak any more sitting down.

"If you will only give me my compensation, let me take you away quietly—I'm a doctor. Nobody will think anything of it—I need say nothing more."

"Take me away! But I'm nearly well now, and there can be no more danger."

"If you come away with me—no!"

"But you forget, I'm not alone. I must consult my wife."

"That is what I don't wish you to do."

"Don't? You mean, go away with you without——?"

"I mean, without Mrs. Armine."

"Leave my wife?"

"Yes."

"Leave Ruby? Desert her after all she's done for me?"

"Yes."

"Why?"

Isaacson said nothing.

Nigel looked at Isaacson in silence for what seemed to Isaacson a long time—minutes. Then his face slowly flushed, was suffused with blood up to his forehead. It seemed to swell, as if there was a pressure from within outwards. Then the blood retreated, leaving behind it a sort of dark pallor, and the eyes looked sunken in their sockets.

"You—you dare to think—you dare to—to say——?" he stammered.

"I say that you must come away from Mrs. Armine. Don't ask me to say why."

"You—you liar! You damnable liar!"

He spoke slowly, in a low, husky voice.

"That you hated her, I knew that! She told me that. But that you—that you should dare to——"

His voice broke, and he stopped. He leaned forward in his chair and made a gesture.

"Go!" he said. "Get out! If I—if I were myself, I'd put you out."

But Isaacson did not move. He felt no anger, nothing but a supreme pity for this man who could not see, could not understand the truth of a nature with which he had held commune for so long, and, as he in his blindness believed, in such a perfect intimacy. There was to the Doctor something shocking in such blindness, in such ignorance. But there was something beautiful, too. And to destroy beauty is terrible.

"If I am to go, you must hear me first," he said, quietly.

"I won't hear you—not one word!"

Again there was the gesture towards the door.

"I have saved your life," Isaacson said. "And you shall hear me!"

And then, without waiting for Nigel to speak again, very quietly, very steadily, and with a great simplicity he told him what he had to tell. He did not, even now, tell him all. He kept secret the visit of Mrs. Chepstow to his consulting-room, and her self-revelation there. And he did not mention Baroudi. At this moment of crisis the man bred up in England fought against the Eastern Jew within Isaacson, and the Eastern Jew gave way. But he described his visits to the Savoy, how the last time he had gone with the resolution to beg Mrs. Chepstow not to go to Egypt, not to link herself with his friend; how he had begun to speak, and how her cold irony, pitiless and serene, had shown him the utter futility of his embassy. Then he came on to the later time, after the marriage and the departure, when he received his friend's letter describing his happiness and his wonderful health, when he received soon afterwards that other letter from the lady patient, speaking of Nigel's "extraordinary colour." He told how in London he had put those letters side by side and had compared them, and how some strong instinct of trouble and danger had driven him, almost against his will, to Egypt, had bound him to silence about his arrival. Then on the terrace at Shepheard's an acquaintance casually met had increased his fears. And so, in his quick, terse, unembroidered narrative, almost frightfully direct, he reached the scene in the temple of Edfou. From that moment he spared Nigel no detail. He described Mrs. Armine's obvious terror at his appearance; her lies, her omission to tell him her husband was ill until she realized that he—Isaacson—had already heard of the illness in Luxor; her pretence that his dangerous malady was only a slight indisposition caused by grief at the death of Lord Harwich; her endeavor to prevent Isaacson from coming on board the *Loulia;* the note she had sent by the felucca; his walk by night on the river bank till he came to the dahabeeyah, his eavesdropping, and how the words he overheard decided him to insist on seeing Nigel; the interview with Mrs. Armine in the saloon, and how he had forced his way, by a stratagem, to the after part of the vessel. Then he told of the contest with Doctor Hartley, already influenced by Mrs. Armine, and of the final victory, won—how? By a threat, which could only have frightened a guilty woman.

"I told Mrs. Armine that either I took charge of your case or that I communicated with the police authorities. Then, and only then, she gave way. She let me come on board to nurse you back to life."

"How could you have known?" Nigel exclaimed, with intensely bitter defiance, when at last a pause came. "Even if it had been true, how could you have known?"

"I did not know. I suspected. To save you, I drew a bow at a venture, and I hit the mark. Your illness has been caused by the administration, through a long period of time, of minute doses of some preparation of lead—almost impalpable doubtless, perhaps not to be distinguished from the sand that is blown from the desert. And Mrs. Armine either herself gave or caused it to be given to you."

"Liar! Liar!"

"Did she ever herself give you food? Did she ever prepare your coffee?"

Nigel started up in his chair with a furious spasm of energy.

"Go! Go!" he uttered, in a sort of broken shout or cry. His face was yellowish white. His mouth was working.

"By God! I'll put you out!"

Grasping the arms of his chair, he stood up and he advanced upon Isaacson.

"I'll go. But I'll leave you that!"

And Isaacson drew from his pocket the letter Mrs. Armine had sent by the felucca, and laid it on the coffee-table.

Then he turned quickly, and went away through the dark garden.

Before he was out of sight of the house, he looked back. Nigel had sunk upon his chair in a collapsed attitude.

From the western bank of the Nile came the shrill,

attenuated sound of the pipes, the deep throbbing of the daraboukkeh, the nasal chant of the Nubians.

And the lights of the *Loulia* were like a line of fiery eyes staring across the Nile.

XLIII

WHEN Mrs. Armine got into the night train at Luxor, heard the whistle of the engine, felt the first slow movement of the carriage, then the gradually increasing velocity, saw the houses of the village disappearing, and presently only the long plains and the ranges of mountains to right and left, hard and clear in the evening light, she had a moment of almost savage exultation, as of one who had been in great danger suddenly and unexpectedly escaping into freedom.

At last she was alone, unwatched by the eyes of affection and of perhaps menacing suspicion and even hatred. How had she endured so long? She wondered, and could scarcely tell where she had found her courage. But though now she felt exultation, she felt also the tremendous strain she had undergone. She knew that her nerves were shattered. Only in happiness could she recover. She must have the life she wanted, and she must have it now. Otherwise she was "done for." Was she going to have it?

And soon the exultation passed, and again fear beset her. Even if she found Baroudi in Cairo, what reception would she have at his hands?

With anxious fingers she took out of her dressing-case the gilded box he had given her, and opened the lid. But, having opened it, she dared not look at herself in the glass, and she shut it sharply, replaced it in the case, and leaned back in her corner.

"I won't bother," she said to herself; "I won't worry. To-night I must sleep. I must look my best to-morrow. Everything now may depend on how I look when I get to Cairo."

And she shut her eyes with the determination to be calm, to be tranquil. And soon she went to bed, determined to sleep.

But of course she did not sleep. Quietly, then angrily, she strove to lay hold on sleep. But it would not come to her wooing. The long hours of darkness wore gradually away; the first pale light of the new day crept in to the rocking carriage; the weary woman who had been tossing and turning from side to side, in a sort of madness of restrained and attenuated movement, sat up against her crushed pillow, and knew that there was probably some new line on her face, an accentuation of the sharpness of the cheek-bones, a more piteous droop at the corners of the mouth.

As she sat there, with her knees drawn up and her hands hanging, she felt that she was uglier than she had been only the day before.

When the train reached Cairo, she pulled down her veil, got out, and drove to Shepheard's. She knew an address that would find Baroudi in Cairo, if he were there, and directly she was in her room she sat down and wrote a note to him.

"SHEPHEARD'S HOTEL, Tuesday morning.

"I have come to Cairo for a day's shopping. Can I see you? If so, please tell me where and at what hour.

"RUBY ARMINE."

She wrote in French, sealed the envelope, and told the waiter to have it taken at once by a messenger. Then she ordered coffee and rolls to be sent in half an hour, and took a hot bath. How she wished that she had a clever maid with her! It was maddening to have no help except that of a clumsy Swiss housemaid, and she now saw, with horror, that she was haggard. She scarcely recognized her own face. Instead of looking younger than she was, it seemed to her now that she looked older, much older. She was shocked by her appearance.

But she had had a night journey and had not slept,

and every woman looks old after a night journey. She would be all right when she had rested. On arriving she had engaged a sitting-room. She went into it and had breakfast, then asked for newspapers, and lay down on the sofa to read. At every moment she expected the return of her messenger to Baroudi. He came at last.

"Have you brought a note?" she asked, starting up on the sofa.

The messenger said no; the gentleman was not in.

"Did you leave the note?"

"Yes, ma'am."

"You can go back presently. Go back at twelve, and see if the gentleman has come in. He may come in for lunch. Stay till lunch-time and see. I want an answer."

The man went away. Slowly the morning passed. Twelve o'clock came, but the messenger did not return. Mrs. Armine had lunch in her room, but she could scarcely eat anything. After lunch she ordered very strong coffee. As she was drinking her second cup, there was a tap on the door. She cried, "Come in," and the messenger reappeared.

"Well?" she said. "Well?"

The man looked at her as if her voice had startled him.

"The gentleman has not come in, ma'am."

"When is he coming in?"

"I don't know, ma'am."

"Is he in Cairo?"

"I don't know, ma'am."

"What do you know? What's the good of you? What are you here for? Go back at once, and find out whether the gentleman is in Cairo or not."

The messenger went out rather hurriedly.

Mrs. Armine was shaking. She had felt inclined to attack the man, to beat him for his stupidity, as slaves are often beaten by their masters when they do wrong. When she was alone, she uttered two or three incoherent exclamations. Her body was burning with a sort of cruel, dry heat. She felt parched all over. An hour passed, and at length she again heard a tap. The messenger came in, and very sulkily said:

"The gentleman was in Cairo last night, ma'am."

"What I want to know is whether he is in Cairo now!" she exclaimed, angrily.

"They don't know, ma'am."

"Don't know! They must know!"

"They don't know, ma'am."

"I tell you they must know!"

"They don't know, ma'am."

She sprang up, tingling. She didn't know what she was going to do, but as she faced him the expression in the messenger's eyes recalled her to a sense of the proprieties. Without another word, she gave him some money and turned her back on him. When she heard the door close, she no longer controlled herself, until suddenly once more she remembered her ravaged face.

She went into her bedroom and after half an hour she came out dressed for driving. She was resolved to go herself to Baroudi's house. After all these months of slavish obedience and of fear, something rose up within her, something that had passed for the moment beyond obedience and even beyond fear, that was fiercely determined, that was reckless of consequences. She engaged a victoria and drove to Baroudi's house. It was on the outskirts of Cairo, near the Nile, on the Island of Gezira. A garden surrounded it, enclosed by high walls and entered by tall gates of elaborately-wrought ironwork. These gates were shut and the coachman pulled up his horses. Inside, on the left, there was a lodge from which there now came a tall Arab. Mrs. Armine got quickly out of the carriage, passed the horses, and stood looking through the gate.

"Is Mahmoud Baroudi in Cairo?" she said, in French.

The Arab said something in Arabic.

"Is Baroudi Effendi in Cairo?" Mrs. Armine said in English.

"Yes, I think," replied the man, in careful English, speaking slowly.

"In the city?"

"I think."

She took her purse, opened it, and gave him some money.

"Where?"

"I dunno."

"When will he be back here?"

"I dunno."

She felt inclined to scream.

"Will he come back to-night, do you think?"

"I dunno. Sometimes stay in Cairo all night."

"But he has not gone away? He is not away from Cairo? He is in Cairo?"

"I s'pose."

They stood for a moment staring at each other through the dividing gate. The man's eyes were absolutely expressionless. He looked as if he were half asleep. Mrs. Armine turned away, and got into the carriage.

"Go back to Shepheard's."

The coachman smacked his whip. The horses trotted.

When she reached Shepheard's, she resolved to spend the whole afternoon upon the terrace. By chance Baroudi might come there. It was not at all improbable. She had heard it said that almost every one who was any one, in Cairo, either came to Shepheard's or might be seen passing by in the afternoon hours. She took an arm-chair near the railing, with a table beside it. She bought papers, a magazine, and sat there, sometimes pretending to read, but always looking, looking, at the men coming up and down the steps, at the men walking and driving by in the crowded street. Tea-time came. She ordered tea. She drank it slowly. Her head was aching. Her eyes were tired with examining so many faces of men. But still she watched, till evening began to fall and within the house behind her the deep note of a gong sounded, announcing the half-hour before dinner. What more could she do? Mechanically she began to gather the papers together. She supposed she must go in. The terrace was almost deserted. She was just about to get up, when two men, one English, the other

American, came up the steps and sat down at a table near her. One of these men was Starnworth, whom she did not know, and of whom she had never heard. He ordered an apéritif, and plunged into conversation with his companion. They talked about Cairo. Mrs. Armine sat still and listened. Starnworth began to describe the native quarters. Presently he spoke of the hashish café to which he had taken Isaacson. He told his friend where it was. Mrs. Armine heard the name of the street, Bab-el Meteira. Then he spoke of the rich Egyptians who frequented the café, and he mentioned the name of Baroudi. Almost immediately afterwards he and his companion got up and strolled into the hotel.

That night, quietly dressed and veiled, Mrs. Armine, accompanied by a native guide, made a pilgrimage into the strange places of the city; stayed long, very long, beneath the blackened roof of the café where the hashish was smoked. She was exhausted, yet she felt feverishly, almost crazily alive. She drank coffee after coffee. She watched the dreaming smokers, the dreaming dancers, till she seemed to be living in a nightmare, to be detached from earth and all things she had ever known till now.

But Baroudi did not come. And at last she returned through the dancing quarters, where her sense of nightmare deepened.

Again she did not sleep.

When day came, she felt really ill. Yet her body was still pulsing, her brain was still throbbing, with an activity that was like a fever within her. Directly after breakfast, which she scarcely touched, she again took a carriage and drove to Baroudi's house.

The sleepy Arab met her at the grille, and in an almost trembling voice she made enquiries.

"Gone away," was the reply.

"Gone? Where to?"

"Him gone to Luxor. Him got one dahabeeyah at Luxor."

"Gone to Luxor! When did he go?"

"We know last night."

"Did he get a note I sent him yesterday morning?"

The Arab shook his head.

"Not bin back heeyah at all."

Mrs. Armine telegraphed to the villa, and took the night train back to Luxor.

She arrived in the morning about nine, after another sleepless night. As she drove by the Winter Palace Hotel, she saw a man walking alone upon the terrace, and, to her great surprise, recognized Meyer Isaacson. He saw her—she was certain of that—but he immediately looked away, and did not take off his hat to her. Had she, or had she not, bowed to him? She did not know. But in either case his behaviour was very strange. And she could not understand why he was at the hotel. Had something happened at the villa? Almost before she had had time to wonder, the horses were pulled up at the gate.

She had expected Ibrahim to meet her at the station. But he had not come. Nor did he meet her at the gate, which was opened by the gardener. She nodded in reply to his salutation, hastened across the garden, and came into the house.

"Nigel!" she called out. "Nigel!"

She immediately heard a slow step, and saw her husband coming towards her from the drawing-room. She thought he looked very ill.

"Well, Ruby, you are back," he said.

He held out his hand. His eyes, which were curiously sunken, gazed into hers with a sort of wistful, yearning expression.

"Yes," she said. "I hurried. I couldn't stand Cairo It was hot and dreadful. And I felt miserable there."

They were standing in the little hall.

"You look fearfully tired—fearfully!" he said.

He was still holding her hand.

Her mouth twisted.

"Do I? It's the two night journeys. I didn't sleep at all."

"And the maid? Did you get one?"

"No. What does it matter?"

Infinitely unimportant to her now seemed such a quest.

"I must sit down," she added. "I'm nearly dead."

She really felt as if her physical powers were failing her. Her legs shook under her.

"Come into the drawing-room. And you must have some breakfast."

He let go her hand. She went into the drawing-room, and she sank down on a sofa. He followed almost immediately.

"Oh!" she said.

She leaned back against the cushions, stretched out her arms, and shut her eyes. All the time she was thinking, "Baroudi is here! Baroudi is here! And I can't go to him; I can't go—I can't go!"

She seemed to see his mighty throat, his eyebrows, slanting upwards above his great bold eyes, his large, muscular hands, his deep chest of an athlete.

She heard Nigel sitting down close to her.

"Why didn't Ibrahim come to the station?" she said, with an effort opening her eyes.

"Oh, I suppose he was busy," Nigel replied.

His voice sounded cautious and uneasy.

"Busy?"

"Yes. He'll bring your breakfast. I've told him to."

Then he was in the house. She felt a slight sense of relief, she scarcely knew why.

The door opened, and Ibrahim came in quietly and carefully with a tray.

"Good mornin' to you, my lady," he said.

"Good morning, Ibrahim."

He set down the tray without noise, stood for a minute as if considering it, then softly went away.

"You'll feel better when you've had breakfast."

"I ought to have had a bath first. But I couldn't wait."

She sat up in front of the little table, and poured out

the strong tea. As she did this, she glanced again at her husband and again thought how ill he looked. But she did not remark upon it. She drank some tea, and ate a piece of toast.

"Oh," she said, "as I passed by the Winter Palace, I saw Doctor Isaacson on the terrace."

"Did you?"

"Yes. What's he gone there for this morning?"

"I suppose he's staying there."

Mrs. Armine put down the cup she was lifting to her lips.

"Staying! Doctor Isaacson!" she said, staring at her husband.

"I suppose so."

"But—do you mean he has left here?"

"Yes. He went away last night."

"Why? Why?"

"Why? Well—well, we had a discussion. It ended in a disagreement, and he left the house."

"You quarrelled?"

"Yes, I suppose it might be called that."

In the midst of her exhaustion, her physical misery and mental distraction, Mrs. Armine was conscious of a sharp pang. It was like that of joy.

"Doctor Isaacson has left the house for good?" she said.

"Yes. He won't come here again."

She drank some more tea, and went on eating. For the first time for days she felt some appetite. A shock of fear that had assailed her had passed away. She remembered how Nigel had held her hand closely in the hall.

"But why did you quarrel?" she said, at last.

"Oh, we had a discussion——" He paused.

"I know," she said, "I know! You did what I asked you to do. You spoke about being strong enough now to let Doctor Isaacson go back to London."

"Yes, I did that."

"And about what we owed him?"

"Yes."

"And he was angry?"

"I had been speaking of that; and——Ruby, what do we owe him? I—I must send him a cheque. I must send it to him to-night."

She shrugged her shoulders.

"I don't know. He'll open his mouth very wide, no doubt, now you've quarrelled."

"I think—I'm sure that you wrong him there," Nigel said, slowly.

"Do you think so? Well, I must go up and take a bath. I may be a good while."

"Let me come and sit with you. Shall I? I mean in a few minutes."

"Not just yet. Better try and calculate out your debt to Doctor Isaacson."

She hastened away. Directly she reached her room, she locked the door, went out on to the balcony, and looked across the river to the *Loulia*. She saw the Egyptian flag flying. Was Baroudi on board? She must know, and immediately. She rang the bell, and unlocked the door.

"Ibrahim!" she said, to the Nubian who appeared.

He retreated, and in a moment Ibrahim came, with his soft stride, up the staircase.

"Ibrahim," she almost whispered, "is Baroudi on board the *Loulia*?"

"Yes, my lady."

She could hardly repress an exclamation.

"He is? Ibrahim"—in her astonishment she put one hand on his shoulder and grasped it tightly—"to-night, as soon as dinner is over, you are to have a felucca ready at the foot of the garden. D'you understand?"

He looked at her very seriously.

"Can you manage to row me across to the *Loulia* without help?"

"My lady, I am as strong as Rameses the Second."

"Very well then! Get a small, light boat. We shall go more quickly in that. How long is Baroudi going to stay?"

"I dunno."

"Try to find out. Is Hamza with him?"

Ibrahim looked vicious.

"Hamza him there. But Hamza very bad boy. I not speak any more to Hamza."

"Don't forget! Directly after dinner."

She shut and relocked the door.

She took a hot bath, let down her hair, got into a wrapper, lay down, and tried to rest. But her body twitched with desire for active movement, almost worn out though she was. Again and again she got up, went out to the terrace, and looked at the *Loulia*. She took her glasses and tried to discern Baroudi on the upper deck. But she could not see him. Presently she pulled a long chair out to the balcony, and was just going to lie down on it when she heard a knock on the door.

"Ruby!"

It was Nigel. She felt inclined to rush across the room, to open the door, to seize him by the shoulders and thrust him out of the house, out of her life for ever.

"Ruby!"

"I am coming!" she said.

She waited an instant, striving for self-control. Every nerve in her body seemed to be quivering.

"The door is locked."

"I know. I'm coming! I'm coming!"

She set her teeth, went to the door, and unlocked it.

"Come in! Come in, your importunate man!"

"Importunate! But I haven't seen you for three nights. And I can't get on without you, Ruby. Thank God, to-night we shall be alone together. After dinner I want you to play to me."

Her face twitched.

"If I'm not too tired."

"We'll go to bed quite early."

He shut the door.

"I'll come and sit in here with you. I want to take your opinion about this cheque to Isaacson."

He sighed heavily.

He had a pencil and some paper in his hands, and he sat down by a table.

"I must get this off my mind. After what has happened, I must pay Isaacson, though otherwise I think we——" He sighed again. "Let me see, when did he first come on board to take care of me?"

*　　*　　*　　*　　*　　*

That day went by slowly, slowly, with feet of lead. Whether she would endure to its end without some hysterical outburst of temper Mrs. Armine did not know. She seemed to herself to be clinging frantically to the last fragments of her self-control. For so long she had acted a part, that it would be tragic to break down feebly, contemptibly, now close to the end of the drama.

This night must see its end. For her powers were exhausted. She meant to tell Baroudi so. He must take her away now, or let her join him somewhere. But in any case she must get away from her life with Nigel. She could no longer play the devoted wife, safe at last, after many trials, in the arms of respectability. It was only by making a cruel effort that she was able to get through the day without rousing suspicion in Nigel. And to-day he was curiously observant of her. His eyes seemed to be always upon her, watching her with a look she could not quite understand. He never left her for a moment, and sometimes she had a strange sensation that, like herself, he was on the verge of—what—some self-revelation? Some confession? Some perhaps emotional laying bare of his heart? She did not know. But she did know that he was not in a normal state. And once or twice she wondered what had been the exact truth of the quarrel with Isaacson. But, at any rate, it had not been the truth in which she was concerned. And she was too frightfully intent upon herself to-day to be very curious, even about Isaacson's relations with her husband.

He was gone, and gone without having tried to destroy

her. That was enough. She would not bother about small things to-day.

At last the evening approached along the marvellous ways of gold. As she saw the sky beginning to change Mrs. Armine's fever of excitement and impatience increased. Now that the moment of her meeting with Baroudi was so near she felt as if she could not bear even another second's delay. How she was going to escape from her husband she did not know. But she did not worry about that. She could always manage Nigel somehow, and she would not fail for the first time to-night.

When the moment came it would find her ready. Of that she was sure.

She made up her face elaborately that evening, put a delicate flush upon her cheeks, darkened her eyebrows more than usual, made her lips very red. She took infinite pains to give to her face an appearance of youth. Her eyes burned out of the painted shadows about them. Her shining hair was perfectly arranged in the way that suited her best. She put on a very low-cut evening gown, that showed as much as possible of her still lovely figure. And she strove to think that she looked no older now than when Baroudi had seen her last. The mirror contradicted her cruelly. But she was determined not to believe what it said.

At last she was ready, and she went down to get through the last *supplice*, as she called it to herself, the tête-à-tête dinner with Nigel.

He was not yet down, and she was just going to step out upon the terrace when he came into the drawing-room in evening dress. This was the first evening since his illness that he had dressed for dinner, and the clothes he wore seemed to her a sign that soon he would resume his normal and active life. The look of illness which she had thought she saw in his face that morning had given place to an expression of intensity that must surely be the token of inward excitement.

As he came in, she thought to herself that she had never

seen Nigel look so expressive, that she had never imagined he could look so expressive. Something in his face startled and gripped her.

He, too, gazed at her almost as if with new eyes, as he came towards her, looking resolute, like a man who had taken some big decision since she had last seen him an hour ago. All day he had seemed curiously watchful, uneasy, sometimes weak, sometimes lively with effort. Now, though intense, excited, he looked determined, and this determination, too, was like a new note of health.

His eyes went over her bare shoulders. Then he said: "For me!"

His voice lingered over the words. But his eyes changed in expression as they looked at her face.

"I couldn't help it to-night Nigel," she said, coolly. "I knew I must be looking too frightful after all this journeying. You must forgive me to-night."

"Of course I do. It's good of you to take this trouble for me, even though I—— Come! Dinner is ready."

He drew her arm through his, and led her in to the dining-room.

"Where's Ibrahim to-night?" she said carelessly, as they sat down.

"He asked if he might go to the village to see his mother, and I let him go."

"Oh!"

She felt relieved. Ibrahim had gone to fetch the felucca to take her across the Nile. A hot excitement surged through her. In a couple of hours, perhaps in less time, she would see Baroudi, be alone with Baroudi. How long she had waited! What torment she had endured! What danger, what failure she had undergone! But for a moment she forgot everything in that thought which went like wine to her head, "To-night I shall be with Baroudi!" She did not just then go beyond that thought. She did not ask herself what sort of reception he would give her. That wine from the mind brought a carelessness, almost a recklessness, with it, preventing analysis, sweeping away fears. A sort of spasm—was it the very last?—of youth seemed to leap up in her, like a brilliant flame from a heap of ashes. And she let the flame shoot out towards Nigel.

And again he was saying:

"For me!"

He was repeating it to himself, and he was reiterating silently those terrible words with which he had struck the man who had saved him from death.

"You liar! You damnable liar!"

The dinner was not the *supplice* Mrs. Armine had anticipated. She talked, she laughed, she was gay, frivolous, gentle, careless, as in the days long past when she had charmed men by mental as much as by merely physical qualities. And Nigel responded with an almost boyish eagerness. Her liveliness, her merriment, seemed not only to delight but to reassure something within him. She noticed that. And, noticing it, she was conscious that with his decision, beneath it as it were, there was something else, some far different quality, stranger to her, though faintly perceived, or perhaps, rather, obscurely divined by that sleepless intuition which lives in certain women. Her apparent joyousness gave helping hands to something in Nigel, leading it forward, onward—whither?

She was to know that night.

At length the dinner was over, and they got up to go into the drawing-room. And now, instantly, Mrs. Armine was seized by a frantic longing to escape. The felucca, she felt sure, was waiting on the still water just below the promontory. If only Nigel would remain behind over his cigarette in the dining-room for a moment, she would steal out to see. She would not start, of course, till he was safely upstairs. But she longed to be sure that the boat was there.

"Won't you have your cigarette in here?" she said, carelessly, as he followed her towards the door.

"Here? Alone?"

His voice sounded surprised.

"I thought perhaps you wanted another glass of wine,"

she murmured with a feigned indifference as she walked on.

"No," he said, "I am coming to the terrace with you."

"For a little while. But you must soon go to bed. Now that Doctor Isaacson has gone, I must play the sick nurse again, or you will be ill, and then I know he'll blame me."

"How do you know that?"

The sound of his voice startled her. She was just by the drawing-room door. She stood still and looked round.

"How?" she said. "Why, because Doctor Isaacson doesn't believe in me in any capacity."

"But I do."

Again she noticed the amazing expressiveness of his face.

"Yes," she said, "I know. You are different."

She opened the door and passed into the room. Directly she was in it she heard the Nubian sailors on the *Loulia* beginning their serenade. (She chose to call it that to herself to-night.) Their music tore at her heart, at her whole nature. She wanted to rush to it, now, at once, without one moment of waiting. Hardly could she force her body to move quietly across the room to the terrace. Nigel came up and stood close to her.

"Oh, I must have a wrap," she said.

"I'll fetch it."

"No, no! You mustn't go upstairs. You'll tire yourself."

"Not to-night," he said.

And he turned away. Directly the door shut behind him Mrs. Armine darted into the garden.

"Ibrahim! Ibrahim! Are you there?"

"Yes, my lady."

He came up from the water's edge and stood beside her.

"I can't come yet, but I'll be as quick as I can."

"Yes."

He looked at her. Then he said:

"I dunno what Mahmoud Baroudi say to us. He got one girl on the board."

"On the board!"

BELLA DONNA

"On the board of the *Loulia.*"

"Ruby! Ruby! where are you?"

"Go back! Wait for me—wait!"

"Ruby!"

"I'm here! I'm coming, Nigel!"

XLIV

She met him in the garden, a little beyond the terrace. He had on an overcoat and a soft hat, and was carrying a cloak for her.

"You shouldn't walk out in the night air with bare arms and shoulders," he said, holding the cloak so that she could easily put it on.

She turned her back on him, put up her hands and so took it.

"It's very warm to-night."

"Still, it's imprudent."

"You playing sick nurse!"

But all the gaiety had gone out of her voice, all the liveliness had vanished from her manner.

"Shall we walk a little?" he said. "Shall we go to the bank of the river?"

"No, no. You mustn't tire yourself. Let us sit down, and very soon I shall send you to bed."

"Not just yet."

"I'm——"

"It isn't that I want you to play. Besides, that noise over there would disturb us. No, but I want to talk to you. I must talk to you to-night."

One side of her mouth went down. But she turned her face quickly, and he did not see it. They came on to the terrace before the lighted windows.

"Sit down here, Ruby—near to me."

She sat down. With the very madness for movement thrilling, tingling, through all her weary and feverish body, she was obliged to sit down quietly.

Nigel sat down close to her. There was a silence.

"Oh," she said, almost desperately to break it, "we haven't had coffee to-night. Shall I—would you like me to make it once more for you?"

She spoke at random. She wanted to move, to do something, anything. She felt as if she must occupy herself in some way, or begin to cry out, to scream.

"Shall I? Shall I?" she repeated, half getting up.

Nigel looked at her fixedly.

"No, Ruby, not to-night."

She sank back.

"Very well. But I thought you liked my coffee."

"So I did. So I shall again."

He put out his hand to touch hers.

"Only not to-night."

"Just as you like."

"We've—there are other things to-night."

He kept his eyes always fixed upon hers.

"Other things!" she said. "Yes—sleep. You must rest well to-night, and so must I."

A fierce irony, in despite of herself, broke out in her voice as she said the last three words. It frightened her, and she burst into a fit of coughing, and pulled up her cloak about her bare neck. To do this she had to draw away her hand from Nigel's. She was thankful for that.

"I swallowed quantities of dust and sand in the train," she said.

He held out his hand to take hers again, and she was forced to give it.

"I shall rest to-night," he said. "Because I've come to a resolution. If I hadn't, if—if I followed my first thought, my first decision, I know I should not be able to rest. I know I shouldn't."

She stared at him in silence.

"Ruby," he said, "you remember our first evening here?"

"Yes," she forced herself to say.

Would he never end? Would he never let go of her

hand? never let her get away to the Nile, to that barbarous music?

"I think we were getting close to each other then. But—but I think we are much closer now. Don't you?"

"Yes," she managed to say.

"Closer because I've proved you; I've proved you through all this dreadful illness."

His hand gripped hers more firmly.

"But you, perhaps, haven't proved me yet as I have proved you."

"Oh, I don't doubt your——"

"No, but I want you to know, to understand me as I believe I understand you. And that's why I'm going to tell you something, something very—frightful."

There was a solemnity in his voice which held, which startled her.

"Frightful?" she almost whispered.

"Yes. I didn't mean ever to tell you. But somehow, when you came back to-day, came hurrying back to me so quickly, without even doing what you went away to do, somehow I began to feel as if I must tell you, as if I should be a cad not to, as if it was your right to know."

She said nothing. She had no idea what was coming.

"It is your right to know."

He paused. Now he was not looking at her, but straight before him into the darkness.

"Last night Isaacson and I were here."

At the Doctor's name she moved.

"I had asked him to tell me what my illness had been, what I had been suffering from. He said he would tell me. This was before."

Now again he looked at her.

She formed "Yes" with her lips.

"When we were out here after dinner, I asked him again to tell me. I had had your telegram then."

She nodded.

"He knew you were coming back a day sooner than we had expected."

She nodded again.

"And he told me. I am going to tell you what he said. He said that I had been poisoned"—her hand twitched beneath his—"by a preparation of lead, administered in small doses through a long period of time."

"Poisoned!"

"Yes."

"And—and you believe such a thing?"

"Yes. In such matters Isaacson *knows*."

"Poisoned!" she repeated.

She said the word without the horror he had expected, dully, mechanically. He thought perhaps she was dazed by surprise.

"But that's not all," he said, still holding her hand closely. "I asked him who on board the *Loulia* could have wished for my death."

"That's—that's just what I was thinking," she managed to say.

"And then he said a dreadful thing."

"What?"

"He said that you had done it."

She took her hand away from his sharply, and sat back in her chair. He did not move. They sat there looking at each other. And their silence was disturbed by the perpetual singing on the *Loulia*.

And so it had been said!

Isaacson had discovered the exact truth, and had told it to Nigel!

She felt a reckless relief. As she sat there, she seemed to be staring not at Nigel but at herself. And as she stared at herself, she marvelled.

"He said that you had done it, or, if not that, had known that it was being done, had meant it to be done."

She remained silent and motionless. And now, with her thought of the truth revealed to her husband was linked another thought of the girl with Baroudi on board of the *Loulia*.

"Then I told him to go, or I would put him out."

"Ah!" she said.

There was a sort of bitter astonishment in the exclamation, and now in the eyes regarding him Nigel seemed to discern wonder.

"And he went, after he had told me some—some other things."

Something in her, in her face, or her manner, or her deadly silence, broken only by that seemingly almost sarcastic cry—began evidently to affect her husband.

"Some other things," he repeated.

"What were they?"

"He said he had come out from England because he had suspected something was wrong. He told me that he met you by chance in the temple of Edfou, that you seemed terrified at seeing him, that it was not you who asked him to come to the *Loulia* to see me, but that, on the contrary, he asked to come and you refused to let him. He said you even sent him a letter telling him not to come. He gave me that letter. Here it is. I have not read it."

He put his hand into his coat and drew out the letter, and with it the gilded box which Baroudi had given to her in the orange garden.

"There is the letter."

He laid it on the table.

"I found this in your room when I went for the cloak," he said, "full of Eastern things for the face."

His eyes were a question.

"I bought it in Cairo yesterday."

He laid it down.

"In spite of that letter—Isaacson said—he did come that night, and he overheard us talking on the balcony, and heard me say how I wished he were in Egypt."

He stopped again. His own narrative seemed to be waking up something in his mind.

"Why didn't you tell me then that you knew he was in Egypt?" he asked.

She merely raised her eyebrows. Within her now the recklessness was increasing. With it was blent a strange and powerful sensation of fatalism.

34

"Was it because you hated Isaacson so much?"

"That was it."

"But then—but then, when he was with me, you said that you had brought him. You said that in the temple you had begged him to come. I remember that quite well."

"Do you?" she said.

And fate seemed to her to be moving her lips, to be forming for her each word she said.

"Yes. Why was that? Why did you say that?"

"Don't remember!"

"You don't——?"

He got up slowly out of his chair.

"But the—the strangest thing Isaacson said was this."

He put one hand on the back of the chair, and leaned down a little towards her.

"He said that at last he forced you to let him attend me as a doctor by—by threatening you."

"Oh!"

"By threatening, if you would not, to call in the police authorities."

She said nothing. All he was saying flowed past her like running water. No more than running water did it mean to her. Apparently she had fought and struggled too long, and the revenge of nature upon her was this terrible indifference following upon so much of terror, of strife, of enforced and desperate patience.

"Ruby!"

* * * * * *

"Ruby!"

"Well?" She looked at him. "What is it?"

"You don't say anything!"

"Why should I? What do you want me to say?"

"Want! I—but——"

He bent down.

"You—you don't think—you aren't thinking that I——?"

"Well?"

"I've told you this to prove my complete trust in you. I've only told you so that there may be nothing between us, no shadow; as even such a thing, hidden, might be."

"Ah!"

"And if there are things I don't understand, I know—they are such trifles in comparison—I know you'll explain. Won't you?"

"Not to-night. I can't explain things to-night."

"No. You're tired out. To-morrow—to-morrow!"

"Ah!" she said again.

He leant right down to her, and took both her hands.

"Come upstairs with me! Come!" She stood up. "Come! I'll prove to you—I'll prove to you——"

There was a sort of desperation of crude passion in his manner.

He tried to draw her towards the house. She resisted him.

"Ruby!"

"I'm not coming."

He stopped.

"Ruby!" he said again, but with a different voice.

"I'm not coming!"

His hands grew cold on hers. He let her hands go. They dropped to her sides.

"So you didn't believe what Isaacson told you?" she said.

Her only thought was, "I'll make him give me my liberty! I'll make him give me my liberty, so that Baroudi must keep me!"

"What?" he said.

"You didn't believe what Isaacson told you?" she repeated.

"Believe it! I turned him out!"

"You fool!" she said.

She moved a step nearer to him.

"You fool!" she repeated. "It's true!"

She snatched up the gilded box from the table. He tore it out of her hands.

"Who—who——?" he whispered, with lips that had gone white.

"Mahmoud Baroudi," she said.

The box fell from his hands to the terrace, scattering the aids to her beauty, which he had always hated.

She turned, pulled her cloak closely round her, and hurried to the bank of the Nile.

"Ibrahim! Ibrahim!"

"My lady!"

He came, striding up the bank.

"Take my hand! Help me! Quickly!"

She almost threw herself down the bank.

"Where is the boat—ah!"

She stumbled as she got into it, and nearly fell.

"Push off!"

She sat straight up on the hard, narrow bench, and stared at the lights on the *Loulia*.

"There's a girl on board," she said, in a minute.

"Yes, my lady, one girl. Whether Mahmoud Baroudi likin' we comin' I dunno."

"Ibrahim!"

"My lady!"

"Directly I go on board the *Loulia*, you are to go. Take the boat straight back to Luxor."

"I leavin' you?"

He looked relieved.

"Yes. I'll—I'll come back in Baroudi's felucca."

"I quite well stayin', waitin' till you ready."

"No, no. I don't wish that. Promise me you will take the boat away at once."

"All what you want you must have," he murmured.

"How loudly the sailors are singing!" she said.

Now they were drawing near to the *Loulia*. Mrs. Armine, with fierce eyes, gazed at the lighted cabin windows, at the upper deck, at the balcony in the stern where so often she had sat with Nigel. She was on fire with eagerness; she was the prey of an excitement that made her forget all her bodily fatigue, forget everything except that at last

BELLA DONNA 533

she was close to Baroudi. Already her husband had ceased to exist for her. He was gone for ever with the past. Not only the river but a great gulf, never to be bridged, divided them.

"Baroudi! Baroudi! Baroudi!"

She could belong to Baroudi openly at last. In this moment she even forgot herself, forgot to think of her appearance. Within her there was a woman who could genuinely feel. And that woman asserted herself now.

The boat touched the *Loulia's* side. A Nubian appeared. The singing on board abruptly ceased. Mrs. Armine quickly stood up in the boat.

"Go to Luxor, Ibrahim! Go at once!"

"I goin' quick, my lady."

She sprang on board and stood to see him go. Only when the boat had diminished upon the dark water did she turn round. She was face to face with Hamza.

"Hamza!" she said, startled.

His almond-shaped eyes regarded her, and she thought a menace was in them. Even in the midst of her fiery excitement she felt a touch of something that was cold as fear is cold.

"Yes," he said.

"I must see Mahmoud Baroudi."

He did not move. His expression did not change. The Nubians, squatting in a circle on the deck a little way off, looked at her calmly, almost as animals look at something they have very often seen.

"Where is he?" she said. "Where is he?"

And abruptly she went down the steps, under the golden letters, and into the first saloon. It was lit up, but no one was there. She hurried on down the passage, pulled aside the orange-coloured curtain, and came into the room of the faskeeyeh.

On the divan, dressed in native costume, with the turban and djelab, Baroudi was sitting on his haunches with his legs tucked under him, smoking hashish and gazing at the gilded ball as it rose and fell on the water. A little way off, supported by many cushions, an Eastern girl was lying. She looked very young, perhaps sixteen or seventeen. But her face was painted, her eyes were bordered with kohl, and the nails of her fingers and of her bare toes were tinted with the henna. She wore the shintiyan, and a tob, or kind of shirt of coloured and spangled gauze. On her pale brown arms there were quantities of narrow bracelets. She, too, was smoking a little pipe with a mouthpiece of coral.

Mrs. Armine stood still in the doorway. She looked at the girl, and now, immediately, she thought of her own appearance, with something like terror.

"Baroudi!" she said. "Baroudi!"

He stared at her face.

When she saw that, with trembling fingers she unfastened her cloak and let it fall on the floor.

"Baroudi!" she repeated.

But Baroudi still stared at her face.

With one hand he held the long stem of his pipe, but he had stopped smoking.

At once she felt despair.

But she came on into the middle of the saloon.

"Send her away!" she said. "Send her away!"

She spoke in French. And he answered in French: "Why?"

"I've left my husband. I've left the villa. I can never go back."

"Why not?" he said, still gazing at her face.

He threw back his head, and his great throat showed among the folds of muslin that swept down to his mighty chest.

"He knows!"

"Knows! Who has told him?"

"I have!"

As he looked at her, she grew quite cold, as if she had been plunged into icy water.

"You have told him about me?" he said.

"Not all about you! But he knows that—that I made

him ill, that I wished him to die. I told him, because I wanted to get away. I had to get away—and be with you . . ."

The bracelets on the arms of the Eastern girl jingled as she moved behind Mrs. Armine.

"Send her away! Send her away!" Mrs. Armine repeated.

"Hamza!"

Baroudi called, but not loudly. Hamza came in at the door.

Baroudi spoke to him quickly in Arabic. A torrent of words that sounded angry, as Arabic words do to those from the Western world, rushed out of his throat. What did they mean? Mrs. Armine did not know. But she did know that her fate was in them.

Hamza said nothing, only made her a sign to follow him.

But she stood still.

"Baroudi!" she said.

"Go with Hamza," he said, in French.

And she went, without another word, past the girl, and out of the room.

Hamza, with a sign, told her to go in front of him. She went slowly down the passage, into the first saloon. There she hesitated, looked back. Hamza signed to her to go on. She passed under the *Loulia's* motto—for the last time. On the sailors' deck she paused.

The small felucca of the *Loulia* was alongside. Hamza took her by the arm. Although his hand was small and delicate, it seemed to her then a thing of iron that could not be resisted. She got into the boat. Where was she going to be taken? It occurred to her now that perhaps Baroudi had some plan, that he did not choose to keep her on board, that he had a house at Luxor, or——

The Villa Nuit d'Or! Was Hamza going to take her there in the night?

Hamza sat down, took the oars, pushed off.

Yes, he was rowing up stream against the tide! A

wild hope sprang up in her. The *Loulia* diminished. Always Hamza was rowing against the tide, but she noticed that the felucca was drifting out into the middle of the Nile. The current was very strong. They were making little or no headway. She longed to seize an oar, to help the boat up stream. Now the eastern bank of the river grew more distinct, looming out of the darkness. It seemed to be approaching them, coming stealthily nearer and nearer. She saw the lights in the Villa Androud.

"Hamza!" she murmured. "Hamza!"

He rowed on, without much force, almost languidly. Never could they go up against the tide if he did not pull more strongly. Why had they not two of the Nubians with them? The lights of the villa vanished. They were hidden by the high and shelving bank.

"Hamza!" she cried out. "Hamza!"

There was a slight shock. The felucca had touched bottom. Hamza, with a sort of precision characteristic of him, stepped quietly ashore and signed to her to come.

She knew she would not go. And, instantly, she went.

Directly she stood upon the sand, near the tangle of low bushes, Hamza pushed off the felucca, springing into it as he did so, and rowed away on the dark water.

"Hamza!" she called.

"Hamza! Hamza!" she shrieked.

The boat went on steadily, quickly, and disappeared.

*   *   *   *   *   *

Nearly an hour later there appeared at the edge of the garden of the Villa Androud a woman walking unsteadily, with a sort of frantic slowness. She made her way across the garden and drew near to the terrace, beyond which light shone out from the drawing-room through the tall window space. Close to the terrace she stood still, and she looked into the room.

She saw Nigel sitting crouched upon a sofa, with his elbows on his knees and his face in his hands. He was alone, and was sitting quite still.

She stood for some time staring in at him. Then at last, as if making up her mind to something, she moved, and slowly she stepped upon the terrace.

Just as she did this, the door of the drawing-room opened and Ibrahim came in, looking breathless and scared. Behind him came Meyer Isaacson.

The woman stood still on the terrace.

Ibrahim remained by the door. Nigel never moved. Meyer Isaacson came quickly forward into the room as if he were going to Nigel. But when he was in the middle of the room, something seemed to startle him. He stopped abruptly, looked questioningly towards the window, then came out to the terrace. On the threshold he stopped again. He had seen the woman. He looked for a moment at her, and she at him. Then he came forward, put out his hands quickly, unlatched the wooden shutters, which were set back against the house wall, and pulled them inward towards him. They met with a clang, blotting out the room from the woman's eyes.

Then she waited no longer. She made her way to the gate of the garden, passed out to the deserted track beyond, and disappeared into the darkness, going blindly towards the distant hills that keep the Arabian desert.

THE END

A NEW SPARKLING ROMANCE

The Woman in Question

By JOHN REED SCOTT

Author of "The Colonel of the Red Huzzars," "The Princess Dehra," and "Beatrix of Clare"

**THREE FULL-PAGE ILLUSTRATIONS IN COLOR
BY CLARENCE F. UNDERWOOD**

12mo. Decorated cloth, $1.50

"*The Woman in Question*" is a romance, but not of Valeria nor mediæval England. Mr. Scott has remained home in America, and the scenes are laid in the Eastern United States. The story is distinctly modern in tone and theme, and centers in and around Fairlawn Hall, an old mansion with a marvellous garden, lying on the outskirts of Egerton, where the new master has come with a party of friends—to find mystery, misfortune, and love awaiting him.

Mr. Scott shows steady improvement in each succeeding novel, and he has planned this latest story well, filling it with many surprises and dramatic moments.

"The story has dash and verve."
—*New York Times Saturday Review of Books.*

"There are few heroines in latter-day American fiction comparable with charming Mildred Gascoyne."—*Philadelphia North American.*

"The dialogue is bright and sparkling, the characters interesting, and the plot sufficiently exciting. The woman in question, young, beautiful, and spirited, is involved in mystery, the unfolding of which introduces some thrilling episodes."—*Boston Evening Transcript.*

J. B. LIPPINCOTT CO. PUBLISHERS PHILADELPHIA

THE DAINTIEST ROMANCE IN YEARS

MARCIA SCHUYLER

By GRACE LIVINGSTON HILL LUTZ
Author of "Phoebe Deane"

Frontispiece in color by Anna Whelan Betts, and six illustrations from paintings by E. L. Henry, N.A.

12mo. 348 pages. Cloth, with medallion, $1.50.

SET in 1830—the time of full skirts and poke bonnets—this romance opens upon the wedding preparations for the marriage of a winsome, wilful Kate to strong and good David. On the eve of her marriage she elopes with a young lieutenant and her angry father urges the benumbed lover to wed in her place the younger sister, Marcia. After a period of trials and heartaches Marcia wins her husband's love when he comes to understand her worthiness and Kate's heartless frivolity and duplicity.

The story of the introduction of the steam railway in New York forms an interesting part of the plot.

"One of the most lovable heroines that ever lived her life in the pages of a romance."—*Chicago Tribune*.

"So dainty a novel it has not been our fortune to see for some time."—*San Francisco Argonaut*.

"A pleasant story delightfully told, with a refreshing ring of candor and sincerity throughout its pages, a distinctive local atmosphere, broad, clear-cut characterization, and a suave and engaging literary method and manner."—*Phila. North American*.

J. B. LIPPINCOTT COMPANY
PUBLISHERS   **PHILADELPHIA**

A SANE, SCIENTIFIC, AND INSPIRING BOOK

WHY WORRY?

By GEORGE L. WALTON, M.D.

Frontispiece.   12mo.   275 pages.   Cloth, $1.00 net.

THIS book is no cure-all, but it has a sane hopefulness that should make it one of the most helpful works ever written upon the topic of worry. Never has a subject been treated with a fuller combination of professional knowledge, common sense, clear, concise, and pointed language. This is a book to read and to recommend to your neighbor, as it will prove an inspiration to any one who has found himself curtailing his physical energy by worries, futile or needless.

"A well-thumbed copy in every household where there is the slightest inclination to worry would mean a great addition to the world's present stock of happiness and contentment." —*Philadelphia Press.*

"People who overwork and worry, who consider themselves misunderstood, or what is commoner and far worse, who make themselves wretched by the habit of self-depreciation and introspection, should by all means read this sympathetic book."
—*Chicago Evening Post.*

J. B. LIPPINCOTT COMPANY
PUBLISHERS   PHILADELPHIA

BEAU BROCADE
By BARONESS ORCZY
Author of "The Scarlet Pimpernel," "I Will Repay," etc.

A captivating romance of love and chivalry—the adventures of a charming highwayman of the days of the English Pretender.

"Faith and courage make the story of 'Beau Brocade' a very interesting one. The hero is delightfully fascinating—bubbling over with exuberance of youth; nothing is a hardship for him. He reminds one of Dumas's famous D'Artagnan, and most especially in his fighting escapades. Gloriously dramatic is the fight in the forge, when, by his prowess, Beau Brocade holds at bay a lot of redcoats, escaping on his steed 'Jack O'Lantern.'"
—*N. Y. American Book Review Contest.*

"The story is so well told, so full of life and action, that one never loses interest from start to finish."
—*Pittsburgh Dispatch.*

"Let no one begin reading this tale late in the evening, for there is no stopping-place till the end, and the end is worth reaching." —*The Congregationalist, Boston.*

"The illustrations in color are unusually attractive."
—*Chicago Tribune.*

FOUR FULL-PAGE ILLUSTRATIONS IN COLOR BY
CLARENCE F. UNDERWOOD.
12mo. Cloth, $1.50.

J. B. LIPPINCOTT COMPANY
PUBLISHERS PHILADELPHIA

BY THE BARONESS ORCZY

"I WILL REPAY"

A Romance of the French Revolution

12mo. Decorated Cloth, $1.50

THIS period of the great French Revolution appeals to the imagination in a way that no other historic event does. It was so very terrible and yet so very recent. The Baroness Orczy's story deals with the most stirring moment of that exciting time—when the "Law of the Suspect" was in full force, which gave every French man or woman the right to denounce a fellow man or woman to that awful tribunal of the Revolution which knew neither mercy nor justice. The romance of "I Will Repay" is concerned with the tragedy of a soul-conflict 'twixt love and a mistaken sense of duty. The Scarlet Pimpernel, of her former book of this title, plays an important part in the development of the story of "I Will Repay."

"A good story of action, admirably told."
—*Press, Philadelphia.*

"It will be read eagerly, closed with a long satisfied sigh." —*Nashville American.*

"Clever and well worked out, its details related with dash and spirit, its intrigue and devices adroitly managed." —*Sun, New York.*

"The story is well written, is full of incident and rapid movement, is characterized by a thorough knowledge of the spirit of the time, and displays clear characterization and great power of analysis of human nature. It is worth reading, for it will interest from the first page to the last." —*Public Ledger, Philadelphia.*

J. B. LIPPINCOTT COMPANY
PUBLISHERS   **PHILADELPHIA**

ENTERTAINING NOVELS

GRACE LIVINGSTON HILL LUTZ'S
Phoebe Deane
A romance as modestly refreshing as a whiff of fresh lavender or a handful of old-time clove-pinks, by the author of "Marcia Schuyler."

Frontispiece in color and five illustrations from paintings by E. L. Henry, N. A. 12mo. Cloth, with medallion, $1.50.

ROSA NOUCHETTE CAREY'S
The Key of the Unknown
The last of Miss Carey's popular stories for young women.

Frontispiece portrait. 12mo. Decorated cloth, $1.50.

CAROLYN WELLS'
The Clue
An unusually clever and absorbing detective story.

Frontispiece in color. 12mo. Cloth, $1.50.

ALBERT E. HANCOCK'S
Bronson of the Rabble
A vivid and dramatic romance of old Philadelphia between the years 1812 and 1828.

Frontispiece in color. 12mo. Cloth, $1.50.

CRITTENDEN MARRIOTT'S
The Isle of Dead Ships
A fascinating tale of the mysterious Sargasso Sea.

Frontispiece in color and three illustrations in black and white. 12mo. Cloth, $1.00 net.

MARIE VAN VORST'S
In Ambush
A striking novel of adventure, mystery, and romance, with varied change of scene.

12mo. Decorated cloth, $1.50

RUPERT S. HOLLAND'S
The Man in the Tower
An exciting and highly dramatic novel of love, intrigue, conspiracy, rebellion, and adventure.

Illustrated in color and half-tone. 12mo. Cloth, $1.50.

J. B. LIPPINCOTT CO. PUBLISHERS PHILADELPHIA